THE SEQUEL OF "HEIRS OF A LOST RACE"

RAPA NUI SETTLERS

BY CHOICE AND NECESSITY

DR. FRANCIS F. PITARD

ISBN: 978-1-961078-56-7 (Hardback)
ISBN: 978-1-961078-57-4 (Paperback)
ISBN: 978-1-961078-58-1 (eBook)

Library of Congress Control Number: 2024911466

This book is a work of fiction. Any resemblance to real places, events, or individuals, whether living or deceased, is purely coincidental. All characters, names, and incidents portrayed in this novel are products of the author's imagination.

Printed in the United States of America.

Springer Literary House LLC
6260 Lavender Cloud Place
Las Vegas, Nevada 89122, USA

www.springerliteraryhouse.com

CONTENTS

For my wife, Deloris
For my children
For all my friends around the world

FOREWORD

I know some people will read this book and think of it as a fantasy that took place more than sixteen hundred years ago. So be it! As a good friend of ours, Dr. Janet J. Seahorn put it so well after reading my first novel: "Sometimes you pick up a book thinking it will just be an average reading experience; one that gives you something to do on a normal day where you have a few hours to sit and relax. Heirs of a Lost Race is not such a book. It is much more and demands that the reader pay attention to the greater message. Pitard requires the reader to think about the characters, what is happening and why, and contrasts that information with his/her world. It takes several chapters before the pieces begin to fit into the story and is worth the wait." I kept the same spirit for Rapa Nui Settlers.

The way the transportation of moais is described in this novel may not have been the most efficient. The most efficient way, only used much later in their history, caused the destruction of many endemic palm trees. It is likely indeed that moais were rolled on fragile palm tree logs. However, the way it is described in this novel is at least consistent with what the Rongo-Rongo characters suggest. It is my belief that these mysterious characters hold valuable information about the long-forgotten early ways of Rapa Nui; it makes them priceless.

Then there is the tale told by modern man that the Rapa Nui people destroyed themselves because of warfare, starvation, cannibalism, greed, and even stupidity. This is an attempt to hide the real truth. I strongly disagree with these statements, which are gratuitously made and are blatant insults to great Polynesians. Ancient Polynesians were a lot smarter than this, as studied in depth in Heirs of a Lost Race. Yes, it was difficult to manage ten thousand people on such a small land. Yes, it was a challenge to feed them every day. Yet not only did they do it, but they were beautiful, graceful, and healthy people, at least until 1786, as described by French navigators. The same navigators claim the land was fertile, and that growing vegetables was a relatively easy task. For centuries these creative people found ways to entertain and feed themselves in their peaceful solitude at the world's end. Let's make it very clear: the Rapa Nui people were doing just fine until outsiders came, loaded with arrogance, guns, and diseases on that infamous Easter Sunday in 1722. For the next 150 years, numerous navigators, adventurers, whalers, and slave merchants would rape the bodies, minds, and souls of these wonderful people in the name of civilization. Beginning in 1722 and continuing for over two centuries, a holocaust of unsurpassed arrogance, cruelty, and savagery took place until 110 Rapanuis remained, all relegated below beasts of the field. This was indeed the despair of Rapa Nui; the only reason for the fall of Rapa Nui. The Rapanui had nothing to do with this horrific and undeserved fate. Grazing sheep devastated the land for over 100 years. Western "civilization" brought the sheep. The formidable intellects that wrought ahus and moais were innocent of the fall of Rapa Nui. They can take immense pride in their achievements, and we should seek penance for the irreversible hurt and devastation that we brought about.

This book pays homage to the real Rapanuis, the original Rapanuis, a peaceful group of talented, intelligent, and caring people. Contemporaneous theories characterizing the Rapanuis as a self-destructive society that created the environmental disaster, starvation, cannibalism, and warfare resulting in its downfall is unadulterated slander! In today's society, we often scrape the bottom of the barrel to rationalize what we do around the world. Such is the case for those who cast aspersions on the Rapanuis. Mongers of inaccurate, arrogant, and contrived pseudo-histories have done a criminal disservice to a proud people and to the rest of us who honor them for their magnificent achievements.

Furthermore, as an internationally respected expert on sampling statistics, I also strongly disagree with the findings of some modern archaeologists who revise the dates of Rapa Nui's first settlements from AD 400 to AD 800, or even AD 1200. There is perhaps no other dating technique as susceptible to erroneous interpretation as carbon 14 dating, which can be corrupted by the repeated burning of the land and increasing charcoal leftover from rapidly growing populations. Too often careless or biased scientists confuse their findings with what they hope to find, not what was found. Plain logic suggests it should have taken a long time for Rapa Nui to evolve. Unless we cast aside our misconceptions as scientists, writers, and philosophers, it is unlikely our vision of Rapa Nui will accurately portray the lives of these wonderful people who settled such a long time ago in this isolated corner of the world.

Several self-proclaimed experts have erroneously blamed the Rapanuis for their embroilment in internecine warfare, which precipitated the quid pro quo toppling of moais. As far as this is concerned, there is strong evidence that ahus hosting many moais were built on low land and that tsunamis toppled the moais. Today anyone can see boulders tossed on the hillside everywhere. Since this is still an active volcanic island in geological terms, earthquakes may have toppled some statues on ahus located farther up in the hills. Some statues with slightly rounded bottoms were very vulnerable and may have toppled on their own. There is reason to believe that Peruvian slave merchants who killed chiefs and knowledgeable priests may have knocked them down to further denigrate the few survivors' self-esteem. If the Rapa Nui people toppled any statues, it certainly must have been very few; even then it could only have been caused through the confusion and despair of a people decimated by incurable diseases brought by outsiders. Despite the adversity visited on Rapa Nui, the legacy to us, Rano Raraku's moais, are still standing tall in a mysterious, intriguing splendor.

The following story is a product of the author's imagination. However, I made a strong effort to emphasize the few things they may have done right in the early days, and perhaps we could learn something ourselves about how to cure that which makes us who we really are today.

CHARACTERS OF RAPA NUI SETTLERS

THE GODS

The Great Taaroa
- *The Polynesian people's version of the Mighty*
Make Make
- *The Rapa Nui people's version of the Mighty*
Viracocha
- *The Lost Race people's version of the Mighty*
The Light
- *The Light is a supreme being, personified in many ways over the history of mankind. It is God for many religions. It is Taaroa for the Maohis. It is Viracocha for a lost race from South America. It is worthwhile to mention there may be historical and scientific evidence that light is indeed God or at least a subtle part of the Mighty. Let's make a few pertinent comments supporting this theory: sometimes we reach too far to know the truth, when all along it was with us, talking to us, and showing us the way. A long time ago God said to Moses, "I am the Light..." We thought it was a metaphor. Maybe it was the simple, ultimate truth.*
Closer to us, Albert Einstein said once, "The photon makes intelligent decisions. The photon knows ahead of time things it should not know. I would rather become a cobbler than a physicist if I had to accept that the decisions I observed were made by sheer

chance. For the rest of my life I will reflect on the real nature of light." For readers who are not scientists, light and photons are the same thing.

And today, at some very advanced laboratories, such as those equipped with giant particle accelerators, the behavior of photons baffles scientists beyond everything they ever imagined, and beyond anything they could think possible. Photons continuously communicate between themselves, even after they are sent in opposite directions at the speed of light; therefore, they know how to communicate when they travel away from each other at twice the speed of light. Even more baffling, there is strong evidence photons can read the minds of experimenters, which is truly entering a domain many scientists would rather keep silent, so they can keep their jobs instead of residing in a psychiatric rehabilitation center.

What is the real nature of light? Someone may say it is pure energy. This is too easy. We must make an effort to comprehend light far more in depth: it is worthwhile. After all, light comes from the stars, and without photons our brains cannot work. Therefore every one of us is star stuff. There is no birth. There is no death. The photons that make us work are eternal: they indeed control everything. We are their instruments for a moment. They are on a mission we can discover the meaning of. The conclusion is clear: religion can easily reach science if we accept that we must open our eyes and see the infinite beauty of the Light. But there is a catch: light is from fire, from what we play with and also fear most. With fire we play, with fire we kill, and with light we create and love. There will be a day when we will enjoy the Light and stay away from fire. On that day perhaps, humanity will be at peace.

THE MAOHIS

Hina of the Valley - Sixteen sun cycles old when she arrived at Rapa Nui. She is the young daughter of a Tahitian king. In Heirs of a Lost Race, she became a greatly respected priestess at a very young age.

Hotu-Matua

- A king from a far away island called Hiva who has an important place in Rapa Nui legends

Tamatoa the Great

- A feared king who grew up on Rarotonga, who plotted the revenge of his father's death when he was a boy on the island of Pora Pora. In Heirs of a Lost Race, for good reasons, he became a peaceful man.

Taatamao

- One of Tamatoa's commanders

Mahine

- Tamatoa's daughter

Tupua

- Hina of the Valley's father

Vana

- A great Tahitian priest, mentor of Hina of the Valley

THE VIRACOCHAS

Kama Tici

- Twenty-nine sun cycles old when she arrived at Rapa Nui

Ku

- Eleven sun cycles old when he arrived at Rapa Nui, he was Kama Tici's oldest son

Kane

- Nine sun cycles when he arrived at Rapa Nui, he was Kama Tici's youngest son

Kura

- Kama's daughter

Kora

- A young Viracocha girl who traveled on the same raft as Kama Tici

Taranga Tici

- The old Viracocha ancestor and Kon Tici's grandfather

Rangi

- A Viracocha friend of Kon Tici

Hiti

- A Viracocha friend of Kon Tici

Kon Tici

- A legendary Viracocha priest; the name represents a god of great knowledge for Polynesians.

Kukara Tici

- Eight sun cycles old when she arrived at Rapa Nui. She is a young Viracocha girl who possessed exceptional intelligence.

ACKNOWLEDGEMENT

I am indebted to many people who have supported my work, inspired me, and encouraged me to pursue, day after day, the extraordinary exploration of the human mind at its best. I am especially grateful to Deloris, my wife, for polishing the manuscript, and to Lulu, my daughter-in-law and also professional photographer, who spent a long time creating an inspirational cover picture for the book. I am honored by the work of a good friend, Doug Lange, who helped me find the right words. The novel is fiction, but based on sound archaeological evidence. I am especially thankful for the outstanding patient and factual academic works of Drs. Katherine Routledge, Georgia Lee, and Jo Anne Van Tilberg; their integrity and knowledge is superb and refreshing. I am thankful for the inspiring works of Thor Heyerdahl, for the deeply human and emotional works of Francis and Tila Maziere, for the daring explorative works of Jean-Michel Schwartz, and for the works of many others. I appreciate their work because they deeply loved the Polynesians. Some of us are academicians, or philosophers, or scientists, or dreamers, or passionate idealists, or even lost souls in search of serenity. There should be a place for everyone in a peaceful and harmonious world. We all make mistakes, but through our passionate works we may create a few events in our lives that are worthwhile for many. Therefore, everybody's works have immense value, through an entire book, or sometimes through only one inspired quote. Indeed, only a few well-inspired words can make the story of an entire book worthwhile for humanity, as long as there is pride, sincerity, honesty, and love.

I am especially indebted to one of my mentors and a good friend, the late Charles Oliver Ingamells. He was one of the most intelligent human beings I ever met. He was a world-class analytical chemist and sampling expert; it was in this field that we met. But there was another side of him, deeper, more private, and truly visionary. During his last days, he had been searching for our subquantic identity. Many people may jump right there and wonder how this has anything to do with the exploration of Rapa Nui. Well, there is a possible connection, and the Rapa Nui priest in his ancient meditations was probably a long way from realizing the true nature of his mana concept. Ingamells' work on the "vacuole hypothesis," published in Speculations in Science and Technology, is a daring challenge to mankind and truly opened my eyes. Yet this single published document is only a modest reflection of who the man was. As his daughter Margaret I. Resnick put it so well: "My Father was an Einstein; and it's a shame that he didn't get more recognition. His genteel, selfless desire to learn what's out there made him a valuable asset to the scientists who want to further mankind's sense of awareness." Ingamells' work allowed me to formulate the logical deeper conclusion of this novel. My appreciation of his work is because of his scientific integrity. Oliver would walk one step forward only after he had accumulated enough facts; his work must be taken seriously. Once, Oliver went to Rapa Nui and spent some time reflecting on the secret meaning of moais. He may not have found the answers, but at least I know he was searching in the right direction, and this alone is progress. There is a subtle way to explore and better know ourselves, and there is no doubt that the ancient Rapa Nui's well-initiated priests reached that level of knowledge: this is suggested in some Rongo-Rongo characters shown in this novel.

I am absolutely delighted to dedicate this book, and the previous one, Heirs of a Lost Race, to our unforgettable Rapa Nui friends with whom we shared thoughts, joy, and everyday life— Lucia Riroroko de Haoa, the mother of all; Leandro (Leo) Haoa Pakomio, the very quiet father; Fernando (Nano) Leandro Haoa Riroroko, the carver of his ancestor's mana in a wooden staff we all cherish and called heua; Jose Roberto Haoa Riroroko, who still searches the ways of his ancestors; and Jorge Pio Andres Haoa Riroroko, the soul of a new generation. Also, I will never forget the charming friendship of Maria Rapanui Hooo Pakomio, her silent humbleness for her island, her deep love for her ancestors, and above all, her daring courage to slide down the slopes of an old volcano on banana tree trunks at 60 miles an hour. Deep in your roots you all have this mysterious power of mana, when you want to. We love you all, forever. Finally, this book is for Mayor Pedro Edmund Paoa and many others who are so proud of who they are and who they want to be. You live on a small island perhaps, and very few of you are left; but you most certainly made a huge impression on the entire world. Therefore, we all shall and must help you to keep Rapa Nui as a cherished treasure for humanity: this should be the sacred mission of UNESCO.

Two-thirds of the height of these moais are buried by wind sediments.

*Two-thirds of the height of these moais are buried by wind
sediments.*

Lucia Riroroko de Haoa, our good Rapa Nui friend

*Fernando (Nano) Leandro Haoa Riroroko, the carver of his
ancestor's mana*

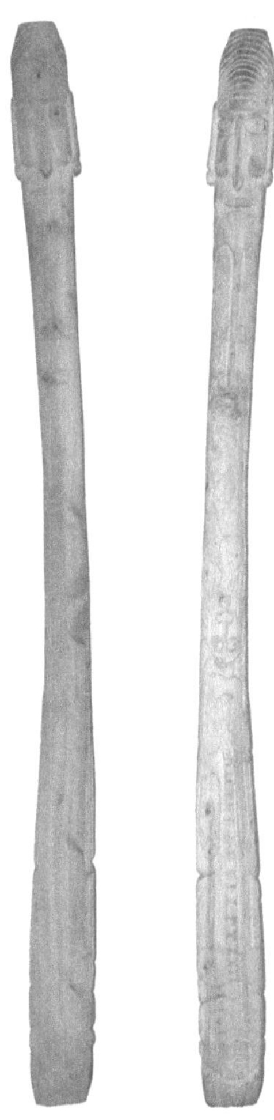

The beautiful, cherished heua he so kindly gave me

Lucia, Nano, and Deloris on a relaxing day

Jorge Pio Andres Haoa Riroroko, the soul of a new generation, and Deloris holding a moai so kindly carved and offered to us by his father, Leandro (Leo) Haoa Pakomio

The stunning view from Orongo of Motu Nui, Motu Iti, and Motu Kao Kao

Partial view of the Rano Kau crater, one of the most beautiful in the world

The author, Francis F. Pitard

109° 30'
27° 5'
Anakena
Ovahe
Poike
Terevaka
Ahu of the sacred
seven souls
Taatamao
settlement
Hanga Roa
Rano Raraku
Rano Kau
Orongo
Orito
Vinapu
Motu Kao Kao
Motu Iti
Motu Nui
N
RAPA NUI
0 1 2 3 4 5 6 7 Km

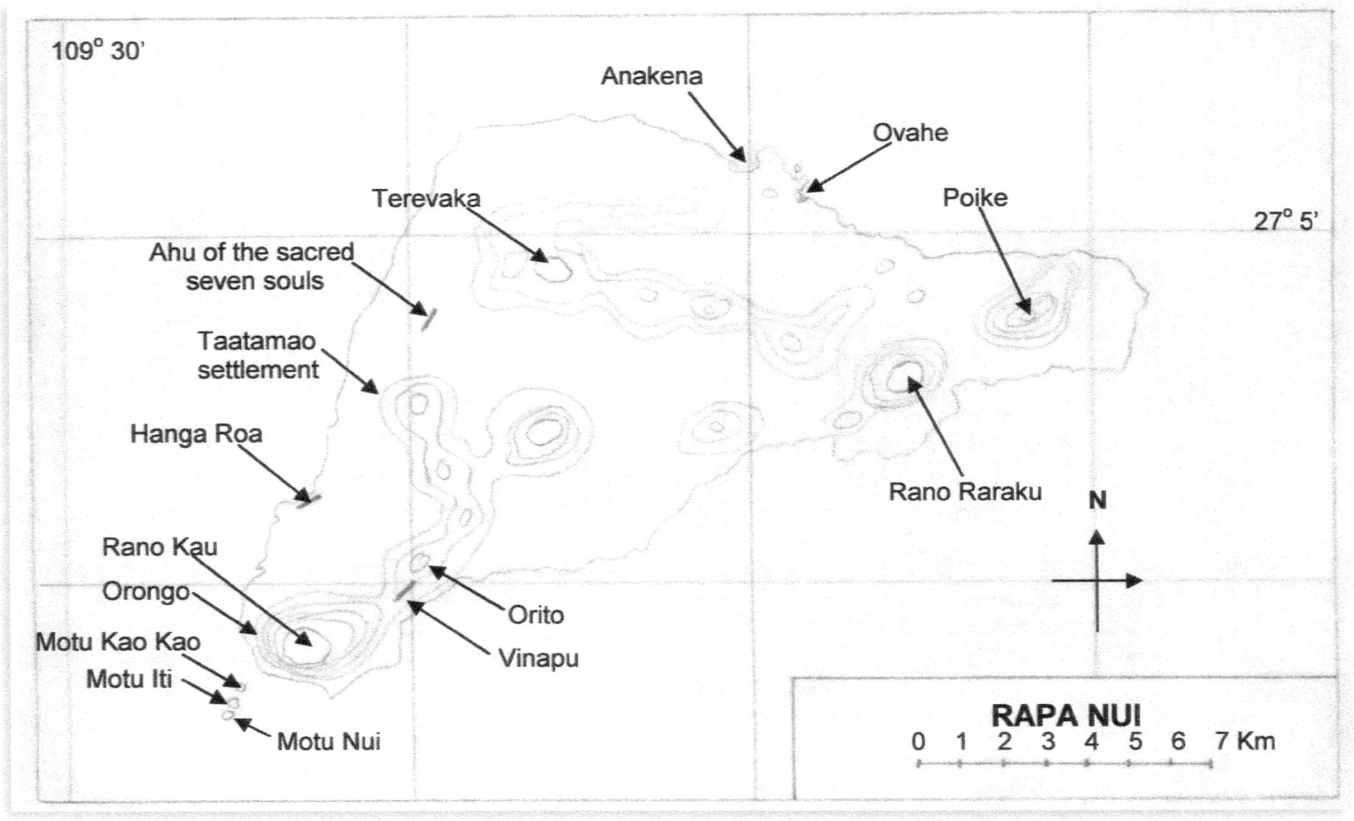

Rapa Nui Map

CHAPTER 1

For us it was the year AD 403, in another world where ordinary time does not exist. It was near an island that had just entered human consciousness. It was an island the visionary Maohi priestess Hina of the Valley had named Rapa Nui.

"Mana lives in my mind. Therefore, I will find a way to communicate with my loved ones and challenge my unbearable solitude on this lost island. My fate shall not destroy me."

Kama Tici Viracocha

Since dawn, the massive raft of balsa logs had followed the north side of the island. Only once along its entire length did a tiny beach of white sand interrupt the rugged, unfriendly coast. At times the Viracochas saw giant caverns eroded deeply inside the cliffs, where large waves incessantly pounded. Kama Tici's eyes swept the western end of the island and its formidable crags, followed by three islets. After the raft passed the third and largest islet, she knew the Awesome Sea would rule their lives again, as it had for the last two moon cycles. They had escaped the continent where the Inca were methodically exterminating their peaceful race. Their nonbelligerent nature was regarded by the rising class of Incan military leaders as subversive and a threat to their power at this still-distant dawn of what would become the largest empire on the surface of the earth. Some would call them fugitives, and others would revere them as the great gods of knowledge who vanished in pursuit of the setting sun.

The fifty rafts, holding all the hopes of the Viracocha race, had been divided into three groups: Taranga's group followed a northwest course, Kon's group headed due west, and Illa's group, by far the largest, followed a southwest direction. Taranga Tici was the old, powerful monarch, and a man of great wisdom. Kon Tici, the Son of the Sun, was one of Taranga's grandchildren. Illa Tici, the Son of Fire, was his older grandchild.

It had been Illa's choice to go southwest so all the lookouts could scan the sea, from the southwest to the northwest, and have a better chance to locate new lands where the sun sets. Illa's raft was the farthest south, so far. After they passed the last islet, Illa had plans to change his course to due west and allow no further drift from the other rafts. In any case, he did not consider this relatively small island an ideal place for them to settle. It was just a welcome distraction along their epic voyage into the unknown.

There were twelve passengers: Illa and his wife, Kama; their three children, Ku their oldest son who was eight sun cycles old, Kane who was the second son, six sun cycles old, and Kura, their daughter, who was three sun cycles old. There were also three older couples and one young woman, Kora.

Kama Tici was a woman of great beauty, tall, thin, and quite strong, considering she was not accustomed to hard physical work. Her flowing black hair caressed her waist. Her penetrating dark blue eyes were extremely observant. Despite being at the top of the Viracocha aristocracy, she was humble. She possessed a keen intellect. She wore a modest white robe split on the sides to allow her legs more freedom of movement when walking. She always wore a thick belt with a few treasured items: a gourd with a two-day supply of fresh water that she had just refilled and three little bags that held a collection of valuable seeds that might prove useful on an unknown land they would eventually call home.

As the raft approached the last islet, the three children played at the aft, near the twin rudders. On this side of the island, the sea was calmer. Everyone marveled at the rocky islet they could almost touch, and the crystalline depths. It was an extraordinary luxury for the eyes after two moon cycles at sea. Young Kura saw a turtle swimming in tiny waves breaking on shore. The animal fed on some green seaweed attached to the volcanic rock. Excited, Kura rushed to the edge of the raft pointing with her fingers, tripped over a coiled rope, lost her balance, and fell overboard. The other children screamed to alert their parents. Kama jumped into the sea to rescue her daughter. Illa and two other men brought the sail down as quickly as possible, and everyone paddled hard to bring the raft back to the islet. But momentum, combined with current, pushed the raft farther and farther away. Illa was ready to dive into the sea as well, but the other men held him and begged him to stay on board. They had been warned that it was possible to alter the course of the raft; however, it was impossible to reverse course. They were all aware of the danger.

"None of us can swim that far to rescue them," one man said. "We are not good swimmers. Kama swims much better than you do. It would be suicidal for you, and we all need you and your sons."

"Paddle east," Illa ordered, changing his strategy. "We may be able to reach the main island farther on this side."

Inexorably, the raft continued to drift farther away from the island on its southerly course. There was nothing that could be done. They paddled as hard as they could, but knew it would be impossible to rescue Kura and Kama. Illa was crushed by the cruel reality of the accident nobody could have foreseen. His mind raced at the stunning implications. He looked at the western horizon, hoping another land would not be too far away. He had no way of knowing they had just passed one of the most isolated islands on the surface of the earth.

Kama swam the best she could, fighting for every inch in an element not hers. She desperately searched for Kura in the rolling chaos of the waves splashing along the islet. She never saw her. She no longer knew where to look and what to do. Exhausted, she reached the islet, sobbing aloud. She found the energy to climb to higher ground and gain a better view of the surroundings. She disturbed many seabirds while scrambling up a small cliff overlooking the inlet. She ignored their wheeling and screeching. Driven by adrenalin, Kama focused on finding Kura. She searched for Kura's white garment, but found nothing. Finally, Kama wiped tears from her eyes, and she searched for the raft. She found it, sail down, drifting far away on the Awesome Sea.

"They are fighting hard, but the sea rules their destiny," she murmured. "They will never make it back."

She fully realized the implications of her vision. She was overwhelmed and devastated. She felt helpless.

"Wherever you may go, my love, live well, and remember me…" All her life she would remember these terrible words. In the blink of an eye, their destinies had irrevocably changed.

She sat near a seabird nest, trying to overcome her emotions. She knew there was no way she would ever find Kura alive; the little one did not know how to swim. She hoped for a miracle. She knew the raft could never reverse its course; it had been a pervasive concern throughout their journey.

Kama Tici Viracocha was alone, and night was coming. She

removed her wet clothes to dry them, and walked around the islet. She found a little cove full of long grass in which she lay down. She covered herself with the grass and cried. Sheltered from the night breeze, she succumbed to a fitful sleep, defeated. Twice she woke and thought she heard her daughter calling, but it was the waves, the breeze, the futile wishing of a mother's mind.

The low-pitched grating of terns declared the dawn. Kama's eyes scanned the waving grass. Her ears strained for a miracle. She was afraid to stand up and face her sad reality. Finally, she dressed and carefully explored the shore around the islet, searching for Kura's body. She found a small depression in the rock that had trapped rainwater. She drank and checked the level of water in her gourd. Drawing from the strength of her intellect, she knew she could not stay on any of these islets; her only chance for survival was to swim to the main island. For her, it was a huge undertaking.

"This is what I have to do… now!" she told herself.

The next islet was very close, which would make her first experience easy. Looking at the high-water mark on the rocks, she could tell the tide was out, and the sea was calm; it was the ideal time of day. She slowly entered the water, and within a short time she was on the next islet; it was much smaller than the one she just left. She climbed to safe ground, disturbing many nesting birds as she circled the islet at the top of a cliff and searched for any sign of Kura. There was no trace of her little darling. She sobbed again, then looked at the next islet. It was a tall, sharp pinnacle that erupted from the ocean floor, leaving practically no place to walk. It was about halfway between her and the main island. As she entered the water, she noticed some of the rocks were obsidian. She was familiar with volcanic formations on the continent. Determined, she walked into the water and started her long journey. She felt the gentle current flowing east of the pinnacle, the same current that had pushed the raft from the island. By sheer willpower she managed to stay on course. Steadily, but not rushing, Kama approached the pinnacle. She circled it to the side where the waves were smaller. The pinnacle was much taller than she had anticipated, and there was no place to walk. She hung on the edge of a crevice, with water to her waist, and rested. She looked at the huge cliff of the main island, and noticed it was fortunately circled by a narrow beach full of boulders and cobbles. Determined, she started her last journey, and let herself drift eastward with the current, which was not as strong as at the other islets. The slow drift allowed her to save energy, and it would inevitably bring her to the beach on the eastern side of a long cove. Several times the thought of a shark encounter crossed her mind, and she began exploring it as a way to end her misery. She fought such negative thinking and persevered.

Exhausted and shivering, she reached the beach and sat on a flat boulder, glancing at the islets. She removed her clothes and let them dry. She was in the shade of the giant cliff and wished the sun would reach her. Slightly to the west, she noticed the cliff was about half as high as in other parts, and more climbable. She knew it would be a daunting task, but she had done that kind of thing when she was a girl. Later in the morning, the sun finally reached the edge of the cliff. Its therapeutic rays invigorated her body; she regained energy and courage. She tightened her sandals, dressed, and started the long and difficult climb.

The nature of the rock was similar to what she had observed on the small islet: definitely volcanic. It was covered with sharp edges and holes, easy to wound feet and hands for the unwary. As a Viracocha, she was an experienced climber. She took her time and smiled at the thought; she, indeed, had all the time in the world. The same characteristic long grass that she had seen on the islets was growing everywhere. She used it to help maintain her balance. It was about midday when she approached the top of the cliff. Finally, out of breath, she reached the edge of another world. Totally taken by surprise, she surveyed one of the most breathtaking panoramas she had ever seen. It was a huge caldera with a variegated bottom covered with green patches of vegetation alternating with beautiful blue ponds. The walls of the huge crater were quite steep and covered with crumbling reddish pebbles. All around the lake near the well-drained slopes, tall palm trees added to the beauty of this awesome natural garden. Kama was not in any mood to admire the spectacular scenery. Nevertheless, it certainly made an impression on her. She carefully walked down the slope full of crumbling pebbles, trying to stay as close as possible to the large patches of long grass. At the bottom, when she reached the first palm tree, she noticed the ground was covered with small nuts. With a stone, she cracked the hard shell. The yellow nut inside was very tasty and helped assuage her hunger. She headed for the first pond, found her way between high reeds, walked above a thick marsh similar to those she was familiar with around Lake Titicaca back home, and finally got to a clear spot by the calm, crystalline water. The pond was very deep. She could not see the bottom of it. The water was unusually clean and not salty. The bank of the pond was very unstable and was sinking under her weight. She drank, undressed, washed her salty, dirty clothes, and took a swim to soften her sunburned, parched skin. She could not help thinking Kura would have loved doing the same. Once more she sobbed with immense anguish. She let herself drift until her mind cleared up. She noticed the inside of the crater was hot and well protected from the prevailing winds. In a mysterious way, her mind told her this place would be of great importance for her. She was a woman with a brilliant intuition. She felt these unmistakable vibrations typical of other sacred places she had been. There was no doubt this place held unknown powers. An uncontrollable shiver ran down her spine as she fought back primordial fear. Silence was absolute, broken only by the occasional chirp of a bird in the distance.

Kama spread her wet clothes in the full sun, and rested for a while in the shade of the palm trees. She heard a seabird, looked up, and saw a red-tailed tropicbird, then a second. They were rare birds that nested in inaccessible places, and to find one there meant the place should be well protected from intruders. She reflected on the shape of the trees and the nuts; far back in her memory she recalled having seen the same trees in the southern part of the continent during a long trip when she was a young girl. So far, no streams were to be seen, and she worried about storing drinking water. She cut a few reeds using a little obsidian knife. She took one and made a clean cut at both ends, and noticed it was filled with tight fibers. There was no space available to store water. She decided to keep them anyway to further study them later on. She tightened both ends together with one fiber of long grass and put the reed around her neck. Selecting four of the tallest and largest ones, she repeated the same procedure. She filled her gourd with fresh water from the lake. She dressed and started her journey up the western ridge.

The climb was long and tedious. The view on both sides was food for vertigo. Kama reached a plateau where she had a good view of the ocean and the rest of the island. There were several well-protected caves that would be good places to spend the night. She studied the island and had a premonition that it was inhabited, but by whom, or what? Earlier, as they had followed the coastline with the raft, no one had noticed any evidence of a human settlement.

The cloudless evening was clear. She would have a very good view of the horizon at sunset and could use the setting sun's backlighting to search for an outline of another distant island. If a nearby island existed to the west, she would have a better chance to find Illa, since he would most likely launch a rescue mission from there.

She had many birds for companions. They were not afraid of her, though they did not seem to enjoy her presence. Following a nonnegotiable argument, she ate two gannet's eggs, then a few more nuts that she had gathered from the crater and stored in her pockets. She took her gourd, drank, and pondered the reeds, wondering what she could do with them.

As the setting sun backlit the western horizon, Kama scanned for other islands: there were none. She searched again for a tiny dot that could have looked like a raft: the sea was empty.

"How far are you going?" she murmured to herself, Illa, and the wind. "How long is it going to take for you to discover other people with better navigation skills? Far away, are there seafarers who could bring you back to me?"

Kama pondered her questions and had no illusion about their wisdom. She laid her head on her arms and knees and sobbed in despair. Although drained of any will, she managed to cut some long grass to make a bed inside one of the caves, to protect her from the cold night. She curled inside her primitive arrangement and let her mind drift into unpredictable dreams. That night she dreamed of a young woman with long black hair and large black eyes. She was an outstanding swimmer, and obviously her people were talented seafarers. It was not the first time Kama had dreamed about her.

The next day she searched the sea and the horizon, hoping and praying for some sign of Illa, anyone. Then she circumambulated the top of the crater, going all the way around until she could again see the beach of boulders far below. A tiny white dot attracted her attention and sent blood rushing to her head.

"Kura! Is that Kura?"

She followed the sharp ridge until she found a relatively safe place to clamber down; even then, it was a daunting and dangerous endeavor. But nothing would stop her. Her resolve to reach her daughter was as strong as the ancient lava she was traversing. As soon as she reached the beach, she ran on pebbles between boulders and cobbles. Kura's body had been left by the receding tide. Kama grabbed her daughter, embraced her swollen, cold face, and held her tight in her arms. Even dead, Kura was an incredible treasure. Kama's plaintive cry echoed off the cold and brooding cliffs. With her eyes raised to the heavens, she thought about the tiny cave where she had slept.

"Yes, I will take you all the way up to that cave and give you a decent burial."

She tied both tiny arms together around the wrists, so she could hang Kura around her neck and not hamper her difficult climb. She started the daring climb, retracing her path from the day before. Kama felt pain in her joints and muscles. She sweated more than she ever did. Kura was heavier than she had noticed in the recent past. Several times she took a rest and looked back at the islets and the horizon for Illa. A brief rain made her journey even more treacherous. At the lower edge of the cliff, she laid Kura on a patch of long grass and went down into the crater to collect more nuts and water.

The sun was already low on the horizon when Kama finally reached the place where she had spent the previous night. She prepared a bed of long grass for Kura, checked the other caves, and selected one where there was the softest soil. She chipped and broke the soil loose from the cave floor, then removed it one handful at a time. She built a grass bed inside the cave and laid Kura's body on it. She looked at her daughter for the last time with immense suffering and anguish. As a mother, she was unprepared for what she had to do next: the most painful act she might have to do in her life. She completely covered her little darling with grass until she would see only her nose and cheeks. Crying loudly, she covered her with more grass and the dirt she had collected. She went outside to collect flat stones she had located a day earlier, and covered the mound of dirt with them. She borrowed a few nice feathers from nearby nests. Just as she had completed her daughter's burial, the sun sank into the western ocean.

In a sad way, she felt better. Kama Tici, the wise woman, had no doubt about the afterlife. She knew her daughter would wander forever on this island in mysterious ways. This island would never again be a lost island. For the time being they were the only two inhabitants of the island. Or were they?

"Have a good journey, my little one," she murmured. "Mana is with you. The Light is with you. You are the Light now, with all its beauty, its power, and its destiny-making will that changes all of us so easily, all the time."

Kama went to sleep feeling a knot of pain in her throat. Again, she was overwhelmed by her intuition that a puissant force was present. She could feel the great power of someone walking around. This time, she did not really care about spirits, as long as Kura's peace was assured and preserved. Kama knew her daughter was now part of this island's spirits for eternity.

The next morning, after scanning the horizon as usual, Kama was ready for a more in-depth exploration of the island. She kneeled near Kura's grave.

"Don't worry. I will be back in a few days," she said. A tiny vortex of dust went by the entry of the cave.

She placed a few nuts in her pockets, four reeds around her neck, verified her gourd was full of water, and started her long journey, heading north along the western coast. Aside from her emotional pain, Kama was in good physical condition. But on that day, after the swim and the climbing and digging of the day before, her body ached everywhere. She had broken most of her fingernails, which were the mark of the high aristocracy in the Viracocha society, where she had a place all her life. Mentally, she was solid as a rock, highly educated, and extremely capable. Yet never had she dreamed she would be challenged by such a dramatic fate. She glanced at her sore hands and feet, then at the mountains that soared far ahead of her.

"Everything has a sacred purpose," she murmured. "It may take me a long time to find out what it is."

As she went down into the valley and followed the coast just above sea level, she walked faster. Palm trees were everywhere. At one point, she felt water dripping on her chest; one of the reeds she had dug and filled with water was leaking. She untied it, drank the drops, and learned they could not keep a significant amount of the precious liquid for very long.

"This is not very reliable," she said. "I should find a good place to plant the seeds I have with me to make more gourds."

Under a cloudy afternoon sky, just before reaching the northern point of the island, she noticed a few tiny ponds of fresh water. She inspected the surroundings, discovered a cave, and decided she would spend the night there. Nearby, she noticed a few palm trees. Rain started to sprinkle. Since it was a warm day, she undressed, placed her clothes inside the cave, and went near the seashore to hunt for a meal. In clear little pools constantly filled with splashing waves, it was easy to collect sea urchins. She was familiar with them from her childhood, and she liked them. She made a full meal of them, cleaned and flossed her teeth with a string of long dry grass, rinsed her mouth with seawater, and went back to the cave. She suffered from sunburns and decided to weave a wide hat. She was a talented weaver. The rain stopped. She went outside to collect long grass for her bed and for her hat. Before sunset, she had a large hat to protect her face, neck, and shoulders. She put it on her head and laughed at how awful she must have looked.

"Well, as long as I don't scare the birds, it will be fine," she said to herself.

She noticed many undisturbed frigate birds were nesting along the wild coast. She attached two woven strips to tie under her chin to keep her hat in place. She looked again at her handicraft and shook her head in dismay. She always liked to look good, but there, alone, she mused on how life's priorities had so horribly changed.

The next day, she climbed to the summit of the island, where she could see all sides at once. She was standing on the edge of a small crater full of reeds, with a crown of clear water surrounding a tiny islet. Farther to the east, she could see the beach with white sand that she had noticed from the raft. At the top of the beach were many palm trees. She noticed another detail that had concerned her for some time: there was no trace of any stream. The freshwater resources of the island were extremely limited. Farther to the southeast she noticed another crater with trees around it. She noted its location and made a mental note to explore it on her way back, after following the south side of the island. She went down, followed the right side of a sharp cliff, reached the seashore, and continued her long trek toward the white sandy beach. At some distance from the beach, she found another pool of fresh water, surrounded by reeds. Early in the afternoon, she reached the beach and was amazed at its beauty. It was a perfect place for a settlement. It was now very clear the island was uninhabited. Humans would never leave such a beautiful place, in such an unfriendly rocky land. She lay in the shade of the palm trees and weighed her options. She thought she would make two settlements: one near Kura's grave, and one here, unless there were other surprises. She bathed in the shallow water near the beach and found many clams in the sand. She had plenty of food, but very little fresh water, and so far she had not found anything more satisfactory to store water in than the fragile reeds she carried around her neck, and her gourd.

The next day, she found another tiny, well-protected pink sandy beach. Then she followed a rugged coast, with an increasingly high cliff that rendered the sea inaccessible to her. The evening found her at the far eastern side of the island, where she located a cave and pool of fresh water. She was exhausted.

The next day she did not find anything of interest. There was a small islet near the coast on the south side. But for a long time to come she would have a distaste for islets. Nevertheless, she enjoyed the calm water near the shore; it was deep and full of fish swimming from crevices to caves. This would be an outstanding place for fishing on a calm day.

Then she headed for the crater she had seen from the top of the island, where she would spend the night. First, she followed the strange-looking outer south side of the crater and found deep enclaves in a pleasing, relatively soft rock. When she reached the edge where she could see the inside of the crater, she was delighted at the sight of a beautiful blue lake, surrounded by familiar reeds, and trees she had never seen before. She had not found any stream or river, but she had found three lakes so far. She found a well-protected cave, not very deep, but good enough to spend the night, protected from the cold breeze.

She looked at the texture of the rock, took her obsidian knife, and made a few scratches. Her guess had been correct. The rock was relatively friable. But at this moment, something happened in her mind. She felt a burst of energy surge from the rock and invade her body. As a Viracocha, she was an adept at discovering the mysteries held by Mother Earth. She realized this mountain, with its rock, its crater, and its lake, was important. She could not explain the reasons. But it was certainly a good place to visit and meditate for the night. She ate a few nuts and a few seeds from the surrounding grass and drank a lot of water. As usual, she curled herself under a thick layer of long grass and let her mind enter a trance in which she could have visions. For most people, there are two steps in their daily life: one when they are awake and one when they sleep and dream. For Viracochas there were three steps: when they were awake, when they slept and dreamed, and when they were in a trance and had visions.

She saw large rocks separate from the mountain and walk like haunted shadows around the lake. There were many. Each of them seemed to have a selected place. It was like a meeting of giants around a sacred lake. All night Kama Tici observed the giants and tried to understand what they were doing. Above the lake the sky was very clear and full of stars. The stars swam in the calm lake. The giants lay slightly on their backs, as if they were looking at the stars. Their mouths expressed some kind of disdainful mood; it was as though they disagreed with something.

It was dawn when Kama woke up. She looked at the lake and the mountain. There were no giants anywhere to be seen. Intrigued by her vision, she approached a flat, slick wall and slowly pressed her hands on it as if she wanted to communicate with it. She closed her eyes and felt the sleeping life forces in the mountain. The mountain was alive with mystery. She took a pebble from the mountain; it would be offered to Kura.

Kama continued her journey. Two days later she closed the circle, having traveled around the island, and was back at Kura's grave. She placed the pebble on the top of the grave, and found it comforting that an island numen would protect her daughter's spirit.

"Mata Kite Rani, my little loved one," she said. "The Light is with you."

"Eyes looking at the stars," she said.

This was Kama Tici's vision, which would have astonishing implications a few sun cycles later. Nearby the cave a tiny vortex of dust went by.

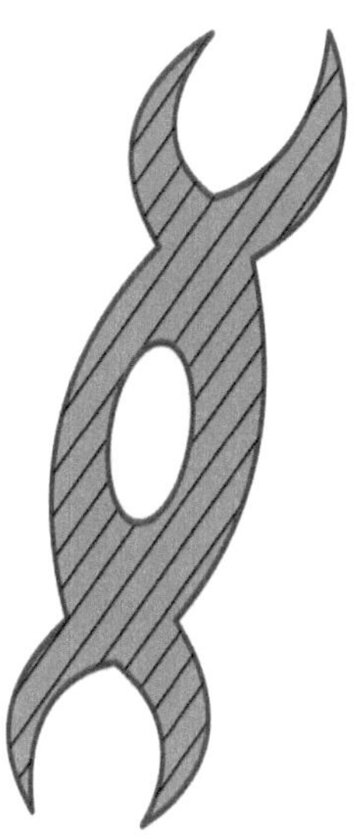

The sacred, supernatural spirit of the first woman is alive
inside and outside her earthbound body: It was never created;
therefore will never die. It is the eternal Light.

CHAPTER 2

"The Light gave us this earth to be part of a wonderful experiment. It is for us to find ways to protect and honor this awesome trust. Explorers with goodwill we must be. Therefore, I was determined to find Mata Kite Rani, an island Hina called Rapa Nui, and perhaps my lost brother Illa."

Kon Tici Viracocha

Almost four sun cycles later, far to the west, during the great religious gathering of Maohis on Havaiki, a young priestess from Tahiti Nui impressed the tribe's elders. Hina of the Valley was a tall, beautiful Maohi woman, about sixteen sun cycles of age, barely out of adolescence, but experienced beyond her years since Kon Tici had entered her world. Her noble posture exuded pride and self-confidence.

"Do you know why I chose Rapa Nui as the name of this mysterious island you want to find?" Hina of the Valley asked with humor in her eyes.

Kon Tici Viracocha and all her relatives and friends stared at the young priestess with rapt anticipation.

"One island was not represented during the Great Gathering," she said.

Kon was from a faraway world in the east. He was from

another race, tall and fair-skinned with long black hair held on the top of his head with a gold pin. He wore a blue tunic and a belt with embroidered red suns and golden condors. A matching headband imparted a charismatic charm to his face. Gold bracelets, gold ear plugs, and a gold necklace with a carved sun awed the priests. To them, there was no doubt he was a god sent by the Great Taaroa, Creator of Everything.

"Which one?" Kon asked with his eyes widening.

"Rapa Iti," she replied. "I think we should visit it before we go east."

"But we went there!" the old Taranga argued.

Taranga Tici Viracocha was the grandfather of Kon. Taranga was regarded as a living god, constantly in touch with the Light, Creator of Everything, by the few remaining members of the lost Viracocha race.

During the last few moon cycles, it had become clear, especially to Hina of the Valley, that Taaroa for the Maohis and the Light for the Viracochas are the same supreme being, the unconditional master of everything.

"Are you sure it was Rapa Iti?" Hina challenged. "Describe the island to Tamatoa, who is familiar with its landscape."

"It was a small, low land with very few inhabitants, that kept to themselves," Hotu-Matua answered.

"What you describe is not Rapa Iti!" Tamatoa retorted. "Rapa Iti has high, jagged summits, like Moorea."

Tamatoa the Great was a giant Maohi, a formidable warrior whose body was covered entirely with intricate tattoos. He was king of the Pora Pora people, on a group of islands north of Havaiki, and king of Rarotonga; he was incredibly strong and a talented navigator. Tamatoa was committed to helping Kon search for his brother Illa. Tamatoa was a good man, and his friendship with Hina and Kon grew stronger with every passing moon cycle.

"This changes everything!" Kon said, pointing a finger at Tamatoa.

"As Hotu-Matua goes to Hiva, as he told us he would, and prepares his trip east with Taranga, we can quickly visit Rapa Iti," Tamatoa suggested.

Hotu-Matua was the king of Hiva, a group of islands in the far northeast of Tahiti Nui. He had saved the lives of several Viracochas and had become a close friend of the old Taranga. As a talented navigator, Hotu-Matua's assistance finding Illa was most welcome; besides, he enjoyed the challenges of exploring new shores.

They conferred and agreed that Tamatoa's plan made good sense.

Kukara grabbed Hina's hand and smiled; it was a gesture that signaled the young girl's happiness about the events taking place in her life.

Kukara Tici Viracocha was about eight sun cycles old. The Inca had massacred her parents and her brother. Hina and Kon had adopted her and cared for her as though she were their own child. The old Taranga taught her many things about mana, and the meaning of some mysterious Rongo-Rongo tablets that Hotu-Matua had given her. Hina, who was continually amazed by unexplainable acts by the little girl, had observed Kukara's precociousness from when she was an infant.

Five days later, after a dramatic farewell, Tamatoa's three best oceangoing ships left for one of the most epic and daring maritime adventures ever. Mehao, Tamatoa's oldest son, would rule the Pora Pora people, and Teahu, his youngest son, would rule Rarotonga. Kon, Hina, and Kukara traveled on Tamatoa's ship. Tamatoa's daughter, Mahine, and her mate, Taatamao, were in charge of one of the two other vessels. The third was loaded with plants, ropes, food, and animals. Five families from Pora Pora were on board the supply ship. Under Tamatoa's regimented command, all three craft sailed at full speed to Rapa Iti.

At the same time, on Rapa Nui, a well-dressed woman headed to the lake around which she would meet shadows from another world. Kama's self-sufficiency and strong will served her well. She deftly wove solid, attractive clothes and ponchos from strong reed fibers and made strong ropes, baskets, and hats from long grass. Kama constructed five comfortable shelters from woven reeds and palm tree fronds at key locations throughout the island, and provisioned them for a long stay. With the hard wood of a native tree, she made small jugs for her excursions and larger ones to store water at each shelter. The vines grown from her seeds produced more gourds than she could ever use.

She was constantly exploring and moving from one shelter to the next. It killed time, and she was actually enjoying herself. At the crest of a tiny hill, she found a large deposit of high-quality obsidian, which could make survival possible.

As if her own voice was her only companion, she took the habit of saying what she was thinking.

"I saw Kon in my visions," she said to herself. "I saw Taranga and Kukara. I saw a beautiful woman from another world with the golden condor around her neck. But I never saw my loved ones. In a way, it is telling me they went to the world of spirits long ago. If this is so, then they became the Light; therefore they are in good hands."

Following her evening meal, she touched the living mountain with her hands, closed her eyes, and turned around. Like a specter, dressed in white, she slowly walked halfway between the mountain and the lake. Sitting on a mat she had used many times at this place, she raised her arms and easily slipped into a deep trance; she saw giant anthropoid shadows disengaging from their mountain niches, moving slowly down the slopes, and assuming the positions they have occupied around the lake since the beginning of time. At the most isolated place on the earth, they were the secret guardians of a cosmic tradition, each with its sacred role and unspoken name.

Kama was communicating with beings she had never succeeded so far in comprehending. She did not mind them having their secrets. She would keep trying anyway, as it was a fascinating experience. She knew her visions would vanish at dawn, leaving no trace of physical manifestations. Kama desperately wanted something tangible, but knew that was wishful thinking. She knew the ways of the Light, with its unlimited energy sent through the ether to enter our eyes, warm our skin, nourish our brain, and create awareness. She knew her body was only a transitory vessel that carried the burdens of universal consciousness. Viracochas were well aware their bodies were only vessels carrying a tiny local consciousness, with a mission to grow, evolve, and create at all cost. They were well aware the universal consciousness was constantly feeding the local consciousness for its mysterious, temporary purpose.

"At this time of my life, I really wonder what my temporary purpose is!" she joked, laughing aloud.

Tamatoa's ship navigated with precision among the coral reefs protecting Rapa Iti's deep bay. The bay was ringed with spectacular jagged peaks and crowned with sculpted terraces. The foothills were covered with luxuriant, verdant vegetation.

"Who could have built this?" Kon asked.

"There are several clans on this island," Tamatoa said. "They often fight between each other. Kon Tici, welcome to the real world!"

Tamatoa admired the peaceful ways of Kon and his people, but knew their utopian dream world was unrealistic.

After crossing the bay, they noticed a crowd waiting for them. As they approached the beach, Kon searched for a familiar face. Two young boys entered the water. They were Viracochas. They were Ku, Illa's oldest son, now eleven sun cycles old, and Kane, his youngest son at nine. He searched for Illa, Kama, or Kura but did not find them. He saw another young Viracocha woman and recognized a few elders. He jumped in the water and went directly to Ku and Kane. They joyously embraced in the waist-deep water.

"Where are your parents?" Kon asked impatiently.

"Mother and Kura are lost on a faraway island in the east," Ku explained. "Kura fell overboard as we were close to the western end of the island. Mother rescued her. We could not stop the raft. We only assume they are alive. Father was killed shortly after we arrived here."

"How?" Kon asked in dismay, his eyes tightly closed in anguish.

"He tried to separate people fighting from two different clans. These people always fight. Also, after losing Mother and Kura, he lost his will to live and became depressed."

Hina held Kon's hand and did not say anything. She knew his pain was terrible. However, she also knew this would help cleanse his mind, even if the reality was impossible to accept. They also knew now that there was an island in the east where a miserable woman might be waiting for a miracle. Tamatoa put a friendly hand on Kon's shoulder. The tattooed giant knew when to stay silent.

"In a few days, we should leave, to search for your mother and Kura," Kon said gently. "Both of you will come with us."

A young Viracocha woman came to them.

"My name is Kora. I know Kama well. She is my best friend. Can my parents and I go with you?"

Kon glanced questioningly at Tamatoa.

"Yes," Tamatoa replied. "We will have to divide everybody equally among the three ships."

Two days later, with a full supply of plants and animals to start a new settlement, the three vessels found their way to the open sea, headed due east, and retraced Illa's route, to the best recollection of two young boys, one young woman, and two elders, by observing starry paths traced in the night skies.

At the same time, much farther to the north near Hiva, Hotu-Matua's five vessels were navigating on a southeast course. On board these ships were the famous Viracochas Taranga, Rangi, and Hiti, good friends of Kon, along with several other Viracocha families, many Maohi families, and almost every plant and animal found on Hiva.

"I don't look forward to this trip," Taranga said with a grin on his face. "Yet I am very excited about it. How do you explain this?"

"You are a pragmatic explorer," Hotu-Matua replied, laughing. "Now there is no turning back."

"You are kind to a useless old man at sea," Taranga said self-deprecatingly while fluttering his fingers with very long nails on his lap.

Thirty-four days later, after a lengthy battle against heavy winds and currents, Tamatoa and Kon relaxed on the deck with Illa's oldest son, pointing out and reading the major stars and constellations blazing in the night sky.

"Are we too far south?" Tamatoa asked. "Do you remember

what your father said?"

"I think the placement of the stars is correct," Ku replied. "But at that time it did not occur to me this would be important one day."

"I know," Kon said. "But even the little you know may help; please do your best."

At dawn they all scrutinized the horizon for any sign of an island. There was nothing. Later during the day, Tamatoa noticed a flock of birds flying north. He looked at the clouds above the northern horizon. There were too many clouds to be of any help. Nevertheless, Kon saw his hesitation.

"Isolated clouds are much better indicators," Kon said.

"The birds were long-range birds," Tamatoa replied. "Therefore it is not clear where they go or where they come from. As for the clouds, there are just too many to be sure."

"Shall we turn north?" Kon asked.

"No, we are going to continue straight east," Tamatoa said. "However, make sure we remember the exact position of the stars tonight. If we have to come back later, I want to be slightly north of here."

On the same day, some distance to the north, on Rapa Nui, Kama cooked a fish for her morning meal a few steps away from Kura's grave. Her eyes randomly scanned the northwestern horizon. She felt faint as blood rushed from her head at the astonishing, unbelievable sight. She counted five white sails, far away under the mist of a large cloud.

Rushing around her campsite, she collected everything that could be burned and piled it on the fire. She cut large amounts of long grass to make smoke. This was a dream she never thought possible. She had hoped for it, but always rejected the thought as unrealistic and depressing. She had been mistaken to give up hope so early, and now she had better hurry to attract attention.

"These travelers must know of the Viracochas! There is no way they can't," she said.

Excited beyond belief, she studied the approaching ships. They were fast and navigated with great skill. She knew they must have seen the smoke, but she decided to wait longer. She continued to fuel the fire with more grass to ensure that they saw her exact position.

"I should have cooked more fish, much more fish!" she chuckled.

She remained near the fire until she could see people on the ships. There were many people. Now she knew they would be able to locate her white garments. The first boat sailed in the south side of the largest islet, where Kura had drowned. Kama Tici struggled her way down the dangerous cliff. Two ships landed at the same time she reached the beach, a terrible beach full of obstacles at the bottom of a formidable cliff. She negotiated her way between sharp volcanic rocks and cobbles. She saw old Taranga walking on cobbles, coming to her. She literally flew to his arms, and in tears, they embraced. She fell on her knees sobbing from joy and pent-up emotions. In many ways it was the triumph of will. Then she backed off a little and looked at his eyes with expectation.

"Where is Illa? Where are my children?"

Taranga looked at her with expectation as well.

"You are trying to tell me you are alone on this island?"

"Yes, I am," she said. "Where are they?"

"We never found Illa's raft," he said. "We never found any raft from his group. But Kon and Kukara are coming through a more southern route. They should join us in a few days, I hope. They went to explore a few islands far in the south, just to make sure you were not on them. So until they arrive, we will not know."

"I am accustomed to waiting by now," Kama replied.

Taranga introduced her to his long-time friend Hotu-Matua, who looked at her from head to toe.

"My garments are not very feminine," she joked.

"On the contrary," Hotu-Matua said, using clear Viracocha words, a sign he and Taranga had spent a long time together. "Many details show me you are a talented woman, as Taranga always told me. It is a great honor to finally meet you."

"It is early in the morning," she said. "May I suggest a place where you can anchor the ships in a safe harbor?"

"Absolutely!" Hotu-Matua replied. "Indeed, that would be most appreciated."

"Follow the coast to the north side until you find the only sand beaches on the island. The first one is quite large, a magnificent, well-protected place for you."

"Come aboard, let's go," Hotu-Matua ordered.

As they passed the largest islet, Kama explained what had happened when her daughter fell overboard, how she tried to rescue her, and how Kura had died.

"My child," Taranga said with sadness, "all the suffering we are enduring is still better than being massacred by the Inca. Therefore, let's be positive and prepare for our new lives."

As they followed the western coast, Taranga told her Kon and Hina's story.

"I will be so happy to see them in reality," Kama said.

Taranga glanced at her, pondering the meaning of her words. She smiled at him, guessing his thoughts.

"There are great powers on this island that even I don't understand yet," she said.

"I would like to know more of these powers some day," he said.

"I will show you, soon," she said.

She heard a rooster crow at the back of the ship, a sound that was repeated by another rooster in a nearby ship.

"They are looking at the island too," Kama said, laughing. "This island will never be the same again. We must be careful; the freshwater supply is very limited and could be polluted easily."

"If this is the case, dear," Taranga replied, "we will use our genius to correct the deficiency. But tell me, you just insinuated we will stay on this island."

"I will, even if nobody else does," she said frowning. "This sacred land is where my daughter died and is her eternal resting place."

There was a long silence following her statement. Suddenly, everyone marveled at the white sandy beach and surrounding palm trees. Immediately following their first steps on the beach, children and women explored the surroundings, while men unloaded the ships. Children took possession of Kama's shelter and all her belongings, and nobody seemed to care. Kama was happy to be with all of them, but on the other hand, she was annoyed at the lack of manners. Taranga knew her thoughts and offered a clarification, albeit a rationalization.

"They are different, but they are good people," he said. "They take what you have, but they will repay you a thousand times in many ways. Remember my words."

"Are they expecting gifts from me after this?" she asked.

"Don't be perturbed," he said. "Give them very little; it will be an immense treasure for them."

Kama went to her shelter, searched under some old mats still undisturbed, and found what she was looking for. She came back with a package in her hands and bowed her head in front of the king.

"This is my present to you," she said gently. "I am sure you will find them useful."

Hotu-Matua opened the package and saw two amazing black obsidian adzes. Surprise was written all over his face. Never in his life had he seen such beautifully made adzes. He tested the sharpness of the edges on some hair on his lower leg and was impressed at the result.

"You did this, all by yourself, on this island," he said.

"It is nothing really," she said.

"You are indeed a talented woman, and I am greatly honored by this valuable gift," he said.

He went to the ship and came back with his own gift for Kama. He handed her a heavy, lumpy bag. She opened the bag and stared at its precious contents.

"Sweet potatoes! Kumaras!" Kama marveled.

She smiled at him, and he smiled at her.

"They grow well on Hiva." Hotu-Matua said.

The king left, showing the adzes to everyone. As Hotu-Matua's people were busy unloading the ships and installing a camp under the palm trees, Kama invited Taranga for a walk.

"I want to show you our water supply," she said. "It is not too far. It will be good for your old legs."

"Yes, after so long on this ship, I was wondering why we have legs anyway."

"They must be good navigators," Kama said.

"This is an understatement. Maohis are geniuses at sea, and you have seen nothing yet. Wait until Tamatoa comes with Kon and Hina."

"Tell me more about Hina."

"Hina of the Valley! You won't believe the kind of person she is. I cannot describe her; nobody can describe her. You have to see for yourself. With you and Hina combined, men would never rule this world."

"Is that so?" she inquired with a broad smile. "Would it be desirable for women to rule all these warriors?"

"Why not! This world needs good brains. Hina and you combined is the best proposition that ever germinated in my mind."

"Would these powerful men accept such a thing?"

"As I said, you must meet Hina of the Valley first, and then you will quickly understand why there is no other way."

"How old is she?"

"About sixteen sun cycles."

Kama stopped walking and looked at him, incredulous that this mighty king would exalt such a young person.

"I know your thoughts," he said. "I could not believe it either."

"She is only a girl!" Kama said.

"No, she is a woman, a priestess, a great lover, Kukara's adoptive mother, a revolutionary, the best swimmer and diver I have ever seen, a sophisticated, independent mind, an unpredictable adversary, the protector of the weak and ill, and much more."

Kama glanced at him, intrigued, but asked no further questions. She would have to wait and see. They came to the edge of a little pond with crystalline deep water. Kama kneeled near it and showed her treasure.

"There are two large lakes, one small lake, and about eleven ponds like this around the island: this is all our freshwater supply."

"No streams?"

"No streams!"

Taranga scratched the back of his neck and reflected, looking at the sea.

"Are there some rocks capable of being hollowed to hold rainwater?"

"Yes, of course, but creating such ponds would be a daunting task. Also, there is a season when the southerly winds dominate; during those times, the weather is too cold for growing crops. However, we can use the lava tubes; they are protected from the wind."

"Lava tubes?"

"Come, I will show you."

They went farther, slightly up in the hills, to the edge of a long hole.

"This is a lava tube," she explained.

"How do you know this?"

"Long ago, when I was a little girl, a friend of my father showed us one."

"I see."

They found a place where they could walk down inside the tube, which disappeared far inside the earth at both ends.

"How far do they go?" Taranga asked.

"Some may start at the top of the mountain and go all the way to the sea."

"No! You are joking."

"It is true. But look, this is where we can make the best gardens. The soil is moist and very rich. It is perfectly protected from the wind, and yet the sun exposure is excellent."

"For you, this island must have no secret."

"Wrong! The more I explore it, the more it fascinates me. I always find something new, unexpected. There are many things I would like to do, but either I am not strong enough or I don't swim well enough."

"Hina will show you how to swim better; she is a fish!"

They walked to a large patch of tall grass, full of seeds.

"Did you plant these?" he asked.

"Yes, they grow sporadically on the hills, but here they excel. The seeds are very good. This is where we should grow sweet potatoes, manioc, and other plants more favorably disposed toward a warmer climate."

"You are something else," Taranga marveled, placing an arm around her shoulders. "Maohis are excellent gardeners, and they learn fast. They are very creative in finding better, simpler ways of doing things."

In the afternoon, when they came back to the camp, they saw everyone gathered around a fire.

"Come, my friends," Hotu-Matua said. "Eat some of that tuna."

Kama marveled at the three large fish cooking on red embers.

"How did you get them?" she inquired. "These are deep-sea fish."

Hotu-Matua gave her a big piece of tuna and put a hand on her shoulder.

"We are Maohis and born seafarers. This fish cannot hide anywhere from us."

Kama shook her head in disbelief and savored a fish that she had not eaten for as long as she could remember. Later in the evening, they all circled around the fire and asked her to tell her story, starting from the first day she tried to rescue her daughter after she fell from the raft. Kama agreed and was surprised at how engrossed all of them became, from children to elders. In their ways, they were good people, considerate, and caring.

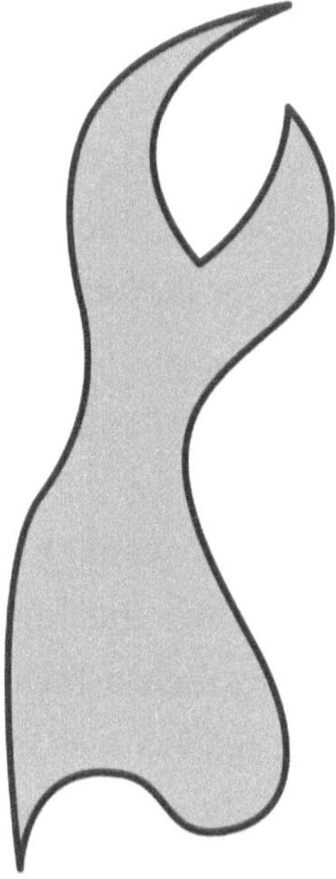

The sacred, supernatural spirit of the first man never dies. It is inside and outside each man of this world, present, secret, and with a mission. It was never created, therefore cannot die. It is the universal consciousness.

CHAPTER 3

"The sea was empty and cold. It was often cloudy and humid, thick with mist and fog. The expedition no longer amused the seafaring Maohis. The time came when they needed a dramatic change for the better."

Hina of the Valley

Another thirty-five days went by on Tamatoa's ship. Navigation was difficult against the high winds, forcing long swings alternately tacking to the northeast and southeast. Such time-consuming zigzag navigation was exhausting to everyone; however, it was necessary if they were to achieve their objective. The technique required arduous training in Maohi seamanship, which mandated an intimate knowledge of the winds, currents, stars, flora, and fauna. The navigator would watch the floating long woven strings at the tip of each mast, which were giving them the exact direction and velocity of the wind at all times. To save time, they had to navigate with the sails at the maximum angle possible relative to the wind, and it was an exhausting battle.

It was clear to everybody that they had missed Rapa Nui long ago. But following Kon's advice, they would continue their journey all the way to the continent. Then they would head north, to a selected point determined by the position of stars. They would wait for Hotu-Matua until the elapsed time would presumably make it apparent he had found an island. Then they would return on a westerly course to find him, a much easier course this time. At least, it was what they thought the scenario would be.

As night descended on them, they gathered as they had done every day since the start of their voyage inside the bamboo cabin, except for the two men watching the sails, watching the course, and watching for the unpredictable. Tehani, Tamatoa's wife, was coping poorly with a bad cough; others, including Hina, struggled as well. Clearly, they were not accustomed to such a cold climate.

"It should not take very long now," said Kon with false bravado. His attempts to bolster their spirits and give them courage were appreciated, but not believed.

"I hope you are right," Tamatoa replied. "Our food supply is nearly gone, except for fish; and our drinking water is low."

Hina was curled up on the floor, her head resting on Kon's lap. Tehani snuggled inside Tamatoa's cape, soaking up the warmth from his chest. Kukara was playing with Ku in the middle of the room; they were fond of each other. Kukara was nine sun cycles old, and Ku was eleven. In dismay, they looked at the adults falling apart one by one. Kukara glanced at Tamatoa looking at her. She went to him and sat by his side. He put his large hand on her tiny shoulder.

"I can feel things," she said. "At dawn watch for the current to change direction."

"Thank you," he murmured in her ear. From experience he knew he should trust her observations and advice, mysterious to many.

They all went to sleep with the hope that their suffering would soon come to an end. At sunrise, everyone went on the deck, expecting the dark outline of the continent on the horizon.

There was nothing. But Tamatoa watched the shape of the waves carefully, and glanced at Kukara, who was smiling at him.

"I love you, little girl," the tattooed giant said. "The current is flowing north."

"This says it all," he added with a thundering voice. "I want every man to paddle, and let these ships do their best."

He took his conch and signaled his orders to the other boats.

"I am always amazed at how contagious his attitude is to everyone around him," Kon said.

"In times like this we definitely need him," Hina replied.

All day the ships sped through the water. Since there was nothing on the cloudy eastern horizon at sunset, they stopped paddling and rested for the night. Not wanting to take any chances, Tamatoa and two other men stood watch throughout the chilly night, always alert for the unpredictable. At dawn they heard Taatamao's conch from the other ship. They all rushed on the deck and looked to the east. Far away, rising very faintly above the horizon, they saw a strand of white cones. Nobody except the Viracochas knew what it was.

"Those are high mountains, volcanoes, covered with snow," Kon explained.

"Tell me what snow is," Hina inquired.

"Frozen water."

"Like the ice we saw on Mount Orohena's lake?"

"Not quite the same. Ice is massive frozen water. Snow is fluffier. It is frozen mist that has fallen to the earth. When it falls, it looks like chicken feathers."

"Whatever," Hina chuckled. "It is pretty on mountains. But it must be very cold there."

"We have had enough of that," Tamatoa added.

"Near the coast it is like here," Kon reassured. "We will not go to the mountains. If we approach the coast between the two largest white cones, we should find a large island with friendly people. We can trade as many fish as you can catch. They like fish, but they are not seafarers."

Pushed by the wind in the sails, the three ships slowly approached the coast. Within a short time they had a respectable quantity of fish, which obviously pleased Kon. He had his reasons. They sailed to the east side of the island and followed its coast until midafternoon. Then they entered a deep bay, at the end of which they saw a village with many houses covered with thick thatch. A primitive canoe with four people paddled out to them.

"Shall we give them two days to leave the island?" Hina chuckled.

Tamatoa and everyone else roared in laughter. One man, well dressed, came on board. As soon as he saw Kon, he fell to his knees and bowed his head all the way down to the deck. Kon took his shaking hands and invited him to stand up. Hina glanced at Tamatoa, intrigued. Kon talked to him in his native language for some time. Then with no further explanation, they were invited to follow the native's boat. The three ships anchored very close to the beach. Smaller boats came out to welcome them. Always concerned with security on such occasions Tamatoa assigned four men to remain on each ship, until their return. The entire population of the village was on the beach; they appeared to be interested in only Viracochas.

"Can you explain their fascination for you?" Tamatoa asked. "Or maybe I should borrow a gold bracelet..."

An old man with a red poncho welcomed them and invited them to an isolated house, more decorated than the others, with nicely carved wood columns. Kon translated that he was the chief of the village, and he wanted to welcome them properly.

"Send someone to get the fish," Kon said. "They are our present to them. They will be impressed because they never go far out in the sea where we caught the tunas."

Tamatoa sent two men to the boats. Kon explained to the old chief what they were doing. Shortly, the two men came back, both holding a huge tuna by its tail.

Their wizened host was overwhelmed and thankful. Humbled, he asked what he could offer to them for their kindness. Kon went to Tehani and asked her to cough. He asked Hina to do the same thing, then asked three other people. The old man smiled, clearly understanding the problem. He called a woman, talked to her for a moment, and she left the house. The old man explained to Kon that he had something that would help them.

"They are going to give us a supply of honey mixed with an extract of fern rhizomes and ground sunflowers," Kon explained. "We should not expect miracles, but it will help you."

"Tell him his gift is appreciated and most appropriate," Tamatoa said, bowing his head in front of the old man, who gave a gesture meaning that it was not much.

Finally, the old man shifted his attention from the Viracochas to the tattooed giant. He walked around him and looked at him from head to toe. He tested his arm muscles and whistled in admiration. He asked something that sent all the Viracochas roaring in laughter.

"What did he say?" Tamatoa asked, amused.

"He asked how many fish you eat in one day," Kon said.

All the Maohis threw their heads back and burst out laughing.

The man asked Kon what else he could do for them. Kon explained they were going farther north as soon as possible, but they needed fruits and vegetables. The next morning, the ships were loaded with fruits, nuts, greens, and sweet potatoes.

In return for the many valuable goods they were given by the natives, Kon gave all the fish they had caught the previous night. Kon and Tamatoa also agreed to give away a little cage with three hens and one rooster they were keeping until they found their final destination. They briefly explained what the chickens were for. The entire village marveled at the unusual birds, and they quickly understood their importance.

"This gift is too much," the old man said. "You will need them."

"No, we have more on the other boats," Tamatoa replied, placing a friendly hand on the old man's shoulder. Kon translated.

With no further ceremony, they bade farewell to the friendly people of the village.

"So far, nobody wants to massacre us," Hina said.

"This is exactly what we should be careful about during our journey along to the coast," Kon explained.

"Why not go west right now?" Tamatoa suggested.

"It is not wise with most of you in bad health," Kon explained. "I know a place where it may be safe and hot, where you will recover quickly. Then we will go west, if Hotu-Matua does not show up."

With the wind in the sails and the current pushing them north, they progressed up the coast at a high speed for six days, at which time they found a large bay, a river, and beautiful white sandy beaches. There was obviously much activity in this area. Plantations could be seen farther in the hills.

"If we can stay here half a moon cycle," Kon said, "I can promise you will all be in excellent health."

"Before we go to shore," Tamatoa said, "let's have a security meeting if something unpleasant happens to us."

"The strategist is talking!" Hina exclaimed.

The three ships came side by side, and sails were taken down. Paddlers held the end of long paddles from the other ships to maintain a short distance between hulls. Then they all crossed over to Tamatoa's ship for their meeting.

"Kon, explain how we should proceed," Tamatoa asked.

"People from only one ship should go to shore at one time. We will take turns. I think we are safe, but the Inca may have spread his influence to here. If the worst were to happen and we are captured for any reason, make no attempt to rescue us. It would be futile, as you would be vastly outnumbered in no time and killed or captured. Instead, patrol the area with the three ships for a maximum of three moon cycles, going back to our new friends in the south for supplies if necessary. Whatever happens, we have three moon cycles to sort out our difficulties, and come back right here. Is that a reasonable plan?"

"I can go along with this with slight deviations to permit greater flexibility," Tamatoa replied. "After three moon cycles, leaving west is not mandatory. We will leave it to the commander of the fleet to decide. Furthermore, the three ships should patrol separately. We should always have one ship near this bay for quick embarkation if necessary. Smoke on the beach will be the signal during the day. Fire on the beach will be the signal during the night."

"Well done," Kon complimented.

They all agreed. They were ready to go ashore. Tamatoa's ship would go first. It was a hot and beautiful day, to everyone's joy. After landing, they cautiously surveyed the surrounding trees for any kind of activity; the lack of contact with an indigenous tribe was disconcerting. Tamatoa, Hina, Kon, and Kukara decided to reconnoiter the immediate sand dunes with sparse trees and left the others to patrol on the ship close to the shore.

As Tamatoa led his team across the beach, they saw a group of people waiting for them in the shade of a tree. A small man in a light white tunic came to them, and was frozen at the sight of Kon and Kukara. He kneeled and buried his face in the sand.

"Here we go again," Hina murmured.

Kon took the man's hands and gently pulled him up.

"I am Kon Tici Viracocha, Son of the Sun. We come in peace to visit you, but for only a few days."

"My master is aware of your visit and wants to welcome you at his temple. But..."

"But what?" Kon inquired.

"He is not aware you are Viracochas. His surprise will be immense."

"Where does your master come from?"

"He is the local Inca governor."

Kon and Kukara instantly blanched in terror. The man saw this and understood their consternation.

"I know what the Inca did to your people," he said. "Have no fear, the old Inca is dead, and his son, Ica, who was bad to you, was assassinated one year ago. The new Inca has always praised your accomplishments."

Kukara translated the conversation to Hina and Tamatoa, who were on their guard. Warriors out of nowhere instantly circled them.

"Don't do anything out of line," Kon said, putting his hand on Tamatoa's wrist.

"Please follow me," the man said.

At some distance from shore, Tehani, Ku, and the others observed the encounter; they instinctively moved closer together and nervously looked at each other and back to the beach.

Kon, Hina, Tamatoa, and Kukara were led far away from

the beach and into the surrounding hills. As the sun started its downward path, they came to a temple surrounded by a massive wall. They passed through a towering gate framed with huge stones carved in pink granite. Warriors were at the cliff top of the fortress. They then entered the temple and went through two successive rooms, where it was much cooler. Tamatoa and Hina were astonished at the immensity of this structure. Finally they came to a closed door, flanked by two guards. The man they met on the beach opened the door. Another old man, lightly dressed because of the heat, came to them, stopped, and glanced at Kon.

"This cannot be!" he said. Kukara translated.

"We come in peace to visit you, just for a few days," Kon said.

The old man walked in a circle, waving his hands above his head in a sign of concern and confusion. He was obviously calculating the significance and ramifications of this sudden encounter.

"You must meet the Inca," the man said abruptly.

"But we don't have time," Kon emphasized.

"You must make the time," the man replied, pointing a finger at Kon. "The Inca is not as far from here as what you may think. He is resting in a small village up in the mountains, about ten days from here. If he learns I did not allow him to see you, I will be executed."

"We don't wish to meet the Inca," Kon protested.

The man came close to Kon and took his hands.

"My friend, I think you don't have a choice. But don't fear; there is no longer any Inca hate for the Viracochas. You will enjoy your stay, and I insist that you do so."

The man beckoned for them to follow him as he moved toward a sunlit terrace that had a breathtaking view of the sea.

"Your boats should come to shore," he said. "Your friends could stay around here until you return." Kukara translated this to the others.

"They are seafarers," Tamatoa replied, with a thundering voice. "They prefer to remain at sea, and I want them to remain at sea."

Taken aback by Tamatoa's demeanor, the old man listened to Kukara's translation.

"As you wish," he said.

"But I need to go to the closest ship to tell them my friends will be gone for a moon cycle," Kukara said, taking Kon by surprise. Kon translated to Hina and Tamatoa.

"So be it," the old man said, hesitating.

Kukara pulled on Tamatoa's hand in a sign of conspiracy. The old man called two guards, who would accompany her to the beach.

"She must go back to one of their boats," he told the guards. They bowed to him.

At dusk, Kukara said farewell to the two Incas. They bowed to her. She swam to the ship nearby. She explained to Tehani what had happened.

"I want to go back in secrecy," Kukara suggested.

"What are you talking about?" Tehani asked, surprised.

"I don't trust them," Kukara replied. "I know the land well. I know their language. I will follow them. They will never find me."

"I will go with you," Ku said.

"You stay here with Tehani," Kukara ordered. "Alone it will be far easier for me to go undetected."

Tehani took the girl in her arms.

"Are you sure about this?" Tehani asked. "I don't want

anything bad to happen to you."

"They need me. Without me, their days are in danger. When it is totally dark, take me close to the beach, and I will take care of myself."

Later that evening, Kukara slid into the shallow water; looking back over her shoulder, she took one long last look at Tehani.

"Take care of the Rongo-Rongo tablets for me. We should be back about one moon cycle from now."

"Mana is with you, little one."

Kukara swam to shore and walked across the beach, dragging a tangle of seaweed to erase her tracks. She had a gourd of water, a few dry fruits, and a little bag of grass seeds tied to her belt. She easily found her way back to the temple and located a suitable hiding place not far away from the temple's massive entrance. She settled in for a long wait.

The sun had just risen over the eastern mountains when Kon, Hina, and Tamatoa exited the temple and headed up a long, rugged valley, accompanied by dozens of warriors, priests, and local dignitaries, including the local Inca governor. The procession was followed by slaves and several llamas carrying tents, food, and water. Kukara quickly understood she would not be able to follow them far without provisioning and a llama of her own to carry it. Farther up in the valley she saw several llamas grazing; an old couple watched them from a distance. She walked up to them, and they fell to their knees when they realized she was a Viracocha.

"I need your help," she said humbly.

"What can a poor man and woman like us do for you?"

"Some of my friends are being taken to the Inca. They are not aware I am following them. I need to borrow one llama, some water and food, and one poncho. I will bring everything back in a few days."

"Are you familiar with llamas?" the man asked, looking at her fragile body.

Kukara smiled and made a very faint whistle. The llama she already had selected came straight to her and smelled her hands. She caressed the animal, to the great amazement of the couple. Moments later Kukara was on her way, with the ability to traverse the high mountains.

"Thank you," Kukara said, waving to her new friends. They bowed to her with big smiles on their faces. They were good, poor people.

Eight days went by. Slowly but steadily they went up, to a rarified elevation unknown to Maohis. Kukara managed to follow the convoy from far away. She hoped the Inca warriors would not concern themselves with a solitary traveler. When she was a little girl, she loved walking and herding llamas. Her new companion apparently sensed the affinity and actually seemed to enjoy her presence. It was Kukara's inscrutable ability to master skills that few others could without the benefit of lengthy training. It was her cosmic gift, a gift of universal consciousness. The young girl had the ability to tap this resource, omnipresent but hidden in most of us.

One evening she saw many lights some distance ahead of the convoy. It was a large, temporary settlement, adjacent to the famous Inca trail. She intuited that they had reached their destination.

The new Inca sat on a large stone, surrounded by two well-armed guards. He wore a red tunic embroidered with many blue, red, and yellow geometric figures. Large golden disks were part of his earlobes. An immense hat looking like a sun made him look much taller than he really was. A headband made of blue, red, and yellow woven strings supported a golden plate from behind which two long condor feathers were rising up. He watched the convoy approach and wondered what made his representative come in person. The Inca was in his forties, ambitious, yet peaceful by nature, and an inveterate gambler, more to add spice to his dull life than for the financial gain. As soon as he saw Kon from a distance, he recognized the unmistakable outline of a Viracocha. He jumped to his feet, clearly excited about this most serendipitous encounter.

"Our name is Manco Pachacuti, Inca. How is it that you come here?" the Inca said using an extremely formal language.

"This is Kon Tici Viracocha," the Inca governor replied.

With a brief dismissive gesture, the Inca silenced the functionary.

"Kon Tici! We knew your father. Come, you and your companions should join me. We have much to discuss."

"This is Tamatoa the Great, king of many islands, far away beyond where the sun sets," Kon said. "This is Hina of the Valley, our great priestess from the same islands. We come in peace to visit you. But we must return to the sea very soon, as our brothers and sisters are waiting for us in our new land. Furthermore, my friends are not accustomed to such altitude, and they feel poorly."

"We are honored," the Inca said with a mysterious smile. "Are you interested in trading with us?" he continued, pointing at Tamatoa. Kon translated.

"No!" Tamatoa answered with a voice that greatly impressed the Inca. "As Kon Tici said, we must return soon."

The Inca beckoned to a young woman servant and whispered in her ear. Minutes later she came back with a beverage in beautifully sculpted gold cups.

"Drink this," the Inca said. "It will help your bodies recover from this hostile environment. We welcome all of you."

"How far does your empire go now?" Kon asked.

"This is no empire yet," the Inca replied, "and we don't know if it ever will be one. As you are aware, we live in a few cities around the Titicaca Lake. Then we have these trading trails, going far north and south, but we do not rule these regions. One day perhaps, our great-grandchildren and their descendants will make an empire of all this."

Kon thought the Inca was modest, which greatly surprised him.

"A great priestess, so young!" the Inca inquired, taking Hina's hand. "What could your best talent be?"

"I protect my people from man's madness." Kon translated.

The Inca's eyes widened in surprise at Hina's swift and urbane answer.

"Then you must not be impressed by the Inca."

"So far, you have been kind to us," Hina replied, adding, "which is unexpected."

"We respect your honesty; it is a hallmark of the Viracochas. Many things have changed, and the Viracocha people may come back to this land any time of their choosing. We would never object to this. But we have to admit that a small minority of people resent the Viracochas... We don't know why."

The Inca looked at Tamatoa's tattoos and admired his impressive size. "Are many people like you in your land?"

"Maohis are a very strong people," Kon answered for Tamatoa. "You would be astonished at what we did together."

"May we ask you to fight with two of our best warriors? We would like to know your capabilities." Kon translated, very nervous.

"I am not interested in fighting with your warriors," Tamatoa replied, pounding on a table with his fist and breaking it in half.

"See! Now we are convinced we want you to fight with two of our best warriors."

"Please, don't do this," Kon asked the Inca. "Please don't force Tamatoa to use customs unknown to Viracochas."

"But they are not Viracochas, and we don't care much about what you think. We want to see this man fight for himself, so we understand you better."

Hina squeezed Kon's hand, not knowing what to do.

"You may tarnish the good opinion I had of you," she said. Kon hesitatingly translated.

"What difference does that makes? We are gamblers, and we always will be. Prepare for the fight," the Inca said, calling several warriors' names.

Ten heavily armed warriors circled the room, while two more pointed their spears at Tamatoa's chest. Tamatoa looked at them straight in the eyes; then he slowly scanned their uniforms, sandals, decorated red and blue bands below and above their calves, modest tunics down to their knees, pointing hats, silver discs in their earlobes, and small square shields to protect themselves from an enemy.

The great Maohi slowly removed his hat, then his cape, and looked at the Inca one more time.

"Are you really sure you want this?" Tamatoa asked in an unusually quiet and calm voice, slowly pushing aside the two spears.

"Absolutely, my friend," the Inca said, signaling the two warriors to proceed.

The two warriors adjusted their spear back toward Tamatoa's chest. The great warrior's eyes were riveted on the coming spears and seemed not to fear them at all. In the blink of an eye Tamatoa took and snapped both spears. With one hand he swiftly grabbed one warrior by his clothes, took him to a swing along which the warrior lost his balance, and smashed him into a wooden post, killing him instantly, his head lying in a pool of blood. At the same time he had taken the first warrior into a swing, Tamatoa's other hand hit the face of the second warrior with full force, literally decapitating him, and his head bounced on a faraway wall.

It happened so fast, the Inca was stunned, and so were Kon and Hina. Following the signal of the Inca, the other ten warriors circled Tamatoa with spears. All spears stopped at the contact of his body, except one, which went all the way through his massive right thigh. In pain, the great warrior sat on the ground with hatred in his eyes. The ten warriors cuffed his hands with a heavy chain made of bronze. The Inca dismissed all the warriors. Kon and Hina kneeled close to their wounded friend.

"Free him," Kon said.

"Absolutely not, he is too dangerous," the Inca replied. "He did not have to kill them."

"It was self-defense," Hina argued with the Inca in the Viracocha language. "You made him angry because of your lack of honor and wisdom."

"Are you questioning my honor and wisdom, Viracocha priestess?"

"Let's take care of his leg first," Hina replied with a dirty look on her face. "Then I will be delighted to answer your question."

Kon broke the spear, leaving only the portion that went through Tamatoa's leg.

"As I pull the remaining spear part through his leg, we must clean the wound at the same time," Kon said. "Please, you gambled on this man, remember, and he won. Now we obviously depend on you; help us!"

Hina took the hands of the Inca in a gesture he did not expect. Her eyes were calm, asking for help. Somehow, as he moved his hands away from hers, he knew she was a great priestess. He felt the power of her mind, combined with her kindness and honesty. She made a great impression on him.

"We know what you need," the Inca said, disappearing to another room. Moments later he came back, handing a little gold rod and a gold string to Kon.

"Attach the gold string to the gold rod and make it very hot on the red embers of the fire. Attach the gold string to the end of the broken spear in his leg. Then drive the gold rod quickly, all way through his wound, as you remove the spear."

Kon understood the procedure exactly.

"What we are going to do is going to hurt a lot," Kon said. Tamatoa agreed with a faint nod. He was aware of similar procedures from his priests.

Hina placed a thick piece of cloth in Tamatoa's mouth. The red-hot gold rod was ready. Kon pulled the spear out of Tamatoa's leg, then the rod went through his leg. The tattooed giant never flinched, to the amazement of everyone. The Inca handed a gold box full of cream to Hina.

"Put some of this at both ends of the wound," the Inca said.

Hina followed his advice, then circled Tamatoa's leg several times with a large bandage and tightly attached it.

"Thank you for your help," Hina said, looking the Inca in the eyes.

"You are welcome. We should not have started that stupid game."

Hina shook her head in agreement.

Then something unexpected took place. The Inca ordered

the warriors to bring the one responsible for wounding Tamatoa. They brought the warrior with his hands cuffed behind his back and made him kneel in front of the Inca.

"Cut his head off!" the Inca shouted, to the astonishment of Hina and Kon.

As one warrior was hefting his axe, Hina inserted herself between the condemned warrior and the executioner.

"Don't do this," Hina said. "It was not his fault."

"Great Priestess, and magnanimous too!" the Inca remarked. Then with a nod, he ordered the warriors to liberate the pardoned man and let him depart. The incident had been a clarifying moment for Hina. She now knew who the Inca was and that he could not be trusted with his many changing moods.

The night was very clear and cold; the bright moon and myriad stars imparted a soft fluorescence to the landscape. From a short distance, Kukara watched the camp and the few guards around it. She saw a little boy about ten years old exit a tent, sit on a stone, and start playing a flute. He was far away from the guards, who did not pay attention to him. At some distance from the boy, several llamas grazed on the scant patches of grass that grew here and there on the pebbly ground. Kukara climbed on her llama, then keeping only one leg on the top of its back, she slid down the llama's side so the warriors would not see her. She let her llama slowly approach the others. At one point, she was hidden from the warriors; however, the boy noticed her and stopped playing. She left her llama with the others and walked to him. The young boy was astonished when he realized she was a Viracocha. But being inarticulate, he gestured for Kukara to join him inside his tent.

"What is your name?" Kukara asked.

The boy understood her and used a primitive sign language

to convey his condition.

"How long have you not been able to talk?" she asked. The boy explained with his fingers that he was ten sun cycles old and he had not talked for five sun cycles.

Kukara took his flute and started playing, sending an enchanting melody through the entire camp. The boy was astonished at her talent and took the flute back, trying to repeat the melody. He stopped, shaking his head in dismay, wishing he could play as she did. Kukara smiled at him and put her hands on his head.

"Try talking with me." The boy shook his head negatively.

"Try to say your name." The boy was not cooperating, so she tried another strategy. She took his hands and placed them on her chest.

"Say my name, Kukara."

"Ku..." the boy said, overwhelmed by the warm chest of the girl.

"Say your name."

"Ma..."

"Say my name, Kukara."

"Kuka..."

"Say your name."

"Manco!"

"Say my name, Ku...ka...ra."

"Kukara!" Joy flooded the boy's face.

"Say father."

"Father!"

"Say, Father, I can talk."

"Father, I can talk." The boy jumped to her in tears and kissed her.

"Who is your father?" she asked.

"The Inca." Kukara glanced at him, wondering if luck had

been on her side.

"Take me to your father."

They went through two adjoining tents and found the Inca with Kon and Hina, and Tamatoa down on the floor.

"Who is she?" the Inca asked, puzzled. "I was not aware of her."

Astonished, Kon and Hina could not speak. "This is my girl," Tamatoa murmured.

"Father, Kukara taught me how to talk again."

The Inca fell to his knees and took his son in his arms. "How is this possible?" Then he went to Kukara and put both hands on her shoulders.

"How in the world did you do this? All our medicine people failed to make him talk again after a bad illness he had five sun cycles ago."

Hina glanced at Kon; they smiled at each other.

"How did you get here?" Hina asked.

"I followed you."

"All by yourself?"

"All by myself and a borrowed llama!"

"You mean you followed all our men for ten days," the Inca inquired, "and nobody ever noticed your presence."

"That is correct," Kukara replied proudly, smiling.

The Inca shook his head in dismay and smiled at Kon and Hina. "This is a very talented girl you have here."

Kukara went to Tamatoa and looked at his wounded leg and cuffed hands.

"What did you do to my best friend?" she inquired, looking at the Inca with peaceful eyes.

The Inca came close to her, and freed Tamatoa's hands.

"For what you did for our son, we can do anything for you."

"Anything?" she inquired.

"Anything, just ask."

"We came in peace to visit you. Now it is time for us to continue our long journey on the Awesome Sea. Please, let us go safely."

Kon grabbed Kukara in his arms and held his treasure against his chest. Hina could not hide her tears. Tamatoa accepted a drink from the Inca, but could not move from the floor.

"You should stay here a few days until your friend heals," the Inca said. "Have no fear and please enjoy our hospitality."

The next morning, a sumptuous feast was spread before the seafaring visitors. Tamatoa battled pain the best he could.

"I will stay here with Tamatoa," Kukara said. "At the same time, I will help Manco practice talking."

Kon and Hina walked to a nearby mountain. They climbed to the summit, where the eternal snow lives. Just below they found a beautiful green valley with crystal clear water burbling its way through the rugged channel festooned with miniature tundra flowers. Guanacos lazily grazed along the way, warily eyeing the intruders.

"These are wild llamas," Kon explained. "They won't let us approach them."

"Even Kukara?"

"Even Kukara!"

As they reached the first patch of snow, Hina bent down and took some in her hand, admiring the tiny crystals melting between her fingers.

"This stuff is cold!" she giggled. It reminded him of the young girl she was when he met her.

The path they followed opened on an alpine lake; they walked around it and sat down on a clean, dry patch of beautiful green groundcover. Wild ducks slowly paddled in lazy circles, dipping their bills under the ice-cold water only a short distance from them.

"It is like the lake on Mount Orohena," she said. "There are even a few ducks, but they are different. This place is so huge. It is endless. The view is overwhelming."

"Do you think it was worthwhile to come here?" Kon asked, putting his arms around her shoulders.

"Yes, but only now am I starting to enjoy it; we must leave soon."

Eight days later, the convoy was ready to depart the Inca's redoubt. Kon helped Tamatoa walk until Kukara showed him the llama.

"The llama is going to walk for you," she said lightly.

Kon laced his fingers together in a cup, braced them on his thigh, and offered to lift Tamatoa onto the llama's back.

"Here, climb up," Kon said, "and carefully lift your wounded leg over the llama's back. Hold the hair around his neck. Everything will be fine."

Tamatoa made one attempt, but was obviously uncomfortable trusting the animal to bear his weight.

"I cannot believe this!" Kukara chuckled. She sharply whistled, and the llama dropped to its knees on the ground, making it easy for Tamatoa to sit on its back. She caressed the cheeks of the llama, the tactile signal to get up. Surprised by the sudden lift, Tamatoa screamed.

"Be quiet!" Hina laughed.

"My ship is far more reliable," Tamatoa joked.

The Inca burst into laughter as well at the sight of the mighty Tamatoa on the llama.

Manco gave his flute to Kukara. "Keep this; you play so much better than me... Something else! I want to give you this present."

The young boy placed a magnificent gold necklace around Kukara's neck and kissed her. She flushed with pleasure.

The Inca gave a small box to Kukara, its precious contents securely protected with an exquisite and finely woven fabric.

"This is a musical instrument for you. It is made of ceramic by our best artisan. Use it only for the most sacred high ceremonies. You must practice extensively before each ceremony, since its fingering is very difficult."

The Inca bade farewell to his visitors, and waved at them as they continued their journey.

Ten days later, they reached the valley where they could see the beach. Glancing on one side, they saw the top of the temple rising in the distance above sparse trees. Tamatoa's three sailboats cruised near the coast. Then they went near a little settlement where many llamas grazed. Kukara asked the local Inca governor for one of his llamas.

"I have to give this one back to my friends," she explained, pointing to the llama loaned to her by the old couple a moon cycle earlier.

Kukara handed the llama's tether to the old man, who beamed with pride and joy.

"Thanks to you, everything went superbly well," she said.

"It was an honor for us," the man said.

"Take this necklace to remember me. I have no use for this where we are going," Kukara said, turning to the old woman.

"But this is too much!" the wizened woman objected.

Kukara draped the necklace around the woman's head and hugged her. "This is what happens when you unselfishly help someone in a desperate situation."

"If this humble peasant is found to have a gold necklace," the governor said, "she would be accused of stealing. Ordinary people are not allowed to possess such fine things."

"This is for you to resolve," Kukara argued, "and I trust that this gentle family will come to no misfortune."

The first man was created by the Great Ancestor, in search of his spirit. With mana's power, he one day must find his spirit, the first woman, and her spirit. Then, from the depth of the earth, they will create and prosper.

CHAPTER 4

"Our last voyage toward the setting sun held all our hopes. No news from Hotu-Matua intuitively told us he had found Rapa Nui. Now it was up to us to carefully plan for a dream to come true."

Hina of the Valley

Moments later, Tamatoa limped his way through the shallow water near the beach, and they all clambered aboard the ship, where Tehani waited. The two other ships were anchored nearby. Tamatoa ordered the three vessels to pull side by side. They told their adventure in the mountains to their relatives, who were astonished at Kukara's performance. Their food and water supply was replenished to overflowing: it was time to go.

"I have a fairly good idea where we made a mistake," Tamatoa said, gently massaging his leg. "It was about halfway between here and Rapa Iti. I am sure that at that point Rapa Nui was slightly north of us. Therefore, we should go straight west from here." And so they did. This time the wind and the current were partly behind them, making the trip considerably shorter.

Eighteen days later, in the evening, they saw a small island on the horizon. Before night they carefully checked their heading and furled the sails to reduce their speed. At dawn the island waited off their bows. It was low in the middle, with small hummocks at each end. They brought their ships ashore at the end of the wide-open bay, bracketed by the hills. They walked all around the island, which was occupied by a diverse population of seabirds. They lazily walked to the top of the western hill and sat on the warm ground covered by tall, flowing grass.

"Let's spend the day watching these birds," Tamatoa said. "Some of them may fly back and forth between islands."

Kon pointed at an albatross passing nearby.

"Not those," Tamatoa said. "They fly too far away from land and sleep in flight. They are not good indicators. We should watch these sandpiper colonies; they often fly among close-by islands."

Several times during the day they observed little flights of sandpipers coming from the west and slightly to the south. The converse was consistent with outgoing colonies.

"See how they land in shallow water, near the beach, and feed right away," Tamatoa said. "They are not tired."

"What does a tired sandpiper looks like?" Hina inquired, chuckling.

"If they fly for more than one day," Tamatoa replied, missing the gentle sarcasm of Hina's question, "they would land on the beach, rest on the sand for a short time, and would then start feeding."

"Fascinating!" Kon said, with a faint smile.

They placed stones on the ground to pinpoint the exact direction with which they would compare stellar alignments during the night. Then they waited for the sunset: they saw no signs of land on the dazzling orange horizon. Waiting to have a better view of the stars, they ate a quick meal, mainly fresh eggs they had found in the surroundings. Then they went back to the ships and continued their westerly journey, very slightly to the south.

And again the next day, they carefully scanned the horizon at sunset, searching for an unmistakable dark outline. Concern and disappointment continued to ebb and flow among the weary voyagers.

At dawn, Hina, who had not slept well, was the first to search the western horizon. Although it was still dark, she saw clouds to the southwest, hovering over something darker underneath. Uncertain, she gave the signal for a sighting by hitting a piece of bamboo on the deck. Tamatoa woke immediately and came to her side.

"It is a quite large island," he said with a booming voice. Tamatoa reached down to his belt and lifted a conch shell horn to his lips and blew a mighty blast, alerting the others.

At sunrise, the massive outline of the island was slowly revealed by the retreating mists. They embraced each other in sheer joy. They knew that day would remain in their memories forever.

As they navigated along the eastern end of the island, they saw angry breakers smashing into huge, rugged volcanic cliffs. It was not a good place to land. Farther west, on the north side, they saw smoke, which clearly indicated a human presence. As they continued along the northern coast, they came upon a small, deserted beach of pink sand. The smoke appeared to come from a point beyond the beach. They rounded the point and saw a large white sandy beach with many people waiting for them. Hina squeezed Kon's hands.

"I recognize Hotu-Matua's ships," she said, noticing the tears flowing down on his cheeks.

"I have been waiting so long for this," he said in a husky voice. "It is a dream come true."

Kukara held Hina's hand tightly. She silently sobbed.

Kon held Ku and Kane's hands. The two boys immediately recognized their mother waiting on the beach. They dove into the warm water and swam to the beach. Kama saw her two boys and fell to her knees, weeping. She joyfully embraced them.

Then the difficult questions came.

"Where is our sister?" Ku asked.

"She drowned after she fell into the water; I found her too late," Kama said with profound sadness in her voice. "Where is your father?"

Kon took Kama in his arms and kissed her neck. "He was killed two years ago trying to negotiate peace between two warring clans."

She looked at him with distress in her eyes, then hugged Kukara, and briefly glanced at Hina.

"I love you, Kon Tici," she said. "I have my two boys and your family to remind me I should be thankful." Kama took her boys and left, weeping aloud. Kukara quietly followed her.

"Take your time, Kama Tici," Hina murmured, looking after her. "Your heart is happy and wounded in the same moment. It is a lot to assimilate in a single day."

"She needs to be alone with them," Taranga said, putting a friendly hand on Hina's shoulder. "She is an astonishing woman. With both of you we will make a jewel of this island."

"So, this is Rapa Nui," Kon said, "Mata Kite Rani: eyes looking at the stars!"

"It is smaller than what you dreamed of," Taranga said. "But I can tell you this island has its charms, and its mysteries. You will see for yourself."

The next morning at sunrise, Hina felt someone touch her shoulder. She turned around on the mat where she had been sleeping and saw two magnificent blue eyes smiling at her.

"My name is Kama Tici Viracocha. We have met before but only in our dreams," Kama said in her pleasant Viracochan accent."

Hina jumped to her feet and hugged Kama as if she had always known her.

"Finally, I meet my sister from another world. My name is Hina of the Valley," Hina said in Kama's language.

Kama felt a current of energy flowing through her, clearly telling her this young woman had acquired Viracocha's powers. She also experienced something unusual, like waves of kindness and care, like the certainty of what needs to be done on every occasion. Hina was quite athletic and exuded a strong charisma.

"What a charming and appropriate name!" Kama said. "There are many vales on this island that echo your name. Eat this food, and drink this water. Afterwards, I will take you and Kon to the top of the island, where I will explain a few things you should know."

"It sounds to me like you already know we will all stay on Rapa Nui," Hina probed.

"It is my home, and I love this island," Kama replied. "The longer you stay, the more you will like it as well."

Hina did not know what to think of that statement. Kama saw that on her face.

"You mentioned valleys," Hina said. "The valley where I was born is full of clear rivers, giant trees, ferns, fruits, and flowers. This looks desolate in comparison."

"You have seen nothing yet," Kama defended.

Following a short conversation, Kama realized the Maohi had a quick, analytic mind. Also, adding to her beautiful physical appearance, Kama thought she was pleasant to be with in many ways, and began to understand what Taranga had told her. Then, Kama sensed Hina had an urge for something.

"If I can do anything for you," Kama inquired, "please tell me."

"I am dreaming about a freshwater bath," Hina said. "Maohis love freshwater baths, especially after having been abused by salted water for so long."

"There are no streams on the island; however, there is a wonderful lake at the top of the mountain that you will enjoy."

"I cannot wait," Hina replied and started walking toward the hills.

Kukara, Ku, and Kane joined Kon, Kama, and Hina walking into the hills. On the way they explored a few lava tubes, which fascinated Hina.

"Neither children nor anyone should venture into these tubes without careful preparation and assistance," Kama said. "They are complex systems that go very far. They often branch out like the streams that feed a river. If you get lost in them, you may never find your way out."

"Have you explored any of them?" Kon asked.

"Very few! Alone, I was afraid. But in the ones that are open, we can make magnificent gardens. They provide excellent protection to the plants from the frequent strong winds that we have, especially during the winter season."

"Look!" Hina said, pointing at the sea. "Hotu-Matua is taking Tamatoa's family around the island."

"I was not introduced to Tamatoa," Kama commented. "He is huge and seems scary."

"Huge maybe, but he is a good man," Hina replied. "He will quickly and positively impress you. His mate, Tehani, and his daughter, Mahine, are wonderful friends."

The sun was nearly overhead when they reached the summit. The sky was clear, and they had a panoramic view of the entire island. Kama pointed out several volcanoes, the lakes, and the various places where they could find fresh water. She also identified the various places where small groups could settle and start their own clans. She pointed out Kura's burial place and trembled slightly.

"I am getting emotional today," Kama said, trying to hold back a few tears. "But I am happy. There was a time when I was convinced I would spend all my life alone in this tiny world."

Then she pointed at the mysterious mountain, where she had communed with its unknown spirits so many times.

"A few days from now, after you get settled, I want to take you to that place," Kama said. "I want Taranga and Kon's opinion about what they will sense there. It is the weirdest place I ever experienced in my life, particularly during the night."

"Maybe you want my opinion too," Kukara suggested.

"Absolutely!" Kama and Hina said simultaneously.

"Maybe you want Hina's opinion too," Kukara teased.

Kama glanced at Hina, who was gazing at the sea.

"Are there good places around the coast to dive?" Hina asked.

"I am not a good swimmer, but I know several places where on a calm day the water is quiet and crystal clear. It is the clearest water I have ever seen during my life. We can see myriad fish of many colors swimming in and out of large submerged caverns."

"She can swim and dive anywhere," Kon said. "She is almost a fish herself."

"I will bet that we can find lobsters along this rocky, tormented coast." Hina suggested.

Kama was not as interested in what the sea could offer. She thought she would change the conversation to something she was curious about.

"You did not have Kon's children yet?" Kama asked, taking Hina's hand gently.

"Not yet! I was not ready for it. So as a priestess, I ate the appropriate plants every day. But here, the priestess is lost. The priestess would have to learn again about the native plants. Perhaps you will help me."

Kama smiled at her. "Alone as I was, I did not need to find such plants here."

Kon and Hina burst into laughter, but quickly regained their composure. Kama looked at them, sad but also amused.

"You can laugh. You can joke with me. I will be your companion for a very long time."

Kon pressed the two women's heads against his chest and hugged them with deep love. It was as if time had come to a stop. It was as if all their miseries, adventures, and daring undertakings had come to an end. Or was it a respite between new unimaginable adventures?

Kukara sauntered a short distance away from the group and stared at the faraway, mysterious mountain to which Kama had pointed. Kon followed and stood close to her.

"I feel it from here," Kukara said. "This mountain is alive. This mountain is talking to me. This mountain is waiting for us."

They all slowly followed the edge of the summit, until they came close to a small lake with crystal clear water. Around it many reeds were growing, and some birds were hunting with half their legs in the water.

"As far as I am concerned," Hina replied, "this lake nearby is waiting for me."

Hina unabashedly undressed and dove into the cool water. Kama was surprised by Hina's freedom to show her naked body.

But she was stunned at her expert swimming abilities. Never in her life had she seen anyone swim so well.

"She reminds me of a dolphin," Kama said. "She is incredible."

Everyone else undressed and joined Hina, except Kama.

"Come!" Hina said.

"No, not today, another day. I like the way you swim."

"I told you she is a fish," Kon joked.

"I will teach you how to swim like me," Hina said. "I am a good teacher."

"I have no doubt."

Hina took a breath, then dove. As everyone waited, Kama started to wonder why it took so long for Hina to come back to the surface, but nobody seemed surprised.

"I told you she is a fish," Kon insisted.

"Amazing!"

Hina surfaced and swam toward Kama. As she came out of the water, twisting the water out of her hair, she seemed contemplative.

"There are caverns underwater, and the lake it is not very deep," she mused.

"Yet we don't see the bottom," Kama replied. "The other lakes are much deeper and much larger."

"I want to settle near a place where I can bathe like this every day," Hina said.

Later in the day, when they arrived at the beach, Tamatoa came to them, going directly to Kama.

"We have not met. I am Tamatoa. People call me by many names: the great warrior, the tattooed giant, Tamatoa the Great. Pay no attention to all that; call me Tamatoa."

Kon translated.

"I am honored to meet a great Maohi," Kama said.

Hina translated.

"Oh! I forgot that one," Tamatao added with a smile on his face.

Kukara translated; Kama laughed.

"I will be back," she said. "I have a modest present for you."

Embarrassed, Tamatoa looked at Kon and Hina. "I have nothing for her."

"Yes, you do," Hina replied, "your friendship."

"She is beautiful!" Tamatoa commented.

"Ha!" said Hina.

"Ha!" echoed Tehani, Tamatoa's mate.

"Ha!" chorused everybody.

Kama ran back. "These are my presents to you," she said gently. "I am sure you will find them useful."

Tamatoa opened the package and saw two exquisitely crafted black obsidian adzes. He lifted one from the package and appraised its workmanship. He bent down and picked a coconut from the stack they had brought to the island. Holding it in his hand, he slightly struck it with the adze. The fibrous husk split easily to its hard core. The result brought an astonished look to his face.

"Did you make those tools yourself with a rock from the island?" he asked incredulously.

"Yes! I thought we would find a good use for them."

Keeping his eyes on the two adzes, Tamatoa put his arm on Kama's shoulder and took her to Tehani.

"I want you to meet Tehani, the woman I have loved all my life. It is my wish that we should be good friends. And this is Mahine, my daughter, and her mate, Taatamao."

"You all seem so nice," Kama gushed, bowing her head in respect.

Tehani took her hand and invited her to the evening meal she and Mahine had prepared.

"Do you know what a lobster is?" Tehani inquired.

"I never saw one."

"They are everywhere around this island," Tehani added.

"See! I told you, I could smell them from the top of the island," Hina said with a smile all over her face. "Let's find out if your recipe is better than mine. Where is the expert? Ho! There he is!"

Everyone glanced at Kon, who was smiling. "This is the kind of contest I like!" he said.

"Unfortunately, we will have to reinvent our recipes here," Tehani said. "Most herbs we used cannot be found here."

"I will help you," Kama suggested.

When Kama saw the cooked lobster halves near the fire, her eyes widened.

"Where did you find these animals? They are like giant shrimps!"

"They live in the dark caverns under the sea," Tamatoa explained.

"But how do you get them?"

"You dive deep and just get them!" Hina answered.

Kama looked at all of them, still perplexed by Hina's answer.

"I told you they are almost fish," Kon explained.

"You people, you are unbelievable," Kama concluded. "Can I taste one?"

"Let me explain how to do this," Kon said.

"Stay away from my lobster!" Kama protested. After Taranga translated, all the Maohis laughed in merriment. It was the beginning of a new era.

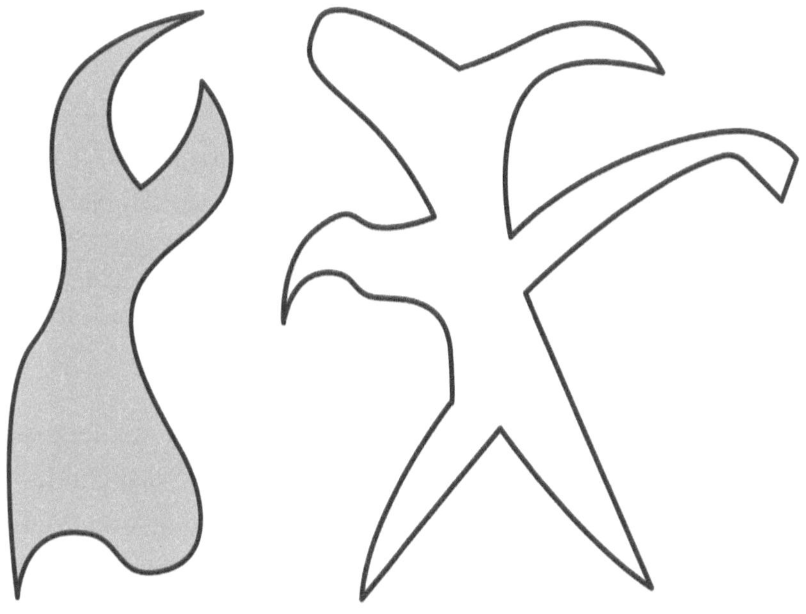

The first man and his immortal spirit were given by the Great Ancestor, so the earth would recognize one day that man would be capable of creating on his own.

CHAPTER 5

"Kama took us to a place where dreams meet the world of spirits. We all felt the same experience she had when she was alone on the island. The meaning was uncertain, but the effects on our minds were vast. There was no doubt this place would transcend our activities for generations to come."

Kon Tici Viracocha

Two days later, Tamatoa and Hotu-Matua went on a deep-sea fishing expedition. Taatamao and Mahine took several children, including Kama's sons, Ku and Kane, to a swimming and diving lesson. They anchored the ship at some distance from the beach where under-the-sea caverns could be seen. Kama invited Kon, Hina, Kukara, and the old Taranga on a two-day exploration of the mystical mountain she had repeatedly mentioned. They were all excited at what they might discover. They walked south through the lowland separating the main part of the island and the eastern peninsula. They climbed a little hill and saw the crater, with the lake at the bottom, a beautiful, deep blue lake, surrounded by reeds, and farther away by diverse species of trees sprinkled with a few giant palm trees. On the opposite side, a majestic cliff of dark volcanic rock awaited them. Farther behind, they saw the sea on the island's southern side.

"I am too old for this," Taranga said. "Go ahead, my children.

I will join you later."

"We can wait for you," Kama suggested. "Nothing will happen before the dark of night."

As they went down the dormant volcano, they maneuvered between trees and thick patches of an indigenous long grass, and walked on a thick carpet of dead reeds.

"These are the same type of reeds as are the ones at Titicaca Lake," Kon said. "They are a valuable resource in this tiny world."

Much to Kama's consternation, Hina again responded to her natural urge to swim in this beautiful lake by undressing and diving into the lake. With Kon and Kukara following, Kama's discomfort was apparent to everyone; however, her people's customs favored propriety over promiscuity.

"These are Maohis' ways," Taranga smirked.

Even the old monarch undressed and went in the water with his friends.

"What are you waiting for?" Hina asked.

"I am not comfortable to reveal myself like this," Kama replied. "It is not our way."

"What are you afraid of?" Hina asked. "Are you afraid to show you are the most beautiful woman in the world? It does not make sense to me, or to the others."

"I don't know!" Kama said, embarrassed.

Hina left the water and walked to Kama and gradually, slowly helped her to undress.

"I don't believe I am doing this," Kama said, her cheeks turning pink.

"Come, my friend," Hina said, holding Kama's hand. "Never have fear of the infinite beauty the Great Viracocha gave you. Honor his gift. Honor yourself and share your body with ours so you can liberate yourself from futile prejudices."

Kama contemplated Hina's words. These were words of great wisdom, and she could not believe a woman so young could be capable of such cerebral depth. The more she knew her, the more she respected her. There was something magical in her simplicity, freedom, and kindness. To many, Hina was attractive and irresistible in many ways. She was tacitly in command.

They started swimming together.

"How do you feel now?" Hina asked.

"It is great! There is a first time for everything."

"Some rules have nothing to do with right or wrong," Kon said, "but everything to do with someone in the past who wanted power to dominate the people."

"I know!" Kama said. "But you never saw me like that before."

"I know, and I dearly regret it," Kon kidded.

Kama splashed water on his face. The little group continued to enjoy the warm, clean water for a while.

After completing their swim, they gently washed their clothes and hung them to dry on some low bushes. Finding a nearby patch of reeds, Kama cut an armload of them and rapidly wove them into mats.

"We will need them tonight," Kama said, motioning for the others to start theirs. "That place can be windy and cold."

Everyone started weaving theirs mats. They were amazed at Kama's speed and the quality of her work. Then they all lay in the sun and napped.

Later that afternoon, they walked to the south side of the lake, dragging their mats to the base of a cliff where Kama thought they would be better protected from the cold night breeze.

"Leave all your things here, and follow me," Kama said.

She climbed to a point where eolian soil had been deposited

at the mountain's base. They looked at the rock, which was similar to a conglomerate of nice, colorful crystals. Kama took her obsidian knife and deeply scratched the rock.

"You see, it is a good-looking stone, which seems very hard at first. But it is easily carved into whatever you may want, if you have patience and creativity."

"Fascinating!" Taranga murmured.

"Now follow me, I want to show you the place where we will meditate tonight."

Kama went to a tall, dark, narrow cleft in the mountain. Both sides were part of the slick cliff. Inside, tall grass grew and waved in the breeze.

"Put your hands on these walls, and close your eyes. Tell me if you feel anything."

They all complied. Only the breeze in the grass could be heard. Kukara was the first one to turn around, looking Kama straight in the eyes.

"Under this mountain," Kukara said, "there is fire with no end."

"Because of the crater, we know it is an ancient volcano," Kon said.

"No, not ancient, it is only taking a nap," Kukara added. "It is alive, under the lake."

"But the lake is full of water, deep water," Hina argued.

"Kukara is right," Taranga said, "way below the water there is fire. I can feel it as well."

"Then let's call this place Rano," Hina suggested, "the place where fire meets water."

"There are several places like this on the island," Kama said. "You saw a smaller one at the top of the island. There is a much bigger one near Kura's grave, where I will take you next. I promise you this one will overpower you."

Kama took them farther to the mountain's west side, where they climbed to the top of the cliff. They followed the cliff to the top of the mountain. The other side of the cliff lunged into a large valley that ended in the sea far below. The view was breathtaking.

"Let's call this place Rano Raraku," Taranga suggested. They all repeated the name to memorize it.

They ate seeds and small nuts from the local palm trees, then chatted quietly as they watched a spectacular sunset. They walked back to their mats. As they positioned their mats, Kama gave to each of them a small rock she had collected from the mountain.

"Hold these rocks, then let's sit in a circle holding hands. Totally relax and let the mountain direct your dreams."

Taranga held Hina and Kukara's hands; Kama held Kukara and Kon's hands; Hina held Kon and Taranga's hands. Five little rocks from the mountain were kept warm in a circle of five remarkable people. As mana slowly permeated them, they could see themselves floating in light. Each of them would experience contact with spirits differently, since they were very different people. Taranga saw the Light in a swirl of faint purple glare. The Light seemed to tell him his earthly voyage had been good, long enough, and soon the time would come for him to experience the great passage from illusion to reality. Kukara saw the Light smile at her. There was no need for words. Kukara knew her worldly mission perfectly well. Kama saw the Light telling her to help Hina in her great mission. Kon saw the Light telling him to build a legend at Rano Raraku. Hina did not see the Light. Several moon cycles earlier, in the sacred cave of Mount Orohena, the Light had told her, "You will never see me again. Use my powers wisely." Hina remembered.

Inside the circle they saw stars reflected in Rano Raraku's

lake. Shadows of giant stones circled the lake. One of them assumed the mysterious face of a wise man, with thin lips, long nose, long ears, deep eyes, and long fingers with very long nails reaching gracefully across his lower belly, giving the shadow a peaceful and preternatural look. This is when Hina woke. Then everyone woke up and gazed at her through the crisp night air, illuminated by only stars' light.

"I recall my commitment to the Light," Hina said, "when I was alone in the sacred cave of Mount Orohena."

They looked at her with expectation.

"Mata-Kite-Rani! One day I will seal that vision in sacred rocks. One day I will make the silent look of a frozen face looking at eternity more powerful than anything alive… I swear!"

"These were my words after I briefly met the Light," Hina added, "and I will never forget."

"Now everything makes sense," Kon said.

"Now you know I am going to need you to find a way to make this a reality," Hina replied.

They covered themselves with their mats. The breeze called their names around the lake in the reeds. It was music to their ears. They knew they had found their home. They went to sleep peacefully among shadows from another dimension. The universal consciousness flew freely within and among them; they were one.

At dawn Kama woke up first, and went to the cliff to inspect the smooth, shiny texture of it. Puzzled by her actions, the rest of the group joined her one by one.

"Let's vie for best shadow artist," she challenged. "Last night we all had visions of shadows turning to dark faces that walked around the lake. Let's draw what we saw on these walls."

Using obsidian shards they sketched their visions on the rock of the mountain. They drew what they recollected, then stopped to inspect each other's work. They all laughed when they looked at Hina's drawing of a grotesque man, kneeling with his buttocks on his heels.

"I guess it is not good!" Hina chuckled with a grin on her face.

All other drawings were consistent, representing a typical Viracocha profile. Then Hina glanced at the old Taranga, who was still working on his sketch, and going nowhere.

"I have an idea," Hina suggested. "But first let's vote for the best drawing."

There was no contest, and they all agreed Kama's was the best.

Hina grabbed Taranga and Kon's hands. "Follow me."

She took both men inside the tall, dark, narrow hole where they had touched the mountain a day earlier.

"Kneel there in the shade, both of you, and look outside."

Hina went outside in the sun, with Kama and Kukara. Then, unsatisfied, she went back to Taranga.

"Join both hands on your belly, so we can see your long nails well... thumbs up. Yes, like this."

She went back in the sun.

"On a much larger scale, don't you think this is what we saw last night?"

Kama was instantly astonished at Hina's observation. Perhaps she did not know how to draw well, but her vision had been most accurate.

"Now, my friend," Hina said, putting one arm around Kama's shoulder, "take these men in the shade as a model, and draw what you see there in the sun, on a grander scale."

Kama went to work, interrupted at times by suggestions from

Hina and Kukara. It did not take long until their stunning vision took life on the mountain's surface. Both men came to admire the fantastic effigy. It was the face of a naked giant with a long torso, and his fingertips barely touching below the navel, realistically presenting the long nails of the old Viracocha. Then there was the face, charismatic, mysterious, stoic, and resolute. The eyes could not be seen in deep sockets, no matter what the sun exposure. Intentionally, it would be impossible to define whom or what the face looked at, at any time of the day. The nose was long, straight, and widening at the nostrils. The ears were long and hanging in the Viracocha tradition, allowing a place for disks in the earlobes. The sullen mouth was long and narrow. The chin and neck were strong, well delineated, adding enormous character to the drawing. There was a mysterious beauty in the face, suggesting a bond between man and the island's spirits.

"Wow! This is truly amazing," Kon exclaimed.

"I like it," Kama said humbly.

"It is exactly what we saw in our meditation," Taranga said.

"This will have a place in my Rongo-Rongo characters," Kukara added proudly.

Hina was silent. She smiled and pointed her finger at Kon. In her mind, a flood of images of present and future events flowed relentlessly. She focused her thought and asked Kon, "How large could a statue like this be? How large could we make it and still move it to its preordained location on Rapa Nui?"

Kon was taken by surprise by Hina's question and thought for a few moments.

"It depends where you want to place it."

"About halfway down the mountain, between here and the lake," Hina replied.

Kon surveyed the mountain, the rock, the slope to the lake,

and guessed.

"About five times the size of a man," Kon explained, using his fingers.

Hina thought for a while, skeptical. "You are serious!"

"Yes, I am!"

"Then we must do it even larger," she added with shiny eyes, stunning everyone. "I want this statue to symbolize our ability to accomplish the impossible to anyone who will ever come to this place."

They were all silent, not knowing what to say. Hina, the Maohi, was in command, irresistible; the three Viracochas noticed.

"Think about it and take your time," Hina added, walking slowly toward the valley.

They walked down the flanks of Rano Raraku, but Kon stayed behind. He could not help exploring all the details of that mountain on which he was going to spend so much time. Reluctantly, he left the mountain behind and caught up with the little group.

They went near the sea and walked east until a very steep cliff hampered their progress.

"See that sharp islet?" Kama asked, motioning to the water. "We should get closer to it. The sea is calm, and you will have a good view of its underwater caves and fish."

It was midday when they found a cove with deep, crystal clear water. Fish of all kinds swam in and out for as deep as they could see. They undressed and all went in the water.

"How would you like to swim to the islet?" Hina asked.

"We are all poor swimmers, except perhaps for Kama and Kon," Taranga replied.

"I guess we will just explore from here then," Hina said.

After a long time in the water, they came out and rested in the sun. Hina was still swimming and ready to explore further. They all admired her skill at diving.

Everyone in the group realized that Hina had been underwater much longer than even she was used to staying.

"She is in trouble!" Kama worried.

"I don't think so," Kon reassured. "She may have found something, and she is taking her time."

"Taking her time! You are joking. Nobody can stay that long underwater."

"Underwater, she has mana," Kukara said.

Finally, they saw Hina slowly rise to the surface. As she broke the surface, she was breathing normally, to Kama's considerable astonishment.

"If I had her skill, Kura would still be alive," the beautiful Viracocha woman said.

"Can you give me a piece of cloth to protect my hand?" Hina asked, giving five large sea urchins to Kon.

"What did you find?" Kon asked, handing her his shabby garment.

"Our dinner!"

With no comment, Hina went back to the abyss and disappeared in the darkness of a cave. Moments later, she came back with one large and one small lobster.

"You are truly amazing!" Kama said. "I cannot believe this. I could never learn to do such a thing."

Hina smiled at the compliment and dove back into the water. They chatted and waited for Hina to return with the next lobster. Time slowly drifted by with no sign from Hina. Even Kon, who knew her well, started to become concerned. He dove into the water, took several deep breaths, and descended to the underwater cave. He saw Hina holding a huge lobster in her hand while tugging mightily at something around her waist. She beckoned for Kon to take the lobster. He grabbed it behind its powerful antennas and returned to the surface.

"Where is she?" Kama asked, taking the flapping lobster from Kon.

"She is fighting with something, but she signaled me to leave."

"You mean she is still staying in the cave on her own free will?"

"Absolutely!"

Taranga shook his head, laughing. "We told you she is part fish."

Finally, Hina came back to the surface with a large animal crawling all around her wrist.

"This is not a moray eel," Hina said. "I never saw such a thing, but it is powerful."

They all stared at a conger the size of Hina's arm, disbelieving that she could have overcome it, in its element.

"Can all Maohis do this?" Kama asked in amazement.

"Most men can, but few women could, like Hina," Kon replied.

They dressed, except for Kon, whose garment was wet. They rolled their mats, took the lobsters and the conger for later, and continued their journey to the west.

"You look funny in the nude," Kama said, teasing Kon.

Hina glanced at Taranga, who was giggling, and so did Kukara.

They walked until late in the afternoon. They climbed a small hill at the top of which Kama told them they would spend the night. They made a fire with the abundant deadwood they found scattered between surrounding trees. They cooked and ate the lobsters and half the conger with great delight.

"You see, this is not a moray eel," Hina commented. "Moray eels are not very good to eat."

"It is more like the eels of Vahiria Lake or the rivers," Kon suggested.

"Yes, but it is still different," Hina said. "It is unique to this island. I wonder how big they can get."

"Maybe you don't want to know," Kon replied.

Tired from their long journey, they went to sleep against one another under the mats that protected them from the cool wind. Silence was absolute in this mysterious land. Kon dreamed about the giant he would carve one day at Rano Raraku. Hina was at peace with her naked body against the man she loved. She felt Kukara at her back, sleeping deeply. Kama lay on her back, her eyes exploring distant stars.

At dawn, they cooked the other half of the conger and inspected some rock formations Kama wanted to show them.

"This is the place where I made the adzes I gave to Hotu-Matua and Tamatoa. This is where I suggest we make the tools for you to carve the mountain."

"There is plenty of raw material," Kon said.

"The entire hill is made of this rock; much of it is buried under the soil. There are many places where you can see it popping out. If you are not careful, you will cut your feet."

They went south, crossed a valley, and started climbing the flanks of the largest volcano of the island. For Kama, this was the ultimate place, with its incredible beauty and its drama, and somewhere on the far side a young girl was at peace with spirits. They followed the giant cliff that plunged straight to the sea. Slowly, as they progressed, the cliff became higher and higher.

Slowly but surely, they were approaching the edge of the volcano. Kama took them to a natural basin full of clear water. They rested until old Taranga recovered his energy. As they approached the summit, Kama stopped them.

"Come around me, all of you. I want to watch your reaction when you see what is ahead."

They slowly approached. First, they saw the other side of the huge crater. Then, they saw two magnificent islets farther west, through a large break in the mountain. The next few steps brought them face to face with an incredible display of Mother Nature at her best and took them by surprise. They looked around, again and again, silent, incapable of expressing any thought equal to the vista's wonder.

"The first time I saw this, it was from the lowest point on the ridge," Kama said, pointing in the direction of the islets. "Though I was very tired and sad, it made an indelible impression on me."

"It is stunning," Kon said.

"I have never seen anything like it," Taranga added.

"This island is not the charming home where I was born," Hina said. "But I think it will be easy to get attached to it. I cannot explain the reasons yet."

"Because it is the perfect place to look at the stars," Kama suggested.

"But we could do this on Mount Orohena; you could do this on the continent," Hina argued.

"Yes and no," Kama replied. "This island is totally untouched by man. When the wind howls, we still hear spirits. When waves slam against the cliff, we still see the majestic power of water. When the crater catches our attention, we can only be humbled by things we will never be able to create. There man can almost become a bird because his soul can soar like nowhere else. Follow me!"

Not saying a word, Kukara reflected on those thoughts from Kama. She knew somehow she must remember them.

They walked around the crest of the crater until they reached the western side, where there was a narrow plateau. On one side was the caldera with its magnificent swamps and lakes. On the other side was the Awesome Sea with its waves pounding far below, booming on the giant cliff hidden from their view. Countless birds of many species enjoyed the solemn majesty of this paradise belonging solely to them. Man had not disturbed their delicate ecological balance or peace yet. Kama went into a nearby cave. Religiously, she kneeled near a shallow mound on which several objects had been reverently placed. They all knew it was Kura's grave. They entered behind Kama and remained respectfully silent in honor of this woman who would come to be their best friend for the rest of their lives. When they came out of the cave, they heard some voices. It was Tamatoa, Tehani, Mahine, and Taatamao coming back from the caldera where they had bathed all afternoon.

"I really like this place," Tamatoa said.

"If you plan to live here," Kama said, "please don't disturb the little cave where my daughter is resting." Kukara translated.

Tamatoa walked to Kama and put both hands on her shoulders. Deep black eyes explored the extraordinary beauty of her deep blue eyes.

"This cave is a sacred place," Tamatoa said solemnly. "It is tabooed for anyone to enter here without your permission. There are plenty of other caves anyway, so do not fear my friend." Kukara translated.

"Thank you!" Kama replied, with a demure smile. She enjoyed having his hands on her shoulders and was most surprised at this feeling.

In the evening, they made a fire and sat around it. They

languorously watched the red sky slowly darken above the western horizon, where many of their memories lived. They were all different. They were all talented people. They were good friends. They were in a dream of peace. The word war was no longer part of their vocabulary. They were happy and candid with one another. For a long time they talked about their findings, their projects, and their friendship, until the wind lulled them to sleep. Sparks from the fire slowly spiraled into the evening sky. Below, at the bottom of the giant cliff, waves pounded the island… relentlessly…

The first woman was created by the Great Ancestor, in search of her spirit. With mana's power, she one day must find her spirit, the first man, and his spirit. Then, from the depth of the earth, they will love, create, and prosper.

CHAPTER 6

"Everyone must come to the top of the island, where we shall establish the rules of a new order. We must elect leaders, decide what they must do, and learn to obey their rules. We are a small group; each of us must have an important role to fulfill for all the others. Let's do this in good spirit and with the verve that characterizes each of you so well."

Taranga Tici Viracocha

Seven days later, they held their first tribunal on the volcano's crest. It was a mandatory reunion for everyone. Taranga was their elected supreme leader; he was charged with guiding them with his wisdom in this small universe in which they were determined to live in peace and harmony, with reality blending into their dreams.

Several individuals were appointed to facilitate discussions. Their first order of business that day was to name the island's many topographical features. The top of the island, where they all were, with its small lake and islets in the middle, was named Mount Terevaka. The mysterious mountain with the lake surrounded by silent nocturnal giants was named Rano Raraku. The big volcano with the magnificent caldera at the southwest corner of the island was named Rano Kau. The mountain full of obsidian rock became Mount Orito; the beautiful beach of white sand on the north side of the island, Anakena, at the request of Hotu-Matua; the smaller beach with pink sand, farther to the east, was named Ovahe; the eastern part of the island was named Poike; and the plateau on the western edge of Rano Kau became Orongo. Now they had a common geographic lexicon. Then came the time to determine and assign responsibilities.

Standing tall and proud, Taranga beckoned for Hina of the Valley and Kama Tici Viracocha to join him. They complied, standing on each side of him. The three of them faced everyone, and Taranga placed a friendly hand on the shoulders of each women.

"Look at them, how special they are. I am your leader today, but I am old and my days are numbered. These two women will be your leaders tomorrow. Hina of the Valley will be your queen and Kama Tici Viracocha will help and guide her and counsel her in every detail of daily life."

"But I don't want to be a queen," Hina argued. "I am a priestess. Why not select Kon, why not Tamatoa, why not Hotu-Matua, why not Kama?"

Taranga turned to face Hina, placing both hands on her shoulders. Silently, he gazed into her eyes. She tingled as the power of his mind probed her soul. She felt her mind rising. She felt the presence of the Light deep inside her being. She realized now that she was his equal in knowledge, will, and more. Everyone saw this in her countenance.

"Now, don't tell me you will not be their queen, in due time," Taranga said.

"As you say, in due time. We shall see." Hina flushed with Maohi pride.

There was no doubt in anyone's mind that Hina would become their queen soon. Kon glanced at Tamatoa, who smiled back at him in mutual understanding.

Taranga placed both hands on Kama's shoulders. "Wife of my late grandson Illa, your knowledge is immense, beyond mine, and you are still so young. You don't have the inherent leadership capabilities so unique to Hina of the Valley, but you will be her friend, and always help her in her complex mission. The Light told us you were sisters born in two different worlds. So, two outstanding women are going to guide our steps and create a stunning example for future generations."

Taranga went to Hotu-Matua. "My old friend who saved our lives a long time ago, I mightily praise your friendship. You should make the northern coast prosper by Anakena and Ovahe beaches. You and your people are the stewards of these beautiful places, where many of us will yearn to visit. At your legendary place we shall rejoice, talk, sing, play, and dance, so our lives will be filled with the products from the sea you know how to gather so well. The sacred sea turtle shall be your totem for generations to come. The sacred sea turtle comes to Anakena and Ovahe every year to mate and lay eggs, so Hotu-Matua can say to his friends: 'Come to me, and I will always feed you with the best there is in the Awesome Sea.' Make sure we all use the sea's abundance wisely. You should have taken my place, but it was your will not to do so. You were the first Maohi to step on this island; your legend will live forever."

Taranga went to Tamatoa. "The tattooed giant, the great warrior, the feared man, but as Kukara once said 'the good man,' you have a prime role in this strange adventure of ours." Taranga's extraordinary fingernails reached the massive arms of the giant. "Kon will become our great architect; he will organize and direct our people to build great things. There will be no such achievement without courage, discipline, and extraordinary will, and this is where you must assist because you have always been a great commander. You are the perfect man for the task. Kon shall be your best friend; then nothing will be in your way. Together as brothers, nothing will stop you."

Taranga took Kon's hands. "My dear and only remaining grandson, this place is your destiny. Delegate all the leadership to Hina, Kama, Hotu-Matua, and Tamatoa. You will use your brain to create a paradise, heretofore unknown to man. This is a place of spirits, living rocks, secret caverns, hidden freshwater resources, and talking winds, where you will excel. They will all help you build, draw, carve, and dig with great creativity. It is your responsibility to keep everyone productive on great and wondrous projects. It is also your sacred obligation to keep everyone at peace. Undoubtedly quarrels will develop because it is the nature of man to disagree, but you will be there to help them with your great motto: 'I shall not fight with my adversary; my adversary shall not become my enemy.' Our heirs must never forget these Light-inspired words."

Then Taranga turned to a shy little girl. "Kukara Tici Viracocha, keeper of the sacred Rongo-Rongo tablets. You are still very young, just about nine sun cycles, yet your mind is a sleeping giant that can benefit everyone; they shall and they will benefit. All of us know by now you are a great favorite of the Light, and I know why." Taranga stopped talking. Everyone expected him to give the reason, including Kukara, who glanced at Taranga with wide-open dark blue eyes. "Injustice was brought to you long ago," Taranga continued. "But you kept being a wonderful little girl. Your mind is swift, you are extraordinarily intelligent, yet you are humble, and arrogance is an unknown concept to you. Create, my little one, be the one who will write on rocks and wood the mysterious legend of Rapa Nui. Your role is significant. You will also have another secret mission on this island, and you shall be the one to discover it, in due time; for that, mana will always be with you!"

"Mahine, Tamatoa's daughter, and your mate, Taatamao, have two responsibilities. Mahine, you shall ensure that all our children receive proper care and an adequate education. Taatamao, you love the sea. You shall develop ways to make magnificent gardens inside the numerous open lava tubes where rich soil has accumulated, where rain can be collected, and where protection against the wind is found. In these endeavors, use

Kama's knowledge to its fullest extent. Tehani, Tamatoa's mate, should also help create these gardens. She will be the keeper of our freshwater resources."

"Rangi and the young woman Kora, who loves you, you will explore the resources of the Poike Peninsula. It is an isolated place, and not fully appreciated. This is a small island, and every place has its purpose; it is your mission to uncover Poike's."

Now speaking to the entire assemblage, Taranga said, "These people I mentioned are the supreme council. They are your leaders. They are the sacred people and they will remain so, provided they continue to protect everyone here and inspire the ones far away. They are the Sacred Circle of Twelve and during any emergency situation they must gather and use their wisdom. This has been said, and it shall be done that way."

Assignments continued throughout the day and were generally consistent with individual strengths and skills. Taranga had been very careful not to impose tasks on anyone that he or she would dislike doing. His dream was to create an egalitarian society rather than an authoritarian, brutal system, which everyone the island had experienced once in their respective worlds.

"What an extraordinary team we have here," Taranga said. "These tasks are not mandated. They are but only recommendations. However, I do command you to work hard and to find time for pleasure as well. You shall enjoy your life. You shall have fun with your life. Love your mate, love your friends, and respect your neighbors. It is all I have to tell you."

It was late in the evening when they all gathered at Anakena, where Hotu-Matua had prepared a great feast to celebrate that epochal day. Kon and Tamatoa sat on the ground near Hina and Kama.

"How does it feel to be the queen?" Kon asked.

"I am not the queen yet," Hina replied. "But if it becomes my duty, I will earn our people's trust to the best of my abilities."

"I think it is you, Kon, the architect, who has the most

important role," Tamatoa said. "Your wish is our command."

"I know it has something to do with big stones," Kama said. "Kon and Illa were always obsessed with big stones."

"As far as I am concerned," Hina said, "the matter was settled at Rano Raraku a few days ago. Think about it, plan it, and do it. But whatever you do, do it to inspire awe in all those that behold it."

"I will," Kon replied, looking at Tamatoa. "We will!" The two men shook hands to seal their mutual pledge.

Kon gazed at the horizon, lost in thought. His mind was thoroughly occupied, busily mulling a private mystery.

"You see, Hina," Kama said, "this is why you should be the queen. These men are clueless as to how our children can be fed." They all laughed in good humor.

"What would be wrong with Kama being the queen?" Hina asked, seriously.

Kama did not reply. They all waited with rapt anticipation.

"I am a broken mother who still hurts deep inside. I don't have the will to command. I enjoy analyzing possibilities. I enjoy solving problems. I enjoy learning new things. Let me be your sister from another world only; then I will be fulfilled with wonder."

Tamatoa pressed a finger on Kama's thigh, to her surprise. "Your pain is immense. I also lost a son, and long ago, my father. I know how you feel. Kon told me once there is a reason for everything because this world is always in harmony." Kukara translated.

"You are not the man I thought you were," Kama said. Kukara translated.

"I sure can witness to this," Hina chuckled.

"Well, I hope to know you better sometime," Kama smiled. "Where is Tehani?"

"I am here, Kama," Tehani replied, coming from behind, "and you are welcome in my home anytime you wish."

Kama glanced at the strong, older Maohi woman. They understood each other and smiled at one another.

Moments later, the Sacred Circle of Twelve was seated and served luxurious seafood and drinks. Kukara sat in the middle of the circle and started to play the flute the Inca's son had given to her. Her inspiring tune charmed everyone, including those sitting on the surrounding hills. It was an enchanting melody from another world. It was so good that Hina felt instant shivers down her spine. She took Kon's hand and held it with love. Nobody talked. Every settler listened. The little girl's long black hair cascaded over her magic fingers and the flute. Kama cried because she was sure that on a faraway hill, in a remote cave, Kura's spirit was listening. Taranga glanced at Kon, who placed one finger across his lips to make sure no words would be spoken. The child was gifted beyond imagination. Every sound would mean something special to everyone, yet something different. Every sound was a mysterious story, exactly like each sign of the Rongo-Rongo tablets; sounds with no words, capable of telling stories and legends to the soul, capable of igniting sentiments and love. This was the true talent of young Kukara Tici Viracocha. Everyone had the deepest respect for the girl, inside whom mana lived.

Kukara stopped and let the flute drop to her chest at the end of a necklace made from tiny shells. She stood up and took Hina's hand, then Mahine's hand.

"Would you show us a Maohi dance done at its best?" Kukara suggested.

A murmur of approval came from the gathering.

Hina took Mahine's hand. "So be it, sister from Tahaa, Pora-Pora, and Rarotonga, daughter of Tamatoa the Great. Let's make Kukara proud of us."

In Hina's words, there was that certainty and propagating confidence instantly igniting Mahine's will.

The two women disappeared, followed by Tehani and

Kama, who would help Hina and Mahine dress. Several of the men quickly smoothed and swept an impromptu dance area. The remaining ten members of the Sacred Circle of Twelve sat in a large circle. All other settlers sat behind them. Borrowed from Hotu-Matua's ships, four drums were placed nearby under a large palm tree. At the powerful blast from a sea conch, the two dancers came, holding a fire torch in each hand. Slowly, the drums started rumbling like in the old days on Tahiti Nui, but with a slightly different beat, probably inherited from Kukara's melodies. Among the settlers, a few women started a song, then some of the men sang a response. In the middle of the circle, standing tall and holding the fire torches high, Hina and Mahine danced to the song. Then in a truly mystical moment, everything stopped. As the echoes played out, the sound of the waves and nearby crickets could be heard; then the grating of terns, far at sea, could be heard. The instant was frozen in time. Kon opened a little bag he had secretly brought to the event. Hina instantly recognized the dry flowers she had given to him long ago after he saw her dance with her sister Fenua for the very first time. She told him at the time that these flowers are sacred and should never be lost. The powerful symbol instantly energized the great priestess, who felt blood rushing to her face. Taranga Tici Viracocha pointed a finger at Hina of the Valley. Now everything was in the hands of the two dancers.

The drums rolled; this time it was different. Some people found something to clap with; many started singing. At first, the tempo was slow, its mood melancholy. Imperceptibly, a crescendo began, imbuing the rhythm with momentum, life, and an unbounded joy. The two young women slightly accelerated the dancing, skillfully and effortlessly moving in one with the music. The tempo accelerated more. Hina and Mahine gracefully swayed with their hips, keeping their arms above their heads. Everyone admired their suppleness, grace, and beauty, even though the two women had very different styles. Hina had charismatic beauty and enormous charm, while Mahine, having the stronger body, was all power. The rhythm accelerated even more, and everyone became involved and excited. Even Tamatoa and Hotu-Matua stood up and started dancing. Everyone clapped with increasing energy. It was a combination of rapid calls between sharp sounds against split bamboo brought from other islands, loud claps against house pillars and trees, and the deep rumbling of the drums. Hina and Mahine swayed so fast that their skirts parted, revealing their perfect legs. Faster and faster, they reached a speed that was breathtaking. Yet it was not the climax. The two women had their eyes closed with pleasure and pain, with power and sweat. Kama's mouth was wide open, as she had never thought that such a rhythm was possible. Finally, swaying, clapping, drumming, and singing saturated the senses. Then everything stopped. The group felt as though every fiber of their beings was magnetically attracted toward Hina and Mahine. There was no music, no song, and no talk, only the waves of the sea pounding on the beach, the gratings of faraway terns, and the surrounding crickets. Covered with perspiration, Hina stood perfectly still in front of Kon, her arms frozen above her head.

Mahine came toward her father and put her lei around his neck and kissed him. Hina slowly took the old lei from Kon's hands and put it around his neck.

"I love you, Kon Tici," she said firmly. "These flowers are good luck for you. Do not lose them. Many years from now, you will remember this moment. These flowers are a symbol of beauty, and they are always given with love. They are the jewels of my island; this new island shall be an inspiration for the world, because of what we are going to create on it. We are all part of this island, and we shall all live on it in peace and love."

The first woman and her immortal spirit were given by the Great Ancestor, so the earth would recognize one day that woman would have the sacred knowledge of perpetuating life.

CHAPTER 7

"Rano Raraku holds secret energy. Its rock vibrates and has a mind of its own. Its shadows gather in a circle under the moonlit night. Shadows of giants travel along its eastern flank as the sun's first rays illuminate the dawn horizon. The mystery is mirrored at sunset. This unique place is inspiring, rewarding, and has a sacred bond to another world."

Kon Tici Viracocha

Six moon cycles went by during which Kama learned the Maohi language. She was an excellent student.

It had been an uneventful period, during which all the settlers had been busy organizing the way they would live for the rest of their lives, based on the Sacred Circle of Twelve's guidance.

"You have been an outstanding teacher for me," Kama told Hina.

"I practiced with Kon," Hina replied.

Sitting a small distance from the two women, Kon scrutinized Rano Raraku and was lost in deep thoughts. They had been fishing, and had just eaten a good meal. Their nude bodies glistened under the warm sun as they rested on large flat rocks near the beach's edge. With Hina's teaching and experience in diving, Kon and Kama became much better swimmers and were capable of independently gathering and hunting their food under the calm seas.

"I need to spend some time alone at Rano Raraku," Kon said. "I know this place waits for me, but I am debating on how to start."

"Do you need our creativity?" Hina asked with a smile.

"Not yet!" Kon replied, kissing the neck of the woman he loved.

"Then we will leave you alone," Hina replied. "I am going with Kama. We will visit Tamatoa and Tehani at the Orongo settlement. Take your time and join us at their place in a few days."

Kon looked at the two women as they got up and started walking to the west; he was surprised when a strong sense of foreboding washed over him. Something of great importance was going to happen, but he did not know what it was. For an instant he debated with himself whether he should go to Rano Raraku or go with Hina and Kama. It was a beautiful sunny day with a gentle breeze. It was around midday. He shook the premonition and ran to Rano Raraku. Having run half the way, it did not take him long to reach the crater. He climbed to the summit of the tallest cliff, while taking in the desolation of his surroundings. Here and there were scattered stands of toromiro, a small tree that provided good-quality wood. Interspersed among them were stands of tall palm trees. Kon inspected the natural fractures in the mountain and determined the best ways to carve the rock, avoiding fissures that could compromise its structural integrity. He had studied these fractures many times and always arrived at the same conclusion: statues this large would have to be carved horizontally, not vertically.

Before sunset, he walked to the west side of the lake and watched shadows slowly spread up the cliff as the sun slowly disappeared behind the mountain in the west. As he stared at the mountain and shadows, optical illusions liberated the great stone giants from the mountain. He smiled at the fantasy, but shivered at its realism. Later that evening, stars appeared to float on the lake's dead calm surface.

"This is another illusion," he murmured. "There are no stars in the lake, yet how do I know the difference? So how do I know if the shadows that travel around that place are not real? Perhaps it is up to us to decipher their message, like the one inside the cave of Mount Orohena."

Lost in his thoughts, he forgot time and his surroundings. Kon Tici spent the entire night watching the lake and spirits of Rano Raraku. In his mind there was often a conflict between the pragmatic reality of everyday life and the secret, enigmatic mystery of something deeper and unreachable inside himself. As a well-trained Viracocha, never once in his life had Kon Tici lost his time in meditation. The faint light from the stars clearly told him this time was no different.

At the same time, farther west and close to Mount Orito, Hina and Kama made a small fire, cooked a few fish, and prepared for the night. They thoroughly enjoyed talking to one another.

"How was it to have children?" Hina asked.

Kama glanced at Hina with surprise. "Are you expecting?"

"No, not yet, but I am running out of the Tahiti Nui herbs to prevent pregnancy. This herb was common in my valley, but I cannot find anything similar around here."

"Why do you want to prevent pregnancy? It is a wonderful experience to have children. And any progeny of you and Kon should be beautiful."

"I was too busy becoming a priestess and never felt the need to have children of my own. I feel I would be a lousy mother. But I know I cannot delay it forever."

"I know of such herbs on the continent," Kama said, "but I have not seen anything like them here. To be honest, after being alone for so long, I have not felt the need to search."

"How could you?" Hina said with a chuckle. "Don't you feel

the need for a man's contact?"

"Sometimes I do. I am still young and passionate. But I went through terrible pain for such a long time. The scars are slowly healing."

Hina went behind Kama and gently rubbed her shoulders.

"That feels good, Hina. Thank you for being my friend."

"Lay down, and I will massage your back."

Kama undressed and stretched out on the mat. Hina sat on Kama's legs and ran her strong fingers along Kama's spine, starting from the shoulders and moving all the way to her lower back. She continued the therapeutic exercise until Kama almost went to sleep. Then Hina undressed, and both young women crawled between two woven blankets, positioning themselves back to back for warmth.

"I miss my valley, my sister, and my parents," Hina said quietly.

"Do you feel the need to go back?"

"Yes and no! I almost lost my life at sea once, another time alone in a deep cave of Mount Orohena, and another time against Tamatoa if Kon had not been on our island at the right time. Therefore, everything considered, I feel happy and privileged to be here with all my best friends and the man I love. Sometimes we must adjust and be content. I could also have been ordered to take a mate, a king from another island. If I had done this, I would have lost my identity. So, my dear sister, I am going to make the best of this island, I swear."

"I enjoy your friendship, Hina," Kama murmured.

"So do I!"

They went to sleep listening to the treet-treet of crickets, at peace with the world and themselves, savoring their unique friendship.

Early the next morning, Tehani went to explore a cave with Manua, one of her servants. Facing the sea, not far from the abyss of the giant cliff of Orongo, she had earlier discovered a place that she believed hid a pool of fresh water. Indeed, every time she went to the cave, she heard drops of water falling in a pool, but she had never found the source. She regarded the cave as her personal secret place. Determined to find the pool's source this time, she asked Manua to join the quest. They entered a very narrow crevice hidden behind a shrub. Although they both had torches, only Tehani's was lighted. They were saving the other for a safety backup. They walked deep into the lava tube. After a long journey, carefully picking their way through the tube, they reached a large chamber.

"Stop and listen," Tehani said. "Do you hear?"

"Yes, I do," Manua murmured. "It sounds like water dripping into a pool."

"Despite several trips down here, I have not been able to find its origin," Tehani said.

They carefully inspected the walls, methodically sweeping them with the light from Tehani's torch. During one pass Tehani noticed the aberrational behavior of the light reflecting on the wall in front of her. The wall had a discontinuity that she had not previously noticed. Handing her torch to Manua, Tehani explored the wall with her hands and discovered a vertical slit in the rock, barely large enough for a person to climb through. Both women held their breath and listened; Tehani smiled with excitement.

"There is no possible doubt: the pool is behind this."

"Be careful, my queen," Manua said. "You don't know what is behind this."

Tehani squeezed her body into the crack and struggled forward. Finally, after several attempts at pulling and pushing, she reached a second chamber. As the torch pierced the primordial darkness, a stunning sight was revealed. They were on a ledge, standing far above a beautiful blue pond. With their need and struggle for good fresh water, this pool was an incredible discovery.

"There is much more water on this island than what we may think," Tehani said. "It is all underground."

Entranced, Tehani inadvertently stepped forward, forgetting where she was. In the blink of an eye, the flat stone on which she was standing flipped over the edge. She tried to find her balance. Manua grabbed the queen's hand, but could not manage her weight. Desperately, Tehani grabbed at the ledge, at Manua, at the air, at anything, at nothing. She felt her body floating freely in space. Twisting her body in midair, she hoped to correct her trajectory and fall feet first into the pond. Fate decided otherwise.

Manua heard the plunk of Tehani's body hitting the ground, mixed with the gentle splash of her hands still searching into the very shallow water.

"My queen! Tehani! Talk to me!" Manua screamed. But silence was the only reply. Terrified, she ran outside the cave and screamed for help. Tamatoa ran to her.

"Master, I tried to help her, but I was not strong enough."

"Show me where!" Tamatoa said with a roaring voice.

"You need ropes. It is impossible to get to her without them." Immediately, two men went to get some ropes.

Manua took Tamatoa into the cave and showed him the narrow passage. His powerful hands tore through the friable, loose rock, and he was soon standing on the ledge. Manua held the torch and pointed to Tehani's body far below.

"Careful, master, many of these rocks are loose."

Tamatoa glanced at Manua's terrified eyes. She was scared of what his reaction would be. To her surprise, he comforted her by taking her arm.

"I know it was not your fault, woman."

Two men came with ropes, and Tamatoa immediately started the descent. "Stay there and hold the rope while I climb down."

When he reached his wife, he found she was still breathing.

He hurriedly tied a small loop at the rope's end. He took Tehani in his arms, placed one foot in the loop, and seized the rope with his free hand.

"Pull us up!" he shouted.

Outside the cave he gently placed Tehani on a carpet of green grass, and blew his conch to signal the terrible tragedy. Far to the north, Mahine and Taatamao heard the message. Farther to the east, Hina trembled at the terrible news.

"What is it?" Kama asked.

"Tehani had a bad accident. Tamatoa is asking for help."

"How do you know this from the sound of a conch?"

"Sounds are like words," she said. "The Maohis language includes many words, some made by man's voice, others by conches and drums. Those made by conch are succinct, yet provide enough information for us to get a general sense of the meaning."

Gathering their goods quickly, Kama shook her head skeptically.

The two women ran as fast as they could to the summit of Rano Kao, circled the caldera, and ran to Orongo. As they arrived out of breath, they found Tamatoa sitting near Tehani, surrounded by several Maohis. Manua explained what had happened. Hina kneeled next to Tamatoa and cradled Tehani's head. She saw that Tehani's skull was badly fractured; her breathing was labored and irregular. Kama silently pointed at Tehani's broken legs and started to sob. The queen opened her eyes and forced a smile. Tamatoa took her hands and leaned closer and looked into her eyes.

"We...," she started. "We had a good life together...," she whispered. Then in an instant, her life energy left her body. Tehani was gone.

The great warrior held his wife, put his face in her hair, and cried like a young boy. Mahine joined them, holding them both.

"Mother! My dear mother, it is not fair! No!… No!" she sobbed.

Hina stepped back a few paces and started to cry. Kama went to her and put her arms around her shoulders.

"She was a good friend, like a mother to me," Hina said. Kama had never seen Hina in so much sorrow.

Kama went back to Tamatoa and saw that Taatamao was comforting him. The tattooed giant turned around and said, "All of you go! Leave me alone in this place for a few days."

"Father, I want to stay with you. She is my mother!" Mahine objected.

"You may stay a little longer to help me, and then you will leave as well. This place is for Tehani's spirit."

As Kama left, Tamatoa stopped her. "Would Kura's cave be a good place for Tehani?"

Two dark blue eyes looked at him with compassion.

"It is the best place of all," Kama replied, bowing in front of him.

It was much later during the afternoon when the Sacred Circle of Twelve convened. With Tehani, Tamatoa, and Mahine missing, the group felt ill at ease. The revelation of their vulnerability helped them explore their destiny in a better perspective.

Kukara wanted to go see Tamatoa; they told her to let him mourn in private.

"You may comfort him in a few days," Taatamao said, "like I will comfort Mahine later today."

"Mahine is devastated," Kama said.

"So am I!" Hina replied, finding solace on Kon's chest. "She did not die in vain. Indeed, she died for our collective well-being."

"What do you mean?" Taranga asked, raising his long, shaking fingers. Kon noticed the trembling hand, as did Kukara and Kama.

"Manua, the servant, told me that Tehani had found a large

underground pool of pure, fresh water," Hina explained. "It is a place that should be considered sacred; we should protect and conserve it for the future."

Concerned, Kon took Taranga's hand, and asked. "How do you feel?"

"Not good. Today I fell twice as I was hurrying here. I know I will leave this life soon; my heart is weak."

"So will I!" Hotu-Matua replied, taking everyone by surprise.

"What do you mean?" Kukara asked.

"You may notice I have lost weight during the last two moon cycles."

"So, you look better that way." Kukara replied.

"No. Something is eating at me slowly from inside. I know. I have no energy."

There was a long silence. They all realized they would never forget that day. The Sacred Circle of Twelve was atrophying. They all looked at one another, measuring the implications, and the necessity for a new order. They all looked at Hina of the Valley. Her time had come. It never crossed the young priestess's mind that this time would come… so soon.

One moon cycle later, Taranga departed this life, uttering these last words to Hina: "Hina of the Valley, my dear, now it is all yours… I wish you well…"

Seven days later, Hotu-Matua called for Kukara. He took her hand and managed a few final words.

"You are the little daughter I never had. All my children were boys. Take care of the Rongo-Rongo tablets. They hold the future of this island. Remember mokohe!"

"Your spirit will always be alive within the characters of the Rongo-Rongo tablets," Kukara replied, wondering why he was referring to mokohe, the frigate bird they had observed together so many times.

"They are incomplete," Hotu-Matua murmured, pointing at the Rongo-Rongo tablets in her hands. "You must add to them."

"I will!"

"Call Hina, I have a message for her."

"I am here, my good friend," Hina said.

"Listen to what I have to say. In my dreams I have seen Hina of the Valley sent by the Great Taaroa. The whiteness of your dress was like a beautiful cloud next to a rainbow that passed from Anakena to Ovahe. Ovahe will be the place of the future queen; it is your place. The Teke family gave me a home." Like many other Maohis, he could not pronounce Tici. "Kukara, in many ways you are my adopted daughter. Remember how I used to call you Teatea? You did not like that name, I know. My little Teatea, I love you immensely. Prepare a drink of water for me; I will leave this world when I take the last sip."

Hina placed her gourd of water in his hands and lovingly closed his fingers around it.

"Soon there will only be seven left in the Sacred Circle. You should call it the Sacred Circle of the Seven Souls. All members of that circle are my adopted children, never forget. The Great Hotu-Matua created the Sacred Circle of the Seven Souls."

"We never will," Kukara murmured near his ear.

"The legend of the Sacred Circle of the Seven Souls must live forever. Many sun cycles from now, you must build a special place for it, so future generations will never forget King Hotu-Matua."

"Your words are sacred," Hina said. "I, the queen, swear such a place will be built."

Hotu-Matua took the last sip of water, then slowly lowered the gourd to his side.

"I return to Hiva where... The rooster... Beware of the Awesome Sea..."

The legendary navigator exhaled for the last time. Outside the house, a rooster crowed, sending the sad news from Rapa

Nui to Hiva. Kukara closed his eyes and collapsed on his chest in tears. She recalled he had told her once she would be the one who would close his eyes for the last time.

The Circle of Twelve was down to nine.

Several days later, when the moon was a full circle, they met as usual.

"Shall we add new members?" Kon asked.

Hina faced the Awesome Sea from the top of Orongo, reflecting on Hotu-Matua's strange last words. There was something in his words that did not make sense. And yet she knew he had not spoken these words for naught. They were to be taken seriously. Kukara knew exactly what she was thinking.

"I have given a lot of thought to this," Hina said. "I have decided that we will not add new members until such time as we become less than seven."

"Why is that?" Kon asked.

"There are seven sun cycles between each Great Maohi Gathering on Havaiki. It is important that we don't forget this. Also, because Hotu-Matua had seven adopted children in his heart, and we will know their names soon. In the meantime, beware of the Awesome Sea. Those were Hotu-Matua's final words."

The queen had spoken, and nobody dared question her words.

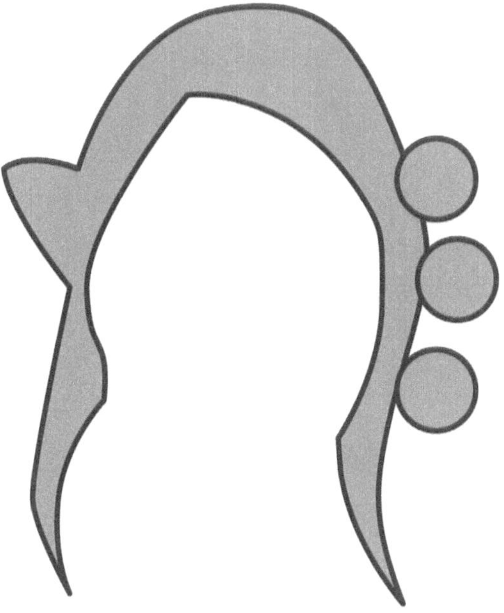

The sacred, supernatural spirit of the great god Make Make, with its mysterious origin from the stars, was present in all of us. It is the Light. It is everywhere. It is all of us. It is eternal.

CHAPTER 8

"Following a devastating and unpredictable act of nature, more loved ones went on their eternal journey. It was hard for the survivors to accept the cruel reality. Being the queen, and responsible for the well-being of my people, I adopted the concept of the Circle of the Seven Souls. From now on, the wisdom of the Seven Souls would determine Rapa Nui's future."

Hina of the Valley

A few days later at Orongo, Kukara carved the new characters she had recently created on a beautiful piece of wood Tamatao had given her.

"Is the wood too hard?" the tattooed giant asked.

"No, it is perfect," Kukara replied. "I like it a lot. The characters will last forever on this wood."

"One day you will explain to me the meaning of these characters."

"Of course I will! May I ask you something personal?"

"Sure!" Tamatoa replied, with a surprised look on his face.

"You are always alone. You don't seem to enjoy the presence of your old friends, not even that of Mahine, your own daughter. You barely put up with me. What is wrong with you?"

Tamatoa sat down, took Kukara's tablets and tools from

her, and set them aside. Taking Kukara's hand, Tamatoa said, "I lost the woman I loved. I have done many things wrong during my life. I have lost the motivation to be a leader. I feel empty and despondent. I fear it will take many moon cycles for me to recover."

"You are lonely, and Kama is lonely."

Tamatoa took the child by the shoulder and brought her head close his chest.

"Kama is a beautiful and intelligent woman. She has no desire to associate with a man like me, for many reasons."

"Would you?"

"No, not now."

"But," she stammered, "I know she likes you."

Kukara abruptly stood, shading her eyes with her hands. She silently gazed at the eastern horizon.

"This is not right!" she murmured after a short time.

Tamatoa sensed her growing distress.

"What is it, child?"

"The Awesome Sea! It is coming, all the way from the continent. It will destroy everything near the shore."

Tamatoa knew Kukara too well to ask for more details. He grabbed his conch and blew it as hard as he could. The carefully blown notes alerted the well-trained Maohis of a danger. All Tamatoa's ships were at sea fishing and could not hear the conch. But were they far enough from shore? Hina and Kama were at Mount Orito making obsidian knives. Instantly, Hina's eyes narrowed.

"What is it?" Kama asked.

"Kukara must have told Tamatoa to have the people evacuate the shore now; the Awesome Sea is coming."

Kama panicked.

"My children, they are at sea with Taatamao and Mahine."

"Don't worry; they are far away from shore. They should be safe, and Kon is at Rano Raraku; he should be safe too."

Tamatoa's message was retransmitted around the island. The Maohis ran rapidly from the coast. Even from the top of Orongo, Kukara and Tamatoa could easily see the unusually low tide line. Tamatoa had seen this phenomenon before; he knew what was coming. His fingers tightly gripped Kukara's shoulders.

"It is coming!" he said. "But from which direction?"

"I told you, it comes from the continent."

"Therefore, it comes from where the sun rises. All the northern, eastern, and southern coasts will be affected."

"Rangi, Kora, and her parents are at the very end of Poike," Kukara said. "They don't understand your conch language. I hope they are not at the bottom of the cliff collecting sea urchins and clams, as they often do."

"I hope they will realize the reasons for the unexpected low tide," Tamatoa said, grimacing.

"There is nothing we can do," he added absently.

They stared, mesmerized by the huge, long swell forming near the coast. It pummeled the shore with a devastating shock, catapulting water high in the hills. The rolling waters madly raced far inland, inundating every low-lying area. They heard the awesome roar as the water battered the base of the Orongo cliff. Shock waves from the onslaught reverberated under their feet. Part of the cliff collapsed and slid into the retreating seas. Two smaller waves followed, and then everything seemed to return to normal.

Tamatoa and Kukara set about reckoning the damage and counting the survivors. This would be a devastating day to the Viracochas: Rangi, Kora and her parents, and Hiti had been killed by the first wave. Their entire settlement at the eastern side of Poike was obliterated when the cliff on which their settlement was located collapsed into the sea. Only two Maohis at the Anakena beach were killed; all others had time to run to safety in the hills. However, all five boats from Hotu-Matua's group were destroyed or missing. Tamatoa's group had no casualties, and their three boats, far at sea, barely felt the waves passing below them. Kon, Hina, Kama, and Kukara were devastated by the loss of Rangi's family.

Next evening, the survivors of the Sacred Circle of Twelve met at Orongo.

"We are now down to seven, just as Hotu-Matua's prophecy told us," Hina said, with sadness on her face. "But it could have been far worse, if not for you, Kukara."

"I did not do anything. Tamatoa blew the conch."

"Thanks to you too, great warrior," Hina added. "Hotu-Matua had warned us, but I never made sense of his words. I am very sorry about my first failure as your queen."

"There is nothing you could do about it," Kon argued. "We all discussed these words, but none of us could make sense of them either."

"I disagree," Hina replied. "I could have been better prepared."

"I am sorry we did not teach the Viracochas to understand the conchs," Tamatoa added. "I take that as a personal failure as well."

"We should remedy these shortcomings as soon as possible," Hina replied. "We lost too many lives in a very short time. I am concerned about our future."

"Shall we elect more members to the circle now?" Kon asked.

"No," Hina replied, "I am changing the name of the circle.

From now on, it will be called the Sacred Circle of the Seven Souls. We will be equals, each of us with our respective fields. The Seven Souls are Hotu-Matua's legendary children."

"Can you be more specific?" Kon asked.

"Kon, my mate, you are the supreme architect of everything that will be built on this island: in other words, you set the protocols. Tamatoa, an erstwhile adversary but a good friend today, you will make sure everything is built correctly: in other words, you are in charge of implementing the protocols. Kama, my sister from another world, you are responsible for researching everything that we can grow, gather, fish, eat, and drink, whether it is found on land, under the land, or in the sea; your responsibility is immense to all of us. Mahine, my very dear friend, you are in charge of educating our children; I count on you to mold peaceful, creative, and dedicated young adults. Taatamao, the best navigator after Tamatoa, you are in charge of gathering all the resources we need from the sea: without the sea resources, we cannot survive for long. You shall also manage the crops we cultivate in the lava tubes. Kukara, the gifted one from the sacred, supreme Light, your mind is a treasure that we cannot afford to lose. You shall be prohibited from doing anything dangerous. I am sorry about this, and you may be annoyed about this at times. But always know that we love you. Your responsibility is to create the Rongo-Rongo characters carved on the sacred toromiro wood to help us remember and pass along our knowledge. We will carve the rocks of this island with your symbols, inspiring future generations; I want them to be extraordinary in scope and beauty. I, Hina of the Valley, solemnly swear this Sacred Circle of the Seven Souls will create the most extraordinary civilization the world has ever known: Great Light, Taaroa, Viracocha, or by whatever name you will reveal to us, please inspire me and help guide me in this brave endeavor. My dear friends, this is what we owe to all the loved ones that we have lost, those who went to the world of spirits and those who are still alive but far away."

Hina's words stunned them all. They were all silent and stared at her. She had been beautifully prepared. There were no doubts that Hina was their beloved queen, and for a very long time to come.

Two days later, Hina of the Valley walked alone from Anakena to Ovahe. "The whiteness of her dress was like a beautiful cloud beside a rainbow passing nearby." This was another prophecy from Hotu-Matua. Anakena had been Hotu-Matua's favorite place for a long time. He thoroughly enjoyed resting under a palm tree and watching the children and naked women playing and bathing. He was a great man, but introverted and with modest desires. Ovahe was Hina's favorite place. She puzzled how he could have known that. She had never told him. On the other hand, how could he have known about the Awesome Sea coming and killing so many? Many questions raced through her mind. Near Ovahe, she sat near the cliff and looked at the pink sand beach, then to an islet's nearby shore. She liked the idea of making her settlement there.

"Would Kon and Kukara approve this idea?"

She smiled at her thoughts.

"Who cares? I am the queen!"

She grabbed a piece of grass, swept her arms with it, then bent over and picked up a stone and flung it as hard as she could toward the sea.

"This is my place. This is where I will live!"

She caressed the sacred green pigeon feather on her chest, fully aware that she did not need to be told by anyone how to rule her life. The sacred green pigeon feather was the mark of the great priestess she had earned on the islands of her childhood a long time ago; she always kept the feather with her, especially for the important moments of her life. Only at the sight of that feather, all Maohis would bend to her. In many ways, she dearly enjoyed being the queen.

That evening she walked down to the pink sandy beach and found a cave covered with dry sand. She decided she would spend the night there, alone. It was a warm night. She undressed, curled up on the sand, and rapidly sank into peaceful dreams.

She woke up during the night and wondered about the wisdom of sleeping near the Awesome Sea so soon after the tsunami that killed so many of her people. She rejected these negative thoughts, and went back to sleep. She dreamed that a rooster was feeding inside Hotu-Matua's skull. Afterward, the rooster mated with many hens. Many more hens flocked to the rooster. The hens laid many eggs. Many chicks hatched. The king's skull created a prolific fertility among the chickens. The familiar grating of terns rudely roused her.

She walked to the sea, reflecting on the silly dream, then she swam for a while, diving into the crystal clear water and collecting several clams and sea urchins for breakfast. She ate them, dressed, and went back to Anakena to join her family and friends. Her meditation had clarified her mind about many things; for the time being she was content.

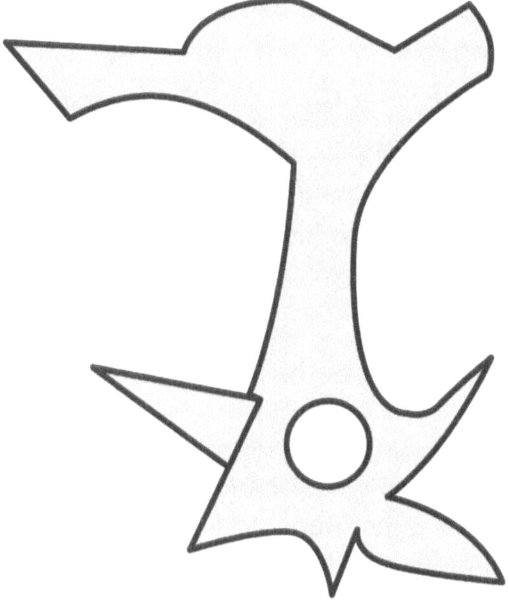

The Great Ancestor with the circle of knowledge given by mana propagated awareness and capability. The sacred bird flying between earth and the stars is forever the symbol of Make Make. It is eternal and universal consciousness.

CHAPTER 9

*"Kukara's words were most interesting: she told me
I should talk alone to the Great Tamatoa. Interestingly, the
thought had crossed my mind more than once. On that day,
I freely decided to change my destiny by exploring the soul of
a man who would have terrified me a few moon cycles earlier.
On that day, I felt liberated from prejudice."*

Kama Tici Viracocha

The early morning light roused Kama from her fitful sleep. Many thoughts raced in her mind. She got up, added a few dry branches to her campfire, and cooked a few sweet potatoes and cakes, using flour she had milled from seeds of the tall grasses she found on the island. She carefully wrapped the food in strips of delicate, handwoven fabric and placed them in an old basket. As she left Anakena, she glanced at Kon and Hina busily exploring the pleasures of life the Light had given them. She smiled, amused that she could have walked over them and they would never have noticed.

"I have to admit I am jealous," she thought to herself in a gentle way.

It was a long walk from Anakena to Orongo. She spent a night at Mount Orito, a favorite place of hers. It was early in the afternoon when she reached Orongo, Kura's sacred resting place. First she looked for Tamatoa and found him alone, sitting and watching the western horizon. The man looked older, thinner, and more depressed than ever.

"Do you mind if I go to the cave and talk to Kura?" she asked. "Tehani can listen."

"I don't mind, woman."

Kama bridled at being called "woman." It sounded very pejorative when said by the tattooed giant. She shrugged it off and went to the cave where she reflected on fond memories of her beautiful little girl that she had loved so much. Nearby, Tehani slept in eternal peace. Kama's thoughts slowly drifted back to the poor man outside the cave. She lovingly caressed the large stones above Tehani and felt her spirit enter her body.

"Please, take care of my man," Tehani said. Did Tehani really speak? Or was it just Kama's wishful thinking?

"Either way, it makes no difference; this is my place where I lived alone for a very long time."

She gently smiled at Tehani's grave and walked out of the cave and sat next to Tamatoa. He continued to gaze blankly at the horizon.

"It is always empty," she said. "But we never get tired of watching the horizon."

"It is all I have left," Tamatoa replied.

"May I speak with you?"

"Sure!" he replied, shifting his eyes from the horizon to her face.

"First, never call me woman again. My name is Kama. I have suffered too, the same as you. But life goes on, and you have an important mission to fulfill. I would like to help you work through your sorrow, so that you can resume your leadership role."

"Why should you care about me, the lost tattooed giant?"

"Perhaps because I like you, and perhaps because I am lonely myself."

To her surprise he took her hand with his huge fingers and looked into her eyes. Never before had she seen him this close.

She was fascinated, but not afraid of his tattooed face. Although in his early fifties, he was still an attractive man.

"I brought something for you to eat," she said.

She unwrapped the fabric protecting the contents of her basket and handed him a sweet potato.

"I like sweet potatoes," he said. "The first time I tasted them was the day I lost my son, Tera, on Mount Orohena."

"I am sorry for all these losses of loved ones. But we cannot change the past."

"What else do you have in the basket?"

"Some cakes I prepared with the seeds of tall grass. I used to make many of them on the continent, with seeds from a different type of grass. I don't know if you will like them."

She handed one cake to him. He took a small bite and savored the flavor for a short time, then smiled broadly, a beautiful smile, and then ate the entire cake.

"Remarkable!" he complimented.

She flushed with pleasure and modesty and gave him a friendly smile and another cake.

Famished, Tamatoa silently ate the remaining potatoes and most of the cakes.

"How can I return the favor?" he asked.

"Just be nice, friendly, and yourself with me. I want to enjoy our time together. And don't ever call me woman."

They both laughed. He studied her face and saw a mixture of extraordinary beauty, humbleness, kindness, and irresistible appeal. For the first time in several moon cycles, he felt happy; he felt life was worth living. He slowly reached out and delicately moved her long hair away from her face, to her back.

"You are beautiful, Kama Tici Viracocha. Why did you come to me?"

In response to his question, she stretched out on the ground and laid her head on his thigh so that she could see his face outlined by the sky's deep blue background. Kama's spontaneity sent a shock wave through the giant. Never in his wildest dreams would he have thought that Kama would have done this.

"May I stay with you tonight?" she asked.

It took all of his training to control his libido in the midst of an overpowering urge to take her then and there. But he surprised her by his gentleness and humor.

"You honor an old man; you make me feel like a young warrior again."

She burst out laughing, and so did he.

She grabbed his neck with one hand and pulled him toward her face as she moved closer toward him, impelled by her own desire. Her nose met his; she slightly laughed at the cumbersome contact. Their lips met. She nibbled his bottom lip and then explored his mouth with her tongue. She felt his hand on her breast and his other hand on her upper thigh. His mouth passionately responded. Then to her surprise, he pulled away from her. She looked at him, confused. He took her face between his hands and spoke the most caring comment she had ever expected:

"I will make love to you tomorrow morning, after we bathe in the deep lake below. I want to honor you properly, Kama Tici Viracocha. In the meantime, I want to know you better."

"You really surprise me," she said, looking at him with amused wonder. "You are more different than I ever imagined."

She glowed with passion. Her self-confidence astonished him. He knew from the first day he met her that she was a strong woman. He measured the depth and the certainty of what she wanted. She wanted him. He wanted her. The sound of people approaching broke their reverie. It was Taatamao, Mahine, Ku, and Kane.

"I brought some food for you, Father," Mahine said, looking at Kama with surprise. "But maybe Kama already took care of you."

"She sure did. I am not hungry anymore."

"We had good luck fishing today," Taatamao said. "Your

sons are becoming excellent fishermen."

"It was a lot of fun," Ku said.

"But these boats are getting old," Tamatoa mentioned. "We better repair them soon. It will not be easily done with the materials from here."

"You seem in a good mood, Father," Mahine said with a smile. "I have not seen you like this for a long time."

"It is Kama's magic medicine that did it," Tamatoa joked.

"Whatever it is, it pleases me immensely," Mahine replied, poking Kama with her elbow. They all burst into laughter.

"You had a good time," Mahine said. "We should go to our settlement. Ku and Kane, come with us and leave your mother alone for a while."

"They love to be with both of you," Kama replied, giving a hug to Mahine.

"They are remarkable boys," Taatamao said. "I need their help cultivating the lava tubes."

Tamatoa and Kama were alone again. They looked at each other, not saying a word, until the sunset brought a cool breeze.

"Come inside my cave," Tamatoa said.

They made a small fire at the entry of the cave, giving off just enough light for them to see their surroundings. The inside of the cave was modestly furnished. Woven mats covered the floor. Several full wooden water jars stood next to the cave's rear wall. With no sense of embarrassment, Tamatoa undressed, and to Kama's surprise, took water from one of the jars and proceeded to wash his body. She was impressed by the Maohi's attention to hygiene. While he scrubbed, Kama admired the tattoos normally covered by his clothes.

"You like them?" he asked with a smile.

"They are fascinating. Do they have a meaning?"

"Yes, they do. I was sixteen sun cycles old when I wanted to attract Tehani's attention. At the time she did not care for me. I went to the artist, part of the Rarotonga royal family, and volunteered my entire body for tattooing. He told me it would be a painful, long, and hazardous ordeal. For two sun cycles, I spent two days every moon cycle being tattooed. He made tiny cuts with a shark tooth, then filled the cuts with paste made from charcoal and water. The cuts often became infected, making me very sick. I had until the next moon cycle to recover."

"Why did he use a shark tooth?"

"A shark tooth has many tiny needles along its sides, which creates many small punctures where it strikes the skin. The tooth is attached to a wood shaft that enables the artist to repeatedly strike my skin and create the desired image."

"My son Ku learned the art on Rapa Iti, but they used chipped bone blades. What do the spirals mean?"

"Most of the designs came from the artist's imagination. However, I wanted the tattoos to intimidate my enemies and impress the woman I loved. The spiral is also a symbol of knowledge, as Hina may have explained."

Kama's hand went up Tamatoa's thigh until she reached his manhood. She caressed it gently, admiring the tattoos that completely circled it, which made her laugh.

"What an idea to do this to a man! Actually, it has its charm."

As she continued to caress him, she saw his pleasure rise and his breathing quicken. Her eyes wide open, she had a radiant smile on her face, showing warmth and desire. Then he recovered control of himself, showing her a bucket full of water.

"You can use this bucket to cleanse yourself the same way I did," he said gently.

Shocked that he could interrupt his passionate urge for her so abruptly, she stood up and slowly undressed. She had learned Maohis have great respect for their bodies, and even greater respect for the bodies of their siblings. Being naked never shamed anyone. Never in her life had she felt so excited, so inspired, undressing herself. She washed herself with such wonderful erotic skill that Tamatoa could not resist. He grabbed her hand, took her against him, and helped her complete her lavation. After the fire died, they lay on Tamatoa's woven mat, and he pulled another mat on top of them. Naked, they enjoyed the contact of one another. Again, she caressed his chest, and he could not resist her attempts to give him pleasure.

"You really think we can wait until tomorrow," she whispered.

"Yes, we must. Trust me."

"I trust you."

At peace with herself, she removed her hand and drifted into a deep sleep with her head resting on his shoulder. He slowly caressed her hair, reflecting on a day he would never forget. She was beautiful. She was self-confident. She was direct. She obviously was in love with him. He knew he could spend the rest of his life with Kama Tici Viracocha.

Kama woke up to the din of frigate birds' clacking and screeching. She was alone. She dressed and went outside. Tamatoa sat on the cliff nearby, looking at the islets where she had struggled a long time ago.

"This morning we are going to swim to the islets, you and me," Tamatoa said.

"You are kidding! I thought we would go to the lake."

"We will do that afterwards; it will be good for us."

Kama reflected on his plan for a while, and then brought him the remaining cakes in her basket.

"Why not! I never went back to these islets; it is a long swim."

"It was at the time, but after what you have learned from Hina, it will be an easy swim for you."

After they finished eating and drinking, they each attached a gourd of water to their belts and started their long way down to the shore full of cobbles. She knew the cliff much better than he did, so she led the way. At the beach, they undressed and drank copiously before entering the calm water.

"A long time in seawater will completely clean our bodies," Tamatoa said, "then we will remove the salt in the lake."

"Is cleanliness before making love an obsession for all Maohis?"

"It is part of good manners we teach our children. I feel I can honor you better that way."

"Let's go!" Kama said, shaking her head in disbelief at what she would do to please a man she found so different from what she had envisioned. But this was her life, and she was willing to take risks to complete the exploration of her new world. She knew that Maohis were willing to take enormous risks with their lives, which was a dramatic counterpoint to their calm, peaceful demeanors. To her, the challenge was most interesting.

The first islet was familiar, a tall, sharp pinnacle. She knew there was no place to walk. She managed to maintain Tamatoa's pace. He often looked back, checking on her. Enjoying the benefits of Hina's swimming lessons she was astonished at how easily they reached the islet. Her first experience, a long time ago, had been a long, life-threatening race against small currents. They rested for a while, hanging against the steep walls of the pinnacle. Rested, they kicked off and swam toward the next islet. This time, Kama made an attempt to get to the islet first. Tamatoa did not react and let her have her win. She was proud of herself and teased him for being too slow and too old.

"How are you, Grandfather?"

"Mad at you, woman!"

They both laughed. After resting a short time, she showed him an outcrop composed of good-quality obsidian that she had noticed a long time ago.

"It is as good as the outcrop at Mount Orito," she said.

"This is a very valuable observation. You are observant."

Finally, they swam to the last islet, disturbing many flocks of seabirds: tiny sandpipers, arrogant terns, fast gannets, and majestic frigates. The smell of these birds was difficult to get used to.

Kama went directly to the place where she had lost contact

with Kura. She sat, and silently wept. Tamatoa came behind her and tenderly rested his huge hands on her shoulders. There were no words that could improve on the surrounding silence and salve her pain. But she was thankful he had forced her to come to the sacred place. After a long pause, he took her hand.

"This is a sacred place," Tamatoa said. "Every time you come here, you must acquire an inspiration for your future and your loved ones. This is our way. I will leave you in peace. I will wait for you farther around."

"Thank you!"

Kama watched long algae dancing in the ocean's ebb and flow, entranced by their rhythmic motion and the swish of water on a tiny patch of sand. Her attention was piqued by a type of algae that was greener and prettier than the rest. Walking over to a tangled pile that had just washed up, she pulled one out and studied it. She took a small bite of the plant and found it pleasant to her palate. She took some to Tamatoa, who also found it agreeable.

"This is my inspiration of the day," she declared.

"Let's eat some every day for a moon cycle and study the effects. Your discovery may have deep implications for all of us."

She went back in the water and explored the surroundings. She was astonished at the water's clarity and marveled at the many colorful fish that lived in so different a world. This is what had attracted Kura's attention; therefore, Kama had a special desire to admire the blue world's enigmatic beauty. She understood now why Hina spent so much time exploring these nearby treasures.

They swam slowly back to the main island and climbed Rano Kao's steep cliffs, then descended to the swamps, floating islands, and ponds at the bottom of the crater. They picked their way through tall reeds and emerged at the edge of the deep blue water near the crater's center.

Tamatoa and Kama slowly and respectfully undressed each other. Holding each other's hands, they entered the pure, blue water of a well-protected paradise, their paradise.

They swam facing each other. He took her close to his chest, holding her hips. She put her arms around his massive neck. Her eyelashes fluttered, and she looked into his eyes. He touched her nose with his, and kissed her in a surprisingly gentle way. She parted her lips and raised herself in the water to meet his tongue. She lost her balance and sucked in some water; she did not care. She just wanted more, now. She pressed her hard nipples into his chest and slowly rotated her torso against his chest to further intensify her desire. His hand glided across her breasts and abdomen. He came to rest on her thigh and then slid gently upward, where he massaged her. She moaned softly, caressing the back of his neck. Firm and persuasive, she guided him inside her. He slowly entered her sacred temple, and she moaned in sweet anticipation. She felt his own pleasure, his long strokes, as she had never experienced before. She moaned aloud, feeling an orgasmic tremor rise from deep within her. Her moment of ecstasy lingered as she savored his passionate feelings when he reached his peak and full satisfaction, sending roaring fury throughout the caldera. Even in love, he was the tattooed giant and the commander. He was her king, and she was his queen. After silence reigned again in this place of extraordinary beauty, they looked at each other for a long time, swimming entwined in each another's arms.

Such moments remain in the memory of people as a private treasure. As a result, there was absolutely no word to improve on the surrounding silence; therefore they did not say anything.

Two dark blue eyes and two large black eyes explored each other's soul. This was a day they would remember all their lives.

They took their garments and went up to Orongo. Tamatoa went to the sacred underground pool discovered by Tehani and came back moments later with two gourds full of the sacred water.

"During a normal time, only the four of us can drink this sacred water," he said. Then he emptied half of one gourd above Tehani's grave and the other half above Kura's grave. Kama drank the first half of the other gourd, and Tamatoa drank the remaining half. In this simple ceremony, she felt her heart jolt with a tremendous feeling of thankfulness and love. The man was truly regal and was considerate and caring. She saw a new joy of life in his eyes. The despair of the last few moon cycles had evaporated. Tamatoa the Great was back in full command. From now on, he was going to assist Kon Tici Viracocha in an endeavor no human had previously dreamed of.

Early the next morning, naked against each other between mats, Tamatoa and Kama heard Kon, Hina, and Kukara approach the entry of their cave. When Tamatoa and Kama came out from the mats, Kon glanced at Hina with immense pleasure on his face.

"Maybe we are too early," Hina joked.

"You are here at the right time," Tamatoa replied. "You are the first people we wanted to share our joy with."

"Why is it that I feel Kama will live here from now on?" Kukara added, pulling on Hina's skirt.

"Why is it that I have that strong feeling that you, little girl, are partially responsible for all this?" Kama added, smiling at Kon.

"Now, my dear friend," Kon said, looking at Tamatoa and holding Kama by the shoulder, "I know I can show you something, and then ask for your valuable assistance."

It was the beginning of what would become the foundations of one of the most intriguing mysteries generated by humans.

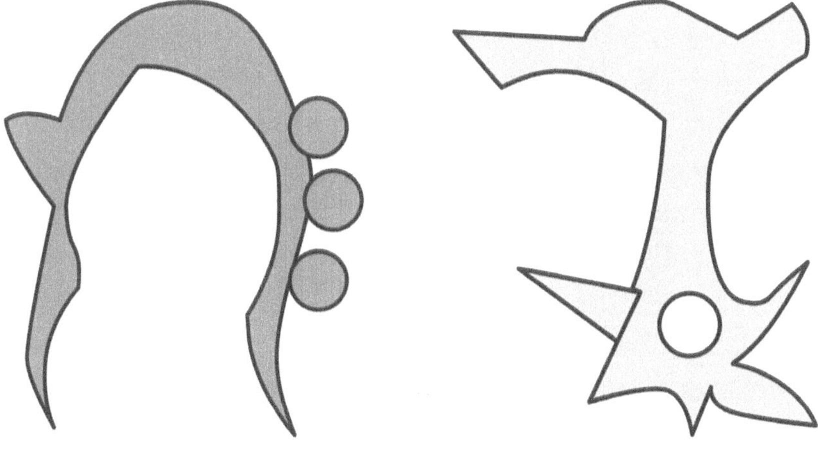

The Great Ancestor and his spirit holding the secrets of life and forever the rulers and inspiration of men and women constantly flow from stars to our soul. Nothing good on this earth is

CHAPTER 10

"At the top of Orongo, while watching Tamatoa and Kama love each other, I had a spontaneous vision of the Great Flying God, half man and half woman. A passing frigate bird gave me even further insights for a new sign for the sacred Rongo-Rongo tablets. I knew I would carve that sign in stone for eternity."

Kukara Tici Viracocha

The next day, Hina, Kama, and Kukara visited Mahine and Taatamao with whom Ku and Kane, Kama's sons, lived. They explored the gardening potential offered by the collapsed lava tubes.

Kon and Tamatoa went to another world, to Rano Raraku. Tamatoa had no idea what to expect, since he had not been to the sacred volcano for several moon cycles.

Long before arriving at Rano Raraku, Tamatoa heard the sound of adzes slamming into hard rock, perfectly complemented by the songs of men in perfect harmony with their work. They went over a small hill and saw the blue lake surrounded by reeds; at that moment the sounds seemed to become amplified, raising Tamatoa's curiosity. Kon guided Tamatoa toward a tall cliff, then through a narrow shaded defile in the mountain. As they pursued further, without warning Tamatoa was face to face with a vision of incredible proportion. Visibly shaken, the tattooed giant stopped in his tracks. Never in his life had he seen such a sculpture. As they approached, four men stopped their work and bowed to the two most important men of the Sacred Circle of the Seven Souls. Tamatoa gently patted their shoulders with his right hand, smiled, and nodded for them to relax and continue working.

"This is incredible," the giant warrior said, "this is unimaginable." Tamatoa slowly and reverently walked around the giant reclining stone man, which was waiting for the sculptors to sever the narrow keel holding it to the mountain and set it free. The statue was about six times the height of a man and about five times as wide from shoulder to shoulder.

"It is unbelievable that all the material missing between the statue and the walls was removed one tiny chip at a time," Tamatoa said. "The patience and skill required to do this is mind-boggling!"

"It is the same thing as digging a canoe inside a large tree trunk," said Kon.

"It is the same concept; the same thing it is not!" said Tamatoa emphatically.

Tamatoa let his fingers trace the long ears. Placing a foot on the ear, he climbed to the top of the statue. Walking by the nose, he stopped and peered into the deep, mysterious eyes. However, no eyes had been set in their compelling sockets; it was as though they were under a secret taboo of the gods. The thin lips seemed to express disagreement about something mankind would often do. The face was commanding and magnetic. Considerable thought had obviously gone into the creation of this being that melded such powerful magic with its imperishable beauty, elegance, force, and mystery. Both hands barely touched one another under the statue's belly; Tamatoa was intrigued by its long fingers. The statue was still unfinished, but well on its way to the day when it would be moved to its ordained location. The thought deeply intrigued him, so he went to Kon and poked one finger on his chest.

"Can you tell me where this will rest?"

"We want to raise it halfway between here and the lake, to look forever at the stars at night. This is the place where Hina and Taranga have chosen. After it has been erected, we will place Taranga's remains behind the statue, at its foot. It will be his final resting place for eternity. The statue will be spectacular. During clear nights with full moons, we will be able to see its face reflected in the water from the other side of the lake. On dark nights, we will feel its profound presence and eternal soul."

Tamatoa placed a friendly hand on Kon's shoulder. "You are far crazier than I ever thought. I suppose you want me to help you to do this.'

"Absolutely!"

"What are these flat monolithic slabs and these large rock cylinders?" Tamatoa inquired, pointing at them lying some distance from the statue.

"We will need more of those. They will be used to move the statue down to its final resting spot."

"When you break the statue's keel, you will unleash an earthquake."

"It will not happen that way; this is why I need you."

"I know I am strong," Tamatoa chuckled, "but there is a limit. This statue is heavier than all my three ships combined. Do you know how many men it takes to transport one of my ships to the water?"

"Don't worry; it will not be done how you are thinking."

"Then tell me. You have my full attention."

"With mana!"

Tamatoa walked away, thrusting his arms into the air,

shaking his head in disbelief.

"I will train you!" Kon added, momentarily embarrassed. Since the procedure he envisaged was innovative, he knew he would have to wait until he could demonstrate what he had in mind. For the time being, he accepted his friend's skeptical reaction.

Calmer, Tamatoa walked back to Kon, then went over to the statue and took another good look at it.

"If you show us a way to bring that behemoth out of that corridor, then I will feel that I am a little boy again, helpless, and impotent."

"I will show you, trust me!"

"When do we start the training?"

"In a few days we will meet near Ovahe, where I will show the Sacred Circle of the Seven Souls how to move a heavy rock ball out of a rock bowl using only a single finger."

Tamatoa threw his head back and roared with laughter, then rested his forearm against the wall, in tears. His unexpected laughter quickly spread to the others, including Kon.

Mahine welcomed Hina, Kama, and Kukara to her settlement on the island's west side. They hugged each other in close friendship. After all, they were the four women of the Sacred Circle of the Seven Souls. But circle or no circle, they were intimate friends first.

"Where are the boys?" Hina inquired.

"Gardening in a lava tube with Taatamao. We can go see them; it is a short distance from here."

"Not before I tell you something," Kama said with a smile on her face.

"What is it?"

"I am out!" Hina said, going away. "It was not my fault."

"I am out too!" Kukara said, going the other way.

"Yes, especially you!" Kama joked.

"Now you have my curiosity," Mahine said with a deep chuckle.

"Your father and I made love yesterday," Kama said peacefully.

Mahine's black eyes glittered, honored by Kama's trust, but she was only half surprised by the revelation.

"Do you love my father?"

"Yes, I do!"

Relief came to Mahine's eyes, since she had been worried for her father for quite some time.

"Was he good for you? He is such a large man."

"Your father, despite the awesome power of his body, is a very gentle man. He was patient. He was considerate. He was concerned for me. He was delightful in all imaginable ways."

Mahine warmly embraced Kama. Tears of happiness welled in their eyes.

"May I come back?" Kukara inquired.

"Kukara is partially responsible for all of this," Kama said, "but sooner or later, we would have done it anyway."

"He liked you the very first time he saw you at Anakena," Mahine said. "We all saw it, even my mother. Let's go see the boys."

Along the way they saw two circular structures the men had constructed using lava boulders brought up from the shore. The walls, about the height of a man, protected the thriving banana trees from the frequent winds. Hina pointed at the green fruits hanging from the trees.

"This was Taatamao's idea," Mahine said. "There are six different banana species growing in there."

"I think we should copy the idea around the island," Hina

replied.

"They could also be used to protect our hau-hau bushes," Kama added. "The bushes would then produce stronger fibers, enabling us to make better quality ropes and deep-sea fishing lines."

"The same applies to the mahute bush," Hina said. "They should yield softer and better bark to make fabric for our clothes."

They approached a deep, open lava tube, where Kukara spoke a name.

"The gardens of the depths!" Kukara said, admiring the scenery down below. This description would remain forever in the Rapa Nui culture.

"The gardens of the depths!" Hina repeated slowly, emphasizing every word. "I like what you said young girl, because it has all the charm of something that has never been seen by anyone before, anywhere. Your words impart a sense of beauty mixed with the unequaled mystique created by this world below."

"We shall remember these words," Kama stated.

The three adult women slowly repeated Kukara's words: "The gardens of the depths." The little girl blushed with pride.

They walked down to the gardens, using narrow stairs carved into the lava rock, then walked along meandering trails pleasingly covered with tiny pebbles that had been patiently collected from the coast. On either side of the path, lush patches of sweet potatoes grew. Kama counted five different species. There were many patches of beans, tall cereal grasses full of seeds, vines with valuable gourds, and flowers. There were several areas covered with luxuriant taros with huge, healthy leaves. Hina saw seven different species. Toward the end of the path, they came to a large area covered with tall sugar cane stalks.

"This is a garden of all the best vegetable species gathered from the island or brought by us moon cycles ago," Hina said.

They stopped in front of a large pool. Taatamao, Kane, and Ku were working hard inside it to make it deeper. When they saw the women, they stopped working and joined them.

"The deeper we go, the more water we find," Taatamao said. "It is a lot of work."

"But very worthwhile work!" Kama added.

"This pool is for swimming, cooking, and cleaning," Mahine said. "At the other end of the gardens, in the upper area, there is a smaller pool of drinking water. It must not be used for anything else; it must be kept pure and unpolluted."

"When it overflows, we use the water for the gardens," Taatamao added.

"How far do these tunnels extend?" Kukara asked.

"We explored them a little," Taatamao said. "But we never found their ends. At times it is difficult to progress, as they become very narrow, or diverge in different directions. They are dangerous; you easily lose your way or your balance on slippery rocks. If you became lost or hurt, nobody would be able to find you. The boys like to explore them, but I told them never to do that without supervision."

"I know how to find my way in them," Hina said. "I used long ropes to mark my path."

"You would need very, very long ropes," Taatamao added skeptically.

"We should explore the tubes some day," Hina argued. "We may discover important things, such as more water."

They walked to the upper part of the lava tube, to the little pond of pure water, where they all drank the sacred beverage. They carefully ladled the water using coconut shell halves, being careful not to touch the surface of the pond with their fingers.

"I have to congratulate you," Hina said. "Within the last

seven moon cycles, you have done some amazing work in this place. This will serve as a model for the other families."

"Several other families, using lava tubes farther north, are already doing well," Taatamao added.

Later at sunset, they were talking around a small fire when they heard Kon and Tamatoa approaching. Hina jumped into Kon's arms, and Mahine went to congratulate her father on his relationship with Kama.

"What is Mahine talking about?" Kon asked, looking at Kama.

"I will show you what she is talking about," Kama answered. She went to Tamatoa, who encircled her midriff with his muscular arms. They rubbed noses. His lips captured hers. Kama sighed with pleasure. She put her arms around his neck, jumped up, and clamped both legs around his waist.

"You did not tell me all this," Kon said with a smile, glancing at Tamatoa. "This is great!"

Now the Sacred Circle of the Seven Souls consisted of three couples truly in love and a little girl. They were a team of extraordinary power and talent that would set the course for later accomplishments on this isolated, tiny island.

At dawn Tamatoa took Kon and Taatamao for a walk by the seashore, and south of the settlement. They were at the lowest point of the isthmus connecting the main part of the island with Rano Kau peninsula. Tamatoa had an idea involving the well-protected little bay.

"I believe that this bay will provide excellent anchorage for our boats," Tamatoa said. "The eastern shores are vulnerable to tidal waves. This was a fact that I noticed on other islands when I was a boy."

"Therefore, we should make our settlement here, on the western coast," Kon said.

"Not only that, but something much more important."

"Explain!"

"I want to build an impregnable seawall," Tamatoa explained. "It would be a reminder to everyone that they must react rapidly when the sea recedes abnormally. Then, constructed along its side, I want a narrow channel of calm water where we can bring our boats up on a ramp."

"I see," Kon said, scratching his head. "You want me to help design and build it."

"Yes! I will call this place Hanga Roa."

"We don't have many men to do this," Kon argued.

"We don't have many men to build and transport your huge statue either," Tamatoa argued, placing a powerful hand on Kon's shoulder.

"Who takes priority?"

"I determine priorities!" Hina said, coming to them. "Tamatoa's project is essential to protect the few remaining boats. We need them for fishing in the sea. We also need a reliable place to repair them. The spirits of Rano Raraku's nights are patient; they will wait a little longer. Besides, the statue is at a critical point, and we have not been properly trained to move it. We will use Tamatoa's project to train our people on the techniques needed to move the much larger and more cumbersome statue."

Kon and Tamatoa glanced at each other, amazed by Hina's flawless argument.

"Give me three days to organize my thoughts," Kon said.

"No problem!" Hina replied, giving a conspiratorial wink to Tamatoa. "We are going to stay at Taatamao's place for a few days. Personally, I want to see the other families 'gardens of the depths.'"

Taatamao left with Hina and returned to his place, while Tamatoa and Kon stayed behind and discussed several ideas and approaches they might use.

"I believe that we need a large breakwater to absorb impacts from large waves, common on some days," Tamatoa said. "I am not talking about tidal waves, which I believe will always strike the other side of the island."

"What is the purpose of such a structure, besides being a ramp for the boats?" Kon asked.

"It would serve as our burial place, gathering place, religious place, landmark, and protected harbor."

"Perhaps after the wall is built, we could bring one of our statues onto it, from Rano Raraku."

After a long silence, Tamatoa looked at the sea, shaking his head in disbelief.

"My dear friend, I truly think you are slowly losing your mind on this island."

"Well, we will build a slightly smaller one!"

"Let's do the wall first; then we will see."

"Could you build a small model of the entire complex you have in mind, using these pebbles from the coast? In the meantime I will reconnoiter the area for an appropriate source for the massive stones we will need to construct this monument."

All day they compared ideas, visited nearby cliffs for a possible quarry, and finalized their recommendations. Tamatoa himself would have never dreamed of the cyclopean project Kon now envisioned.

"Everything you do must be colossal, and never previously achieved," Tamatoa said.

"By definition!" Kon replied, with a smile on his face. Raising a finger, he continued, "This has always been the Viracocha's way. Each block will be precisely cut and fit to the others; this technique will give incredible strength to the entire structure."

"Like some of the walls we saw on the continent."

"Yes! But where we went, you saw only the little ones," Kon chuckled.

In the evening they joined their friends at Taatamao and Mahine's settlement. They saw the women weaving fishing torches with dried palm fronds. Two fronds were cut at their butt ends. Their leaves were then gathered in bunches and woven into a strong braid. Usually these were used on dark nights to attract fish in shallow rock pockets near the shore. But tonight they had something different in mind.

"Mahine found out that it was easy to catch lobsters that way," Hina explained. "Taatamao excavated a large hole near shore, where unusually large waves wash water in once in a while. We can use this depression to store lobsters and fish; they will stay alive in it for more than a moon cycle. Then we can easily catch them as needed. Tomorrow night I want everyone on the island to gather with us here. We will need a lot of food."

Hina had been elusive about the reasons for the gathering, but nobody would ask her why; that is, except Kukara who found an opportunity when she was alone with the great priestess and queen.

"Why are you having this gathering, Mother?"

"I want people to have freedom. On another hand, I want people to focus on several grand projects for which we need their help. I need to convince them of this, but I don't know for certain what to tell them yet. I must find out before tomorrow night. Will you help me?"

"Of course I will help!"

"But you must keep it secret, between you and me."

Kukara always enjoyed little secrets. They went to Kama, who was busy building a fishing net based on an idea from her sons and Taatamao. They sat near her, intrigued by the new fishing tool. It was a hand net attached to a large hoop frame made of toromiro wood. The pointed, narrow end of the hoop was attached to a long handle made of the same wood. The net was made of long, strong braids woven from strands of a long, dry indigenous grass. The net was attached to the hoop using the same long woven braids.

"Test its strength by trying to catch Kukara with it," Kama said, handing the net to Tamatoa.

The little girl ran away laughing. But Tamatoa was swifter and swooped her up in the net. She moved her legs and arms helplessly, laughing and kicking.

"That net is really strong," Tamatoa said, releasing Kukara, who was unsuccessfully trying to regain her composure.

"Please, don't wound my little counselor," Hina said, laughing until tears formed in her eyes.

Then she walked over to Ku and Kane and watched as they busily wove sandals on their loom. Sharp rocks and venomous and biting creatures made walking in shallow water near the seashore a dangerous exercise, especially at night.

"Kon, look at how they are making their sandals," Hina said, holding up one of them for him to inspect. "See, it is a simple, clever design."

A long loop, made of a strong braid woven from long, dry grass, was fastened to the top bar of the loom and the bottoms of the loom posts. As they wove the base of the sandal within the loop, the loom helped maintain the desired shape. The base of the sandal was also made from braids of long, dry grass, tightly plaited to create a strong, protective sole. The circular end of the loop was placed over the back of the heel to keep the sandal in a correct position, while the loose ends of the loop were passed between the toes, then tied around the legs.

"It is quite primitive," Kon said, "but it is so easy to make new ones."

At nightfall everyone put on their new sandals and came together to hunt under the fishing torches' light. Taatamao held one torch and went in the water first, walking until the tiny waves of the night lapped under his arms. Mahine was near him and would show everyone how to catch lobsters. They were all watching the couple, intrigued by the technique Mahine had discovered. To not miss anything, little Kukara climbed onto Kon's shoulders.

Shortly, they started seeing fish coming, soon joined by crabs, then lobsters, many lobsters. Taatamao and Mahine did not move until a few large lobsters were almost at their feet. Then Taatamao pressed his foot on top of the largest lobster, and Mahine immediately dove in and grabbed it by the back, where only a few tiny spines could hurt her hand. She came up with the magnificent animal flapping its powerful tail fins. Somebody else took it and released it in the storage pond.

Now every couple was trying to repeat what Taatamao and Mahine had done. The first ones to succeed were Tamatoa and Kama, then Kon, with Kukara still on his shoulders, and Hina. Soon many lobsters were flapping in the little pond. In sheer joy they pursued the hunt until the torches completely burned out.

"This hunting technique is far more effective than my demanding diving," Hina said.

"We still like to see you dive," Kama replied. "It is a pleasure to see your body glide to the abyss, where few people can go."

"I know that these skills will slowly fade away in future generations. Diving here is much less friendly than in my old blue lagoon. Simpler, better, and less dangerous techniques shall prevail."

The three ancestors and their spirit

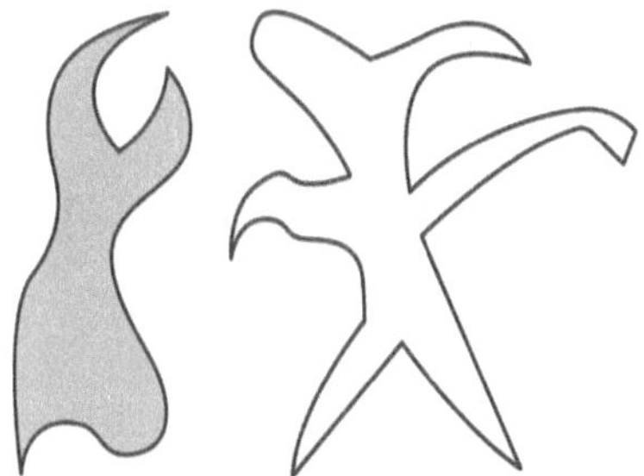

the man and its spirit

the woman and her spirit

the great god Make Make and its spirit

The sacred team making everything possible: the choice is ours.

CHAPTER 11

"With my special flute from the Inca, I will make sounds capable of opening their souls. With drawings on the ground, I will show the face of a new god they will never forget. With signs engraved in the Rongo-Rongo tablets, I will record their knowledge. These are my contributions to Hina of the Valley, our queen."

Kukara Tici Viracocha

Kukara was now ten sun cycles old, no longer a little girl, but not yet a woman. She was attractive but did not have the extraordinary beauty of Kama, the charismatic beauty of Hina, or the athletic beauty of Mahine. However, her mind was extremely creative, unequalled by anyone, woman or man. Her intelligence seemed to belong to another world, perhaps the world of the Light. She was respected by the children, adults, and elders. She was constantly thinking about new ways, untested ideas, and seeing things that nobody ever dreamed possible. She was the little darling of the Rapa Nui colony. At the center of the Sacred Circle of the Seven Souls, she was sacred to the circle and protected by them. Yet she was always very humble about her talents. On this day, when Hina called for an important gathering for the evening, Kukara decided to spend some time with Kon. He knew her words would be all substance. She was up to something. He enjoyed her immensely and always found time for her.

"You were a celebrity in Tahiti Nui," Kukara said, holding Kon's hand. "Since we are here on Rapa Nui, we take your extraordinary Viracocha skills for granted. You live in seclusion, at Rano Raraku."

"I know; Hina told me the same thing. My time will come and I will need you."

"For what?"

"To build the ahu of Hanga Roa and the giants of Rano Raraku, I will need to teach them everything we know about mana."

"I know nothing about mana," Kukara said.

"You know more than they do, and no one learns as fast as you."

"Kama knows about mana; Hina knows a little."

"I know, but I am the only one left with the mana knowledge they need. I must pass it to you quickly so that we can have them trained in half the time."

"So I will have to teach four women how to lift Tamatoa with only one finger!"

"No, not that! That was only an introductory game."

"When do we start?"

"A few days from now, at our place near Anakena."

"What will you teach me first?"

"You will look at a stone bowl containing a heavy stone ball, much heavier than you. You will have to learn how to move the ball out of the bowl using only one finger."

The young girl smiled, but remained silent. She knew where Kon was heading. She knew that mana was the key to moving the giant stones, just as they did when building their cities on the continent. She recalled watching the men using mana's magic, orchestrated by the old Taranga Tici Viracocha, to move giant balsa tree trunks to build the rafts on which they had traveled for so long. She even recalled a few secrets that she had learned from watching Taranga carefully. She smiled at the thought that she knew far more than what Kon ever suspected. She smiled knowing that she could help him by learning what he knew, but also by what she could teach him.

Suddenly, Kukara stopped and tugged Kon's arm.

"Look at that bird sleeping nears the water's edge by that little pond," Kukara said. "Hotu-Matua called it a mokohe."

"It is so close to the water that it almost touches its reflection," Kon remarked.

"Then it is a mokohe mokohe!" Kukara exclaimed, laughing. Then she looked at the bird in more detail, until her eyes widened with emotion. She recalled being at the top of Orongo and seeing Kama and Tamatoa making love in the lake. An incredible thought had taken shape in her mind. But for now, she would keep it to herself. She finally realized what Hotu-Matua had tried to tell her just before he died. She would reveal it to Hina, in front of everyone, during this evening's ceremony. Looking at her face, Kon knew Kukara had found serenity.

Later that day, as the camp prepared for the evening festivities, Hina and Mahine personally supervised a group of women cooking the many lobsters.

"Our recipes can be combined," Hina said, "and modified to incorporate the local spices that Kama has discovered."

"I miss all the spices we had on our islands," Mahine replied.

"On the other hand," Hina said, "if we were in Tahiti Nui today, we would miss the many things we do different in Rapa Nui."

Every lobster was split lengthwise, using a large shark tooth. Some of the internal organs were removed. Each half was placed on a banana leaf. The meat was lightly scored with a square pattern. A mixture of ground palm tree nuts with spices was carefully rubbed into the cuts. Kama had prepared the spices by mixing ground dried algae, a potent condiment, with the ground dried roots of tiny shrubs and ferns. Then the meat was covered with a thin layer of tiny seeds gleaned from various grasses growing on the island. Finally, thin banana slices were laid on top of the seeds. Then carefully, without rotating the lobster, the banana leaf was wrapped several times around it. The well-wrapped lobster was placed directly on hot coals for a short time. Using sticks, they would pull and push the packets from the coals. Carefully unfolding the leaves, they would enjoy their royal meal.

"Can we cook one now?" Kon asked, pointing at a big lobster.

"Absolutely not!" Hina replied.

Tamatoa went to his daughter, completely addicted by the wonderful aromas coming from the preparations.

"Can we cook one now?"

"Go away and sit down!" Mahine said with mock sternness.

Frustrated, Tamatoa put one hand on Kon's shoulder and guided him toward the fire.

"This new world is ruled by women," Tamatoa whispered.

"I heard that. Father!" Mahine said, glancing at him.

"So did I!" Hina replied.

Kama broke into a wide, open smile, but she did not say anything.

"My friend, I think we are defeated," Kon said. "Have a drink."

Tamatoa grimaced in good humor.

Lobsters were only an appetizer. Nearby, another fire heated stones that had been collected from the seashore. When red-hot, they were removed and dropped to the bottom of a small, nearby pit. Rapidly the women placed banana tree leaves on top of the stones. Sweet potatoes, taros, other vegetables, fish, and chickens were carefully arranged side by side on the top of the banana tree leaves. The last layer of banana tree leaves was placed over the food, followed by another layer of smaller red-hot stones. The pit was then covered with a layer of dirt and left to cook. Later that night their truly magnificent meal would be ready.

Slowly, everyone gathered in a circle a short distance from the fire. There were about fifty families in their small colony. The vast majority of people were Maohis; there were only five Viracochas left: Kon, Kama, Kukara, Ku, and Kane. Near the fire, Hina assembled the Sacred Circle of the Seven Souls. For her, it was an important moment. She was well prepared, and so was Kukara Tici Viracocha.

Hina signaled the drums to begin. Everyone sat on the ground, except Hina and Mahine, who stood. They removed their woven capes, beautifully decorated with shells, and handed them to nearby people. They wore only very tight, short skirts, split to the thigh on each side, that revealed the entire length of their superb legs. A narrow braided belt held their skirts in place. On Hina's chest, the golden condor glittered in its eternal beauty and mystery. Long black hair covered their young, firm breasts. They wore tall headdresses consisting of circular bunches of split black frigate-bird feathers sewn to a crown of vertical white tropicbird tail feathers. On her forehead, Hina wore six additional red tail feathers of the sacred, larger tropicbird, which designated her high rank. On Hina's belt, just below her navel, two feathers from the green pigeon of her valley in Tahiti Nui identified her as a great priestess. Some people started a rhythmic clapping, using pieces of wood they found in the surroundings; many others started singing. At first the song was slow-paced and melancholy, almost sad. The tempo increased slowly, and as it did, it became more joyful. The two young women started dancing, moving skillfully to the music. As the dance's pace increased, Hina and Mahine's graceful hips swayed to the beat, their arms slowly waving above their heads. Everyone admired their suppleness and beauty. The rhythm continued to accelerate, whipping the younger people into an ecstatic reverie. Even Tamatoa, Taatamao, and Kon stood up and started dancing. More of the people joined the clapping with increasing energy. The primal symphony of rapid calls merged with the sharp sounds of split bamboo sticks rubbed together, combined with loud claps against house pillars and trees and the deep rumbling of the drums was exhilarating. Hina and Mahine swayed faster and faster, reaching breathtaking speeds. Yet it was not the climax. The two women had their eyes closed from pleasure and pain. Kama encouraged them by clapping loudly with her hands. It was not the first time she had seen the two young women perform, and each time she became more and more astonished. Finally, swaying, clapping, drumming, and singing reached their zenith. Then everything stopped at once. There was no music, no song, and no talk, only the waves of the sea pounding on the rocky cliff and the grating of a petrel. Covered with perspiration, Hina stood perfectly still in front of her audience, her arms frozen above her head: she was ready to talk.

"People of Rapa Nui," she said, recovering her breath, "my people, it is an honor to be your queen, your great priestess, and to be of service protecting your welfare."

As though a single person, the entire body stood and gave her an ovation.

"As long as I live, there will be no arrogance in your queen's behavior and no enemies in this land. As you all know, this fascinating place, lost in the Awesome Sea, is a rough place. We love it, yet it challenges us in many ways. Each family has its territory, but each family works for all families, and all families work for one family. This is the way we shall live, so we protect the ones nearby and inspire the ones far away."

She received another standing ovation.

"Her words are so appropriate!" Kama commented, more astonished than ever about this young Maohi woman.

Hina raised her arms to silence the audience.

"The main reason for this gathering was to ask you a favor. Kon and Tamatoa will soon need your help at Rano Raraku and at Hanga Roa. Many men will be required to work on sacred projects; their women must feed them. At the sound of the conchs, you may volunteer. I insist it is not an obligation for you to come if you are busy with other important matters. If you come, you must be very healthy. For those of you who will be present, working or watching, you will have a story to tell for the rest of your lives. Now, enjoy your meal."

"Finally!" Kon exclaimed, grabbing the nearest lobster.

Kon glanced at Tamatoa and congratulated Hina, Mahine, and especially Kama, for her outstanding combination of spices.

"I am impressed," Tamatoa said, wiping juices from his face with his forearm.

Kukara ate her lobster with delight as well, but it was obvious to everyone she was anxious to proceed with a little entertainment of her own. She washed her hands with sand, then water. She dried her hands and reached for the special ceramic flute that the Inca had given to her. Alone, she had practiced for days on her instrument, which was composed of seven parallel tubes of different lengths. She placed her six peers from the Sacred Circle of the Seven Souls between her and the fire, so they faced the audience, looking at her. She sat cross-legged and started to play. Kama felt an instant chill in her back, recalling her life in the Andes, her dead husband, Illa, and her daughter, Kura. Kon wished he had learned to play so well when he was at the summit of Mount Orohena in Tahiti Nui. He recalled helping Taaroa the leper to be born again. Hina recalled the extraordinary dream she had in a cave when she saw the Light. Mahine recalled her father being magnanimous at the summit of Mount Orohena. Taatamao recalled his hand holding Kon's hand the day he was supposed to die during a daring race to the summit of Mount Orohena. Tamatoa recalled Hina saving the life of his son Mehao at sea, at the risk of her own. Everyone in the crowd recalled a seminal moment. This was the magic of Kukara Tici Viracocha. Her enchanting melody was conjuring different meanings for everyone, exactly like the signs on the Rongo-Rongo tablets would mean something different to every reader. Nobody talked. Everyone listened. The young girl's long black hair enveloped her magic fingers as she played the flute. Sounds with no words, capable of telling stories and legends to the soul, capable of igniting sentiments and love, were her true talent, and everyone on the island respected that. But they had experienced nothing yet. Earlier, when the queen had asked Kukara to help her, the adopted child had committed to repay Hina's love by bringing the most unimaginable gift possible.

Four men quietly brought heavy bags full of white pebbles from the seashore and dumped them into two piles on either side of Kukara. With anticipation, Hina smiled at Kukara's imagination. One pebble at a time, Kukara drew the contour of a frigate bird standing up, and with the beak up as well. She drew only one big eye, emphasizing the profile view of the bird. It was a magnificent white drawing in the black lava sand.

"Mokohe!" Kukara exclaimed. It was the name of the frigate bird on Hotu-Matua's land.

She went to the other pile of white pebbles and started to draw another bird, exactly the same. Both birds touched each other with the tips of their beaks, wings, and feet. Their other two wings hung by their sides, similar to the arms of a man. Kon immediately recalled the frigate bird's reflection in a pond during an earlier walk with Kukara, and truly admired her imagination. Then came the moment of truth, when she gave the final clue to the audience. She drew the eye of the second bird. Instantly murmurs of astonishment came from the crowd and from her peers from the Sacred Circle of the Seven Souls. There were no birds, but the face of a god looking straight at the audience. Sitting at the base of the extraordinary face, Kukara Tici Viracocha stared at the crowd, silent, perfectly still, like a living copy of the face. Several people stood up and ran. But Hina of the Valley stopped them.

"Do not fear, my people. This is the face of a friendly god, as Kukara is going to show you."

Kukara stood up and went to Kon, took his hand, and brought

him near Hina.

"Face each other," she said, "join one hand, one foot, and touch each other's nose, almost as if you were going to make love… like this. Yes! It is perfect. This is like the first man on the earth; I will tattoo this spirit on your arms later on. This is like the first woman on the earth, and I will tattoo this spirit on your arms as well."

Kukara repeated the same ceremony, slowly and religiously with Tamatoa and Kama, then with Taatamao and Mahine. It was a superb, loving, and inspiring ceremony.

"Mokohe Mokohe!" Kukara said, pointing at the two birds on the ground. "There are two birds that symbolize the weightless nature of mana: two human beings loving each other for the promotion of a good life, just like the very first man and woman may have done in another time. See how the single face of the god looks at us; he verifies that we live well."

"Mokohe Mokohe!" she repeated, pointing at the sacred couples preparing to make love. "Each of you is a first man and a first woman, as time does not exist. The Light told me there is no past, no future, nothing was created, and nothing will ever die."

"Moke Moke!" the three sacred couples repeated, slightly mistaking the true name from Hotu-Matua's land.

"Make Make!" the entire crowd repeated, again and again, until all the couples present joined together in love.

"Close enough!" Kukara murmured to herself. "It is the idea that counts, and they all got it."

A new god was born. Kukara Tici Viracocha walked alone into the night, to the seashore where the great Ahu of Hanga Roa would be built, content. Tamatoa and Taatamao removed the dirt from the little pit, then the hot stones and the banana leaves. A wonderful smell invaded the surrounding air, and everyone was ready for the long-awaited meal following the lobsters.

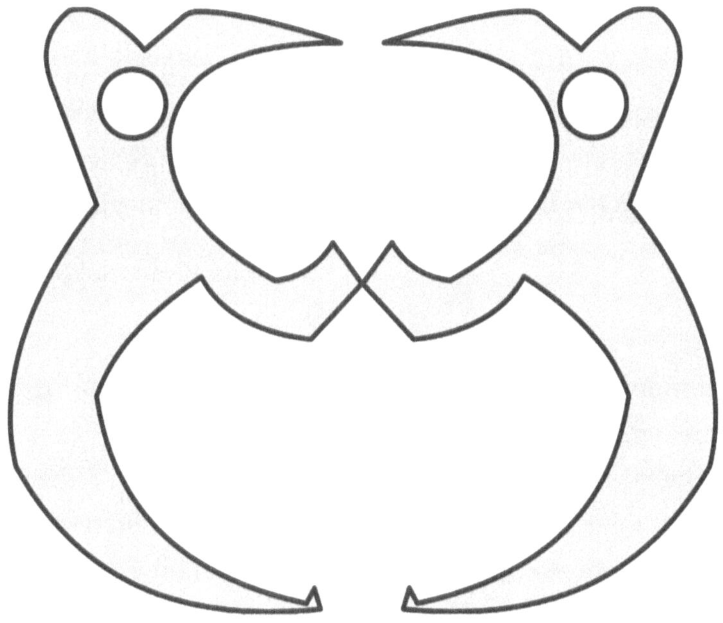

The frigate bird would forever be the symbol of the Great Ancestor with the circle of knowledge given by mana. The great god Make Make became the equivalent of the Light for the Rapa Nui people

CHAPTER 12

"Mana is simple, yet it is uncommon to Maohis. It is supernatural to them, and they fear its powers. It is my duty to educate them until they no longer fear. Then, and only then, mana will live with all of us, helping us in everything we do."

Kon Tici Viracocha

Kon and Hina had carefully selected the location for their settlement. It was easily accessible, situated on top of a cliff above the northern side of the Ovahe beach. Hina loved the place because of the superb view of the pink sandy beach on one side, and a nearshore islet that looked like a crown on the other. The waters inside the islet were protecting a world of colorful corals, inside which Hina loved to swim and dive. The place reminded her of the blue lagoon she missed so much. Furthermore, between the beach and the islet there was a small peninsula with many ponds between rocks that were nicely sheltered from the ocean waves. It was the perfect place to go fishing at night. Hina called it Ure Mamoe Point, after a favorite childhood fishing spot located at some distance east of her Papenoo village.

Two days later, at Kon and Hina's settlement, Kukara had prepared a mixture of black ashes with oil extracted from little nuts and stored inside a gourd. She mixed a small dab of the paste with an equal amount of water in a coconut shell. She firmly held Kon's right arm while dipping the end of her shark-tooth tattooing tool into the black mixture. She brought the tool to the upper part of Kon's arm and tapped, using quick, sharp blows, and continued until it started to bleed. She repeated the painful pricking at another place on his arm. Kon found painless refuge deep in his mind with mana. Upon completion, a cryptic glyph, similar to those on the Rongo-Rongo tablets, was revealed. It looked like a walking, headless ghost with raised arms pointing to the sky. The sign was elegant, simple, and carried mana's powers. The impression it made on people was signature of its indisputable power.

"You are like the first man on this earth," Kukara said, "and this sign is that of your eternal spirit. It is a reminder that the powers in your mind are unlimited, contrary to your ephemeral, weak body."

Then Kukura took her tattooing tool and ink to Hina. She took her right arm and started to prick it. Hina grimaced slightly, but managed to concentrate her mind on the vision of the Light she had at Mount Orohena. It helped her to bear the pain. The sign, also from the Rongo-Rongo, tablets was different. It somewhat resembled the walking ghost on Kon's arm; however, its open arms encompassed a larger part of the sky. Toward the lower part was a little circle. It was the sacred circle of divine knowledge given by the Light.

"You are like the first woman on this earth," Kukara said, "and this sign is your eternal spirit. The little circle is a reminder that only women carry the powers to bring new life into existence. Man may start life in you, but without you, nothing is possible."

They simultaneously recalled that Make Make's eyes are two perfect circles.

Kon and Hina would carry their tattoos for the rest of their lives. Kukara's symbolism was positive, inspiring, and a necessity for the Rapa Nui colony's survival. Now the time had come for Kon to teach mana to the members of the Sacred Circle of the Seven Souls. Each of them would use mana's powers and would wisely teach only some necessary portions of it, as needed, to the others.

That day Kon wore his best old blue garments, in odd contrast to the gold rings in his ears, gold bracelets, gold sun emblem on his forehead, and gold pin holding his long black hair.

"This is my man!" Hina murmured to herself.

"Hina of the Valley, pragmatic and analytic woman from Tahiti Nui," Kon said, looking at Hina, "you always want unambiguous and accurate explanations for everything. You have always been somewhat skeptical about mana's powers, only because you require a logical explanation, as is the Maohi nature. Therefore, the teaching process, systematic, progressive, and factual, is an absolute necessity. This goes for Tamatoa, Mahine, and Taatamao as well."

They all noticed he had not mentioned the Viracochas. Kama sensed the Maohis' uneasiness and came to the rescue.

"All Viracocha's children were taught about mana's powers," she said. "This is the reason Kon did not mention our names. The great master was Taranga, but he is gone; you knew him well and he was a good man. Now the great master is Kon. I only have minor skills, nothing physical, just mental. Kukara is far more advanced, and in some cases, her knowledge may even surpass Kon's. Above all, relax. For the seven of us, this will be stimulating."

"First, unconditionally accept that if we are to survive on this island, we must master mana," Kon said. "Mana is a necessity for us, an absolute necessity. Without mana, Rapa Nui cannot exist, and we will not exist. Without mana, everything will be chaotic, and nothing great will ever be achieved."

Every member of the Sacred Circle of the Seven Souls verbally accepted Kon's proposition that the acceptance and use of mana had become a precondition of living well on Rapa Nui.

"The idea is simple," Kon started. "Each of us is endued with at least one exceptional talent. My skills at climbing are exceptional. People say I have mana when I climb. I say to them: I became that way because I studied climbing techniques for many years, and there is no magic in this at all. Hina, your skills at diving deep, to fish for lobsters, moray eels, congers, and octopuses, are truly exceptional and totally unsurpassed. People may say underwater you have mana, and you do, indeed. I say to them: Hina worked hard at this skill because it was one of the greatest joys in her life; there is no magic in this. Kukara, your skills at the Rongo-Rongo tablets, at the glyphs on rocks, and at playing your flutes, are exceptional. People may say you always have mana in you. I say to them: Kukara is passionate at everything she does; therefore, she developed exceptional skills. There is no magic in this. Tamatoa, your skills at reading the shape of the waves at sea, the shape of clouds, the migration of birds, and the stars at night to find your way from island to island are exceptional. People may say you have mana at sea. I say to them: Tamatao worked hard all his life to develop those skills; there is no magic in this. Kama, your skills at finding new plants unnoticed by the others is truly exceptional. People may say you have mana when you study the ground. I say to them: Kama is passionate about flora; therefore, she developed exceptional skills. There is no magic in this. Mahine, sitting on the sacred white monolith in Havaiki, you saw visions in your mind that were astonishing to the high priest Mato himself. People may say you have mana when you close your eyes. I say to them: Mahine played alone all her life with mental fantasies because reality did not fit her dreams; therefore, she developed exceptional skills. There is no magic in this. Taatamao, in battle you were an exceptional commander, strategist, and organizer. People may say, in battle you have mana. I say to them: Taatamao is passionate in his contact with people. He is always kind, therefore gets noticed. He is always planning, therefore gets noticed. He is always creative, therefore gets noticed. There is nothing magic about all this."

"I understand your point," Hina replied, impatient. "Now what should we do different?"

"The lesson is that every time a passion arises in your mind, you can become exceptional at it. This means, consciously or not, you let the Light shine into your minds with astonishing results. Now, explore how you did it and why you changed. Then we might be able to apply this principle to many other skills, perhaps even to new skills that we will need to survive. However, we must be aware that people often learn new skills but become complacent and lose them through disuse. With mana, we will never stop. With mana, it is impossible to stop. With mana, you will discover your unknown limits, if there are such things. Without mana, if you learn, you will do nothing with that knowledge. With mana, you will create, invent, and go where no one has gone before."

"I think I am starting to understand," Tamatoa replied. "Can we do a simple experiment?"

"Yes!" Kon said. "Look at this large bowl carved from lava. See the heavy lava ball that I placed in it: it is heavier than Kukara."

"I wondered what that is," Mahine said.

"Each of you can take that heavy ball out of the bowl," Kon said. "But this is not the point. Instead, I want you to move it from the bowl using only one finger, while using only a minimal physical force."

"You must be joking!" Hina said, pressing the ball with one finger.

Kon pressed the ball with one finger at the very top and started to make little circles. After a while, the ball slowly responded by rolling in tiny orbits inside the bowl.

"Make sure the pressure is always there, circling," he said, pointing to the top of the ball with his other hand, "so that you can easily increase the ball's momentum with progressively faster rotations."

Now the ball was making large circles inside the bowl. The circles induced by Kon's finger were getting larger and larger. The ball increased its momentum to the point when it clearly started climbing closer to the rim of the bowl. Kon's finger was making larger and larger circles. The ball was near the rim. Suddenly, the ball flipped out of the bowl and fell on the ground, to everyone's astonishment.

"As you have seen, there was no magic, "Kon said. "It is simply the harmonious coordination of what your finger is doing and what your mind wants it to do."

Hina tried, but barely succeeded in moving the ball the width of an ant's leg. Tamatoa tried, but it was only through sheer brute force that his finger moved the ball at all. He did not succeed in making the ball climb up the bowl's wall. Mahine and Taatamao tried, but failed as well. Kama tried, and successfully got the ball halfway to the rim.

"My turn!" Kukara said.

Her tiny finger was like magic at the top of the ball, making swift, tiny circles. The ball quickly gained momentum. Now her finger was turning so fast that it looked like she had many fingers making the same circle. The ball's momentum increased dramatically, much more than what Kon had induced. It was clear to everyone that Kukara would succeed, and in a big way. Afraid they would be hit by the jumping ball, they all backed away from the bowl. At the right moment, centrifugal forces lifted the ball up the bowl's wall and shot it across the rim with incredible energy, landing much farther from the bowl than anyone had anticipated.

"By all the spirits in the sun!" exclaimed Tamatoa, who did not believe in spirits in the first place.

"If you are not careful, mana can kill," Kon added.

"I am impressed," Hina said.

"Let Kukara teach you how to control your finger," Kon said to the Circle's women. "In the meantime, I want to show something to Tamatoa and Taatamao. We will be back shortly."

The three men walked close to a cliff located inside a small crater, slightly east of Kon and Hina's settlement. Kon pointed to the large cubical monolith he had patiently cut in the basalt during the last moon cycle. The monolith sat on a flat surface, as if it were waiting for the men.

"Right now, there is no mana in this block," Kon said, "nor in any of you. Try to move it."

With great effort, Tamatoa and Taatamao made several attempts to move the block. They succeeded in moving it half the length of a man's foot. Then Tamatoa got an idea.

"If we put logs under it, it could be moved much easier."

"I know what you mean," Kon said. "But if we start cutting every tree in sight to build our monuments, the island will be barren in no time. We must find another way."

Tamatoa and Taatamao contemplated for a long time and finally gave up.

"Within one moon cycle, you will know how to move this monolith, just the two of you and two other men, all the way across the crater," Kon said, pointing at the flat area inside the crater. "And it will take you no more than one morning to do so."

"Explain!" Tamatoa demanded, his powerful hands resting on the monolith.

"Look at the top surface. Do you see something different from the other surfaces?"

"It is convex," Taatamao said, pointing at the slightly curved surface.

"That is the key to building and moving monoliths for the Ahu of Hanga Roa," Kon said. "Let's give mana to that stone by flipping the curved surface to the bottom."

Slowly, the three men succeeded in flipping the monolith twice. The curved surface now rested on the ground.

"Don't tell me anything!" Tamatoa said, with a broad smile on his face. "I think I understand what we are going to do."

"Now there is mana in the stone," Kon said, "and perhaps in you as well."

Tamatoa tilted the monolith and pushed it forward all by himself.

"Great!" Kon said. "Now we only need to get a lot better at this. Let's go back to see the women."

They found the four women laughing in sheer joy at their accomplishments.

"Mahine and Kama succeeded in flipping the ball out," Kukara said.

Now Hina was trying again, but she was giggling and not seriously trying to succeed. Furthermore, the other three women were laughing at her. It was a healthy game, and Hina did not mind being the butt of their humor: she had other talents.

That night, Kon and Hina enjoyed being alone at the Ure Mamoe Point. Their temporary home consisted of a flimsy structure built with weathered toromiro branches and protected by only a thick thatch made of tall woven grasses and reeds. It was humble, but they liked it. Kon had put a lot of thought into how their future home would be designed and constructed. He would spend the next few moon cycles cutting lava stones exactly the way he wanted, to make a solid and reliable foundation.

Following a light meal of fish, roasted grass seeds, and nuts, they walked to the crater, where Kon had dug a hole in the lava, allowing fresh water to flow naturally. Several men had helped him with the digging, using the opportunity to cut stones for future projects. For talented climbers, going down the hole was an easy matter. The pond was divided into two parts, a lower, smaller pool, separated from the slightly higher, larger pool by a wall made of small lava stones mixed with gravels. Kon had planted many rapidly growing reeds around the wall to consolidate it. Water from the upper pond slowly seeped, pulled by gravity to the lower pond, which naturally overflowed, drop by drop, through a lava tube. The water disappeared then to an unknown destination. Slightly above the surface of the water, capillary ferns that Hina had found in some nearby lava tubes thrived in their new setting. In the upper level, closer to the entrance, she had planted the wild flower seeds Kama had brought from Orongo. There were very few flowers on the island, but Hina was determined to propagate the few she could find.

They drank fresh water from the upper pond, undressed, and slowly entered the lower pond. The water was high enough to reach their shoulders. They could touch the opposite sides of the pond with both hands. Nevertheless, on Rapa Nui, this was an unbelievable luxury. They had worked hard at creating it.

Hina pulled Kon against her firm breasts. Then she held his hips. Slowly, she put her arms around his neck. To him, the message was clear and irresistible. He brushed his lips against hers and kissed her in a surprisingly gentle way, delicately brushing her lips from left to right. She parted her lips and raised herself in the water to meet his tongue. She playfully flicked her tongue against his, backed off for a short time, then clamped her legs around his waist and voraciously explored deep inside his mouth with her tongue. Water splashed all over, but she did not care. She wanted more. He felt her nails being planted in his back. There was passion in her like he had never seen before. She was dominant: she was the queen. Her nipples pressed hard into his chest, merging with his being. He slowly entered deep inside her temple. She closed her eyes and erotically moaned with sweet delight very special to her. He went in and out, with long, slow strokes. She followed with swivels as if she was dancing. He knew how powerful and experienced the lower part of her body was. It had never occurred to him she would use her dancing skills in lovemaking. Yes, he thought, this is what the dance is all about. She moaned aloud and thrust her head backward. Her eyes were wide open, looking at the stars.

"Mata Kite Rani," she murmured slowly, several times.

She moaned louder and louder with every gyration. The golden condor danced on her chest. The wind howled inside the crater, mixing with loud cries of passion. In this incredible land of spirits, the queen enjoyed the gifts of life the Light had given her. She was healthy, strong, beautiful, and climaxed. Her head collapsed softly on Kon's shoulder. She knew he had reached his full pleasure slightly before she did. She was happy, fulfilled, exhausted, and full of glistering sweat. They both took a deep breath and submerged until they needed to breathe. When they came to the surface, they were quiet and listened to the land. No words could describe the absolute silence. The wind had died completely, as though it were exhausted as well. They listened to the sound of water dripping slowly into the depths of the earth and to the grating of a late tern. They were at home.

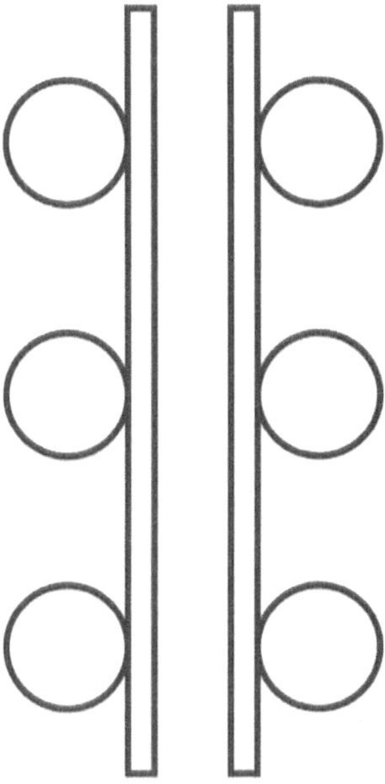

The Earth's eyes: the Earth is between the lines.
Make Make's eyes, woman's eyes, and man's eyes are the Earth's eyes.

CHAPTER 13

"My new home was a small piece of heaven situated on a cliff from where I could see a beach of pink sand, fish swimming, birds flying and nesting, the light blue of the sea above the sand, ponds in the lava where large waves rarely splashed, and a crater that provided building slabs and fresh water. With little resources on my new land, I was content."

Hina of the Valley

Hina woke up to the sound of birds fishing in the lower ponds. Kon was still asleep. She dressed and walked to the top of the cliff and looked at the cove below and at a crown of rocky islets some distance offshore. She sat on a rock, peacefully enjoying the view while reflecting on her astonishing destiny.

They had traveled for many moon cycles, constantly discovering new and wondrous landscapes, plants, and animals. They had found this incredible island, rough, limited in natural resources, mysterious in many ways, yet charming, appealing, and irresistible to the soul. During the early days it was chaotic, with people settling randomly throughout the island. The people were confused with many new ways and things to learn. Then several unfortunate accidents had taken place, changing the destiny of many loved ones forever; old leaders died too soon, Tamatoa's mate fell to her death in her attempts to find fresh water, and a devastating tidal wave decimated the already thin Viracocha race.

Hina reflected randomly on how she and Kon were totally consumed with their projects and how communications were degrading between couples and between parents and children. Interesting, she thought, the entire population is composed of fairly young people. The oldest, by far, was Tamatoa, who was still in exceptional physical shape. Actually, she reflected, things were changing, slowly falling in place. Now they had several clear objectives, and they were getting much better at communicating. Also, the people no longer rushed about trying to accomplish everything overnight; slowly, surely they had established a stable infrastructure to provide the fundamental needs for everyday life. Somehow Hina knew the next few moon cycles would bring fascinating developments, and she was ready for them.

She took a little stone and threw it into the air. A passing frigate bird dove after it, inspecting it as it fell to earth. Determining that it was not edible, the bird swooped off to pursue better opportunities.

"Make Make," Hina murmured, watching the bird fly behind the cliff. "Make Make is a very interesting concept to us humans. Yet I would bet anything this bird is not concerned with it."

"I cannot agree more," Kon replied, approaching from behind.

"Did you know the night Kukara introduced Make Make was the first time the women of this island, including me, ran out of herbs from Tahiti Nui to prevent pregnancy?"

Kon glanced at her with a broad smile on his face.

"Is this a problem for us?"

"I guess not. It had to happen sooner or later."

"I would be the happiest man on the island to father and raise your children."

"Kukara's timing was perfect. I bet you anything she is responsible for half of the women of this island becoming pregnant on that night."

They both laughed in sheer joy.

"I am going to test my new nets," Hina said. "The sea is calm. It is the perfect time. I may catch a few mauros."

The mauro fish, Hina's favorite, was relatively small, approximately the size of her hand, with large eyes. The bright red fish was unmistakable. She had caught many in the lagoon in Tahiti Nui, so she knew their habits well, and they reminded her of her childhood. They lived in small colonies inside dark caverns, at an easily reached depth. Wrapped in a banana leaf and cooked on an open fire, two fish were enough for a delightful meal for one person. Kukara and Kama's sons, who were not fond of fish, thoroughly enjoyed eating mauros.

Kon inspected the two traps. They were cleverly designed and consisted of a light frame made from toromiro wood. The trap was completely covered with a coconut-fiber twine net, which would easily capture fish larger than a fingernail's width. A trapdoor built into the trap's top could be used by Hina to access whatever became trapped inside. A hole located in the center of the trap door was the size of a man's fist and provided the fish with an entrance. Four light stones were used to anchor the trap at a place Hina would select. She placed a dead fish in each trap.

Holding a trap in each hand, Hina swam to the crown of small islets a short distance offshore. Inside the lava crown, a large pond of blue water was a fishing paradise. On the seaward side of the pond, the water was very deep. On the landward side, the water was relatively shallow, and little caverns provided sanctuaries to many species of fish. She selected one cavern in which she saw a school of mauros. She knew that these fish were curious and would quickly find a way inside the trap, but not easily find their way out. Then she looked for another cavern, with its school of mauro; locating one, she deposited the trap and swam back to shore. She would check the traps in the morning.

"That was fast!" Kon commented, as Hina walked toward him.

"It is an experiment. I have never done this before. I got the idea the other night when we fished for lobsters. Now I would like to find a pond where we can store our fish and lobsters, like Taatamao did."

They walked to the rocky point and selected a pond isolated from the large waves that occasionally occurred during high tide. The rim was high enough to keep the fish from jumping out. However, there was one short stretch that needed to be built up. To remedy this problem, Kon build a small dam with large cobblestones. The pond was about ten long steps across and waist deep. Hina liked the location and Kon's workmanship.

As they returned home, they noticed a man and a woman walking toward them. The woman was holding her jaw, obviously in tremendous pain. Hina recognized them as being from Hotu-Matua's colony, at Anakena.

"What has happened to you, Tila?" Hina inquired, putting a friendly hand around the woman's shoulder.

"A tooth has been bothering her for some time," her mate replied. "Now it is getting worse."

Hina inspected Tila's tooth. Severe wear from a rough diet had led to an abscess on one side of the gum. She also noticed that a lot of food was trapped between her other teeth, revealing poor hygiene and dental care. Hina knew the infection would most likely spread, threatening the woman's life. When Hina was a novitiate, her mentor, Vana, instructed her that the best treatment for an abscessed tooth was to extract the tooth and let the resulting bleeding carry away the evil humors. She understood the theory, but had never practiced the technique, which concerned her.

"Would you help me extract her tooth?" she asked Kon.

"Sure, tell me what to do."

"Build a fire. Heat some cobblestones to boil water in a basalt bowl. Then boil a few strips of bark cloth to cleanse the wound after the extraction and stop the bleeding. Also boil some of the coconut-fiber twine that I made for the fishing lines and nets. Select the finest ones that can fit between teeth and check their strength; they must be very strong."

"What can I do?" the man asked.

"Just comfort her and show your love. When we remove the tooth, you will hold her hands. Kon will immobilize her head so I can work."

"Will it hurt?"

"If we do not extract the tooth promptly, she may die, which would be far worse than bearing the pain for a short time."

"Please, Hina of the Valley, do it!" Tila said, flinching with the pain.

The abscessed tooth was next to the last molar on the left side of her lower jaw. Before starting the extraction, Hina flossed Tila's teeth with a long grass string. Then she took Tila to the seashore and asked her to rinse her mouth several times, first with seawater, then with boiled water. Hina vigorously scrubbed her hands with sand, rinsing them with seawater, then with boiled water. She took a woven string, tied it around the base of the infected tooth as deeply as she could, pushing down on the gums where the tooth is narrower, and tied a knot. She tied a second knot in the string. Then she took a second string and repeated the process, but in the opposite direction around the tooth. She placed a small folded piece of bark cloth between Tila's teeth on the opposite side of her mouth; this would keep Tila from biting Hina's fingers and clamping down on the strings. She attached the four ends of the woven strings around a wooden rod, then rolled the rod until the strings were completely secured around it. Now was the critical moment when she would rotate the rod until the tooth came out.

"Tila, are you ready?" Hina asked.

The young woman nodded with her eyes.

"Kon, help him to hold her. Make sure she does not move: I don't want to break her tooth."

Hina slowly but firmly rotated the rod. Tila closed her eyes. A crushing sound came from Tila's tooth, as a flow of blood filled her mouth. The tooth was out, dangling from Hina's rod.

"I got all of it!" Hina said happily. "Wash your mouth with seawater several times, then with boiled water saturated with this sea salt that I make by evaporating seawater in a shallow basalt bowl."

During Hina's instruction, Vana had told her that salt has reliable antiseptic properties. Hina had observed this fact many times in the past. She also knew it could be used to preserve some food for long periods.

"Drink a lot of water now."

Tila complied, happy it was over.

"Lightly bite on this boiled bark cloth until you return home. Then don't drink anything until tomorrow morning. You don't want to lose the blood clot. Start eating only after tomorrow, then only very soft food for several days. Make sure you chew on the other side of your mouth."

Hina gave Tila a friendly hug and continued.

"After every meal, remove the food between your teeth using

long grass, rinse your mouth with seawater, then with boiled water saturated with salt. Do this for half a moon cycle."

Then the young couple went away.

"Well done," Kon said. "Vana would be proud of you."

"Thank you. I will go check on her the day after tomorrow. But I am concerned. How many are like her and will wait until they are half dead before asking for help?"

"It is easy to find out," Kon said.

"How?"

"Organize a gathering like the one we had the other day, to educate our people on the importance of dental hygiene and care."

Hina looked at the sea, then at Kon.

"So be it!"

Early the next morning, Hina went to check her traps. Relaxed, she swam to the caves. The first trap was empty; however, the dead fish had been eaten. Disappointed and puzzled, she checked the second one. There were two lobsters in it and a large conger. She struggled to swim back to the beach with the traps.

"Wow!" Kon exclaimed with surprise. "This must be a strong animal."

"Indeed, and I think that conger was after the lobsters. See, it succeeded in partially eating one."

Hina cautiously removed the two lobsters from the trap.

"I am going to grab that conger by its head. When it comes out, try to bite its tail. That should paralyze it. Act quickly; it is very swift."

She succeeded in removing the animal from the trap, but the powerful animal had twisted itself around her arms. Kon grabbed the tail, but the slimy animal got away from his hands. He grabbed it again by the middle of its body. The tail quickly slipped through his fingers. Finally, he succeeded in biting the animal, partially severing its tail. Immediately, the conger became docile.

"This is going to feed us for several days," Hina said. "But I did not catch any mauros."

"It is a formidable predator," Kon said, looking at the conger. "It could break your arm."

She cut off the animal's head and tail and baited the trap with them. She grabbed her traps and swam back to the islet. This time she selected deeper caves. A small, fearless shark checked the first trap, circled it, and swam away.

"Quite aggressive, that little thing!" she murmured to herself.

The next morning, she caught many mauros in one trap. Hina laughed in the water, fully enjoying herself. The second trap was empty, with the bait gone again.

"Good catch!" Kon said, as Hina kneeled and opened the full trap.

"Yes, but I must find a better way to keep them in the traps. Some fish know how to find their way out."

They transferred the mauros into their pond, where they would keep them until needed.

"I must go check Tila," Hina said.

"You go. I will wait for Tamatoa and Taatamao. We are going to practice mana."

"May I wear your gold pin to keep my hair up?"

"Sure!"

Hina went to their campsite and changed into a tight, short skirt, nicely decorated with shells, which better displayed her rank. For short walks, she liked her breasts to be uncovered. But for longer walks, she preferred to wear a cloth binding made from woven dry grass for better support. Kama had made it for her one moon cycle earlier. She truly enjoyed it. She arranged her hair with the gold pin, which made her look much taller. Since she was going to Anakena, where many people lived, she placed two sacred green pigeon feathers on her belt. It was the unmistakable emblem of the great priestess. Pleased, she started her short journey to Tila's village near the famous white sand beach.

She walked quickly and proudly. Above the green feathers on her belt, her well-toned abdominal muscles mirrored her grace and health. Something about her countenance that morning gave those who saw her a sense that her presence presaged an important event. Along the way, she plucked and chewed a long straw of dry grass and sang a little song.

When she arrived at Anakena, several people bowed in front of her. She asked them where Tila was. They pointed to her, sitting alone on the beach.

"How is my friend this morning?" Hina asked.

Tila turned around, with tears on her face.

"What is it? Is your jaw hurting?"

"No, my jaw is fine. You did a wonderful job."

"Show me your mouth."

Tila stood and opened her mouth. Hina moved Tila's head so the morning sun would better illuminate the socket.

"It looks very good. Be careful not to bite on this side for some time."

Then Hina sat on the sand and invited Tila to do the same.

"Now tell me what is bothering you."

"Lutafu, my mate's brother, raped me last night. He does that all the time. He is much stronger than my mate and intimidates him. So I never receive any justice."

"Did you ever agree to make love with him?"

"Never! I hate him."

Sadly, Hina stood up and brushed the sand off her skirt.

"Tell me where Lutafu is," she asked with a cold steeliness in her voice.

"If you talk to him, he will take revenge on my mate and me."

"Nobody will be mad at you. However, I can assure you that his queen is displeased with him."

Tila pointed to a scraggily hut leaning against one of the palm trees growing on the upper part of the beach.

"Stay here; enjoy the sun, and recuperate. This is the last day anyone will ever touch you without your consent. On this I swear."

Taking long strides, Hina walked rapidly to the hut. Many people watched her, wondering what she would do. With no warning, she burst into the hut and found Lutafu sleeping.

Grabbing him with force, she shouted, "Wake up, boy, and get out of this house, now!"

Terrified, the young man complied.

"Look at me well."

He walked backward, his wide eyes fixated on her. She poked his chest with her fingers.

"Why don't you rape your queen right here, in front of everyone?" she said, poking his chest again.

Lutafu fell to his knees, knowing that to touch the great priestess or the queen was instant death on his land of Hiva where he was born.

"Stand up, man! Or I will lift you up myself," the queen said, poking his chest once more.

The young man started crying. She grabbed his arms and lifted him to his feet.

"I said rape your queen, right here, right now. Let everyone see who you really are."

"I cannot!" Lutafu answered, falling to the ground again.

"Then you better change and become the one who you want to be. On this island, every woman is a queen. Is this clearly understood?"

"Yes!"

"There is nothing wrong with making love to a woman, but it must be by her sacred consent. Is this clearly understood?"

"Yes!"

"Stand up then!" Hina ordered, poking once more on his chest.

This time Lutafu ran away in shame. Everyone around was open mouthed, and immensely impressed by the queen.

"Keep an eye on him," she said. "I expect a drastic change. If he relapses, he will find himself working for a full moon cycle with Tamatoa the Great."

Hina walked away from the village, her face still flushed. She saw Lutafu at some distance.

"There will be no second warning!" she shouted, pointing at the young man.

There was no doubt to anyone that Hina of the Valley was in charge of Rapa Nui, and she needed no escort.

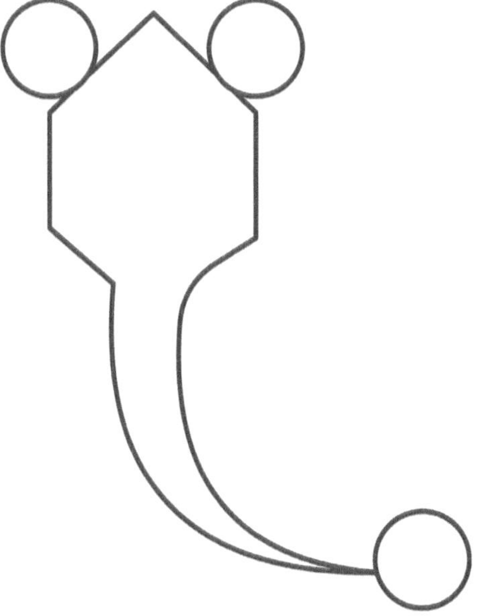

*Words from the Great Ancestor are sacred. Ears must listen
to the sacred words, as it is the only way knowledge can be
transmitted. Knowledge walks transmitted from mouth to ear by
men and women.*

CHAPTER 14

"I thought I knew mana well. But Kukara showed me how limitless mana is. She had learned from Taranga far more than I had imagined. With swift and effective creativity she built a new skills base for the Sacred Circle of the Seven Souls. In many ways she was far ahead of us. Intuitively, I knew her genius would have unimaginable consequences."

Kon Tici Viracocha

"Mother, I need to make better sandals, ones that would give me a safer grip on slippery surfaces," Kukara said.

"What do you have in mind?" Hina asked, puzzled.

"It is a secret!"

"Excuse me!" Then after a short silence, Hina replied, shaking her head, "I will try to think of something with Kama, tomorrow at the gathering." Accustomed to Kukara's daily innovations, she knew the girl would not become involved in any project that did not produce spectacular, substantial results. Ephemeral whims did not exist in her world. Hina knew that any conjecture on her part regarding Kukara's future would be woefully short of reality.

"Who are you, Kukara Tici Viracocha?" Hina asked yet again, speaking to herself.

The gathering at Anakena went well. Several men and

one woman were found urgently in need of having their badly infected teeth extracted. Hina and Kama spent most of the day explaining how the people should take better care of themselves by flossing their teeth after each meal with the long, dry grass growing everywhere on the island and rinsing them with seawater. Overall, the population was healthy and in good spirits.

"Hina told me you wanted to help us move some large stones," Tamatoa said, placing a massive hand on Lutafu's shoulder. "We were just looking for a fourth man."

The young man was surprised and terrified by the tattooed giant's unexpected approach. He glanced at Hina, who smiled to him. He smiled back to her, not too sure of what to think.

"It would be an honor for me," Lutafu replied in a timid way. He could not believe that he, in big trouble a few days earlier, would be selected to join Kon, Tamatoa, and Taatamao, three members of the Sacred Circle of the Seven Souls.

"Join us tomorrow in the crater near Kon and Hina's campsite," Tamatoa suggested. "This is where we will practice."

Happily, the young man walked toward the beach, accidently passing close to Tila. Hina watched their encounter from a distance.

"I apologize for what I did to you," Lutafu said, embarrassed.

"I forgive you, but never do this again, to anyone."

By the way Tila walked and smiled, Hina knew that Lutafu's recent introspection had been profitable. In due time, he will find a way to become who he wants to be, she thought.

That night, Lutafu walked for a long time along the coast, wondering if Tamatoa and the others were honoring him with their invitation or whether they planned to kill him. Driven with angst, Lutafu decided to place his trust in his queen. Although she had devastated his pride, she had given him the chance of redeeming his life. After hating her, he now had a profound respect for her. She had been firm, yet kind. This was how Hina had become the queen in a world of powerful men: self-reliant, intelligent, pragmatic and swift, she cared, she loved, she served, and she solved, in her unique ways, always in harmony with her surroundings. Lutafu knew that Hina of the Valley was incapable of malice and spite.

"I need your help," Hina said, sitting close to Kama, who was meditating on the beach's warm pink sand.

Hina explained Kukara's request for special sandals, and they both agreed they should try their best to help the girl. They were mainly interested in what Kukara was up to, but were clueless. Kama suggested making strong woven ropes from a combination of long dry grass and strong reed fibers. They would reinforce the woven sandals by soaking them in a slurry of finely ground coral powder and seawater and letting them dry under the sun for a few days. It seemed feasible, but they were unsure of the results. Five days later, they gave Kukara their experimental sandals. The young girl inspected them, tried them on, and then removed them.

"They are perfect," Kukara said, as she packed the sandals away in a small bag that she kept next to her mat. "I will keep them for a special occasion."

"Which is…?" Hina inquired.

"I told you, it is a secret."

"Well, excuse me!" Hina replied in mock indignation, glancing at Kama, who was laughing.

The next day, Kukara went over to where the four men were practicing to move the huge block of basalt. She carried the bag containing her new sandals. Kon had cut two deep grooves along each side of the block. A long rope circled the stone and rested in the grooves that would keep it in place as the rope was tightened later. One man was placed on each side of the stone to rock from one side to the other. One man held each end of the rope, ahead of the stone. He would briskly pull the stone forward at the exact time that the stone reached its highest point on his respective side. With each successive rocking, the stone was moved farther forward. By carefully increasing their speed and coordination, they were able to make appreciable progress.

Day after day, they honed their skills and found more effective techniques to increase the stone's momentum. They had learned to improve the accuracy, precision, and stamina of everything they did. Every new day, the stone moved faster and farther across the crater. It was teamwork brought to perfection, so they thought. Until the little girl could not take it anymore, and could not resist making a comment that would devastate them.

"You are pathetic! You don't take advantage of the stone's mana."

The four men looked at each other, not believing what they had just heard.

"I thought we were doing well," Tamatoa said, looking to his companions for consensus.

"What should we be doing differently, young genius?" Kon asked, sarcastically.

"I am tired. I will show you tomorrow." Kukara yawned and walked away, clutching the bag holding her mysterious sandals.

The four men sat on the ground, all energy gone, shaking their heads in disbelief. Having to wait for the young girl's idea heaped insult on their injury. They did not take her comment lightly. They knew her too well. They all suddenly felt like young boys at the mercy of a young girl, a tremendously galling experience. Still licking their emotional wounds, they walked to Kon and Hina's settlement, where they would meet up with the women, while Lutafu walked to Anakena.

Later that evening, Hina and Kon quietly sat and stared at the dying fire. Kon seemed preoccupied and distant.

"What is bothering you?" Hina asked, laying her head on his thigh.

"I thought we were doing very well until Kukara told us we were pathetic."

Hina erupted in spontaneous laughter.

"Did she use her new sandals?"

"No, what are they anyway? She brought them, but did not wear them."

"She patently refused to tell us their purpose."

"Tomorrow, she said, she would show us something."

The next day, early in the morning, they went to the quarry. This time Hina, Kama, and Mahine came to watch, intrigued by what Kukara might do. Lutafu joined them, and his brother and Tila followed, to Hina's great surprise.

"Stay some distance away," Kon said, "so you don't interfere with the team's concentration."

The five spectators sat on a rocky outcrop, away from the monolith's planned path.

"So, genius, tell us what to do," Kon said to Kukara.

"Not yet!" Kukara replied. "Just practice what you were doing yesterday, until you get warmed up."

Kon looked at his three companions with dismay, resigned to becoming very humiliated in front of the women... by a young girl. Hina pinched Kama's leg to get her to stop laughing at the men. The four men started to practice, and everything seemed to go well.

"They have become good at their game," Kama said, impressed.

"Kukara told them they were pathetic," Hina replied.

"I know, Tamatoa told me last night."

Kukara followed a few paces behind the stone, carefully observing each man in action. Then she told them to halt. For the first time, she sat on the ground and shoved her on her new sandals, then stood and walked over to Tamatoa.

"Please, lift me and put me on the top of the monolith."

Tamatoa easily picked her up and placed her on the huge rock. She tested the grip of her sandals on the smooth top of the basalt and smiled with satisfaction.

"The four of you, come close so I can explain how we are going to proceed. Kon and Lutafu, you get on either side of the rock. Tamatoa and Taatamao, you go ahead of the rock and pull your respective ropes."

Kukara pointed one finger at each man beside her, several times.

"When you see my finger pointing at you, or hear one short whistle, push up on the stone."

She repeated several times, until the men clearly understood the sequence.

"When I point at the man ahead of the stone and send a long whistle, that man must pull the stone forward."

She repeated her instructions several times, patiently, until they were comfortable with the sequence.

"Now you understand. Do exactly as I have instructed when

I give you the signal to do so. You have a choice: look at my finger or listen for the whistle. Ready!"

She pointed a finger at Kon on her left and sent a short whistle. The stone rolled slightly up. Immediately her face turned forward to her right, and she pointed a finger at Taatamao and sent a long whistle, giving the signal to pull. The stone went forward. Kukara felt the rock oscillate under her feet and managed to maintain her balance well. Continuing, she pointed a finger at Lutafu, to her right, and sent a sharp whistle. The stone rolled farther up. Her face turned left, causing her hair to sway to the right in synch with a long whistle, which gave Tamatoa his signal to pull. And the stone moved forward.

Awkward at first, they slowly established a cadence in concert with Kukara's commands. Now they understood what she was trying to do. They took a rest and discussed the results.

"The stone has its own mana," Kukara explained, "complementing yours, if you push and pull exactly at the right time."

"I understand," Kon said, "but the stone is going to gain more and more momentum, and we will need to react faster and faster. Looking at you may become difficult."

"Yes, to a point," she said with a smile on her face. "You may have to go by my whistle alone. My fingers and my hair are my own references I use to maintain harmony with the moving stone. Ready!"

They all agreed that the forward ropes should cross one another to provide more leverage to rotate the stone: up on the left, forward on the right, and vice versa.

This time the process was far more effective. The stone took on an impressive life of its own, to the point where Kukara started to have a rough time keeping her balance.

"Now I know what she was up to," Hina said. "What a girl!"

One particularly aggressive cycle caused Kukara to be bucked from the stone. The men immediately stopped and walked around to Kukara, sprawled on the ground. Somewhat embarrassed, Kukara recovered her composure and laughed, rubbing her backside.

"This is excellent!" Tamatoa beamed, patting Kukara's head. "Really good indeed!"

"I need to improve my stone-rocking mana," Kukara joked. "Kon, please place me on that thing again."

Kon swooped her up and set her on the rock in a single motion.

"Ready!"

For each finger pointing on one side, she sent a short whistle. For each finger pointing forward to the other side, she sent a long whistle. The stone took life again, rolling higher and higher, going forward farther and farther. This time Kukara maintained a good grip and balance with her sandals. In no time, they were going three times faster than the day before, mana powering the gestalt built of movement, men, a girl, and stone. There was only one mana, and they progressed in perfect unison, as one body and one mind. Soon only the grating of the rock moving across the crater's floor and Kukara's soft whistling was heard, like a mute conductor.

Kukara directed this lithic symphony with slight flipping of her fingers when needed or the occasional blink of an eye and a barely discernible nod of her head. Soon the whistles were so close together that there was no need to give commands. Her whistled melodies were etched in their minds: they only had to watch her harmonious dance on the top of the rolling monolith to maintain the coordination and speed. Brute force and fatigue vanished; they were irrelevant vestiges of a different time, a different philosophy. To the few spectators, it was an astonishing performance that they would never forget. It was the birth of Rapa Nui's spirit of creation, inspiration, and being different from the rest of mankind. To the uninitiated, what happened that day would be held in awe as an inexplicably magical event. For the Sacred Circle of the Seven Souls, it would be mana at its finest, a concept well learned, nothing less and nothing more.

The rope around the stone was the link with men. Bouncing on a curved base would give mana to the stone. The rest was only a matter of coordination, balance, and speed. Strength was never an issue.

CHAPTER 15

"After the first ahu had been built, every settler knew the past would remain the present forever. Future generations would be less substantial than the powerful ancestors, the Sacred Circle of the Seven Souls. Every man and woman committed themselves to projects celebrating the gods. They all felt they were part of something growing, necessary, and inspiring. Bonds between each other had become so strong that trivial quarrels, petty jealousies, and egotistical arrogance were eradicated."

Kon Tici Viracocha

The Sacred Circle of the Seven Souls charted the little colony's destiny: to create a place for the gods, a place where the living could proudly gather, a place where the dead could rest in eternal peace, a place where children could master the challenges of becoming adults, a place where boats would be protected, and a place where men and women could dream, create, and prosper. Such a place was the Ahu of Hanga Roa. Tamatoa had the vision for it, Kon engineered it, and the rest of the Sacred Circle of the Seven Souls enthusiastically supported it with their talent and encouragement. The Maohis had never seen such a massive structure, much less built one. But there on a tiny, isolated island, the most remote bastion of humanity on earth, this dedicated band of Maohis, aided by a little girl's genius, created a massive structure that would defy earthquakes and the tireless onslaughts from the Awesome Sea.

The huge megalithic structure ensured that the memory of its builders would never die.

First-time visitors were profoundly affected by their experience and invariably recounted feeling a strong tingling sensation penetrating them to their core, imbuing them with mana.

Under Kon's supervision, the workers constructed a formidable breakwater of man-size boulders that had been scattered along the waterfront by centuries of wave action and erosion. For generations, the energy of the waves would roll the boulders up and down before the seashore slope before dying on the rocky coast of the island. This dynamic seawall was a natural protection for the ahu they would build. At a short distance beyond the natural rocky barrier, they had dug a wide trench all along the tiny Hanga Roa bay. At one end, a long ramp of well-cut slabs would be built all the way below the sea level, so Tamatoa could bring his boats to shore during high tide. The bottom of the trench was carefully covered with cobblestones, then flat slabs to make a good foundation for a formidable wall of massive monoliths, about fifty of them, many times the size of the one they had practiced with under the guidance of Kukara's mana.

Higher inland, in a crater, they cut cube-shaped chunks of basalt, following the natural fractures created when the rock cooled in very ancient times. But each cube, convex side down, was still far away from the seashore, where they were to be precisely assembled.

Ready for the day's work, Kukara wore her special sandals, their laces tied tightly around her calves. Kon grabbed the little girl and helped her climb to the top of the first block. For a moment, she sat and enjoyed the view. Then she told the three men on the left side to roll the monolith up on their side when she raised her left hand, and the other three to do the same on their side when she raised her right hand. The rock rolled only very slightly at first, then it gained momentum. She knew it would work eventually, but she was not happy and stopped them.

"Add another man to each side," Kukara directed.

Following a careful selection of two more men and a brief training session, she was ready for another go at it. This time the monolith rapidly reached the desired momentum. Kukara gave the signal for the other two teams of four men each to pull the long rope looped around the monolith, making certain the long forward ends crossed each other. The team on the left would pull when the right part of the monolith reached its highest level, and the team on the right would do the same when the left side reached its maximum height. To help Kukara ride the great stone as it was walked down the hill, Kon made a framework of ropes and anchored it to the monolith's top. When the rocking motion became so severe that it required Kukara to abandon her hand signals, she would revert to her whistled directions to guide the teams.

Under Kukara's command, the rolling commenced again, very slowly at first. Mana was slowly filling the giant stone. The stone started moving forward, slowly at first. Kukara stood on her toes and commanded the men to increase the rolling frequency. Instantly, the stone picked up speed. Women and children followed behind the huge block, chanting and clapping to Kukara's rhythm.

At these relatively high speeds, the monolith became a potential killer, filled with lethal momentum. If any of the rope pullers or rockers lost their concentration or disobeyed Kukara's signal, they could be fatally injured. When workers felt tired or needed to stop, they were to whistle sharply. At the signal, Kukara would gradually slow the pace before coming to a complete stop. Many times some of the men, including Kon, Tamatoa, and Taatamao, tried to take her place, but nobody ever reached her mastery. The stone could easily move twice as fast with her: it was as though a secret understanding existed between her mind and the stone. Everybody respected her for this unsurpassed talent. They especially admired her humbleness. It made her childish kindness a powerful incentive for the others to accept changes and progress.

Hina placed her hand on Kama's shoulder. The firm grip was a signal of concern mixed with admiration.

"In my wildest dreams," Hina said, "I never thought a stone of that size would obey the orders of a little girl. I knew about mana for a long time, but this goes far beyond anything I had imagined."

"I know; you have to see this to believe it," Kama replied. "But it appears to be very demanding on her legs and hips."

"She does not care! Look at her face. She smiles, her eyes closed. She is in a deep trance. Everything is in her fingers and in the songs and rhythmic claps of people."

At the end of the day, one monolith was on site, ready to be placed in the huge trench where it would stay for thousands of sun cycles.

****

Two moon cycles later the Ahu of Hanga Roa was completed, giving the little colony an immense sense of pride, accomplishment, and destiny. They regretted they could not show their marvelous work to the rest of the world. But it did not matter; they had found peace. Their concerns were with themselves, and not the rest of the world. They were in a different world… their world, a happy world, far away from the outside and its persecutions.

On inauguration day, every settler, living or dead, had their personal stone solidly anchored in the ground, along the side of the ahu that faced the island's interior. Twelve large stones topped the ahu; they were perfectly aligned along the ahu's longitudinal axis, evenly spaced, from one end to the other. Each pedestal represented a founding member of the Sacred Circle of Twelve. Hina, Kon, Kama, Tamatoa, Taatamao, Mahine, and Kukara sat on their respective stones, facing east, toward the people. Each of them wore a round woven hat, on top of which a circle of white feathers had been sewn: it was the symbol of sacred knowledge. A few paces inland from the ahu, everyone sat on their respective stones and watched the Sacred Circle of the Seven Souls with profound respect and expectation. Here and there, the pattern was disrupted where the stone belonged to a deceased member. The audience knew something wonderful was about to happen, and they knew the secret would not be revealed until the most propitious moment. They had never been disappointed in the past; today would be no exception. For many moon cycles, everybody had worked long and hard. Today was the time to forget the physical pain and to receive whatever blessing the Circle had planned for them.

Kukara stood and raised her arms, the signal to be silent and listen. Her index finger flexed imperceptibly, and the drummers started to beat their huge drums with large padded drumsticks; their deep voices boomed and reverberated up and down the coast, until everyone was silent. The beat slowed and came to a complete stop; only the sound of waves pounding the shore could be heard. A gorgeous sunset backlit the ahu and those on it. To those seated in line with the ahu's center, Kukara appeared to be crowned with the rays of the setting sun; the event had been perfectly staged to provide maximum theatrical effect.

"I have an announcement to make," she said with her tiny voice.

Everyone waited expectantly. Kukara let their anxiety build for a few moments, then announced with a broad smile.

"Mahine is pregnant!"

The audience burst into spontaneous cheering and applause over the great news.

"I did not know that!" Taatamao exclaimed.

Kukara, laughing, raised her arms to silence the crowd. The drums called again for everyone to be silent. Drums slowed down and came to a complete stop. Crickets could be heard.

"I have another announcement," she said with a broad smile.

Everyone waited with expectation, baffled by what could happen next.

"Kama is pregnant!"

After a short silence, the people again erupted with chanting and dancing.

"I did not know that!" Tamatoa exclaimed, with a roaring voice.

Ecstatic, Kukara raised her arms once again. As the drums stopped, a grating tern could be heard.

"I have a final announcement to make," she said with a stronger voice. She smiled broadly and made a subtle sign of respect to the queen.

Everyone waited with expectation, but intuiting what would be said next.

Kukara shouted, "Hina of the Valley is pregnant!"

There was instant pandemonium: this time no one would stop the crowd's revelry and celebration of the long-awaited news.

"I did not know that!" Kon said, looking at the woman he loved.

"Women have their ways of doing things," Hina replied with a sidelong, conspiratorial glance in Kama, Mahine, and Kukara's direction.

The tattooed giant hugged Kon and Taatamao, literally crushing their noses with his.

"My friends," Tamatoa pursued, "we the men have no idea how arcane things work in the world of women. They constantly communicate together in secret ways that I have never understood."

"To understand something," Hina replied with a radiant smile, "you have to actually live what you are trying to understand."

"This is my woman!" Kon said. "But all of you in the Sacred Circle of the Seven Souls, do you know what Hina just said applies to many things?"

"So all this is the result of your teaching," Tamatoa said.

"My friend," Kon smiled, "It has been a long time since I have needed to teach anything to Hina of the Valley."

"You are a quiet man, when living in peace." Tamatoa said. "But your quiet silence is as great as your charismatic quest for peace."

*************_______

Deep in the windy hills of Rano Raraku, Kon's giant moai, cleverly cut and patiently wrought from the island's hard volcanic rock, was slowly coming to life. Its life force would become entwined with theirs and forever affect their destiny. Unknown to anyone at the celebration, the great moai had already acquired its soul. And it was roaming the island. And it was becoming insinuated in every aspect of the island life. And it was in the person of a little girl named Kukara. No one knew, not even Kon. But the realization had been developing slowly in Kukara's young and fertile mind. Although its form and purpose were unclear, Kukara let the presence know that she willingly waited for its revelation. Throughout her agitated life, she had been a very patient girl.

"You have seen nothing!" she murmured to herself. But for the moment, her mind was on a much simpler concept, based on what she had learned from Hotu-Matua and the Rongo-Rongo tablets. She took Hina's hand, then Kon's hand, and raised them as high as she could.

"People of Rapa Nui, look at the tattoos on my parents' arms. On Kon's arm, you have the living spirit of the First Man. On Hina's arm, you have the living spirit of the First Woman. These spirits are joined together in care, love, and pleasure, which one day soon will bring them a child. And such is the situation with Tamatoa and Kama, Taatamao and Mahine, and with so many others among you all. May Make Make be with you and the sacred beings you have created."

Kukara patiently drew the two Rongo-Rongo characters on the top platform of the ahu, using little white coral stones. Kon's spirit was a very simple sign; it had two short pointed legs and two long pointed arms reaching for the sky. Because it was a spirit, it did not have a head. Hina's spirit sign was similarly shaped, but had a tiny circle added to its center, signifying woman's life creation knowledge. Kukara placed it to the right of Kon's. Then she joined both characters using a larger stone. She drew the Rongo-Rongo symbol for a man next to Kon's spirit and the symbol for a woman next to Hina's.

"Now I am happy," Kukara said. "But there is one more thing you must do to enable Make Make to look at you and say: 'They are living well.'"

Once again, the little girl got everyone's attention. No one took her ideas lightly.

"To understand something," Kukara said, repeating Hina's words, "you must become what you are trying to understand."

On the side of the man symbol, she drew a new sign nobody had seen before. It was like a walking woman with ears and arms pointing at the sky. Although no one understood why, the sign seemed to evoke a subconscious, primordial terror.

Kukara had listened to a conversation held among Hina, Kama, Mahine, Kon, Tamatoa, and Taatamao regarding the Tila and Lutafu incident. While the others discussed the event, Kukara had searched the Rongo-Rongo tablets for answers. But until then, she had no idea that Hina of the Valley would deliver the answer in such a powerful way. Kukara correlated Hina's statement of people, their spirit counterparts, and the universal force to what she found in the Rongo-Rongo characters. Kukara was not necessarily a genius; she was simply a well-prepared little girl, always.

"Each couple is made of one man and his spirit, of one woman and her spirit," Kukara said, "and something else that never dies, something that walks among the dead and within the womb where new life begins, something powerful that controls your life, and your destiny."

Everyone stared at the little girl, waiting for the name of the new Rongo-Rongo character. She anticipated their thought.

"This new character has no name yet," Kukara said. "But it is the amalgamation of the five named characters."

They all waited for the name.

"It is your aku aku, the means by which you shall live."

The crowd murmured the name aku aku many times, until its echo was repeated from the farthest hills.

"This still does not explain what the Light wants us to do," Hina said, recovering her way of thinking faster than anyone else.

"It is simple," Kukara replied. "It is called friendship, but I have no sign for it yet. Before I can name it, I need to better understand its characteristics: I need you to experience friendship so that I can better understand it."

"Then, and only then," Kon replied, "will we be able to find better answers to the Tila and Lutafu incident."

"How do we do this?" Hina asked, intrigued.

Kukara took Hina's hand and placed it with Tamatoa's hand, took Mahine's hand and placed it on Kon's, and finally placed Kama's hand on Taatamao's; it was an interesting proposition that took everyone by surprise.

"You shall live together for a few days, in isolation," Kukara explained. "You will not create life, since it already grows in these women. The purpose of this union is to care, share, support, and help each other in many ways. It is to learn to love each other in a way that would not only please you both, but also please your respective mates. It is a fine balance only you can find."

Hina glanced at Kon, overwhelmed by the concept and also concerned about how to put it into practice. Kama found the answer.

"Hina can visit my place for a few days, when I visit Mahine's place, and Mahine visits Hina's place—simple!"

"I am going to give you a hard time, like I have always wanted," Hina said with a chuckle, kicking Tamatoa's arm very hard.

They all laughed in good camaraderie. They also agreed to the new task, anxious to learn its outcome. The three couples of the Sacred Circle of the Seven Souls had the mission of living something they all wanted to understand better, and that would better enable them to establish sound rules for their people. The Tila and Lutafu incident had alerted them to how fragile their peaceful lives were. Something as simple as daily sexual behavior and jealousy could threaten their way of living and have terrible consequences for what they had worked so hard to create. They thought the experiment was bizarre. Yet they immediately saw its value and importance, keenly aware that none of them had thought of it. Only the little girl, after moon cycles of careful thinking, came to the conclusion that the answer could only be obtained from the behavior of the people she loved most. She knew the dangers attached to the experiment, but she trusted their maturity to create healthy, livable, and ethical mores and guidelines for the others. Satisfied beyond any doubt, Kukara vanished into the night.

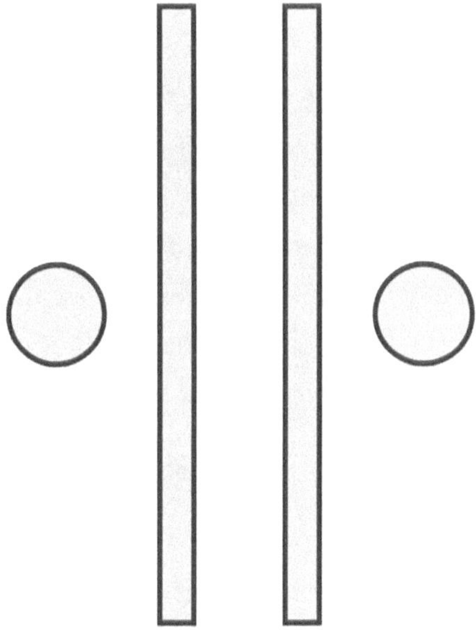

Between two narrow lines there is life. One line is birth, and the other line is death. Beyond birth and death resides the infinite knowledge of the Great Ancestor, Make Make.

CHAPTER 16

"A pact of friendship between a man and a woman must be the ultimate form of trust and tolerance a human being can be challenged with. If all the people I loved could transcend that test, they would live a better life by finding an unlimited source of support in their daily temptations and worries. It is a domain they ought to explore for themselves, at the edges of the dark abysses where so many human beings often sink in the shame of lust, guilt, perjury, and jealousy."

Kukara Tici Viracocha

It took Kukara most of the night to walk to Rano Raraku's quiet seclusion. She found companionship with the isolated moai. She felt the huge ropes tightened around the giant. With feet and arms clinging around one rope, she climbed to the top of the reclining statue still attached to the mountain. She sat on its neck and looked into its deep, secretive eyes farther up. She knew her body and the rock making the statue was only one, an integrated, intimate, and subtle part of the Light.

"I hope the people I love most will pass this test," she murmured to the cold, sightless giant.

There was no doubt in her mind they would, but she also knew there were many unknown forces that influence relationships between men and women; but having no experience in such matters, she knew that she, personally, was entering unexplored territories. Despite the night's chill, the reclining giant under her tiny, warm body felt good. She was comfortable with what would, one day, be the living image of Taranga Tici Viracocha. The first moai was designated to stand and guard over Taranga's bones, in the near future, not too far down the hill, reflecting the tranquility of the nearby peaceful blue lake.

"Taranga! Please, help me," she said, climbing farther up and staring into the water pooled in the eye socket, which was large enough to hold her tiny body.

For a fleeting instant, Kukara saw an ephemeral spark transit the pool. Was it the reflection of a shooting star? Or was it a sign from the Light? Shooting star or not, she knew the Light always rules coincidences in time. The Light never needed to talk, answer, or comply. The Light was far above these concepts. Kukara took the spark of light in the moai's eyes for what it was. It was Taranga communicating through the Light: "Yes, my child, I will help you."

Kukara used a little piece of cloth to sop up the water in the eye, and when it was dry, she crawled into it, curling her body like a puppy would do, and closed her eyes. She could only hear the ululating wind in the hills and feel the extraordinary energy stored in the moai's hulking mass. Far inside the stone, she heard the steady impact of very hard basalt adzes magically shaping the daring monument, and screeching sounds of sharp obsidian finishing its delicate surface. The feeling was so realistic and powerful that there was no doubt in her mind that an omnipresent life force existed there, memorized in stone. Before she slipped off into a peaceful sleep, she vowed, "One day, I will make you walk… I swear!"

When Hina arrived at Orongo, she saw that Tamatoa was

sitting in front of a fire next to the cliff. Using the opportunity provided by Kukara's mandate, Hina resolved herself to exploring and understanding the evolution of her feelings toward Tamatoa. She reflected on their first encounter, the one when Tamatoa had smashed Kon's face with his mighty hand and throttled her throat with his powerful fingers. She was extraordinarily intrigued about spending some time alone with the man she had hated so much a long time ago. Her feelings about the tattooed giant had greatly evolved after, along an immense journey, she discovered the real man. But she could not help think that, once, the only thought she had in mind was to find a way to destroy him.

She sat near him and placed her hand on his leg in a friendly gesture. Without saying anything, he placed one hand on her shoulder in response.

"You and I have been on a most fantastic journey," she said. "Do you recall when we first 'met' on the beach near Papenoo, the day prior to the Mount Orohena race?"

"Like it was yesterday," he replied with his usual thundering voice.

"For many moon cycles I recall having shivers of fear race up my back every time I heard your voice."

"And now?"

"Now! I like your voice. It keeps order in the colony," she added.

Tamatoa shook his head, laughing.

"Are you hungry?" he asked.

"Yes! I am starving."

"I prepared some fish for you," he said, pointing at the fire.

She was very surprised, since men rarely cooked for their wives in the Maohi culture, but for Hina of the Valley it was different. Tamatoa removed a large bundle from the fire and carefully brushed off the many layers of charred banana tree leaves. He slowly unwrapped more layers of green, steaming leaves. Finally, ten little red fish were revealed, surrounded by cooked bananas.

"They are mauros, my favorite fish," Hina said with joy. "How considerate; thank you!"

"I am glad this pleases you. But truthfully, it was not my idea. Kama suggested it."

Speaking under her breath, Hina said. "Kama, my dear friend and adopted sister, I love you for everything that you are."

"You have made an extraordinary impression on her," Tamatoa said. "She talks about you all the time."

"How is your life with Kama?" Hina inquired, taking a fish from the banana leaves.

"She is an unbelievably talented woman, with both her mind and her hands."

"And? What else?"

Tamatoa hesitated, wondering what Hina was probing for.

"She is so beautiful," Tamatoa said, "that I become perturbed whenever any man looks at her."

"In love and jealous! What a combination."

"I am not jealous."

"Really? Yet what if?" she asked.

"If she goes too far with Taatamao?"

"For example."

"I would not like it, but I would accept the outcome."

"Are you sure?"

"No, not at all," he replied, gazing absently into the embers. "Taatamao is like a son to me, and he is also a good friend."

They ate several fish in silence until Hina spoke.

"If she consents and he makes her happy, why should you

be unhappy?"

"This is the way I am. There is still the old warrior inside me, and at times I may lose control if people push me too far. Do you understand me?"

"So you love her. Yet you could act in a way that would make her unhappy."

"Why all these questions?" he asked, becoming irritated.

"We are exploring, remember? For our people! We cannot give them precepts without us, the Circle, understanding the rationale. We must both live by example and provide examples, everyone who is part of the Sacred Circle of the Seven Souls."

"Would Kon consent if you and I were to go too far?" he asked.

"I don't know!" she replied. "I think he would approve, if it pleased both of us."

"Would it please you?" he asked, with a broad smile.

"No! You are a good friend, and I like you, but nothing beyond that."

"What would you do if Kon made love with Mahine?" he asked.

"It is fine with me if both consent, do it well, and leave considering themselves only as good friends. I told Kon, so he knows."

"In other words, I may be the only one with a problem," Tamatoa said with a chuckle.

"Not necessarily! The others could be discussing their respective thoughts on it as we speak."

"You, my queen, what do you think?"

"We must learn to be tolerant of the people we love. Grief, hate, and jealousy do not belong in any relationship where the couple loves each other. Additionally, even if she loves you immensely, you cannot always be the center of the world for her, or vice versa."

"How should this precept be placed into practice?"

"The key is openness, trust, and honesty. If you are ridiculously possessive, it becomes an invitation for lies, distrust, anger, and jealousy: you are slowly killing the love you have for each other. Passion takes over, with devastating consequences. Passion has nothing to do with love. Passion is a killer; love is life."

"I don't know, Hina," the great warrior said. "I don't know if I am capable of conducting myself in such a manner. There are subtleties in your words that I do not fully understand."

"If Kama is perfectly honest with you, I am sure you will have no problem."

"Do you think she is going to make love with Taatamao?"

"I honestly don't think so," Hina replied. "But this is irrelevant. What is relevant, right now, is how you feel."

"I don't want to think too much about all this. I would rather think about my child being carried by Kama. It must be very early; none of you show any signs of pregnancy."

"To you, we don't. But for me, the mornings are becoming more difficult. I can assure you that something is happening inside me."

They continued eating their meal and chatting about many mundane things throughout the day. At times they teased each other, kicked each other, and chased each other around the fire. Finally, they paused at twilight. Tamatoa covered the fire with cold stones. The night would be very dark. The cool mist, mixed with a gentle breeze from the Awesome Sea, portended a chilly night. They went inside Tamatoa's dwelling. He took a torch and went to light it in the few embers left outside. They went back in. Hina sat down on several layers of very soft and comfortable floor mats that Kama had patiently woven during her lengthy isolation on the island. Their shadows danced on the walls. Tamatoa undressed and cleansed his body in the way of the Maohi. He handed another jar to Hina so she could do the same thing. Ignoring Tamatoa's presence, she undressed and started the thorough process. Then they stood next to the burning torch and briskly rubbed their own bodies to dry off. The smoke escaped the room through a narrow hole at the center of the corbeled ceiling made of heavy flat stones. When substantially dry, she turned her attention to a display of obsidian tools.

"These are Kama's experiments at tool making," Tamatoa said.

"She has made all types of implements: adzes for carving moais, hooks for fishing, knives for cutting meat, and sharp miniature tools for precise surgery," he continued proudly. "She is incredible."

"It is one of her many passions," Tamatoa said. "You never get bored around Kama. She is always busy doing something, either with or without me."

Tamatoa walked to Hina and put his arms around her, from the back, just below her breasts. She turned around, slowly meeting her nose with his. Then she gently kissed his lips and looked him straight in the eyes.

"Friends only?" she said, poking one finger on his chest.

"Friends only!" he replied, looking down at her firm breasts and the golden condor resting between them. He noticed that the sacred feathers of the green pigeon were intertwined with the necklace. They were the symbol of a great priestess and queen, the supreme ruler that no one could transgress. He knew that he could never take advantage of Hina of the Valley without her sacred consent, though at this moment he found her immensely attractive. In total control of herself, she smiled knowingly, and slowly stepped away from him. Now more at ease, they lay down together on the floor mats, side by side.

"Do you have any desire to sail back to Pora Pora for the next Great Gathering," Hina asked.

"Kama has no incentive to make such a trip. I would rather stay away from so many people that don't particularly care for me. Would you go?"

"I often wonder. I miss my parents and sister. Yet here I have great responsibilities. I think I will never return to my birthplace."

"Maybe we should send Taatamao and Mahine in due time. I would like for them to bring back new ships to replace the old ones. We don't have the necessary timber resources on this island to make new, reliable vessels. Only the trees that we find in the rain forest are suitable."

"I like your idea," Hina replied, yawning. "I am tired."

Hina's thoughts slowly drifted to the deep significance of the experiment. She loved her people and carefully observed them. Her people, as contrasted to the more austere Viracocha, were much more carefree, which was apparent in their day-to-day activities. The dancing, the chanting, the religious rites, the tattooing, the sexual life, and many other aspects of their lives were characterized by good humor and happiness. The last thing Hina wanted to create were precepts that would ultimately stifle happiness, and thence health. Excessive ruling would only suppress this magnificent joie de vivre, and ultimately crush their valuable heritage. On this issue, she was at odds with the old Viracocha traditions, even though she deeply respected many of their traditions. However, Hina was a pragmatic, caring woman. She would never implement a system that espoused sadness, grief, jealousy, and reprehensible acquisitiveness. She knew her ancestors had been correct. She knew she was correct. She knew it was her responsibility to create precepts that would blend tolerance, trust, and honor, keeping joy in everything they did, including sexual activities. She was determined to protect these inherent pleasures from the bigotry of arrogance that would only lead to a world of shame and deceit. There was no place for such a social disruption in her world.

Hina's thoughts drifted to the other couples and to mentally speculating at what they might be doing now. Side by side, holding hands, Hina of the Valley and Tamatoa went to sleep. For the moment, the two great Maohis were at peace.

Much earlier that evening, Kama reached Taatamao's place, where the handsome, peaceful man was waiting for her. Taatamao had been the most able commander Tamatoa had trained during the dark days of his revenge in Rarotonga. Taatamao was a native of Rarotonga. He was slightly taller than Kama, the tallest woman on the island. Taatamao was in his late twenties. Although Kama was in her early thirties, her face and her body appeared ageless. She was an extraordinarily beautiful woman: many men fantasized about her. Taatamao was no exception. Kama was unaware of Taatamao's attraction and had no preconceived notions regarding what would happen during Kukara's experiment.

Taatamao had prepared two magnificent lobsters, following Mahine's well-known recipe.

"They are beautiful!" Kama said. "You knew I love them. Thank you."

"And so are you!" Taatamao added.

"So am I what?" Kama asked, surprised.

"Beautiful!"

She blushed slightly and gazed at him with an intrigued look.

"Where are my boys?" she asked, looking around.

"We sent them to the neighbors up the hill so we can be alone, you and me. I have been looking forward to this for a very long time."

Now Kama was becoming concerned by Taatamao's increasingly licentious attitude. She tried to change the conversation.

"I am very thankful for what you have done for my children. You and Mahine have been like parents to them, especially you. They admire you and want to be with you all the time."

"I like them both. They have great potential, and they learn fast."

They sat around the fire and ate their meal, chatting about many things. Kama relaxed and started to enjoy herself. After awhile, her earlier apprehensions diminished, but her subconscious continued to be on alert for any untoward behavior.

"Your assortment of sweet potatoes is remarkable," she praised. "They are all delicious."

"I have enjoyed experimenting with them. They grow so well in this volcanic rock."

"I did not know you could cook," she said, amused.

"This is true. In our society, men rarely cook. But I enjoyed doing this for you."

After the meal, Taatamao gave her a complete tour of his garden of the depths.

"Your arrangement of the gardens and their abundance are truly amazing," she said.

They stopped next to a little pond where Taatamao and Mahine bathed at the end of the day. Taatamao spontaneously undressed and walked into the pond. Kama did not mind, recognizing that this was natural for the Maohi.

"Come join me," Taatamao suggested.

Concerned he might become offended if she refused, she undressed and joined him in the cool, crystalline water. With water up to her neck, she truly enjoyed the opportunity of cleaning herself. There were very few places around the island where this luxury was available.

Taatamao looked at her, overwhelmed with lust.

"I must tell you something," Taatamao said. "I want to be honest with you."

She did not reply, but looked questioningly at him.

"For many moon cycles," Taatamao said in a low nasal voice, "you have been causing increased passions in me. I would like to satisfy those passions. Would you consent for me to give you pleasures?"

Kama was stunned at first, then slowly recovered from Taatamao's brazenness.

"Mahine is a beautiful and loving woman. Is she not enough for you?"

"I know, and I do love her immensely."

"Then why me?"

"I cannot help it. It is the way I feel. I told Mahine."

"And what did she say?"

"She told me that with your consent, she would have no objection. Would you consent?"

"Absolutely not!"

An awkward silence filled the air. Kama brusquely left the pond, grabbed a handful of soft tapa, quickly dried her body, and started to pull her clothes on. Taatamao rushed out of the pond and put his arms around her, pinning her arms under his. He kissed her with passion, while continuing to tighten his grip. Remaining perfectly calm and in control of herself, she anticipated his move.

His tongue attempted to explore her mouth. But he felt nothing, no passion, no sharing, and no love. She did not fight, she did not remonstrate, and she did not yield to his brute strength.

"How far are you going to force me, without my consent?" she asked, placing an emphasis on the last three words. She continued looking straight into his eyes.

"Why did you come here if you do not want to share pleasures with me?"

"I came here as a friend, on a mission for our people."

"Hina is having pleasures with Tamatoa."

"I doubt that very much," she replied, with a fiercely defiant look on her face. He had never seen her like this before.

"Kon is having pleasures with Mahine; she told me so," he attempted weakly.

"My name is not Kon, nor Mahine. My name is Kama Tici Viracocha, and I am and always will be a one-man woman."

She pushed him aside, and finished dressing. In a way, she liked him, and she felt sorry for his misjudgment. But nothing would excuse his boorish behavior.

"Despite what just happened, I still consider you as a friend," she said. "I understand how emotions can get out of control, but thought that you were above that."

"I am sorry. I was never trained in such niceties between man and woman. I am a warrior."

"I better leave."

"Please, don't," he pleaded. "Sleep there on the mats near the fire until dawn. I will go to the seashore and think about all this. You are safe. I will not bother you anymore."

Without further notice, Taatamao abruptly left the garden of the depths. Kama was alone. She sat on the floor mats and reflected a long time about the evening happenings. She grudgingly acknowledged that he had honestly disclosed his feelings early on, which showed some courage on his part. Now that his passion was out in the open, and he felt somewhat comfortable discussing it, he now might be more amenable to accepting the facts regarding their relationship. When she left at dawn, Taatamao had not returned.

About the same time Kama and Taatamao met, Mahine reached Kon and Hina's settlement. Kon watched as she walked along the seashore, coming from Anakena. She was not as tall as Hina, but her body was more muscular, favoring her father's build. There was understated beauty in her athletic look, and she was known to be very sexually demanding. He knew she would be all over him; Hina had told Kon so. Without so much as a word of greeting, Mahine sensuously kissed Kon's mouth, confirming what Hina had said. Kon liked her, and loved her warm honesty. He perfunctorily returned her kiss. She looked at him, surprised and delighted.

"I did not expect you would do that," she said.

"Why not? You are my guest, and I was waiting for you."

"Hina told me you would be more reluctant."

"Do you want me to be more reluctant?"

"Absolutely not! Please, enjoy me with no restraint of any kind."

Her powerful openness actually raised his desire, much to his surprise. After a quick and light meal, she took his hands and looked him straight in the eyes.

"Before we go any further," she said, "I want to discuss something with you, something that I have never discussed with anyone, not even Taatamao."

"I am listening," Kon said, intrigued.

"A long time ago, a few days before we met in Tahiti Nui, I

meditated on the top of the sacred white monolith at the Marae of Taputapu-Atea, remember, where we had the great gathering. I saw you during that meditation, and your mind, or your spirit I should say, entered my body, invaded my privacy, and learned my secrets. I was possessed, but not afraid. I smiled with candor, and traveled with you in a timeless universe. I truly enjoyed the experience, until… until you showed me who my father was. You used me to find a way to stop him. I felt like I was only an object to achieve your means, and I was not important to you. Do you remember this?"

Kon listened to her, absolutely astonished. He indeed recalled having done this. However, he did not recall using Mahine in person. But obviously, she had not imagined what she had seen and felt.

"Why wait until now to tell me this?" Kon asked.

"I did not think it was important until now, when I am prepared to share pleasures with you. I thought that if you knew about it, it would make you feel different about me. In a way, it would not be the first time you have given pleasure to me."

"But," Kon remonstrated, "we did not have pleasures!"

"No, I was a depressed girl at the time. You gave me hope. That, in and of itself, was a great pleasure. As I said, I know only too well that I was never important to you."

"You are important to me as a friend and as a part of the Sacred Circle of the Seven Souls. Besides, you never told me."

"I am telling you now, and it feels good to do so."

He gently pulled her close and kissed her with passion. She was far more capable than he had ever dreamed, and she was extraordinarily modest regarding her talents. He knew that Mahine would always be a very dear friend, one with whom he could share the many mystical forces. He was so thrilled about this new understanding that, yes, he would make love to her to honor who she really was. Hina had always told Kon that he had underestimated Mahine. Now he knew what she really meant. He also recalled that long ago he had underestimated Hina's sister Fenua in a similar way.

"Did you ever tell Hina about this?"

"I just told you I never told anyone about our spiritual encounter. But I told Hina about my depression and some other experiences I had during my meditations."

"Hina approved about what we are going to do?" Kon asked, almost ashamed.

"We both discussed it," she replied. "And Taatamao gave his consent as well. But give me one favor, Kon Tici Viracocha."

"Which is?"

"Never, I mean never, be ashamed of what we are going to do tonight. It is the ultimate form of trust between friends. It is to honor Hina and Taatamao's trust."

Kon was astonished at the pure beauty of her way of thinking. She was devastatingly irresistible. It would be morally reprehensible not to make love to her. He took her by the hand and led her to the little pond he had built a few moon cycles earlier.

"Now, after talking about all this, I have another request," she said. "If you ever need me again the way you did at that time, please tell me face to face. Do not invade my subconscious without my sacred consent."

"I promise. At that time, I was desperate to find a solution for your father."

She did not reply, but raised her arms and shrugged as gesture of forgiveness.

"I know this is Hina's favorite place and that you and she enjoy each other here," Mahine said.

"You seem to discuss many things together."

"She is my best friend. We share many confidences."

Mahine quickly undressed and entered the cool water. Kon did the same thing. As she pressed her voluptuous breasts on his chest, he felt her warmth throughout his body. He felt her desire, and her free spirit.

"With respect to my best friend," she added, "we should not have pleasures here. We should find a better place on the grass, somewhere on the cliff above the beach."

"As you wish!"

Kon no longer cared where he would make love to her. Concupiscence ruled his mind, for good. After they found a comfortable place above the beach, Mahine sat and invited him to sit next to her.

"Kon, make this unique for me! Only you can do what I am going to ask."

"Yes, whatever you ask," he said, gently caressing her naked body.

"Go to this other world with me, as you did a long time ago, and we shall then share truly wonderful pleasures. Please, try this with me, as nobody else can."

To him, it was an honor, and a thrilling idea. He moved around her, so she could sit between his legs, turning her back to him. He rested his chest on her back, kissing her neck and held her breasts in his hands. She lifted her body and positioned herself to feel his love deep inside her. She instantly reached her first orgasm. He could not believe how fast and how intensely she could reach that ultimate bliss. And she was immediately ready for much more. She became calmed and felt a powerful stream of energy entering her neck where he kissed her. She closed her eyes and sought that other world. Soon she saw a massive shadow coming toward her, through the night's mist. She heard a deep, distant resonance coming from the ground. Slowly, the shadow took form, and the tremor became more intense. Suddenly, she realized the shadow was the giant moai of Rano Raraku. Scared, she opened her eyes.

"Do not be afraid, no matter what happens," Kon said. "I am with you, and it is only a dream."

She relaxed and went back to her vision. The moai was moving very close. She felt Kon's hands reaching for the lower part of her body, the tips of his fingers touching each other. The moai was so close that she could no longer see its mystical face. She could see only its very long fingers as they reached to touch a tiny square near the ground. The moai stopped when it came within Mahine's reach. She bent over, reached for its hands, and kissed the little square. Instantly, she climaxed again. But this time it was different. She knew something inside her had changed. It was a fundamental change. She knew the moai's mana had reached the new life she was carrying. She relaxed her body. The moai vanished from her vision. She felt as though she were floating in space. She felt Kon and heard his climax as well. She knew she would have another orgasm at the exact time Kon would reach his primal rapture; and so they did, filling the night with the sounds of unbridled ecstasy. Then everything became silent. They heard each other's blood coursing through their veins; their heartbeats sounded like timpani. They lay down in the tall grass and breathlessly looked at each other. Her face was filled with happiness. His face was as inscrutable as ever.

"You are my secret spirit," she murmured. "Thank you for what you have done."

At dawn they went to the pink sand beach and swam together in the clear, calm water. Mahine gave him a long last kiss and went back to the beach, dressed, and returned to the hills.

Kon reflected throughout the day on what had occurred, and how it had occurred. He knew that he had learned something he had never imagined, and it was contrary to his Viracochan beliefs. In his culture, the power of the mind was totally independent of the living body. He had been taught that to reach maximum performance with his mind, he had to completely forget his body. Mahine, in her very simple and honest way, demonstrated that everything the mind does is dictated by what the body wants. The body could actually control the brain and cure the spirit, a concept that he had never thought of. Only a healthy and balanced body could create a remarkable, stable mind. These were the Maohis' ways, and they were indeed beautiful ways.

A few days later, the Sacred Circle of the Seven Souls gathered again at the Ahu of Hanga Roa. This time they were alone. They all joined hands, and Hina asked the first question.

"What did we learn from our experiment? Tamatoa?"

"Hina and I had a good time, but we could not, should not, and did not share pleasures because Hina did not give her consent for us to go that far," Tamatoa said; Hina smiled.

"Taatamao?"

"I had a secret passion for Kama that she did not know of. She was angry when she discovered my desire for her. Then she let me know she was a one-man's woman only, and thus it would always be. Therefore, we could not, should not, and did not share pleasures, to my great disappointment."

"Kama?"

"I was not angry at Taatamao, but I was surprised and totally unprepared. He is a good friend, and always will be."

"Kon?"

"We had pleasures. We both consented. Furthermore, Hina

and Taatamao approved and were happy for us to share such a treasure."

"Mahine?"

"Long before I met Kon in Tahiti Nui, I had a vision of his ghostly spirit. Ever since then, I had a fantasy of sharing pleasures with him. The experience was beyond expectation, and I am thankful that Hina and Taatamao supported it."

"Hina?" Kukara asked.

"I think I am a one-man's woman also. But, contrary to Kama, I would keep my options open. Now we know consent and approval are the necessary essences of extramarital sexual activities."

A long silence took place.

"I think we know now how to guide our people in this matter," Hina said. "Does everyone agree?"

Everyone agreed, but Kukara wanted to ask a question.

"In this matter, beyond my understanding for now," she said—and everyone laughed— "what would be the worst rules we could create for our people?"

They all looked at each other, not too sure how to answer. It was an important question. Finally, they stared at Hina, their queen.

"The worst would be to impose rules that would kill the beauty of sexual activities. When the ruler is ignorant of such beauty, greed could take place, and the people would lose the sacred play instinct so dear to them. They would die in sadness in a world full of grief, deceit, jealousy, lies, and crushed feelings. At all costs, I don't want to live in a world of misplaced and irresponsible arrogance caused by out-of-control ambitions. In my world, good morality will never suffer from fraudulent bigotry; our people deserve better."

They were astonished at the passion with which she spoke these words; however, they were destined to become Rapa Nui's rules for a very long time. The swiftness of her answer showed them she had thought about the subject for a very long time.

Kukara tattooed the five Rongo-Rongo characters that had started the idea of the experiment on the three men's chest and around the left breast of the three women. The tattoos were light and discreet. Everyone liked them.

"Kukara," Hina asked, "can you create a Rongo-Rongo tablet on which everything that was said today could be transmitted to future generations?"

"Yes, but I will need your help to remind me of the details."

"So be it!" Hina of the Valley said. "Written it shall be."

"I am not finished," Kukara said, giggling.

"Yes?" Hina asked.

"What if…" she started, and she burst into laughter.

"What if two men want to have pleasures together?"

They looked at one another, surprised by the question.

"Did you ever see two roasters chasing one another?" Hina asked. "One thing is sure in that case: hens are safe and can live in peace. Kukara, they are called mahoos where I was born. They are very different from us, and we should let them have their ways. They make good friends for women.

"That is what I need!" Kama said.

They all laughed, especially Taatamao, who was the apparent butt of the comment.

"But what if two women want to have pleasures together?" Kukara asked.

"Mahine?" Hina inquired, pointing at her friend with a big smile on her face. "Do you find me attractive?"

"Yes, as a matter of fact, I do," Mahine immediately replied, astonishing everyone, and crawled toward Hina with provocative hands. "I think you are beautiful!"

"But what if I do not consent?" Hina chuckled, a little defiant.

"I will have my way with you, anyway," Mahine exploded, pulling at Hina's clothes.

Tamatoa threw his head back and burst out with laughter that could be heard all the way through the hills. In turn, they joined in his hysterical laughter. Little Kukara blushed, her eyes closed, choking. These were Maohis' ways.

*Dance is a way for man and woman to relate the sacred
knowledge of their spirit to the surrounding world. It is the
necessary liberation for the body to create a healthy mind.*

CHAPTER 17

"At Rano Raraku, the giant moai was ready to be born with mana's formidable power. Its silent face, frozen in time, will never be forgotten by anyone who looks upon its visage. The eyes were filled by the last rain, which heightened the profound sense that an omniscient being's all-seeing eyes were observing us, judging us. Its thin lips melded the complex emotions: pain and love. The moai's authoritarian chin and long ears were a mix of Maohi pride and Viracocha will. The giant was impressive, not only because of its size, but because of its simplicity — a simplicity that accentuated the importance of the mysterious message it carried. It was beauty combined with the unknown, the sacred territory of the gods that guided my hands as I carved the great being."

Kon Tici Viracocha

Kon and his two helpers spent the day with their mallets and chisels giving the great statue its final dressing, completing the work they had started many moon cycles earlier. The name Rano Raraku would soon have a new meaning. It would become the name of a place where the impossible was created. It would become a place where silent giants would scrutinize the star-filled night sky. It would become a place where any visitor would be humbled. Regardless of talent and intellect, great men would feel like ignorant children again. "Why did they do this?" would echo through the ages.

Uphill and on each side of the moai, Tamatoa and his men had dug two deep holes in which their massive basalt winding drums were installed. Ropes, thicker than a man's arm, were wound around the drums to regulate the moai's descent speed after it had been liberated from the mountain. Two ropes were wrapped around each of the two winding drums, for a total of four ropes. A team of ten men were assigned to each rope. These forty mortals were about to make history and an historic mystery. Kon and Tamatoa inspected the four drums and ropes for the last time. They then inspected the rigging around the base of the moai, which would plow the mountain on its way down. The ropes were secured away from the neck and the face, which were the most fragile parts of the sacred monument.

The long carving of the moai had been only half the work. The other half consisted of cutting and paving a long pathway to its final place, downhill. There the great moai would be raised, marking Taranga Tici Viracocha's eternal resting place. The avenue was slightly deeper in the middle, to keep the moai on track. Basalt slabs and rollers had been placed at regular intervals along the pathway to reduce excessive braking friction caused by the moai's tremendous weight. A deep trench, backed by excavated dirt, had been dug at the end of the course to act as a stop, against which the statue would be pulled to an upright position. The moai was still attached to the living rock by a narrow longitudinal keel. The moai rested at the same angle as the general slope of the hill. As soon as the keel was broken, the moai would start to slide downhill with incredible momentum. Kon had to keep all motions tightly controlled, using the four winding drums to slowly lower the moai. The access channels carved around the moai were partially backfilled with cobbles to the top of the keel. This not only prevented a sideways roll of the moai when the keel was severed, but would also act like ball bearings, further reducing friction on the uneven ground. Six holes had been chiseled through the top of the keel. Each of these had a wooden beam inserted through it; the beams would be used later to slowly break the keel, one at the time.

The much-anticipated day finally dawned. The entire population had gathered for the event. Sitting and standing along the pathway, the crowd was mostly composed of women and children, since most able-bodied men had tasks to perform. Half of them would hold the ropes that restrained the tremendous kinetic energy of the moving moai. It was an operation that none of the people had ever attempted. The many unexpected aspects of the event were an enormous source of wonderment and excitement to the people. To Kon, it would provide valuable information. Kon turned his attention to the women who watched.

"Stay far away from the moai's path," he said. "It will crush anything that it runs over."

Hina, Kama, and Mahine made sure his command would be followed. Kukara sat on the side of the talus, behind the trench.

"Step aside!" Kon ordered. "The moai may totally destroy the talus. I am not too sure what that thing is going to do."

Kukara nodded and moved to a safer location and sat down.

"Do not sit on the ground," Kon ordered, "be prepared to run away at any time."

Kukara complied, as did the other women.

Once more Kon checked the ropes, the uniformity of their tension, the winding drums, the winding-drum anchors, and the locations of each man.

Satisfied that everything was in order, he said, "I am going to slowly break the keel. Be alert and listen to my commands."

Kon pulled on the upper wooden beam, cracking the upper part of the keel. Nothing happened. The moai was still solidly attached to the living rock farther down. He pulled on the second beam. Nothing happened. He pulled on the third one. Nothing happened, but he waited a little, observing the ground. He pulled on the fourth beam. This time everyone heard the loud crack when the keel almost separated. Gravel started to trickle downhill.

""When I pull on the next beam, it will be on its way," Kon shouted.

Everyone held their breath. They all knew this would become a long-heralded, historic moment for Rapa Nui. A moment stretched into eternity; time itself waited. Staying as far away from the moai as he could, Kon slowly pulled on the fifth beam. The keel instantly collapsed, sending the broken fifth beam into the air. Kon felt the rush of air when the beam shot by his face at an incredible speed. The moai seemed to slump for an instant, then slowly started its journey. At the speed of lightening, the ropes snapped taut, immediately placing a tremendous stress on the four rope teams. They responded to the pull. All winding drums cranked, producing a loud grating sound as they dug into their solid bedrock anchors. One rope popped and creaked loudly as the teams strained to hold their load. A cloud of dust rose from the pit where the moai was born. Kon jumped out of the way. The moai reached the first basalt rollers that had been placed above slabs on the pathway and crushed them. Taking on a life of its own, the huge moai began to accelerate, becoming an unstoppable juggernaut with unimaginable force. All the men worked in commendable unison, faithfully responding to Kon's command, and showing admirable courage in the face of the inevitable. One team, slightly mis-positioned beyond one winding drum, lost control and were dragged down to the ground. One winding drum broke, virtually exploding from the tremendous strain and sending rock chips everywhere. One rope broke with the sound of thunder and was slung up the hill.

"Let it go!" Kon ordered. "There is nothing we can do."

The great statue's momentum was far greater than what Kon had estimated. A deep rumbling noise reverberated from the ground. Slabs, rollers, everything in the moai's path was crushed and thrown in the air like toys. The moai left a deep furrow as it careened down the hill. Finally, the moai came to a brutal rest in the trench at the bottom of the hill. Kukara felt the shock wave smack into her body. Then everything stopped, dust settled and flew away, and silence descended over the place and the people, who would never be the same again. As though guided by a supernatural hand, the great moai lay at the proper angle and the right place, intact. Slowly, the realization of what had just happened sunk into the stunned people. It started with Kon's powerful shout to the gods and was picked up by everyone; the joyful noise rose into the heavens and echoed across the hills for a long moment.

Hina ran as fast as she could to Kon, jumping over rock shards and debris as she ascended the hill. They embraced and kissed each other with passionate relief.

"You could have been killed by the last wooden beam," Hina said.

"I know! But right now I don't care."

Tamatoa came to congratulate Kon, giving him his usual devastating clap on the shoulders.

"This is what I call a good day!" the tattooed giant said, with a radiant smile that stretched from ear to ear.

During the next few days, Kon and the crews excavated the

talus from around the statue and installed flat basalt slabs all around the moai's base, on which it would sit after it had been moved to its final vertical position. Many more slabs were carefully joined. When completed, this area, situated under the invisible feet of the statue, would make an excellent gathering place for the Sacred Circle of the Seven Souls. Two ropes were attached around the massive head, ropes the two teams pulled until the moai rose to its vertical position. Two other ropes and crews pulled from the opposite side to prevent the moai from moving too far the other way. As soon as the moai assumed its final, vertical position, a moment of prayer was observed.

Then, in a single voice, the people joined in the chant, "Mana, mana, mana!..."

During half a moon cycle, the moai was carefully polished. The face, the neck, the ears, and the back were laboriously buffed, using delicate coral stones. Make Make was yellow-painted on each cheek, giving a dramatic additional touch. At the bottom of the moai's back, Taranga's remains were reburied into the final, sacred resting place. Dirt had been heaped to fill the space behind and to the sides of the moai. The front of the moai was left open, permitting visitors to see the hands and long fingers touching together at the giant's base.

After completion, a great gathering took place to celebrate mana's existence in their great symbol. Once more, the Sacred Circle of the Seven Souls met; this time they sat at the base of the giant, just within reach of its very long fingers.

For reasons only known to her and Kon, these fingers fascinated Mahine. She could not keep her eyes averted.

"Mahine, are you feeling all right?" Hina inquired.

"Yes!" Mahine replied, lifting her head toward the sky and staring at the colossal face. "As a matter of fact, I feel at home."

Nobody understood what she meant, except Kon. Mahine was attempting to re-create the conditions of her earlier vision. To everyone's surprise, she undressed and sat at the base of the moai. She placed her hands on the long fingers and her forehead on the little square the long nails pointed to. She waited for a while, trying to recall all the details of her vision. Her peers waited, pondering, until Kukara came to her.

"If you want something to happen, I know what to do," the young girl suggested.

They waited for her words.

"I need to sit on top of the moai," she said. "But I will need your help to do so."

"That is a long way up," Hina objected. "If you fall from that height, you would break all your bones."

"I will not fall; I must do this."

They quickly made a rope ladder. Tamatoa threw it over the head of the moai, and after several attempts, stabilized the ladder at the right place. Kukara started climbing while Tamatoa and Kon held both ends of the ladder. When she reached the moai's neck, Kukara struggled momentarily, trying to regain her balance along one cheek and ear. Standing on a shoulder, she pulled herself to the top of the head. Standing up, she looked down and waved at the applauding members of the Circle. She reverently raised her arms to the sky. She now knew that everything she did would be sacred and observed from the spirit world by the great Taranga Tici Viracocha.

"She looks so small!" Hina exclaimed.

"She certainly provides a unique perspective," Kama said. "I have never seen anything as impressive."

"Mahine, go back to where you were and lay your forehead on the little square, "Kukara said. "Kon will hold your right hand,

and Kama your left hand. Then Tamatoa, Hina, and Taatamao should stand behind you, all joining hands to close the circle."

They noticed Kukara had placed a Viracocha on each side of Mahine.

"Concentrate on the moai, then close your eyes," Kukara said. "Each of you now sees the little square where Taranga's fingers point."

Kukara sat cross-legged, closed her eyes, and placed her hands, palms down, on top of the giant head. She felt the stone's warmth permeate her body as she slowly entered a different universe, weightless, timeless, and filled with radiant light. Mahine felt a surge of energy enter her forehead from the little square and flow down her chest, abdomen, her legs, and out her arms, to the five peers. The energy seemed to expand within them, with no place to go. Kukara felt the moai vibrate. So did Mahine, and so did the five peers. They felt the moai rise above the ground. They felt the moai spinning. They felt themselves spinning around the moai, in a dance from another world, and in another world, until Mahine coughed and choked, pushing herself away from the moai, afraid it would crush her body. They all opened their eyes. The moai had never moved. It had been a figment of their collective imaginations.

"Did anything happen?" Mahine asked, wishing for an affirmative answer.

"Nothing happened," Kon and Kama replied at the same time.

"I am not sure about that," Hina replied, glancing at Tamatoa. "Viracochas are famous for avoiding explanations about what they can do."

But as she spoke, Hina felt a sudden urge shaping in her mind. She wanted her child to see the moai the very first time he would open his eyes. She never had thought about it until this moment, until the moai's mana told her. There was much more to that moai than she ever imagined.

"I will show you what your father has created, the very first time you open your eyes to this world," she murmured to herself, caressing her still-flat lower abdomen.

"I know what you are thinking," Mahine told her, gently caressing her abdomen. "There is a connection between that giant and our children."

"Perhaps we are making this up, as a result of our earlier experience," Hina said.

"I don't think so," Kama replied, caressing her abdomen. "The moai will indeed change their lives, who they are, and who they will want to be."

Tamatoa called up to Kukara. "Are you ready to descend? Do you need any help?"

"No, I can descend by myself," she said, as she grasped the rope ladder and started to return to the group.

As the sun slowly sank into the western ocean, they watched the giant's shadow grow larger and move farther across the land. Inexorably, it crawled across foothills and up to its birthplace in the cliff. It seemed to pause and point to a location.

"It was pointing at the place where the second moai will be carved," Kon said. "It will be called Hotu-Matua."

At that moment, Kukara took Kon aside.

"I need to ask you something," she said, very privately. "I did some thinking up there."

She took his hand and they walked closer to the moai.

"You cut this one in a way that makes it impossible for me to make it walk."

"Why should you make it walk?" Kon asked, surprised.

Ignoring his question, she continued. "If it was very slightly curved and larger at the bottom, I could make it walk the same way we did for the stones with which we built the ahu."

He was stunned by her idea.

"It would be impossible to do this," he replied. "It would be far too dangerous."

"I think it can be done," she insisted.

"Hotu-Matua had a bigger belly than Taranga anyway," she added, giggling.

Kon remained silent for a while, reflecting on Kukara's idea. Initially disposed to discount the thought as a dreaming girl's folly, he knew that she was a genius and he should seriously consider her idea. She knew him too well. She had a radiant smile when she saw him pull on his beard, looking at the giant. She knew, one day, it would be done.

"What did you concoct with your father?" Hina asked, when they returned.

"I asked some questions about how the moai is designed and sculpted."

Her answer was tantamount to saying, "I won't tell you; it is my secret!"

The clear, moonless night sky was sprinkled with many stars. The Sacred Circle of the Seven Souls remained at Rano Raraku for the entire night, while everyone else returned to their homes. Although everyone in the sacred circle had heard Kama's story about the walking giants before, they listened respectfully, instilled with the moai's mana. Long ago when she had been alone on the island, during a similar night, she saw large rocks separate from the mountain and walk like haunted shadows around the sacred lake. There were many. Each of them seemed to have an ordained resting spot. All night, Kama had observed the giants and tried to understand what they were doing. The giant's backs arched backward, as though they were contemplating the stars.

"The giants of my dreams," Kama said, "had a striking resemblance to this moai. Perhaps tonight we may see them again."

Kukara did not respond and left the group, returning to the moai's top. This time, upon reaching the statue's top, she folded both sides of the ladder all the way up. Now she was totally isolated, on her private, tiny island. As her friends wandered around the lake, she thought her experience would become a defining moment in her life. Never before had she been so right, and so prescient. Later that evening the moai would drain her life forces to such an extent that she ceased to be.

"Don't you dare jump from so high," Hina said, checking on her. "You wait for our return to help you down."

"Don't worry! I have the best place."

"Good night, silly girl," Hina murmured to herself.

Sitting in total darkness, on a tiny place surrounded by nothingness, she enjoyed the sense of floating in time and space at the edge of a vast, cosmic abyss.

"Taranga!" she asked. "Take me to the place where you rest. I want to see it."

She gazed at the stars for a while, and then finally realized her answers were not out there. She closed her eyes and placed her palms on Taranga's forehead. Within a few moments, she felt like they both were floating over the ground. She fought to reconcile the floating sensation with a new feeling of slowly sinking inside the stone. She sank all the way through the stone and felt as though she had entered the earth. She now felt that she was shrinking, becoming smaller and smaller, faster and faster. She felt comfortable, gently spiraling down the length a giant string. She kept turning around it, traveling forever. More strings, with regular and unfamiliar patterns, floated in the distance. As she drew close to one, she saw that it seemed to be made from building blocks. She floated toward one block and saw something resembling a doorway. She went in, and drifted to an immense, infinite room, where an inconceivable number of unknown creatures were working. They had no arms, no legs, and no heads. They looked like little floating clouds, always morphing their shapes. They appeared to be well organized, and all were busily pursuing a plethora of strange tasks. She came close to one of the creatures, entered it, was surrounded by mist, and once more her body seemed to shrink, smaller and smaller, faster and faster, until she saw the Light. Kukara knew where she was. She recognized the unmistakable, radiant peace, timeless and omnipresent. She intuitively knew that she had reached the limit of her experience. Then she realized the Light had been living inside her, always. She knew that the Light lived inside of everyone, but at a scale so small the notion of life and death was moot. The Light moved between building blocks that would never die, that would simply change place, adapt, create, experiment, analyze, and evolve. At the scale of these fundamental living blocks, there were no humans, no rocks, no water, no island, and no Awesome Sea. Kukara saw the Light slowly take the shape of a translucent human being wearing a long white robe. The Light chose to assume Kama's appearance, to make her more comfortable.

"The trip you made to come this far inside yourself is truly remarkable," the Light said, in a gentle voice.

"Am I inside myself, the moai, or Taranga Tici Viracocha?" Kukara asked.

"It does not matter. It is all the same. You have transcended the paradigm that rules cogent life. Very few humans have ever come this far, this deep into themselves. Now you are looking at what is and will always be."

"Then what is the purpose of my life, as I know it?"

"To find new ways for beauty, perfection, harmony, and evolution."

"But why?"

"Because at your scale, in your universe, everything is made of intelligent living blocks that search for the unknown and for perfect symbiosis. As we make progress, everything at your scale changes, adapts, lives, dies, and evolves, until one day, perfection is attained."

"What is the objective of perfection? I am not perfect. No one is."

The Light smiled and placed its hands on Kukara's head.

"At a scale far larger than the one you know, there are things that I built that would astound you."

"Can I see them?"

"You cannot, but your descendents will, if they can learn to live in peace. Many generations from now, after they have evolved sufficiently, they will go on a long journey, to a place that they have never seen before. The moai is the test of evolution for them, for now, to challenge every new day of their lives in a positive way. They must transcend, create, and find new ways, always searching for better ways at all costs, just like we are doing now."

"And if they don't live in peace?"

"Then your progeny and theirs will self-destruct, leaving the place for more worthy inheritors. Not only would you have failed, but I would have failed as well; it would give me great distress."

Kukara felt a surge of energy enter her brain, through the gentle pressure of the Light's hands.

"Kukara Tici Viracocha, receive this knowledge, decipher and deliver it to the ones you love; admonish them to make good use of this sacred knowledge. It will be stored in your memory for only a short time."

Kukara saw a flood of new Rongo-Rongo ideograms flashing through her mind. She was anxious to continue the dialogue, but the Light started to fade.

"Live well, my child, and tell Hina of the Valley that I want her to wisely use my powers."

With no transition, Kukara awakened and realized where she was. It was dawn, and the first sunbeams were reaching the moai's face. Had she dreamed, or had she been blessed with an exceptional vision? The little girl smiled, knowing the answer. She stood, flexed her legs, and greeted the sun with outstretched arms.

"One day, I will make you walk… I swear!"

Leaving Kukara on top of the great moai, Hina, Tamatoa, and Taatamao walked around the lake inside the crater and found a comfortable place halfway between the lake and a small wood to camp. They made a fire and hunkered down, enjoying the warmth. They chatted amicably for a long time and then settled in for the night.

At the same time, between the moai and the lake, Kon, Kama, and Mahine sat on an old woven reed mat, facing the distant moai. By squinting, they could just make out the tiny hump that must have been Kukara.

"Once at this place," Kama said, "I saw large rocks separate from the mountain and walk like haunted specters around the lake. There were many, and each seemed to have a chosen place. The moai we built is exactly at the center of where they gathered."

They sat side by side, Kon in the middle, Mahine on his right, and Kama on his left. They joined hands and waited, scrutinizing the distant mountain, the lake, and the moai.

"I have not felt this strange since first sitting on the white monolith in Havaiki," Mahine said softly.

"I feel the hair rising on my body," Kon said. "There is something in the air around us. Close your eyes for now and look at the moai using only your mind's eyes. Concentrate on it, and only it. He is Taranga Tici Viracocha; Kukara speaks for him."

Their minds saw the giant shadow with Kukara at its top, wearing a long, white robe. Why was she wearing a white robe? She did not have a white robe. Then other shadows seemed to separate from the mountain, where the moai had been carved. Slowly they moved down the hill and circled around the moai. Slowly they closed the circle, moving closer and closer to the moai. They started to form a spiral, a vortex familiar to Kon and Mahine, until they disappeared inside it. At that moment, Kon, Mahine, and Kama saw Kukara stand and raise her arms, and heard her say strange, incomprehensible words.

"One day, I will make you walk... I swear!"

Hina, Tamatoa, and Taatamao reflected on how to balance good and evil, light and dark, life and death, male and female, and many other opposing forces that affected their daily lives. They all agreed there was no ideal world, but only a world where everyone attempted to balance good and evil. But the concept did not fit with the Viracocha's belief that they must fight evil at all cost in order to build a strictly good world. Were the Viracochas too idealistic? Were they, the Maohis, looking for excuses to rationalize their weaknesses, or did they have to learn new values? The three great Maohis did not then know the answer. They felt a sudden gentle breeze cause the lake reeds to rub against each other. All three had the sensation that someone, invisible, listened to what they said.

At dawn, the Circle reunited together around the moai. Kukara immediately asked for something to write on. Tamatoa and Kama opened their cloth bags and reached inside.

"These are the wood tablets that I have carved for you," Tamatoa said, handing several to Kukara.

"These are very fine hard obsidian knives that I have made for you," Kama said.

"Perfect timing!" Kukara said, with joy on her face. "Now I need to be alone for the rest of the day."

Kon glanced at Hina.

"Do you believe in coincidence?" Hina asked.

"I am always suspicious of coincidence," Kon replied. "Coincidence is just a handy way to explain things that defy our comprehension."

"Where is your white robe?" Kon, Mahine, and Kama asked in unison.

"What white robe?" Kukara asked, looking at them as if they had lost their minds.

Kukara sat at the base of the moai and rested her back against the long fingers of the giant. She closed her eyes to refresh her memory and then started carving the sacred ideograms revealed by the Light.

"I guess she is on a mission," Hina said.

"I was given new knowledge," Kukara said nonchalantly. "I have been given only a short time to recollect it."

"Who gave you that knowledge?" Hina asked, puzzled.

"Someone who told you once to use the powers she gave you wisely," Kukara answered, without lifting her face from the tablet on which she was writing.

The unexpected statement sent a shock wave through Hina's

mind. Her body quivered with the realization that Kukara had received a message from the Light. Hina remembered too well every single word the Light had told her a long time ago in a dark, lost, inaccessible cave where a great god rests for eternity.

"This place will be sacred forever," Hina declared with all the gravity she could muster, a demeanor that she used only on very rare occasions. "There is a secret life inside the moai that only a chosen few will ever experience. Today, until dusk, nobody, including the queen, shall approach the moai and Kukara Tici Viracocha. This must be, this shall be; these are my final sacred words."

There was so much power and so much conviction in Hina of the Valley's statement that everyone disbanded without a word and went to their respective encampments. The already very highly revered moai immediately received yet more esteem, a veneration that would not falter for many generations. The great priestess had just created a mystique that would never die. It was a formidable caricature of man, cleverly carved in volcanic rock, with an aku aku of its own, and possessed by mana's powers, with all the implications for each member of the little colony.

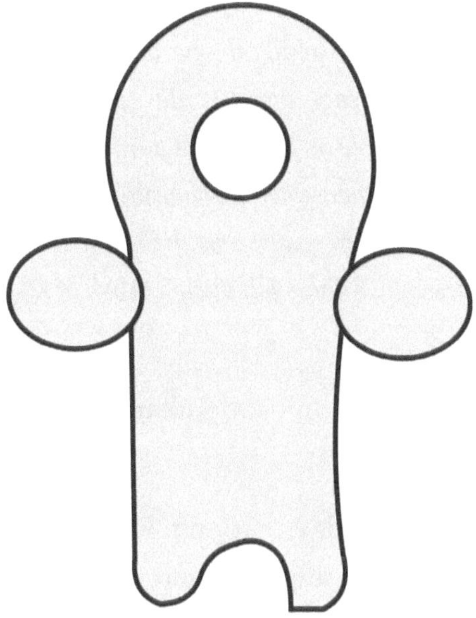

The first initiated priest who had the idea to make a moai walk had been inspired by a divine force. It was a long process involving sacred knowledge, vision, and will. Mana living in him or her would be transmitted to the moai until it would vibrate into life.

CHAPTER 18

"At Rano Raraku, while at one with the great moai, I received a sacred message that I could not understand then. Some characters I wrote on the tablets were familiar, but many were new, incomprehensible, fascinating. I knew that the order in which they were given was the key to discovering the underlying message. I never felt such a crush of responsibility in my life."

Kukara Tici Viracocha

Kukara worked all day, carving Rongo-Rongo characters on several tablets. Late in the afternoon, she reviewed her work. Tired, she wondered if all this was just the product of an overactive imagination, or if she had indeed been given a sacred message. Her experience inside the moai faded away. She smiled, feeling the reassuring pressure of the moai's long fingers on her back.

"Oh, Taranga, what have I done?" she asked rhetorically.

Again, she glanced at all the tablets, overwhelmed. She felt a sense of emptiness. She was alone, and everything was so quiet. She wished she could see at least one bird to break the silence. She felt helpless and totally ignorant in a world far more complex than she had ever imagined. She watched some tall grasses swaying in the breeze a short distance away.

"A tiny blade of that grass is extraordinarily complex," she thought. "Yet it seems insignificant. No one passing near it would ever think of asking questions about its meaning, or what would happen if they could make themselves small enough and look at the hidden universe inside."

Her thoughts drifted to memories she thought were long gone. She vaguely recalled Mahine talking to Hina a long time ago, in Tahiti Nui. Alone, near a white monolith built by their unknown ancestors, Mahine had felt depressed, useless, with no meaning in her life. This is how Kukara felt right now, totally drained.

"I should go, and tomorrow I will talk to Mahine."

She gathered her tablets and tiny obsidian knives and left Rano Raraku at dusk, first heading to home, Kon and Hina's settlement near Ovahe beach. Late that night, she found Kon and Hina asleep, side by side. She knelt quietly and curled up next to Hina. Hina placed her hand on Kukara's shoulder and gave her a slight squeeze. Very tired, Kukara instantly fell asleep.

At dawn Hina woke up first. She sat for a moment and watched a few grunting terns flying nearby. She looked down at Kukara, deeply asleep. She glanced at the recently carved tablets close to her. She reached over and took one and turned it over in her hands, studying small ideograms incised on both sides. Both sides were completely covered with precisely inscribed characters. She recognized a few from Kukara's earlier tablets, but most of them were new. She took another tablet, then another one, and another one: both sides were thoroughly filled. She thought there was harmony and beauty in the tablets, though she did not understand their meaning. Kon woke, and Hina showed him what Kukara had done. Kon knew the old tablets almost by heart. He glanced at the new ones, larger, with many more characters. It looked like an extraordinary amount of information, deeply engraved, with fastidious precision, showing certitude, no hesitation, and extraordinary skill.

"Is this incredible?" Hina whispered.

"Was it her imagination?"

"I know Kukara has a lot of it," Hina chuckled, "but there is more to this, I can assure you."

"She has been working on new characters for many moon cycles."

"I know, but do you realize how much she did in one day?"

Kon and Hina went to the beach for a swim in the sea, which was very calm and placid at that time of the day. After a relaxing swim, they returned to the settlement to prepare their breakfast. Hina called for Kukara to join them. Kukara had apparently left the camp while Kon and Hina were swimming.

"She did not eat anything," Hina noticed. "She did not drink. She left all the Rongo-Rongo tablets, old and new, right there where she slept. Do you think anything is wrong with her?"

"Maybe she went back to Rano Raraku," Kon suggested.

"I don't think so. Why come here just to sleep?"

"Orongo?"

"No," Hina replied. "It was not on her way."

"Anakena?"

"She rarely goes there: too many people! The only place I can think of is Mahine and Taatamao's gardens of the depths."

"But why?" Kon asked. "She abandoned everything she was working on, as though she was irresistibly compelled by something."

"Her intuition often guides her. Let's wait and see."

Hina's motherly instincts were correct; all day Kukara had walked across plains and mountains, straight to the gardens of the depths. She was mesmerized by a mysterious force that told her it was important to keep going. When, exhausted, she finally found Mahine and Taatamao, she immediately asked for Ku and Kane.

"We have not seen them all day," Mahine replied.

"They often visit friends at Anakena," Taatamao added nonchalantly.

"They are not at Anakena," Kukara said with a tone of certainty.

"Were you at Anakena?" Mahine inquired, perplexed.

"No, I don't need to go to Anakena to know they were not there. They are near here, and they need you. They need all of us, now!"

Taatamao looked at the girl, then at Mahine, and finally comprehended what she was saying. He immediately lifted his large conch to his lips and blew it with all his power. Kukara's intuitions were revealed and always correct. All across the island, settlers came together and searched the many endless, dangerous lava tubes, a place where the boys loved to explore.

For most of the day, deep inside the earth, Ku and Kane were exploring a new lava tube that Kane had found when he moved a large rock he wanted for a garden wall. The place was not far from the seashore, only a short walk from Mahine and Taatamao's place. After they had wiggled through the small orifice, they lit their torches and started walking uphill. After a very long and exciting walk, one torch started to sputter and die. Suddenly recognizing their predicament, they reversed directions and hurriedly retraced their steps, or so they thought. Unfortunately, it became rapidly clear that they could not find their point of entry. Using the last remaining light from the second dying torch, they argued about whose fault it was and where they went wrong. The last torch gave a brief spurt of light and silently yielded to the darkness. For a long time they held each other's hands. They made many attempts at retracing the walk they had done. They reversed directions and walked uphill. Then they came to a stop, very concerned. Ku squeezed his brother's hand.

"We have never been here before. The ground goes up too much."

They went down, down too much. They stopped again.

"Brother," Ku said, "we are in deep trouble."

"We have no food and no water," Kane murmured.

"Stay calm and let's walk slowly. Hold my right hand in your left hand. We will use our free hands to follow the wall."

As they continued retracing their steps, the tube became increasingly rugged and more hostile. Their desperation increased with each stumble. As fear and panic closed in on them, they realized they were at the mercy of the unknown, in total darkness, unable to see each other or anything.

"Let's try to remember everything that we touch," Ku suggested. "If something feels familiar, tell me."

"I am sweating. We are lost, we will die," Kane whimpered, with a knot in his throat.

"They will search for us," Ku comforted. "We must search as well."

Tamatoa and several of his men joined Taatamao's search team. They immediately dispersed and searched all the known lava tubes in the vicinity. For half a day they searched in vain. The call for help was answered from throughout the island; with more people arriving, Taatamao decided to wait and coordinate the effort. Hina and Kon finally arrived with many of the people from Anakena.

Hina went directly to Tamatoa and poked him in the chest.

"Do you still have your military leadership skills?"

As he opened his mouth to respond, she abruptly interrupted and silenced him. "The answer is yes!" she said. "Today we need these skills. Command us."

Tamatoa divided the people into three groups: his, Kon's, and Taatamao's.

"Taatamao's group will continue searching all the known lava tubes in the surrounding area. If you are unsuccessful, just expand your search area. Kon's group will form a long line, with each person no farther apart than twice a man's height; you will cover the land moving across the sun's path. My group will do the same, but cover the land moving in the same direction as the sun. Start now!"

Everyone immediately assembled in their respective teams and formed up as directed. That is, everyone except Kukara. Hina went to her.

"Are you going to help us?"

"No, I will stay here for now. I will try other ways of reaching them."

Hina smiled, knowing that Kukara's ways had always produced results.

"Is she coming?" Tamatoa asked.

"No, Kukara said she wants to try alternative approaches. Let's go, and let her have her ways. You never know with her."

All day Tamatoa and Kon's teams crossed the land with perpendicular paths, covering a very large area in the neighborhood of Taatamao and Mahine's settlement. All the next day they did the same thing, and the following day. For three days, they had been unsuccessful in finding any clue to the Ku and Kane's whereabouts.

Little Kukara never gave up her meditation, except to eat and drink what Hina brought to her from time to time. They never spoke.

The next day around midday, shortly after Hina had brought Kukara's food and water, Kukara's eyes followed a colony of ants on the ground. One ant pushed a tiny piece of ash from a nearby cooking pit. Kukara raised her gaze and looked at the horizon: a flood of thoughts and possibilities raced through her mind. She closed her eyes to better concentrate and organize that which could be relevant. After a few moments, she had firmed up a rescue plan. She stood and ran to the camp, where she knew Hina had returned a short time earlier. There she found Hina, Tamatoa, Kon, and Taatamao debating new strategies. She went directly to Taatamao, interrupting everybody else.

"Where can they make fire to light torches?" Kukara asked.

They indignantly looked at each other, irked that none of them had thought about this earlier. Tamatoa blew his conch, ordering everyone to return to the settlement. Within a short time, they all gathered and listened to Tamatoa's new orders.

"We need to start over," Tamatoa roared. "This time look for traces of fresh ashes. They may have built a small fire to ignite their torches before they went into a lava tube. This may give us a clue as to where they entered a tube."

Kukara walked a short distance away from the mobilization area, her eyes sweeping the ground. Catching sight of a small pile of ash and burned grass, she rapidly scanned the surrounding ground and noticed a small opening in the ground, partially hidden by a large rock that had recently been moved. She quickly ran back to the camp.

"I found it," she exclaimed breathlessly. "The entrance is right over there; follow me."

Kukara led the running crowd to her discovery and showed the dark, narrow passage into the earth, hidden by tall grasses and between two large rocks that had been recently displaced.

"Why were you so slow thinking of this?" Hina asked the young girl.

"I know, Mother, I may have failed in my mission to find them in time," she said sadly.

"This is not what I meant!" Hina clarified. "Why in the world didn't any of us see the hole when we were all crossing the land. We obviously passed over this several times. Let's get plenty of ropes, torches, water, and let's get down there, now!"

Tamatoa tried several times to enter the tiny hole.

"It is half your size," Hina chuckled. "You are dismissed, and so are many of you." Kukara easily slipped in the tunnel. Hina jammed herself in. Kon, Mahine, and Taatamao could not. And there was no way they could enlarge the hole in hard lava quickly enough. The lives of the two boys now rested on the abilities of the thinner and weaker searchers to find and extricate them.

"Bring thin men and women, even older children," Tamatoa ordered. "We will provide the logistical support."

Deep in the darkness of Mother Earth, far away in a tributary lava tube that ended at the unknown abyss of the Awesome Sea, two young boys fought dehydration and horrifying hallucinations. Even if they could see, they were incapable of walking anymore. Fatigue and stale air were slowly sapping their brains' cognitive powers. They waited for death. Even if someone had found the entry hole by now, they reasoned, it would take the rescuers too long to figure out which of the many possible ways the boys had taken, unless…

****

Tila from Anakena, whom Hina had befriended earlier, came before Tamatao holding a small dog in her arms. It was one of the very few dogs on the island, brought on Hotu-Matua's boat.

"This dog is very clever," she said. "If he can pick up the boys' scent from their clothes, he might be able to help us find them faster."

Mahine ran to the settlement and found some of the boys' garments. She grabbed a skirt and ran quickly to the lava tube, where everyone waited. Tila took the skirt and scrambled into the hole and found herself in a long, dark tunnel. Hina's torch lit the immediate area as Tamatoa gently handed Tila's dog to her. Tila, Hina, and the dog followed a rope Hina had installed as a guide, apparently leading to a nearby assembly point. The entry of the cave had been slightly enlarged, and women like Mahine could go in. Hina ordered everyone to wrap cloth around their heads to prevent severe injury from the sharp lava rock. Tila found Kukara first, who immediately ran to the others. Within a short time, everyone had gathered around Tila, who rubbed her dog's nose with Ku's garment. Then she released the dog, but kept him leashed with a long rope tied around his neck. At first the dog went in circles, confused, then went back toward the exit of the lava tube where they had entered. The dog found a narrow side tunnel that they had all missed and went in. The tributary tube became larger and led to more branch tubes. The dog stopped, sniffed at the ground, then made up its mind to follow the rightmost tunnel. Shortly they came upon more bifurcated tributaries that disappeared in many directions, much to Hina's amazement.

"Now I fully understand why they got into trouble! Stupid boys! How can they have been so stupid?"

The dog hesitated, went to one tube, then came back, and selected another tube. This time he pulled hard on the rope, sure of himself.

"Make sure you leave tracks behind with ropes, rocks, anything," Hina ordered to several children and women behind her.

"Don't worry, Mother," Kukara reassured her. "I have a keen memory for this kind of thing."

"Well, you know, little girl, this is exactly what these boys thought, and they could be dead wrong."

"You and I are well accustomed to dark caves," Kukara argued. "Remember the Light a long time ago!"

Hina paused for a short moment, reflecting on what Kukara had just said.

"Then make haste, Tila! I will follow you with Kukara. We won't wait for the others, who are busily placing markers to ease our way back."

They entered a large room where several tributary tunnels went up, and two went down. The dog became confused, perhaps because the boys had tried many of these ways themselves, often retracing their steps. They quickly ruled out the upward sloping tunnels since they ended in narrow passages, too narrow for the boys to have passed.

"We are wasting time," Hina said.

The dog hesitated before the two down-sloping tubes. They followed the largest one, but it ended on the shore of a subterranean beach and a large pond of fresh water.

"This could have saved their lives," Kukara murmured.

"They are alive!" Hina insisted emphatically.

With only one choice remaining, they all entered the last unexplored tube. It penetrated nearly all the way to the sea—which judging from the deep rumbling of the waves was close by. Unfortunately, this exit was too far under the surface for the boys to have used it as an escape.

The dog continued to snuffle the ground while Kukara and Hina chatted. It cocked its head and tugged against the rope, giving an excited yelp. There, directly in front of them, was a shapeless mass on the tunnel's floor.

"Here they are!" Kukara screamed.

Hina took Ku, the oldest boy, in her arms. His body was very cold, alarmingly cold. She knew there was no hope for him. He had been dead for quite some time. Kukara tried to force some water between Kane's lips while Hina briskly rubbed his hands. He was warm. Hina felt a weak and irregular pulse.

"He is breathing," Kukara said, "but he is unconscious. I cannot make him drink."

Hina took him in her arms and they struggled to the tunnel with the pond of fresh water. After checking the water's depth, she unceremoniously dumped Kane into the water. The immersion in cold water had the desired effect. He immediately opened his eyes, gasped, and started to flail the water with his arms.

"By all the spirits in this world, drink... Drink!" Hina commanded. The boy almost choked on the water, but clearly regained consciousness and drank a few sips of water. Then he collapsed in the water, unconscious again. They pulled him out of the water and laid him on the ground.

Kukara had tears in her eyes, obviously very upset at Ku's death. She had been very close to and fond of him. Hina warmed Kane by vigorously rubbing his back. He slowly opened his eyes and looked around. Seeing Hina and the others standing over him, he gave them a weak smile and started to drift off again.

"Drink! I am not going to lose you," Hina said.

She forced more water in his mouth, until the boy coughed. He drank a few more sips and seemed to regain a little energy. Finally, the rest of the searchers found them. Plenty of help was now available.

"Get them out, now!" Hina ordered, her voice echoing in all directions.

****

Kama was devastated at the loss of her oldest son. Yet she had feared that she would lose both sons. Now Kane was safe and recovering, but did not talk much. The death of Kama's son was a great shock to everyone. They all loved the boy very much; he had been peaceful and had an inquisitive spirit, always smiling, always happy.

At some distance from the cliff where the Awesome Sea waves perpetually pounded lava into black sand, Kama sat in the tall grass, resting her head on her knees, and silently wept. Kukara joined her and sat by her side, resting her head on Kama's chest. Kama wrapped her arms around the young girl; in many ways she was her daughter.

"I loved him," Kukara murmured, "but I never told him. I was too shy." Then she collapsed into an inconsolable grief.

A short distance away, Hina and Kon watched them, helpless.

"Once more, I failed to protect my people," Hina said with sadness.

Kon put his arms around her waist. "Don't say that. There is nothing more that you could have done."

"I disagree! We could have made the lava tubes taboo, like walking to the top of Mount Orohena. This is how we could have better protected our people."

"A long time ago," Kon said, "you and I won the peace. Here we are all at peace: this is your victory. But you will never stop anyone from exploring. It is man's inquisitiveness that makes us different."

"Perhaps, but I should have provided some guidelines on

how the lava tubes could have been more safely explored. Anyone can explore caves, but always make certain that someone knows what you are doing. That would have saved Ku… and Tehani."

Kon ran out of arguments. Hina took his silence as a sign of approval with what she had just said. She walked to the cliff and sat alone on the grass. Her eyes scanned the horizon. Her thoughts moved among distant memories. The young woman had greatly evolved in strength and wisdom. There were no tears in her eyes; there, fierce determination blazed. Her long hair, pinned on the top of her head with the gold pin, flowed in the breeze. New tattoos on her arms, symbols of the first woman's spirit, gave her a sacred and absolute authority that she intended to use. Her black eyes, half closed, were locked on the Awesome Sea, as though she were challenging nature itself. A new leadership strategy was slowly taking shape in her mind. It would be more responsible, more authoritarian. She knew what she wanted to do, but she was still debating how to implement it. Ku's accident brutally and abruptly settled her mind. There was no longer any doubt in her mind: she needed to create a new order, one that everyone must obey. She stood up, walked with determination to Taatamao and Mahine's settlement, grabbed her gourd full of water, and stared at everyone with a look of resolute determination.

"Three days from now at sunset, we shall all convene at the Hanga Roa Ahu. This is my order, and so it shall be."

With no further word, she drank a sip of water, turned, and left. Her face, her body radiated anger.

****

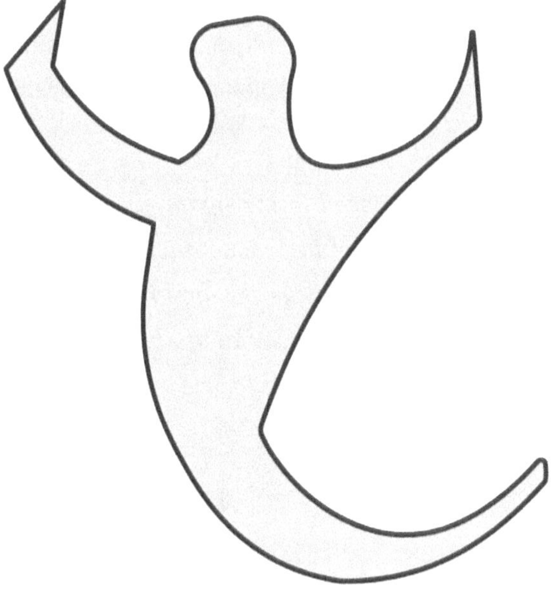

The most worrisome knowledge of all is death dragging the spirit of a loved one into another world where profound eternity reveals its content.

CHAPTER 19

A red-tailed tropicbird, called Tavake, circled around Hina of the Valley, as she stood alone at the top of Hanga Roa Ahu.

"All my life, I listened to the signal given by the sacred Tavake, which has always helped us during bad sea storms and harsh times. Its presence is the approval of the Supreme Being for what I am about to say to my beloved people. This moment is immensely important for me and for our future. It is a moment to help a lost soul."

Hina of the Valley

Hina stood serenely on the ahu, wearing a white blouse and skirt, loosely tied with a cowry belt that emphasized the slight bulge of her pregnancy. Her hair, held in place with a gold pin, made her look much taller than usual. She quietly watched her people slowly walking toward her and the ahu. Hina glanced up at the circling tropicbird. She wistfully studied its white body, red bill, black eye-stripes, narrow black edges along the wings, and two spectacular red streamers that projected far beyond its white tail. The bird added to Hina's image and prestige today, and she knew it. Everyone saw the bird, and knew that this was a favorable omen, since the Tavake avoids contact with humans. They knew it was a sign portending the sacred message from their beloved and respected queen. But they were all demanding, expecting something extraordinary from her. Having few diversions on the island, Hina's people expected their queen to rule and to entertain. Today was such a day.

A day earlier, Ku had been buried alongside Kura and Tehani in the sacred cave at the top of Orongo. Kama, hardened to emotional and physical pain, accepted Ku's death remarkably well. Young Kukara did not accept the fact so easily, and ceaselessly blamed herself for not having been more effective in the search. She grudgingly accepted a modest level of consolation from Kane's survival.

The Sacred Circle of the Seven Souls were now seated on the ahu, except for Hina, who stood at its center. Every islander sat on their respective stones, most of which had a small dip carved in their middles, making them more comfortable to sit on. A few stones were unoccupied, inhabited only by the spirits of those who were now in another world. Their emptiness added even more theater to the event. Water from a recent rain filled the slight depressions in the unoccupied stones. The islanders left the water as their gift to the birds that often drank it. The circling tropicbird flew away toward the formidable cliffs of Orongo.

Hina's slight flick of a finger signaled the drums to start their deep, resonant rumbling. Everyone stopped talking and turned toward the ahu, the Circle, and Hina; the drums slowly faded away. It was very silent. The only sound was the timeless rumbling of the waves pounding behind the ahu. Hina slowly and methodically fixed the gaze of each person in the audience. She was wearing a new white headband, woven with Rongo-Rongo characters describing how men and women were created. The band held a small green feather from the well-known sacred green pigeon. In her younger years, an apparition from another world had told her this: "Hina of the Valley, use my powers. However, always make sure you use them wisely." Since then, Hina had failed only once. She knew she would never fail again to make the right judgment and follow what the Light had instructed her. The rule was easy for her to follow, since she was naturally a kind, sincere, and humble person.

After looking into the last face, Hina started her eulogy. "Ku was a nice young man we will all miss for the rest of our lives. But as part of the grieving process, we may openly and unashamedly express our sorrow. However, before we leave, we will have accepted his life and death; then we must finish this day in joy. Today Ku gave each of us a little part of his mana; therefore, today each of us is a little stronger." She paused to let her words sink in and gently caressed her abdomen.

"Birth and death are nothing more than the boundaries that enclose that which we are permitted to experience. On each side, a universe exists, far beyond what we can imagine. If we could see these alternative universes, we would be so overwhelmed that life as we know it would be made instantly irrelevant: that is why we are not allowed to see them. As humans, we must live and fulfill our cosmic mission. Unfortunately, we don't know our mission either. We must always follow our instincts to strive for the best; otherwise, we will most certainly fail our mission. Every Rapanui must become a role model, to yourself and each other. At the end of every day, you must look at yourself and ask: 'Was it a good day for me? Am I pleased with what I have done?' If not, you must change yourself and become a more fulfilling person. How do you change yourself when necessary, you may ask? Explore your mana, and you will always find an appropriate and sublime solution. Kon Tici will now explain how to explore your mana."

Mana was feared by many because they were ignorant and afraid of what it could bring to them if they were weaker than what their queen expected. As a result, they all listened carefully. The word mana, when spoken, carried authority and great prestige.

"You all know the power of mana," Kon said. "However, many of you only know the physical attribute of the power. That is, when it is used to break a rope or a hard wood stick, or move huge stones. Did you know that there is another side of mana? One that is even more important for you to know. It is its spiritual aspect."

Again, silence. Kon thought they were either skeptical or were waiting for more information. Whichever was the case, he let the silence hang in the air. He wanted them to wonder and think; that way he could capture their attention better, deepen their interest, and intensify their desire to learn.

"Everyone has physical power, but very few have spiritual power. Yet everyone can learn how to enrich themselves with mana's awesome spiritual power. If you focus your physical mana on a given objective, you know that some very impressive results will occur...ephemeral, of course! You can do the same with your spirit. If you are sincere, if you love enough, if you believe enough, you can reach the spirit of departed ancestors, talk to them, be enriched with their knowledge, and reach the source of their wisdom."

Kon paused to gauge the audience's reaction. Everyone sat still, barely breathing. But silence again reigned: this time he thought he had totally lost them. They were pragmatic people and intelligent as well; Kon was at a loss as to how he could deliver the message more effectively. Sensing the problem, Kama Tici Viracocha came to his rescue.

"I know plants very well," she said with a timid voice, "and so does Hina of the Valley. Let us show you the power of the spiritual mana."

Almost simultaneously, the entire audience sat a little straighter, looked a little brighter, and seemed to reengage their minds. This time they were attentive. A few murmurs rose from the crowd. Drums rumbled for a moment, the signal for everyone to observe and respect the sacred silence.

Hina quickly collected her thoughts and understood what Kon and Kama were after. They had given her an idea. She went into the crowd and looked for someone physically weak, depressed, or otherwise physically or mentally ill. She finally found a short, middle-aged man who always avoided work and seemed to be a chronic worrier. He was the little society's consummate loser. His name was Kanui, from Hiva. He had lost all his children during warfare between the islanders, and his wife had died in the tidal wave that struck Rapa Nui a few moon cycles earlier. He had lost every shred of his will to live.

"Kanui, mana shall be with you!" Hina said loudly, surprising the man and everyone sitting nearby. "Stand up and walk with me to the Sacred Circle of the Seven Souls. Kama and I shall heal your wounded spirit and guide you to a new, more meaningful life."

Kanui, humbled by the honor and attention, was immediately uplifted. Timidly, he took Hina's hand as she reached out, and walked with her to the most honored place on the ahu.

"One moon cycle from now," Hina said looking at the crowd, "Kanui will be healed from his lengthy bout with depression. By my command, Kama Tici Viracocha will rebuild this man. She will give him mana's power to become one of our best gardeners; he will find, protect, and propagate the rarest plants on Rapa Nui. This shall be remembered and accomplished by the time we meet again during the new full moon."

Kama took Kanui's hand. Kukara took his other hand. Then the Sacred Circle of the Seven Souls joined hands and sat. Drums rolled, loudly at first, then slowly faded to total silence. Kanui felt a current of energy enter his hands, his arms, and his entire body. A shiver ran up his back. It was a feeling he had never experienced before. His face felt hot. His brain felt the assault of alien waves. He listened to the sea's waves pounding behind the ahu. He felt the resonance of his soul with the Awesome Sea. Fear gripped him. The seven elite had their eyes closed and seemed to be frozen in time and space. Kama and Kukara felt his fears course through his shaking fingers. They reassured him by holding his hands tighter. He stopped shaking and surrendered his trust to them. He closed his eyes and let the Circle deliver its mana. He was at peace, floating among clouds and soaring with tropicbirds. He sensed the ethereal presence of his children and wife's spirits. Slowly, as mana built in Kanui, the specters became more corporeal. He took flight and soared among birds, with them. He heard their voices, their joy, and their laughs. He felt his wife's touch and heard her voice whispering into his ears.

"My husband, I am always with you, despite being in another existence. Know that I continue to love and care for you. Do not be sad, as the day will come when you will be with me again after your destiny on Rapa Nui has been fulfilled. Live the remainder of your earthly life as an honorable man. Diligently discharge your duties and become the best at what you enjoy doing. Perfect your bond with what Mother Earth has created. Create the best nurseries for endangered, fragile plants, as life is everywhere and we are the stewards of that life."

He felt her depart and saw her essence dissipate. He could no longer soar with birds. He opened his eyes as if awakening from a long dream. Hina took his hands and commanded him to stand up.

"Strong man in a weak body, look into my eyes," she said firmly and gently.

He saw peace, beauty, and command in his sacred queen. He saw gentleness, care, and expectation. In her eyes there was irresistible power, joy, and simplicity. He felt overwhelmed by her femininity. For anyone in need, Hina had always been magical. As a child, long before Kon met her on Tahiti Nui, she provide succor and solace to children, the elderly, and the ill, often through the invocation of a single word, a truly magic word. As a healer she had always been the great priestess. Her gifts were received from the great god Taaroa, and then from the great Viracocha, the Light, and the great Make Make, who were all persona of the supreme creator of everything.

"Look deeply into the eyes of each member of the Circle, one by one," she commanded.

He first stared into Kukara's eyes, where he saw mystery and confidence in a young girl still at play with the world. He looked into Kon's eyes and felt the great man's assessment of his worth as a person. Kon's lips showed a trace of disappointment, similar to the moai looking upon the world. He felt Kon's hand reaching his shoulder; instantly an incredible surge of energy entered his body. It was as though he had been hit by lightning. Frightened to his core by such spiritual power, he blinked the termination of his contact with Kon and went to Mahine. Looking into her large, gentle black eyes, he perceived a no-nonsense woman conveying the message to shape up or lose the opportunity to join his family in their bliss. Totally shaken, now he looked into Taatamao's eyes and recognized the gentle, quiet man who occasionally patted his back as a sign of powerless compassion because of his inability to help the poor man relieve his depression. Then he found himself in front of Tamatoa and looked up at him, intimidated by his majestic physique. But for the first time, Kanui felt no fear. A powerful hand capable of crushing him flat to the ground grasped and held his shoulder. A clear, unspoken message passed from Tamatoa to Kanui, a message of care and support. Kanui taciturnly communicated his thanks for Tamatoa's gracious generosity. Then spontaneously, Tamatoa took Kanui's face in his hands and pressed his broad tattooed nose onto Kanui's. In Rarotonga this action signified friendship and trust. Never in his wildest dreams could Kanui have imagined Tamatoa doing this. In itself, the act passed mana-like power to the newly reborn man. Everyone present shared some of Tamatoa's mana from this wonderful gesture. Stunned, Hina of the Valley smiled her approval. Lastly, Kanui looked into Kama's eyes. Never before had he seen her deep blue eyes this close. As he stared at her, he was amazed by the beauty of her face. Hina placed his hands into Kama's hands.

"She will be your instructor during the next moon cycle," Hina said. "You must show excellent progress by the end of the cycle. During your instruction, Kama will take you to the edges of an unknown. Don't despair; what you will learn can change your life for the better. Do not waste her time."

"Come, my friend," Kama said with a gentle, comforting voice, "let's start now."

Holding hands, they both walked past the sitting crowd. Everyone witnessed the transformation in the man's countenance and bearing. The transition, from the sad and uncommunicative wretch that ascended the ahu to the happy, confident, and optimistic man, was truly miraculous already.

"You have seen nothing," Hina said to the crowd. "One

moon cycle from now, you will meet a new man, cured from his sickness. This will prove that you may bring your problems, your torments, your misery, and your misfortune to the ears of the Sacred Circle of the Seven Souls. I swear to you that you will be instilled with mana and cured." Her words were delivered so strongly that none of the audience would ever forget them. Many experienced personal raptures in stunned silence. Tears freely flowed. Their love for Hina of the Valley grew as they felt Mother Earth rise from the depths and enter the body of their sacred queen and beloved great priestess. There were no longer any doubts in their mind that she, Hina of the Valley, was to be their ruler until the end of her days. With a smile full of hope, Hina watched Kama and Kanui disappear over the crest, high in the dry hills overlooking the ahu.

****

Kama took her charge to the eastern edge of the Rano Kao caldera, a naturally enclosed garden in which many indigenous plants were carefully protected from temperature and wind extremes. They slipped and slid their way down the steep slopes until they reached a narrow ledge and a cave.

"There," Kama said, sweeping the panorama with her right arm, "you have a beautiful view of this breathtaking lake, with its deep blue water and its many green floating islands, its giant palm trees and numerous fruit trees. I never become tired of enjoying the Light's awesome creation. It is a gift for wise men and women."

Kanui watched his tutor as she talked with her gentle voice. Pregnancy did not diminish the fascinating beauty of her long black hair, dark blue eyes, and well-carved nose, which had a subtle, barely noticeable bump that added even more charm. Her delicate hands and long fingers with fastidiously manicured long nails gave her the aura of a goddess from another world.

"Here," she said, "you are high enough to see the sacred motus offshore: this is the place where I first came to the island, swimming to save the life of my lost child."

He noticed sadness in her words.

"Here," she continued, "you shall remain for two days, alone, until I return. I will give you food and water. Now listen carefully."

The humble man looked at her, at her thin lips, her chest, her hips, her legs, then back at her eyes. She smiled at his visual appraisal.

"I never realized how beautiful you are," Kanui complimented.

"I am your mentor; enjoy my company and respect me. I am honored that you find me beautiful. However, I need you to help me care for the most precious plants on this island."

In a timid way he took her hand. "Thank you for placing your trust in me. I will not fail you. Thank you for assuming the burden of my remediation."

"It is my pleasure. For the next two days you will do only two things. First, when you look at the lake, think about all of us, about yourself and your role on this island. Then come, I will show you…"

They went inside the cave. She pointed at a little plant up in the wall, in the shade. "This unique, fragile fern is the only one of its kind on the island. I challenge you to find another one. On this island there are three kinds of plants: the ones we brought, the ones you find everywhere and they own the island, and the ones that are rare, searching for unique places and struggling for survival. This is one of them; I want you to help me to help them."

Kanui inspected the rare fern with respect, avoiding any

physical contact. He knew Kama considered the plant sacred. He felt honored that she had shown him its hidden place.

"Every time you look at that fern," she said, "I want you to think about the loved ones you lost long ago." For him, these were magic words, the secret power of kindness.

Kama took his face in her hands, and like Tamatoa, she pressed her nose to his. He instantly flushed, flooded with unexpected pleasure. She turned and departed.

Kanui sat on the ledge and looked at the lake and its surrounding crater, the many floating reed islands, and the crown of giant palm trees well protected from the prevailing winds. Secluded in the hills behind Anakena, he had never taken the time to visit Rano Kao. He knew Tamatoa and Kama had settled on the other side of the crater at Orongo. He wondered if she would spy on him from the other side for the next two days. He went back to the cave and watched the little fern for a moment. Why did she bring him here? Then he recalled his wife's words from the vision: "find the best places for the plants at risk." Were these really his wife's words, or were they hypnotically planted by the powerful seven elites manipulating his mind? Suspicion grew and festered in his mind. He left the cave and climbed the cliff, then wandered on the high plateau that sloped gently to the cliff above the sea. He returned to the cave at dusk, sat among tall grasses, and looked toward where the tiny fern was hidden by the darkness. More questions seeped into his mind.

"Why is this important to me?" he murmured to himself. With no answer, he slowly drifted into a deep sleep under the little fern.

The little fern drifted in and out of his dreams. He saw it floating in the clouds, its delicate, tiny fronds morphing into legs and arms. The unfolding heart of the newest frond assumed the shape of a familiar face, long gone and dear to him. He collected sphagnum and water and nourished the fragile plant in nearby cracks and tiny pits everywhere he could see the evidence of thin tendrils scrabbling to expand its tenuous life.

When Kanui woke up at the first sound of seabirds, his first concern was for the rare, tiny fern hanging above him. His dream had been so vivid he recalled every detail and everything he had done. He also noticed something new had happened in his dream: never before had he dreamed in such vivid color. At first, the phenomenon seemed trivial. He explored the plant's roots in nearby cracks and pits for places where he could deliver valuable nutrients without disturbing its present growth. He went outside and searched for rich soil. He filled the cracks and pits to his best ability. He lightly blew on the delicate fronds to let the plant know it was loved, a sharing of the love he had for his departed wife and children. All day he sat and reflected on his incredible experiences. The next night he hardly slept, wondering if Kama would come back, and what she would teach him next. There was a little light of hope in his life, finally, and he was grateful to Hina of the Valley for her caring and compassion. He knew he had been a purposeful choice. He glanced at the little fern and smiled at the fact that such an insignificant thing two days earlier was now preeminent. Smiling to himself, he reflected that he had never paid attention to ferns, or any other plant for that matter.

"I like what you did," Kama said, taking him by surprise. He had not heard her coming. "You gardened without disturbing the roots. Good job!"

"It is nothing really!"

"Oh no! It is an important matter to me, because now I know you care."

"I dreamed the unfolding fronds were my children and wife."

"Mana's ways are subtle, yet profound, Kanui. There is much more to life than what you and I can see. Come with me. I will show you more plants that you need to know about."

Obligingly, he followed her steps. He deeply enjoyed her presence and hoped to earn her friendship.

"Does Tamatoa mind your being with me?"

She stopped and looked him in the eyes, puzzled by his question.

"Tamatoa the Great, despite his reputation, is a good and trusting man. He is honorable and gives magnanimously to everyone who deserves it. He cares for you the same way I do, as does Hina of the Valley."

"Why am I so important to all of you? I am worthless. I am nothing. My life is desolate, with no possible resolution on the horizon."

"I disagree with you, my friend," she objected, grabbing his arm and sensing negative powers at work in his mind. "Remember the words of wisdom from Kon Tici Viracocha: 'Who you are is irrelevant. What matters is whom you want to be.' I know you have dreams; let's work on them, you and I."

After walking a short distance around the top of the crater, they reached a new steep cliff. She struggled on small pebbles, then scrambled to reach a nearby ledge. Kanui observed that a few boulders had been arranged in a circle, ostensibly protecting another unknown plant. She crouched and gently cupped its leaves with her hands, as though she were holding a delicate and fragile treasure. Her gentleness and caring impressed him. He thought she must have known all the plants on the island.

"How did you acquire your knowledge of plants?"

"I have studied plants all my life," she replied. "Then when I was alone here for several sun cycles, they became my only companions. I talked to them."

He felt the grief in her heart; he knew that they shared a common pain. With compassion, he cupped her hands in his, and they both looked at the plant.

"What is it?"

"Kanui, this is a rare plant. There are a few more on inaccessible cliffs. If you eat the flowers, they make you sweat very much. It is good when you catch a cold."

"How did you learn, here alone?"

"Observations and comparisons with other plants I knew on the continent. Taranga was a master of medicinal plants. All my life I learned from him. Now you can learn from me."

"Why should I do this?"

She looked at him in surprise, sensing again negative forces at work in his mind. "Don't learn if you don't want to. Your purposeless life was much better, wasn't it?"

Shocked by her facetious answer, he watched as she gently lowered the plant, got up, and walked away.

"Why should I be interested in plants? I have always been a fisherman?" he asked petulantly.

"You were nothing," she replied, not even stopping. "I have more important things to do than listen to your whining. If you decide to make something of yourself, you know where to find me."

He wandered alone around the island, regretting his behavior. She was a nice, kind woman, and he enjoyed being with her. But in this process, he found out that he still carried considerable emotional baggage. He tried to rationalize that she was being overly sensitive. He had sincerely not meant to hurt her.

Kama visited Hina and Kon at Ovahe. She described Kanui's behavior and did not hide her frustration.

"He will be back to you," Kon said.

"But I have a deadline of one moon cycle to teach him."

"It will be slow progress for a few days," Hina replied. "He will become more effective and willing to learn more after he sheds his demons. I went through this once myself."

Kama was very upset. Hina noticed a moist rim around her eyes that revealed that she was ready to cry. Hina glanced at Kukara, who was silently listening. Silently, the young girl took a garment and started walking to the hills.

It took a long time for Kukara to find Kanui. She went around the Rano Kao crater, then along the southern cost, around the Poike peninsula, then finally back to the northern coast, west of Anakena. She was irritated at herself that it took her two days to figure out that he was not far away from where she had started her journey. She saw him sitting on a rock next to a tidal pool where only the largest waves lapped occasionally. He idly watched gorgeous purple corals and black sea urchins, his mind lost in distant memories. He did not hear Kukara approach until she called to him from a distance, clearly in a foul mood.

"Why are you not willing to learn from Kama, you ungrateful man?"

"Why should this concern you?" he replied, defiant.

"This is exactly the way you behaved with her. Now I know why she had tears in her eyes."

He turned around, facing her, concerned.

"Kama is the most gentle and caring person on the island," Kukara admonished. "You spurned her good intentions, you unappreciative lump."

"I am alone. I always was alone," he whimpered. "I lost the ones that I have loved. Therefore alone I should remain. I don't want to cause more pain to anyone."

"I like to be alone, too," Kukara said, regaining her calm. "It gives me strength instead of selfishness. Your mind is sick, and solitude works against your recovery. You need Kama, and you should go to her. You should apologize to her."

"I apologize to nobody!" he replied defiantly.

"You apologize to no one," she sneered, angry again. "You make the ones who care about you sad. You enjoy wallowing in your self-indulgent pity. Your life has no meaning, you avoid hope, and you have no reason for being."

"You all prey on me; you use me for your own sick entertainment," he said. "I am like a wild animal being baited for your sport. It is a game for all of you. I am not willing to play your perverted game."

"For the sick, it may seem a game," Kukara replied, now really irritated. "For the queen, it is a necessity; it is not a game. For the great priestess, it is a mission; it is a cause she pursues for all her people, not just you. For Kama Tici Viracocha, it is a sacred obligation. I love Hina and Kama, and it distresses me to see them in pain caused by the man whom they were trying to help."

Kukara turned around and walked rapidly into the rocky hills. After a few moments, he saw her returning. He noticed the incongruous smile on her face. She walked up to him and gently took his hand.

"I am sorry," she said, incapable of lasting anger. "Come, I want to show you something."

They went toward the entrance to another cave, where he saw a circle made of boulders, similar to the one that Kama had shown him a few days earlier. In the middle, a recently planted palm tree was growing.

"This is Kama's work," Kukara said. "Look at it and be inspired by it. She did this for our survival. Without such care we, you and me, are all plants at risk."

They were magic words to his ears. How did she know these were the words he had heard in his dreams? Was she the creator of these words when they joined hands with the Sacred Circle of the Seven Souls? His suspicions of conspiracy grew even deeper. Yet she was kind to him, and she was only a child. Furthermore, he knew Kukara had lost everything, parents and brother, when she was a few years old; that by itself reversed the tide in his bipolar mind.

"Take good care of Kama's gardens," Kukara said, walking away.

He went back to Orongo, wondering how he could approach Kama. He knew that he did not have anything of worth to tell her, certainly nothing that could put him back in her good graces. No one would fault her if she refused to teach him any more regarding the sacred plants. Halfway up the crater he met Tamatoa, who was gathering several other men to go fishing. Tamatoa did not move toward Kanui but pointed toward the top of Orongo.

"She is waiting for you," he roared with a powerful voice that literally electrified Kanui, as though he had been hit by lightning.

It was an unambiguous command that said "stop your self-pitying nonsense." But to a minor degree, he was comforted by the fact that she was waiting for him. As he approached, he saw her combing her hair near a small fire, silhouetted by the rising sun. She smiled at him but did not say anything; she was expecting him to speak first.

"I am sorry for the other day."

"You can be," Kama said, "and I forgive you. Maybe too many things were happening too fast. You needed some time for introspection, which I believe you have done. We all have our weaknesses, and it is hard to shed our demons sometimes."

"I found a circle of stones where you planted a new palm tree. It is growing well it would seem."

"Palm trees are a great concern for the queen and me. We have cut far too many, and not enough have been planted to replace those that we have harvested."

"I can find places for them to grow where it would be nearly impossible to reach them."

"You underestimate these men," Kama replied. "They will reach them on the moon if necessary. However, it is a good thought."

"Where do we go today?"

"Down inside the crater, to explore its steep slopes. I want to initiate you to all the endangered grasses. They are a food source to us, as well as being used as raw materials for many projects."

Seen from the upper edges of the crater, the steep slopes appeared uninviting and hostile to anyone unfamiliar with the volcano. Yet even with her pregnancy coming to term soon, Kama took him down paths to places that he did not know existed. She knew the best, easiest way to caves everyone else would have struggled to reach. They went to numerous ledges covered with long, sturdy grass, whose texture was agreeable to the touch. Its elasticity was unusual. She sat and took a few long blades, wove them into a rope, and asked him to test its strength. He was surprised at the ease with which she wove the rope. It must have something to do with the grass, he reasoned, but it also had much to do with her experience. Kanui took the rope and, after repeated tries, finally broke it.

"We can fish with this! Ropes made with this grass could be invaluable for Kon at Rano Raraku," Kanui said.

"The problem is that the amount of this grass on the island is very limited. We must learn how to cultivate it before we use it. So far it has only been found here, at Rano Kao."

Kanui collected a few seeds from a healthy cluster. "The seeds are very small, but numerous. Do you want me to find other places to plant them?"

"You do what you want, where you want, and when you want. But if you succeed, I can assure you it will make a few important people very happy. I have tried to propagate the plant, but with limited success."

Every day until the day of the full moon, Kanui combed the island searching for rare plants and inaccessible locations. Several times Kon, with his remarkable climbing skills, had to help him reach dangerously out-of-reach places and get him out of there alive. Somehow danger helped him fight his demons. Once he invited Kon to visit a secret place he had shown no one before. It was deep inside Rano Kao on an inaccessible ledge.

"I planted a very rare tuber my grandfather gave me in Hiva a long time ago at this place," Kanui said. "I never shared it with anyone else. It is called uhi. I think it is better than the popular kumara, cultivated in the gardens of the depths."

Kon saw a few mounds of loose soil on which little bushes were growing.

"And you have never shown this to Kama," Kon said.

"No, if I tell her she would insist on coming here. She is in no condition to do this for now."

"I agree."

"But I planted more of those near Rano Roi, many moon cycles ago, before the tidal wave."

Kanui easily dug the soft soil, collected three large tubers, and gave them to Kon.

"Try to grow them near Ovahe, in your gardens. They need a warm place, well protected from the wind."

"I am honored that you have given these to me," Kon said.

"I hope they will grow. I tried several other places than here, but with no success, except Rano Roi, where I planted them originally. Don't show anyone until you succeed."

Slowly but surely, Kanui developed a bond with nature, with plants, and with places that the queen would declare as sacred and taboo. He looked younger, better groomed, and healthier. Kukara and Kane had tattooed Rongo-Rongo characters on his chest indicating he was the chosen one to bring life to rare plants. His transformation was well-known and witnessed long before the gathering day at the Hanga Roa Ahu. Dressed in a simplified priest's robe on the gathering day, Kanui was a new man, respected, and everyone thought Hina of the Valley had performed yet another miracle. For anyone who knew Hina well, there was no miracle; there was only care and immense kindness: this was the true reason she was the greatest priestess and the queen.

"The key for his success is a combination of several things," Hina said, holding Kanui's hand. "It is trust in others. It is friendship. It is the nature of the mission. But above all, it is the ability to learn to talk with Mother Nature at all times. In this respect, it is Kama Tici Viracocha who did very well, not me. Each of you has access to this kind of mana… if you really want it."

She surveyed the audience, sitting on their respective stones. She was not finished, and they knew it. She pointed a finger at one Rongo-Rongo character on Kanui's chest.

"I want everyone to recall this sign and what it means. It is easy to remember. It represents a woman's womb, the place where life grows. On many remote places on this island, Kanui will carve this sign on a stone. An area of five large steps from these marked stones is taboo. Within this area all living plants are sacred; damaging any of them is taboo. The sign will mean that sacred life is growing there, and will eventually feed, clothe, and serve us."

They all seemed happy and comfortable with her explanation. But something was missing. She knew it and purposefully kept it for the end of the gathering.

"You recall we have also gathered today to remember our loss when Ku departed to the other world."

She went behind Kanui and placed her arms around his shoulders.

"My dear friend," she said, "I know the pain you endured during your life. But we all have these terrible moments at various times during our lives. Don't be sad; our loved ones live, in a much better place, far beyond our imagination. They see you, and they are proud of you for a very simple reason; you are fulfilling your mission well."

She was silent again, but not finished.

"Discipline, my friends! I should emphasize self-discipline! We must obey the rules of the land. There are things you should not do, to protect yourself, to protect your family, and to protect others. You are well aware of the taboos imposed during the many moon cycles you have been here. Transgression is a serious matter that the Sacred Circle of the Seven Souls will not take lightly. Do not fear possible punishments; however, you must fear the devastating consequences to your consciences: you will no longer be able to be who you want to be! Remember this, reflect on this, live by this. Those are my words."

The sun, water, and earth are the sources of all life. Men and women are thankful that the Great Ancestor had the knowledge to make these fundamental building blocks for the universe we know.

CHAPTER 20

Somewhere, in a secret place in Hotu Iti Valley, Kon Tici and his friends had arranged an underground cave where women of the aristocracy could give birth to their children. When Hina saw the place for the first time, she said: "Mahine, Kama, and I will deliver our children soon. This place is so well made and furnished that anything that might go wrong during our sacred birthing moments can be remedied and provide for our steady recovery. I look forward to the first of us who brings life into this unique sanctuary: well done, Kon Tici."

Hina of the Valley

Three days later Mahine was brought to the sacred cave when her labor began. The cave had a low, secret entrance that was hidden by a thick wall of ferns. The cave was situated close to the sea and over a deep grotto that disappeared far underground; ocean waves crashing onto the grotto's walls rhythmically reverberated throughout the cave as though from a living, breathing beast. When selecting the location, Kon felt the respiration effect would help the women relax and breathe during birthing. Access to the place was possible only by moving two well-hewn, heavy stones. A long corridor surfaced with flat stones, carved from the island's best pink basalt from the Ovahe hills, led to the sacred place. Mahine was impressed that she could see her face reflected in the highly polished floor and mentioned that to Hina and Kama, standing at her side.

"I have never seen anything like this!" Hina exclaimed.

After walking crouched over a short distance, they reached a room where they could stand. The place could accommodate the mother and up to three additional persons. Since the delivery was imminent, the men were dismissed. Hina, Kama, and Kukara remained to help Mahine. The room, covered with highly polished basaltic slabs, was designed to channel any blood spilled on the ground toward a central channel where it could be easily washed down a drain hole the size of a man's fist. The place was easy to clean. One slot in the ground held special red clay that one of the attendants could use to paint sacred Rongo-Rongo characters on the mother's body. The clay could also be used in a poultice to heal wounds or to seal a freshly cut umbilical cord. The baby's delivery would take place on a large stone located in the middle of the room. A shallow niche had been carved in the stone. Mahine was helped by Hina to a squatting position on the top of the stone. The indentation in the stone was covered by a fresh layer of new fern fronds, creating a warm, soft bed to receive the newborn. The Maohis' practice of squatting during birth was thought to ease the child's delivery. Kama, coming from a different culture, and the mother of several children, agreed that this practice was good, since it used natural forces to aid delivery. A small, short coral table held several elaborate obsidian tools for minor surgeries, if deemed appropriate by the attendants. One attendant held a gourd filled with partially evaporated seawater, which would be used as a disinfectant for wound cleansing. Three other gourds, filled with clean, fresh water drawn from the sacred underground pond at Orongo, were kept on another small coral table. Immediately behind the delivery table was a higher stone table carved like a miniature ahu, on which a small statue was placed to witness the transient suffering of many women during their childbearing. The statue was a naked, squatting woman who looked on as her newborn discovered its new life home for the first time. It had taken Kon Tici more than nine moon cycles to carve the intricately designed figurine.

"I am glad to be here," Mahine said. "I will no longer have to eat the chicken intestines prescribed by my father; he was convinced they are beneficial for pregnant women. Tehani told him so before my birth and my brothers' births."

"I know," Kama replied. "I am on the same diet!"

"It is supposed to be good for you," Hina chuckled. "Vana always told me during my training to become a priestess that it is good for the unborn child as well. And as you know, the sacred leftovers the mother cannot eat are given to the other members of the family so they can honor the coming child. I think it did not go too well with Kon."

They all laughed.

"Oh, it hurts!" Mahine complained, but still laughing. "Stop, don't do this to me."

Taatamao, Tamatoa, and Kon, who sat outside the cave, facing the sea and coping poorly with the wait, listened to the women.

"I wonder what is so funny," Tamatoa sighed in exasperation.

Hina and Kama were massaging Mahine's belly to help her through labor. Several times they made her push hard. It became increasingly clear that Mahine would have a relatively easy and quick delivery.

"I hope it will be this easy for me," Kama said teasingly. "I believe my child will be large, because Tamatoa is so big; I am concerned that I may have difficulties due to the narrowness of my womb."

"But you already had three children, with no problems," Hina said.

"I know, but they were not Maohis."

Mahine gasped in pain from another contraction.

"Push now," Hina said, "as hard as you can!"

They saw the face of the child coming out, then one shoulder, one arm; then in a last burst of Mahine's energy, the baby fully emerged and was gently laid on the fern leaves. Hina grabbed the child by the feet and gave its buttocks a tiny spank. The child instantly started to cry, a sign it was breathing and healthy. Mahine looked down and saw it was a boy; she raised her eyes to the heavens in gratitude.

Outside, at the sound of the child, Taatamao grabbed Tamatoa's arm with a radiant smile on his face.

Hina placed her lips on Mahine's mouth and sucked the mother's saliva. She went outside and did the same thing with Taatamao. Returning to the child, she severed the umbilical cord with her teeth, while simultaneously imbuing the baby with her and the parents' mana. Then she carefully tied the baby's umbilical cord with a string, sealing the baby's mana into its body, where it was now starting its long life journey as an honored member of the little colony.

Hina sat with the child's face against her cheeks. She closed her eyes and listened to its heart. As a priestess, she had to recall the last dream she had prior to the delivery: this sacred ritual of recollection would augur the young boy's life.

She gave the baby to Mahine for a moment, then took him back, cleansed him with fresh water, and took him outside to his father.

"Taatamao," Hina of the Valley said, presenting the baby to

him, "this boy will be a master carver of the wood from the giant palm trees growing on this island. We will have to teach him to use this exceptional resource wisely."

Not hearing Hina, Taatamao joyously took the boy and raised him a high as he could, facing the pounding seas. The young Maohi, a feared warrior of another time and place, broadly smiled as he freely cried with joy; it was one of the best moments of his life. Tamatoa and Kon clapped him on his shoulders for his good fortune.

"Tamatoa the Great," Hina said, "for the first time, you are a grandfather."

In great joy he took her face and pressed his powerful nose on hers in celebration and respect. Then he kneeled and kissed her right knee.

"Taatamao," Hina said, "bring the baby inside with me; we need to tend to the mother."

They wrapped the severed umbilical cord and mother's placenta in fresh banana tree leaves and securely tied the package with twine. Hina took it to the cliff, where the waves of the Awesome Sea pounded. She threw it as far as she could and uttered the sacred words, "Go, and return to Havaiki and Hiva, the sacred lands of our ancestors!"

Returning to Mahine, Hina joined Kama and Kukara, who were warming some smooth stones on a small fire. They picked up the rocks with their bare hands to make certain the stones would not burn the new mother's skin. They placed the stones on her belly to force out all residual birth liquids and blood left inside her uterus. The procedure was also necessary to prevent stretch marks on the skin and encourage muscles to heal faster. Finally, Taatamao was invited to give food and fresh water to Mahine, who was rapidly recovering. This was the time they would name the baby. All eyes were on Taatamao, who was to make the announcement.

"The name of my first son is Kohau. He will help us preserve and transmit knowledge through Kukara's Rongo-Rongo characters."

They all repeated the name, taking their turn raising the child toward the evening stars.

A few days later, it was Hina's turn to deliver her baby. She was carried to the underground cave as soon as she broke water. No sooner she had assumed the crouching position above the delivery bed of ferns than she was already having powerful contractions. The contractions were becoming increasingly painful.

"After my delivery," Hina said, tugging at Kama's arm, "I want you to remain here. You may have bigger problems than we did; therefore, you must not return to Orongo until your time has come. We will stay with you..."

Pain returned, and she closed her eyes with a strained grin on her face.

"Push!" Mahine commanded. Kukara and Kama firmly held Hina's hands while gently massaging her shoulders with their free hands.

"Mother, imagine you are diving very deep into the dark blue abyss," Kukara suggested.

"I am diving very deep all right," Hina chuckled. "This really hurts!"

Her face became livid. Her eyes closed. Muscles in her neck contracted. Sweat ran over her naked body.

"Think about Taaroa," Kukara suggested, "and the words he gave you during the last moments of his earthly life."

These were magic words to Hina of the Valley. She opened her eyes wide and stared at the young woman, still a girl. She recalled her vision of the Light in Taaroa's hidden cave. She recalled the Light had taken Kukara's appearance to make it easier on her: As a result, she always listened carefully to Kukara's words. Her intuition told her that the Light was alive and working in Kukara's mind; in many day-to-day occurrences it seemed that Kukara's mana was exceptional, omnipresent, and gave her continual directions.

"Perhaps," Hina said with a grin on her face, "I am the great priestess. But I know that you are well ahead of all of us. You must record the knowledge of how babies should be delivered."

Going through a new contraction, Hina squeezed Kukara's hand so hard that the young girl fell to her knees, moaning in pain.

"The child is coming," Kama said, as she cupped the little head entering a new existence. Then the entire child came out, followed by a powerful shout from Hina.

"It is a boy!" Kama said.

Mahine placed her lips on Hina's mouth and sucked the mother's saliva. She went outside and did the same thing with Kon. Their eyes met, full of good memories. She returned to the child, where she severed the umbilical cord with her teeth, while forever sealing her mana and the mana of the parents within the child's body. Then she carefully tied off the umbilical portion still remaining on the child. Thus did mana start its long journey within the newest Rapanui.

Hina rose to her knees and took the child, while the other women were busy extracting the placenta and cleaning her vagina with highly concentrated salt water.

"Maui, my son!" Hina said in Taaroa's memory.

Then they thoroughly cleaned the child's body, went outside, and presented him to Kon Tici Viracocha, who took him in his arms and raised him toward the sky.

"When the Sacred Sun rises, Maui, my son, you will open your eyes for the first time and feel the magic of being alive. Then the Light will live in you."

For the nonce, only the gibbous moon and the stellar canopy celebrated the precious new life.

Tamatoa the Great and Taatamao kneeled in front of Kon, offering their congratulations, friendship, and respect. It was the first time that they had ever seen tears in the Son of the Sun's deep dark blue eyes.

Kon went inside the cave and walked over to where Hina lay; kneeling by her side, he gently kissed her hands.

"I love you, Hina of the Valley. I loved you even before we met. Our son is beautiful. Thank you for this wondrous gift; he will shed light on our lives for a very long time."

Kama, Mahine, and Kukara were busy warming the smooth stones on the fire. They made sure they could hold them with their hands so they would not burn the mother's skin. They placed the stones on her belly to force out all liquids and blood left inside her uterus. Then they carefully cleaned her body, inside and out.

"These stones feel so good!" Hina murmured.

Kon fed Hina some of her favorite fish, the mauros, along with some nuts, a banana, and copious quantities of fresh water.

"It looks like you are starving," Kon teased her.

She grabbed his arm, pulled him against her, and gave him a long kiss. They were happy parents.

Outside, Mahine wrapped the leftover umbilical cord and the mother's placenta in fresh banana tree leaves and tied the package firmly with thin cords. She took it to the cliff where the Awesome Sea pounded much stronger than usual. She threw it as far as she could and said the sacred words.

"Go, and return to Havaiki and Hiva, the sacred lands of our ancestors, and may Hina and Kon Tici's mana travel with you!"

Ten days later, Kama, who stayed near the birthing cave, broke her water and started her contractions. Hina, Mahine, and Kukara feared that moment. They were well prepared, but worried about the unpredictable. Her thin body was not built for giving birth to the tattooed giant's children. They laid her down at the same place, in the same position, as they had for Mahine and Hina. After a half day went by, Kama gave signs of exhaustion and passed out twice, which began to worry her attendants. This did not portend a speedy and healthy delivery. Hina explored Kama's vagina with one hand and discovered that the child was coming out one foot first. There was no way Kama could deliver the child that way without jeopardizing both lives. Hina removed her hand, closed her eyes, and stayed silent. Never before had she faced that case, and Vana, hurried by time to train her as a priestess before the Great Gathering, had been elusive about such a possible development.

"What is it?" Mahine asked, worried.

"We have a problem," Hina replied. "The child is coming out one foot first. It is unlikely that either Kama or the baby could survive such a scenario."

"Maybe Kama knows what to do!" Kukara suggested. "She helped other women deliver their babies."

Kama squeezed Hina's hand. Hina bent her face close to Kama's mouth.

"Get inside me, and turn the baby around...," Kama said, and passed out again.

Hina stood up, looked at her hands, their size, and could not imagine doing what Kama had just suggested.

"If I do this myself, I will kill her."

Hina went outside to breathe some fresh air and clear her head. The men saw the anxiety etched on her face and started to pummel her with questions.

"Shut up, all of you," she screamed. "Go away. We have enough problems without your blithering."

The order was strong, and full of certitude: Hina of the Valley was not to be disturbed. Kon meekly added a few words.

"If you need me to help in any way, I will, and remain calm. You know me."

"Thank you. But I think we can handle this." The men turned and started walking from the cave. Tamatoa was obviously upset.

"If you want to help," Hina said to Kon and Taatamao and pointing at Tamatoa, "take care of him."

Hina went back to the cave. "I swear I am not going to lose her," she murmured to herself. She grabbed Kukara's arms and looked at her straight in the eyes.

"I am the brain, and you, young girl with tiny hands, will do exactly as I instruct you."

"But…!"

"There is no 'but', do you understand me!" Hina said forcefully. "I am the great priestess. I am the queen, and I want you both to be obedient, all the way. Is that clear?"

Never had Kukara and Mahine seen Hina in such an agitated state of mind; neither knew that side of her.

"Yes, Mother," Kukara murmured in a shy way.

Hina took Kukara aside and explained the procedure systematically.

"You are right-handed."

"Yes!"

"I will cut your right-hand nails short, and polish them so

that you will not accidently scratch Kama. I will wash your hand and arm with salt water several times and lubricate abundantly with precious oil. You will slowly insert your arm into Kama and search for the narrow passage where the child will come out. At this point, you will feel his foot. Take that foot in your hand and push him back inside very slowly and cautiously. You will find your way inside Kama. Keep the foot in your hand and push it in as far as you can. By doing this, we hope the child will flip over, with its head down. At that stage, you may release the foot. But do not remove your hand from inside Kama yet. Carefully search for the umbilical cord. When you find it, follow it slowly to make sure it does not interfere with the delivery, and be especially certain that it is not wrapped around the child's neck. Then let the cord go. Open your fingers as wide as you can, as if you wanted to cup the child's head. Make sure you keep your fingers spread that way. Then slowly remove your arm from Kama and use your spread fingers to enlarge the narrow channel as much as you can. All of this must be done very slowly. Then the child's head should naturally follow the depression you created. If everything goes well, the head will come out, followed by one arm. At this point, we can handle the rest of the delivery. Do you want me to repeat? Do you understand what I am saying?"

"I understood everything."

"Good! I will repeat these instructions as you proceed."

Hina took a sharp obsidian knife and carefully trimmed the long nails on Kukara's right hand. In her society, long nails were a mark of high rank. But for Kama's good, Kukara did not mind. Then Mahine thoroughly buffed them to a high gloss using a volcanic sponge. They cleaned her arm in the salty brine several times. Finally, Hina lubricated her hand and arm with coconut and sandalwood oils.

"Are you ready?" Hina asked.

"Yes, Mother!"

"Mana be with you!" Hina murmured gently.

"The Light is with me!" Kukara replied, looking Hina straight in the eyes. Hina was convinced it was true and caressed the girl's head in recognition.

Mahine sat behind Kama and rested Kama's head and back on her lap. Hina spread Kama's legs wide, so they would not interfere with Kukara's mission.

"Go for it, girl!" Hina said.

Kukara kneeled between Kama's legs, laid her left hand on her hip, and slowly inserted her right hand into Kama's vagina, biting her lips. She searched for a moment, then smiled.

"I have the foot. It is wiggling its toes!"

"This is a good sign," Hina replied. "Hold the foot. Use it as your guide to go inside Kama; progress steadily, but very slowly."

Kukara closed her eyes to better concentrate. By looking at her slim arm going in, Hina could tell she was doing just fine. Slowly Kukara's arm slid into Kama's body; when her arm had penetrated to her elbow, Hina started to become concerned. Kama was moaning in pain, but both women were holding her.

"Are you still holding the foot?" Hina asked.

"Yes, but the child is moving a lot, maybe complaining."

"No, I think he has flipped over by now," Hina said. "His head must be at the right place. But I am not sure. Release the foot and slowly retract your arm. As you move back, slowly search for the umbilical cord. You should now be able to tell the baby's position."

Kukara did not answer right away.

"I cannot find it!"

"It is not important. Come back a little more until you find his neck. Check around the neck and make certain it is not being choked by the umbilical cord."

Kukara searched carefully.

"There is nothing around the neck. But I know his head is facing down as it should."

"Now, spread your fingers and come out very slowly, enlarging the birth canal, as I told you."

The procedure made Kama scream. In a last surge of all the energy she had left, she rose on her elbows and looked at what Kukara was doing.

"Push hard now. We are almost there," Hina stated.

Kama closed her eyes and with a painful grimace complied with Hina's directions.

"I feel his head in my hand," Kukara said.

"Keep pulling out very slowly."

"I am not strong enough to keep my fingers spread as you told me."

"Then slow down!"

"The child is pushing," Kukara said. "His head is in the canal."

"A little more!"

"His head is out of the canal," Kukara said. "I have one of his hands."

"Close your fingers and come out slowly," Hina said. "Kama does not need you anymore."

Kukara complied, then looked at her bloody arm. She rose to her feet and started to sob against Mahine's chest.

"Everything is fine," Mahine murmured gently. "You did superbly well."

"Kama!" Hina said. "Don't give up on us now. You must remain strong all the way to the end. As soon as you feel a new contraction or the child pushing, give it your all. It will be the last time you have to do it."

With a new burst of energy, followed by a primal scream that could be heard outside, Kama Tici Viracocha finally gave birth to a baby girl. She rose and sat, looking at the child. She could not help smiling and crying in joy. Then, completely sapped of any remaining energy, she collapsed on the ground.

"This is a big girl," Mahine commented.

Hina placed her lips on Kama's mouth and sucked the mother's saliva. She went outside and did the same thing with Tamatoa. Back to the child she severed the umbilical cord with her teeth and at the same time enclosed forever her mana and that of the parents inside the little girl. Then she carefully tied the umbilical cord part remaining on the child, so mana would start its long journey within the new member of the women's colony. This age-old repeated ceremony of mana sharing was extremely important to Maohis.

Hina rose to her knees and took the child, while the other women were busy extracting the placenta and cleaning Kama's vagina using highly concentrated salt water. Then they thoroughly cleaned the child's body and went outside; there they presented her to Tamatoa the Great, who took her in his arms and raised her toward the sun.

"My daughter," the giant said crying, "all the rest of my life I will love you and care for you. May the gods protect your mother. Your name is Marokura Rapanui."

Kon and Taatamao kneeled in front of Tamatoa, offering their congratulations, friendship, and deep respect."

"Can I see her?" Tamatoa asked, worrying about Kama.

"Yes," Hina said. "She needs to rest. She lost a lot of blood."

Hina, Mahine, and Kukara were busy slightly warming some

smooth stones on the fire. They made sure they could hold them with their hands so they would not burn the mother's skin. They placed the stones on her belly to force out all the liquids and blood left inside her uterus. Then they proceeded to carefully clean her body, inside and out.

Kama grabbed Tamatoa's hand. "I will be fine in a few days!"

Outside, Hina wrapped the leftover umbilical cord and the mother's placenta in fresh banana tree leaves and tied the package firmly with thin cords. She took it to the cliff on which the waves of the Awesome Sea pounded. She threw it as far as she could and said the sacred words.

"Go, and return to Havaiki and Rarotonga, the sacred lands of our ancestors".

The next few days, Kane drew a second row of tattoos around Kukara's waist, accurately copying a series of Rongo-Rongo characters she had given him that represented everything she had learned about delivering babies.

"Like methods used to transport heavy stones," Kukara said, "such knowledge shall never be lost!"

The great priestess would cut and tie the umbilical cord of the newborn child. Her dreams prior to the sacred birth would decide what the child's life would be.

CHAPTER 21

"It had been my wish for some time to one day build a house like no one has ever seen. It would have to please my queen, but also to be a fortress capable of sustaining the frequent, strong winds that buffeted us during the cold, rainy months on Rapa Nui. This house should become a model for generations to come."

Kon Tici Viracocha

With patience, Kon meticulously carved the many stones he would use for his house's foundation. He was very secretive about the house's design. Hina was busy taking care of their new son, Maui, who was about one moon cycle old. They prepared for the dreaded Rapa Nui winter that often brought misery to the islanders with its powerful winds and cold, rainy days. For days, Kon placed and anchored the long carved stones into a giant oval on a flat area that Hina had chosen. She enjoyed the view of the islets where she loved to swim, dive, and fish. Kon had drilled each stone to provide deep anchors to hold the main roof arches that he had made from carefully selected branches of the toromiro tree. He tied a layer of horizontal branches to the arches, to create a strong structural base. Above the arches he wove thick layers of totora reeds, which he had harvested from Rano Raraku, covering them with several layers of tightly woven, long grass. Each layer was sealed with muddy clay. Then he covered the final layer with a good-quality soil and planted grass seeds that he patiently watered every day. Within half a moon cycle, the top of the house was solid green and ready to withstand the coming winter. The grass roots secured the reeds and provided a living carpet to absorb the rain that would percolate deeply into the roof. Kon's innovative use of the strong hardwood arches ensured that the building's structural supports were adequate to carry the roof's water-saturated load. Although he was not too sure about the efficiency of his living roof, he was confident it would take a huge storm to prove him wrong.

The house's entryway was as high as Hina was tall, and two persons wide. The approach to the entry featured a large, semicircular terrace that extended from one end of the house to the other. The terrace was covered with highly polished, flat basaltic stones that were pleasant and cool to bare feet. Joints between the stones were filled with a thin green groundcover that Kon had patiently transplanted from the surrounding nooks and crannies. Overall, the house looked like the upside-down hull of a huge outrigger, which pleased Hina. The building's interior space was divided into several functional areas. The narrow, cramped ends were difficult to reach, and were used to store their infrequently used belongings. The adjacent areas were used to store food and frequently used tools. Several calabashes filled with drinking water hung from the ceiling next to Kon's tools. The family and guest sleeping areas flanked the large center area that they used for gatherings of up to eight people.

Kon's design included a series of narrow canals dug into volcanic slabs, assembled all around the base of the roof, and more buried across the terrace, that channeled precious rainwater into a little pond he had carved in the volcanic rock. The family often bathed in the pond. Overflow from the pond was used to water two concentric rows of taro plants that grew throughout the year.

It was their first night in their new house. Maui slept peacefully on a bed of woven totora covered with several layers of the precious tapa cloth. Outside, a fierce, blustery wind and a steady downpour since early afternoon had been testing Kon's design to the limits. Kon and Hina sat together and reflected on their new home.

"So far, the roof seems to work," Kon said.

"I never had a doubt," Hina replied, kissing him. "You are the silent perfectionist of this island."

"It is not perfect, but it is considerably less depressing than the deep, dank caves that we have been living in."

"I like the deep, dark caves," Hina argued. "They are the ultimate shelters. They make me feel closer to Mother Nature."

"But you do like to watch the sea waves' assaults on the lava cliffs."

"Yes, I do! So now I have everything."

Kon went to the entry and placed several layers of woven totora reeds over the entryway, sealing it off from the cold wind. Now they were in total isolation and could barely hear the surf's roar and the wind's mournful drone.

"'It is so quiet!" Hina said. "I like it."

Kon lay near her naked body, rolled her into his arms, and gently caressed her lower back.

"This feels really good," she said, slowly falling asleep.

"Have sweet dreams, my queen…"

Kon enjoyed his new life. It had been his dream since childhood to forget conflicts, wars, murders, warriors, and unprincipled people. He rejoiced that he had finally realized his dream. On this isolated island, Kon was the quiet man, happy, always exploring new challenges, and was an incredible architect. Tamatoa the Great was passionate about Kon's new ideas and often sought his counsel. Hina and Kama often studied them from a distance and enjoyed commenting on their friendship. It was a life during which they had plenty of time to think about the inner nature of who they really were. They had attained serenity and were capable of being positive role models to the new generation. In a deep philosophic way, they were living for challenges that transcended the daily quarrels of ordinary men and women.

At dawn the rain had stopped. Kon went outside to check the condition of the roof. The thick layer of green grass had performed as expected. Hina checked for leaks inside and found very few; the causes were quickly found and eliminated. Outside, the little pond was full and overflowed into the taro plantation. They walked toward the hills, a short distance from where they had planted many banana trees protected by circular walls made of volcanic boulders. They bathed in their favorite pond and watched the low, thick clouds that clearly foretold more rain later in the day. Hina carried Maui in a back bag that Kama had woven for her. She found the design most convenient, since carrying Maui on her chest was painful when her breasts were full of milk. They walked farther up into the hills, following a collapsed lava tube that was used to grow several kinds of sweet potatoes, gourds, yams, many kinds of grass, and sugar cane. The lava tube ended farther up the hill. Farther up, a plateau, inside what was left of an old crater, collected a large volume of water during heavy rains and channeled it into known and unknown lava tubes. This was the settlement's main source of water. The plateau was covered with a fertile, rich soil that supported virtually every agrarian endeavor. Obtaining food near the sea was never a problem. A few chickens followed Kon and Hina on their walk, with a commanding rooster leading the flock. Kon went to a large circular stone pen that he had made to hold several pigs he would get later from a friend in Anakena. Ginger tubers grew in abundance throughout the plateau and provided an ample food source for the pigs. While Kon rolled a few stones into place, Hina sat on one stone and breastfed her son.

Later that morning, they went to the summit of a small peak on the west side of the plateau, where Kon had earlier discovered a small outcropping of the precious obsidian. They stayed there until the afternoon, when a sudden cold wind whipped a fine mist into a numbing fury. They hurried to their settlement, knowing that a strong rain would descend soon. They found Kukara busy with her Rongo-Rongo tablets. The young girl always wandered around the island in unpredictable ways. Sometimes for a few days, she would happily stay with her adoptive parents, who let her have her ways. Kukara truly enjoyed her total freedom, yet she helped them in every way she could; she was easygoing.

In their house they sat near the open door and watched the bad weather outside. That evening Kon Tici Viracocha had been upgraded to be their cook, much to his delight. It pleased him to let Hina and Kukara relax and talk together. The relationship between the two women was immensely enriching. Kukara did not talk much with people around the island, but she knew exactly what was going on everywhere and was happy to tell Hina everything she saw. It was a mutually beneficial and informative alliance.

The spirit of the turtle going back to Hiva or Havaiki, the sacred land of the Great Ancestors, was a yearly event, when young turtles struggled to evade the seabirds at Anakena and Ovahe to reach the Awesome Sea just in time.

CHAPTER 22

"I did not return to the islets for the entire winter, ever since Maui's birth. On the morning that I returned, I felt excited, like a young girl on her way to play with her friends. I wanted new adventures in my life, and I knew that this would be the day when something of great significance would take place. A day with a challenge was my definition of a good day: I was ready."

Hina of the Valley

Four moon cycles later, at the end of the Rapa Nui winter, Kon's house had proven its worthiness by protecting his family and frequent guests throughout the season's wind, rain, and chill. The house was admired by everyone. Tamatoa, Taatamao, and several other high-ranking islanders paid him the ultimate compliment by building their own houses based on Kon's design. It was a sunny morning when the complete Sacred Circle of the Seven Souls gathered at Kon and Hina's settlement for a two-day meeting. Today nannies kept the babies, permitting the Seven Souls to go swimming and fishing at Hina's favorite islets. Tamatoa brought Hina a wonderful gift on his huge double-hulled vessel. Hina watched Tamatoa's ship as he maneuvered it closer to the shore and offloaded a sleek, beautifully crafted two-person outrigger. He beckoned for Hina to inspect it. It would be perfect for her; she could leave it in a little cove at the base of the cliff, just a short distance from the house and the islets. She would teach her child to respect and enjoy the Awesome Sea as much as she did.

Kon, helped by several men, had carved a narrow ledge in the lava from the top of the cliff all the way down to the tiny beach in the cove. Like the larger Ovahe beach, it was covered with pink sand and rocks, eroded over the years from the surrounding pink lava. He had anchored posts along the steeply inclined ledge and joined them together with a safety rope, making access to the cove safe and easy for everyone. On that morning, the Seven Souls used the path to go down to the sea and prepare for their swimming, diving, and fishing expedition. The sea was calm; no waves splashed on the rugged lava coast. Hina pulled her outrigger to the water and sat in it. Kon joined her and admired the craftsmanship. Kukara sat on one of the arms of the outrigger, and they paddled to the islet and admired its purple coral formations, which blossomed in the crystal clear water. They also joked, teased, and laughed at each other along the way. The sun warmed their brown skin, which they had earlier protected with a mixture of rare oils. A narrow platform made of woven totora reeds that spanned the two outrigger arms provided a convenient place for Hina to store her fishing traps. Always the practical person, she never went to the islets without them. This time Hina brought two long, finger-thick ropes.

"What are those for?" Kon asked for the third time since leaving the settlement.

"You will see, in due time!" Hina replied.

"When Mother plays with long ropes," Kukara joked, referring to her daring adventure in unknown caves in Tahiti Nui, "I usually get worried."

"I know!" Kon replied. "That is why I have asked."

"But you taught me how they can save lives," Hina chuckled. "Don't you remember going up Mount Orohena?"

"Yes, I know that too!" Kon said, laughing. He knew Hina had probably planned for this day during the winter months. She was up to something, and was savoring the air of mystery her silence created.

Tamatoa anchored his ship close to the main islet, on the protected side facing the island. Hina moored her little outrigger to it. Then the entire group dove into the water and swam through a deep, narrow passage that led to an unusually large pool inside the islet. It was as though Mother Nature had created this sea life preserve for the islanders' personal enjoyment. Hundreds of species cohabited, thrived, and evolved in this peaceful, relatively protected environment. On calm days, the pool was a paradise for the Seven Souls. However, on windy days, the pool's dark side turned the idyllic haven into a horrific nightmare for even the most skilled mariners. Strong, unpredictable currents and spontaneously formed maelstroms, large and powerful enough to shred and suck a two-person outrigger into the deep lava tubes crisscrossing the pool's floor, were things for adventuring swimmers to be careful of.

"There are deep caves on the far side," Hina said, "but I have never ventured into them alone. Today I would like to do that."

"So that is what you are up to!" Kon said.

Taatamao took a deep breath and dove into the deep blue waters over the abyss. Hina followed him. The others swam peacefully around the pool, relaxing in the shallow landward areas. Taatamao stopped to inspect the narrow entrance to a lava tube. Hina pulled his hand and pointed at two other, much deeper entrances. They both dove deeper to a very dark opening, a secret door leading to ancient, hidden mysteries perhaps. Taatamao took two sea urchins, twice the size of his fists. Hina grabbed three more, then swam slowly back to the surface.

"I love sea urchins," Kama said, as Hina broke the surface holding her prizes.

"I call them vanas," Hina replied, "in memory of my friend and mentor Vana, who taught me how and where to find these big fellows on Tahiti Nui. They are common around Ovahe." They placed the urchins into a basket that hung inside a tiny tidal pool.

"The first lava tube where you stopped," Hina said, "goes nowhere. I went inside that one, and it is a dead end filled with crumbling rocks. It is a good place for congers and lobsters. But I am intrigued by the two farther below, where we picked the sea urchins."

"Is that why you took these long ropes?" Kon asked, amused at Hina's adventurous mind. In this respect, she had not changed since she was a young girl.

"We will go one at a time," Hina said to Taatamao, who was the next-most-skilled diver on the island. She liked diving with him because of his expert skills. "Tamatoa will hold this rope and sit there. You will take this second rope and dive down to the cave entrance. Then once you get here, you will tie the two ropes together. You wait at the cave entrance holding both ropes. I will swim by you and take the end of the second rope and dive into the lava tube. If I pull once on the rope, everything is fine. Once I get there, I will give a single tug if everything is fine or two tugs if the rope is too short. Tamatoa then will release his end, which in effect will double the rope's length for me. If I pull three times, pull me out of there. In the unlikely event that you pull the ropes up and I am not there, don't worry; I could have reached a room where I can stand and breathe…I hope!"

"You are crazy!" Kama said. "Why are you doing this?"

"Because it is there!" Hina replied, smiling.

"I will go first to clear the way," Taatamao insisted.

"Do you remember the sequence?" Hina asked.

Taatamao repeated the sequence.

I will wait for you at the entrance," Hina stated.

They both dove at the same time and headed into the unknown for another adventure.

"I don't like it when they do this," Mahine said. "None of us have the skills to save them if they get into trouble."

"They are the best, and they are the most obstinate," Kon replied. "Nothing or no one can stop them. With all of us here knowing their plan, it will be a lot safer, I hope."

"I don't think so," Tamatoa replied. "Where they go, none of us will be able to help them. Mahine is right. We can only pull on the rope. That is not much, if you want my opinion."

Hina let Taatamao enter the unknown. She held the rope and waited for signals. She lightly held the ropes so that the others, far up on the surface, could also feel his signals. She felt one pull. Everything was fine. She felt two pulls. They released the first rope. Hina felt half the second rope go between her fingers.

"He is at his limit," she thought.

Shortly after, she felt three pulls. She pulled on the rope. Responding to the prearranged signal for extraction, they all pulled on the rope. As Taatamao was dragged up from the lava tube, Hina helped him to the surface by blowing a few air bubbles in his mouth. When they finally broke the surface, it was clear that Taatamao had exceeded his limits. They took him to the shore, where they placed him on a flat ledge, slightly above the water line. Mahine gently massaged his back and neck and then let him regain his breath.

"You did not have to go that far," Hina said. "What did you find?"

"For one thing, there are many lobsters in there, just before you reach the end of the first rope. Then after that, it gets very dark. The room is large and you can swim up, but I never could break the surface. It also goes deeper, but I did not attempt to go that way; it was too much for me. It is too much for you as well."

"I shall find out for myself," Hina replied, more determined than ever. "Tie this cloth around my eyes, so I can get accustomed to the darkness before I dive."

Kukara complied by wrapping several layers of cloth around her eyes.

"I will remove it only when I get to the main entrance," Hina explained.

She waited for a long time, until she thought she could discern a few details in the fabric. Hina had been diving deeply into dark abysses since she was a child. She had been taught by priests about the secrets of maintaining good vision, both in water and at night. She went through the necessary preparation ritual, for her eyes, for her lungs, and mainly for her mind. Taatamao had opened the way. She knew she could easily swim directly to the cave where he had gone. Then, the unknown would be hers.

"I will wait for you at the exit of the main entrance," Taatamao said.

"I disagree," Tamatoa said with a roaring voice. "If Hina gets into trouble, you will too. Then none of us can help either of you at that depth."

"He is right!" Kon said. "The ropes are not good enough."

"I agree as well," Hina replied, dismayed.

"I have a better idea!" Kukara said. "Attach both ropes together now, which will save time for Hina. Then let Taatamao dive only when Hina gets to the end of both ropes. He will hold the end of the rope from the main entrance long enough after Hina starts her dive so he can stay to help her if necessary."

"You are a genius," Hina replied with approval.

"Good luck, my friend!" Taatamao said, worried.

Hina went down like a falling rock. She removed the cloth around her eyes as she entered the main entrance at full speed and stared at the head of a huge conger baring its razor-sharp its teeth. She glanced around and saw large lobsters. Finding a conger eel and lobsters together was not a surprise to her. She knew congers kept lobsters like cattle; they would maneuver a lobster into a hole and then feed the lobster until it was too big to escape from the hole. Then, when the conger became hungry and the lobster shed its shell, it would enjoy its long-awaited favorite meal. Otherwise, these powerful crawling killers were scavengers most of the time, occasionally preying on wounded fish. Hina entered a large room and looked around. She stopped and pulled once on the rope: Taatamao pulled once and dove. Hina continued her exploration. In the far distance, she saw dim light. Before going to investigate the source of the light, she decided to see if there was an air pocket at the cave's ceiling. If there was, she could recharge her lungs and continue checking the light. She reached the ceiling and felt its rough surface, but found no air pocket. She swam back down, until she could see the dim light again. Her only explanation was that the light came from an opening beyond the islet. She quickly reached the extent of both ropes. She had a choice, to pull three times and be pulled back to the surface or to risk her life by going to the light and, hopefully, air. She pulled once on the rope and dropped it, trusting her fate to mana. On her way to the light, she saw the silhouette of a familiar predator as a large shark swam by. Instinctively, she reached for the obsidian knife she kept in her belt. She did not fear sharks and knew the behavior of the species that inhabited this islet very well. It was only a reflexive action. She swam as fast as she could toward the light, knowing that she was pushing her limits; she had no time to spare.

Taatamao reached his limit and pulled on the rope three times. He then realized Hina was not pulling; she had abandoned the rope. Forced to go up, he reached the surface very concerned and agitated.

"Where is she?" Kon asked.

"I don't know! She apparently dropped the rope and swam deeper into the lava tube. I could not hold out any longer."

They all looked at each other. Tamatoa dove into the water and attempted to reach the main entrance and failed. Mahine attempted and failed. Taatamao went down again and was able to enter the cave and locate the rope. He followed it for a short distance but ran out of breath and had to ascend.

"She must be trapped farther back in the cave or may have found an exit!" Taatamao offered.

They all left the large pond and climbed the islet, looking for a better view.

"She should be at the surface by now, or perhaps she found a room with air pockets," Kon said.

"There should be no such thing before the main island, which is way beyond what she can do," Kama argued.

"Trust my mother," Kukara said in a soothingly calm voice. "She is very resourceful and a skilled swimmer."

Deep under them Hina struggled with very little remaining oxygen. She concentrated, focusing her mind on gathering mana's powers. Time slowed, and she felt a pervasive sense of peace fill her body; her analytical side sounded a warning that she might be hallucinating, with dangerous consequences. She shook the reverie, more confident and stronger than ever. But she was running out of air, with virtually no reserves left. The tunnel started to slope upward; she could tell by the light's increased luminescence that she was nearing the surface. Her lungs ached, her body was cut and bruised from the rough rock walls, and she was close to passing out, but she made three powerful strokes and burst through the surface on the far side of the islet. She was amazed at the distance she had covered. She saw her companions looking at her and limply waved.

"I am fine," she gasped, pulling huge breaths of air into her oxygen-starved lungs.

"See, I told you!" Kukara said to the group. "But I have to admit I am considerably relieved now."

Tamatoa reached for Hina's hand and helped her out of the water. "You did something you should not have done."

"I am sorry, but I could not resist the urge to explore further when I saw the light deeper in the cave. This place is incredible, but rest assured, I have no desire to return. From now on, I will stick to the pond where I have been many times."

"I certainly hope so!" Kon said, a little irritated. "Anyway, today you broke your record. I don't know of anyone capable of staying under water that long."

Kama gave Hina half of the big urchin that she was eating: "It will energize you."

"I don't think she needs to be energized," Taatamao commented, with a smile on his face.

"Shall we get some lobsters for tonight?" Hina asked, her mouth full of delicious sea urchin.

Kukara glanced at Kon and Kama, who were rolling their eyes.

Hina went to get one fishing trap on her outrigger and came

back to the pond.

"Do you want me to get the other?" Tamatoa asked.

"Yes, I need both."

They attached one rope to each trap and tied a wooden float to the opposite end to make it easier to recover the traps the next morning. Hina put some sliced fish into each trap. Then she dove into the water and placed one trap at the mouth of the tube where she had seen the big conger. She placed the other trap in the shallower water where she usually caught the large-eyed red mauros. They dove and caught a few lobsters and played until the midday breezes started to churn the water. They chatted amicably about the day's adventures as they headed back to land. During the rest of the afternoon, Tamatoa and Taatamao helped Kon build a chicken house made from large volcanic rocks.

"I don't think the roosters will bother you in the middle of the night anymore with a wall like this," Tamatoa joked.

"The problem is training them to go in there in the evening," Kon replied.

"I can do that!" Kukara said, listening from a distance. "They obey me quite well."

On the terrace, close to the boat house, the women were busily preparing the evening meal and sharing stories. Although they often met, just a few days' separation could result in a plethora of gossip and news. It was easy to become lonely on the island, and these reunions were cherished. On that night the conversation turned to the statue being carved at Rano Raraku. This would be their second moai, and it would be the reincarnation of the great Hotu-Matua. The moai was larger than its predecessor, particularly at the base, since this would be Kukara's first attempt to transport a moai upright. The men listened attentively to their conversation.

"It cannot be done that way," Tamatoa argued. "You make things unnecessarily complicated."

"Then how would you do it?" Hina inquired.

"By rolling the moai on large palm tree trunks," Tamatoa replied.

Kama had a sad look on her face. "How many do you need to cut for a single project?"

Tamatoa showed his five fingers.

"Do you know how long it takes to grow a palm tree?" Kama asked rhetorically. "It takes a lifetime. They don't grow nearly as fast as coconut trees."

"Coconut tree trunks would be useless for the giant stone," Kon added. "They would be crushed to fibers."

Hina stood and raised her arms toward the sky.

"I can stop the argument right here," she remonstrated. "As long as I am the queen, we shall not cut our valuable palm trees unless absolutely necessary for the common good. We will not cut palm trees to transport moais! We can live without moais. If we must build moais, let's keep it challenging, let's keep it fun."

Hina could not know…, could she? That the descendants of this group would one day desecrate her will and, on a day in the future, would kill the last remaining palm tree. Hina's intuition was again proven, albeit too late. However, she knew that her mana intrinsically demanded that she do her best to protect Mother Nature's many blessings on this little island.

"This brings me to another subject," Hina said, sitting down. "How many seabird eggs do we destroy every day?"

"Way too many," Kon replied.

"So we should raise more chickens!" Mahine suggested.

"That would be an excellent solution," Hina replied. "However, I don't want to create a controversy on such a nice evening. But it is something we should think about and promulgate appropriate rules to protect wild birds."

"Personally," Tamatoa commented," I have felt for some time that I overharvested the Rarotonga forest when I built my war fleet. Mato, the old priest, warned me of this, and I ignored his admonishments. Today when I think about it, I know he was right. He was a wise man. Hina is correct; let's use the wisdom of the Sacred Circle of the Seven Souls and avoid repeating our mistakes."

"However, there is a risk to all this," Kon said. "The population of this island will increase rapidly, making today's friendly discussions become tomorrow's violent confrontations."

"That is an excellent reason why we must act now," Hina replied. "We must establish intelligent, sustainable rules to guide our conduct on this island; to protect our resources and prolong our enjoyment of this wonderful place."

"But how are you going to enforce these rules?" Tamatoa asked, placing his hand on her shoulder.

"You have to say one word," Hina joked, "and everybody leaves the island!"

They all laughed, remembering the old days of Tamatoa's powerful war machine and authoritarian rules.

"It works," Tamatoa said, "but we can do a lot better than that. I agree with Hina; I have often rued my actions at the time. I was a sick man."

"But extremely well organized," Taatamao, one of his former commanders, added.

"I know how to do this," Kon suggested. "Self-discipline has always been a big issue for the Viracochas. We must create incentives for people to apply self-restraint. It is easier said than done, but I believe it is possible."

"We can do that among ourselves, in our enlightened circle," Taatamao said, "but I doubt that the ordinary people will readily subscribe to our rules, regardless of how well-intentioned they are."

"I strongly disagree!" Kon argued. "Let's educate them. Hina can tell them about your people's wonderful legends. They like to hear them. Hina knows that all the way back to her childhood. She can shorten the great legend narratives into short parables that will interest the people and remain memorable. Also, the ordinary people like the mysteries behind these legends."

"We are already doing this," Hina said. "But we can create more. Kukara's Rongo-Rongo tablets are a powerful way to do it, and they will provide a permanent record that can be passed from generation to generation."

Kukara opened her eyes wider and flushed red with pleasure. "I will give them a legend from the Rongo-Rongo tablet as they wait for the spectacular Hotu-Matua's release from the mountain."

"Can you tell us which legend you want to use?" Hina asked.

"No, but it will be a montage of Viracochan and Maohi legends; I need to work on it. Make Make will help me."

Kukara came to Hina and touched her cheek gently. "Mother, may I tattoo this cheek for you?"

Hina took her hand, defensively. "Absolutely not!"

"You are the powerful queen and priestess. I want to draw our god Make Make on your cheek. This alone will bring discipline to the people, I assure you."

Hina stared at the young woman and then glanced at her companions. "What do you think?"

"Well, if you look at me, the tattooed giant," Tamatoa joked, "I think the people would respect and love the result."

"Kukara can draw it first to see if the Sacred Circle of the Seven Souls likes it," Hina said. "Then it should be removed until we conduct a special ceremony with all our people in attendance. We will then, and only then, enumerate the rules and taboos that will guide their lives."

"Only the queen should be allowed to be tattooed with Make Make's face," Kon suggested.

"I have other ideas for the rest of you and me, all of us except for Tamatoa," Kukara said, looking at the giant.

"And why is that?" Tamatoa asked.

"Because there is no place left anywhere on your body!" Kama replied, laughing loudly.

They all burst into laughter, led by Tamatoa, enjoying being the joke's target.

"I noticed you coughed many times today," Hina said to Tamatoa. "How long have you been doing this?"

Kama answered for Tamatoa, saying, "He had a cold a half moon cycle ago, but he has not been able to rid himself of the cough."

"I know something that may help him. Kukara, Mahine, and Kama, come with me. I will teach you this old recipe from my ancestors in Tahiti Nui."

They walked under a bright full moon toward the hills and Hina's favorite pool. Near the pool, Hina pointed to a small glossy nightshade shrub.

"That shrub was grown from seeds that I brought from my homeland. We call it popolo."

She collected a few leaves and many of its tiny black berries. Then she went to another shrub, a mulberry, and collected some young leaves. They went back to the house, where Hina picked up a little bag full of seaweed.

"This is what you use for colds," Hina said, pointing at Kama. "I will mix a little of that with my mixture."

She pounded everything into a pulp in a basaltic bowl. The liquid was then squeezed, strained, and placed into a calabash. Hina then warmed the mixture by placing three small, red-hot basalt stones into the calabash. After the liquid cooled, she placed it in a coconut cup and took it to Tamatoa.

"You drink half of this now and the other half in the morning. Then we will repeat this for five days. After that, you will be cured."

****

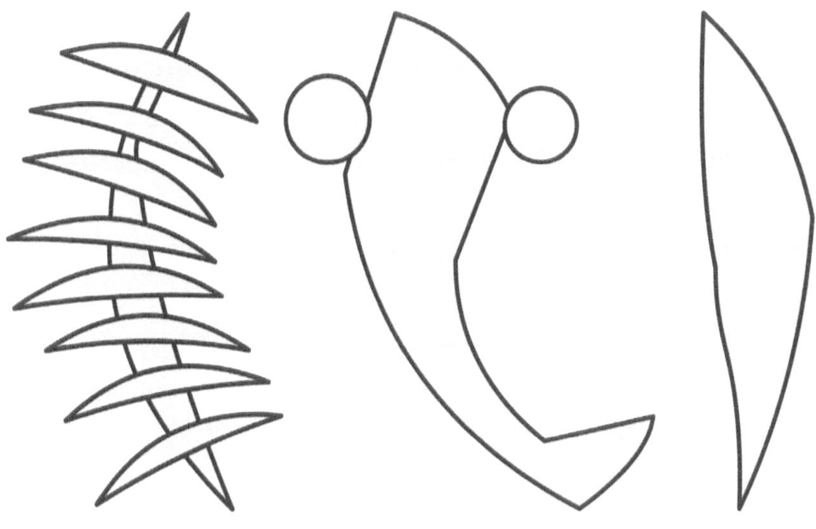

The first woman and her immortal spirit were given by the Great Ancestor, so the earth would recognize one day that woman would have the sacred knowledge of perpetuating life.

CHAPTER 23

"Until this day, the powerful Make Make god was manifest in nature as a flight of frigate birds, its symbol carved on rocks by Kukara and her friends, or held in the people's imagination. Now this potent symbol would be on the most powerful ruler's face. From this day forward, Hina of the Valley would personify the strength of Make Make, a power that no one would ever dare to challenge. Hina of the Valley would never be the same again: she would enter Rapa Nui's legend. From now on, she would become one with Make Make."

Kon Tici Viracocha

The next morning the Circle went to retrieve Hina's fishing traps. The first trap held dozens of red mauros. In the other trap they found the huge conger that Hina had seen the day earlier and three lobsters. The tiny red mauros she loved so much excited Hina.

"We should build some traps like Hina's," Tamatoa told Taatamao, while killing the conger by choking it between his awesome fingers. "These are quite effective."

They placed the mauros and lobsters in storage pools near the shore.

"Half a moon cycle from now, we will proceed with the

tattooing ceremony at the Hanga Roa Ahu," Hina said, before her friends left Ovahe. "Pass the word around the island."

****

Using charcoal, Kukara drew the Make Make glyph on Hina's right cheek. Kon, the only observer of this event, was impressed with Kukara's speed and precision; clearly, she had practiced for a long time.

"By all the spirits in the world, this is absolutely remarkable!" he said.

The drawing seemed alive and in harmony with Hina's face, adding to her natural beauty.

"I want to see it!" Hina said, curious to see how it turned out.

"Patience, Mother, I am not finished."

Make Make's eye was close to Hina's right eye. The top of its head was above her eye, and the beak reached to the top of her forehead. The back and wings followed the natural contours of her cheek, and its long tail reached far down her neck and ended on her muscular shoulder. The design was simple, narrow, and elegant, and gave her face surreal grace. Hina went to the pool and looked at her reflection in the quiet water.

"Oh Taaroa!... What has she done?" she asked the supreme God of her childhood. "This drawing gives me chills up my spine. I already feel mana's power in it. Would the tattoo be as good as this?"

"It will be better, Mother. This is nothing!"

"How could it be?"

Kukara took a wet cloth and erased her drawing.

"Because, Mother, I will make the tattoo ink from the ashes of the sacred Mokohe bird's egg; thus Make Make's mana shall live in you."

Hina looked at her face in the water again, reflecting on Kukara's words. With the drawing gone, she thought her face looked dull. More than ever, she knew the Light inspired Kukara Tici Viracocha in everything she did.

"It is the difference between a dullard and an enlightened master!" Hina exclaimed. "I will never be the same again."

"You will be the same again," Kukara said, "if you let people look at the other side of your face."

"Oh yes! I forgot. I like that…"

"Me too," Kon added sadly. He liked Hina just the way she was.

The next few days they went to Taatamao and Mahine's settlement, and then they went to Orongo to show the drawing to other members of the Sacred Circle of the Seven Souls. They all agreed on the design and affirmed Kukara's genius at Rongo-RongoRongo-Rongo symbolism.

"Could we carve the same design on the right cheek of Hotu-Matua's moai?" Kon asked.

They all looked at each other.

"Yes!" they exclaimed in unison.

"This is going to be very interesting," Hina concluded. "Hotu-Matua's name is going to remain a part of this island's legends much longer than we ever thought possible."

"I know," Kukara said, as she had thought about this for a long time. "I loved him so much! For the many years before I was reunited with you, he was like a father. After that, until his last day on Rapa Nui, he became my best friend. He always said I was the daughter he always wanted. He had seven sons that he loved, but they never cared about him. Many times he asked me to be the one who would close his eyes after he left his temporal body and flew away to join the gods. When we erect his moai at Rano

Raraku, all will behold the powerful visage of a god possessed by mana."

**************______

On the morning of the full moon day, Tamatoa, Kama, Kon, and Taatamao swam to Motu Iti islet in search of a sacred egg from the Mokohe bird, the sacred frigate. Kon was the first one to find one, and thereby earned the honor of bringing it to Hina, at Orongo. Kukara ordained that the egg must not be broken, or Make Make's mana would escape. Before leaving the islet, Kama securely wrapped the egg in a cloth and then wrapped the cloth around Kon's forehead. They escorted him to shore and assisted him, when necessary, to climb the dangerous cliff. It was early in the afternoon when they reached the little fire Kukara, Hina, and Mahine had prepared at Orongo's summit. The egg was roasted very slowly in embers of the sacred sandalwood tree that had been brought to Rapa Nui by Hotu-Matua, who enjoyed its powerful scent. Kukara made sure the sandalwood she used had been in Hotu-Matua's hands many times, so some of the wood was him. The egg and sandalwood ashes were placed into a little bag that Kukara secured to her forehead with the same cloth Kon had used to transport the egg earlier that day. They departed to Hanga Roa Ahu for the long-awaited evening ceremony.

****

Before sunset, Kukara mixed a small amount of oil extracted from little nuts found on the island with the ashes. Then she mixed a dab of the mixture with an equal part of water in a coconut shell. She took the usual shark tooth tool. Hina lay on the ground with the right side of her face up. All Rapa Nui settlers watched reverently, sitting on their respective stones. The drums started a slow, deep beat, while Kukara carefully dipped the end of the shark tooth into the black mixture. She confidently pricked Hina's face with quick, sharp blows, striking the handle of the shark tooth implement with a small stick. She continued the tapping until the skin started to bleed. Then she dipped the shark tooth in the black mixture again and repeated the painful process at another place. Hina's eyes started to well up because of the pain. Kon placed a cloth in her mouth to help her. Holding tightly to Kon's hand, she sought refuge from the pain in her mana. She chose to concentrate on what she would say to the audience after the ceremony was completed. Under Kukara's skillful hands, Make Make slowly formed on Hina's face. The sign was elegant, simple, and yet carried mana's powers. The impression it made on the people watching validated mana's awesome power. One by one, audience members filed by the queen to admire the progress of what would become the symbol of ultimate power. Shortly after, the most serendipitous event occurred.

Kukara made the last prick on Hina's face and said, "You can sit up now, Mother."

As the young girl closed her eyes and raised her arms toward the setting sun and invoked mana's power, a sacred frigate flew over the crowd and made several low passes. Then to everyone's amazement, the bird glided to and landed on Hina's right shoulder and inspected the tattoo. The crowd was hushed in reverent awe of this most sacred event: a divine coronation that confirmed Hina's role as the earthly representative of their supreme god, Make Make. Hina felt mana surge and flow throughout her body, while imparting a sublime humility and sense of peace.

As the sun touched the horizon, the frigate took off and flew toward the steep cliffs of Orongo. Hina's pain was replaced by a warm tingling. She walked toward the crowd, stopped at the edge of the ahu platform, and turned sideways to show the right side of her face to everyone. They all stood. A powerful chant of "Hina, Make Make" resounded throughout the island and rolled far out to sea, calling on everyone and everything to witness Hina as Make Make's surrogate.

When the sun vanished below the horizon, a brilliant, supernatural flash bathed the Circle on the ahu in a bright emerald green light. The crowd fell to their knees in silent wonderment. The members of the Sacred Circle of the Seven Souls lit oil torches around the queen; she was ready to give her words.

"People of Rapa Nui, today your queen evolved into a new person, as you have witnessed. You know me well. I am your queen. And, I am your friend. And, I am an ordinary woman. Despite my rank, as a person I have always been humble about who I am."

She was silent for a moment and motioned to the drummers; the drums started the slow roll that commanded the people to listen. Only the waves of the Awesome Sea breaking on the lava coast behind the ahu could be heard. Rapa Nui was listening.

"When I address you with the right side of my face facing you and with my hair standing tall above my head, as you see now, you must listen to what I say. You must listen and you must remember exactly what I tell you."

She pointed to the gold pin holding her hair tight above her head and said, "This is the gold pin I was given by the Viracochas. You can see it from far away; you will be reminded that I am your queen, the representative of Make Make."

The Make Make symbol on her face created a new persona that projected a melding of beauty, mystery, authority, and self-confidence that intimidated her subjects.

She removed the gold pin and shook her hair. It partially

obscured the Make Make tattoo as it cascaded gracefully over her shoulders and flowed softly to her waist. Then she turned the left side of her face toward the crowd.

"Now I am your friend, and the ordinary woman who lives and loves as you do."

It was magic. No one could resist her magnetism. They all crowded close to her, joking, talking, and treating her as their friend, just another ordinary woman, much to the surprise of the Sacred Circle of the Seven Souls.

"This is Hina!" Kon said. "She has always been this way."

"This is Hina!" Tamatoa, the great warrior, repeated. "It makes her greater yet, and in a way that would humble any king or great priest."

The drums rumbled again, commanding everyone to go back to their respective stones. The drums rumbled louder, commanding total silence. Hina took her hair and raised it above her head with the gold pin. She wiped away a few tears that flowed down her cheeks in response to the immense joy her people had given her. Then she slowly turned the right side of her still-bleeding face to the audience.

"These will be my last words for the night. I am going to recite a legend that our great god Taaroa gave me a long time ago, when I was a little girl. Later on, a similar legend was given to me by the great Viracocha. Today I will combine these legends for you. From this day forward, this will become Make Make's legend about how this world was created."

The crowd, especially the children, became quiet and waited with rapt anticipation.

"A long time ago, there was no land, no sea, no sky, no clouds, no rain, no air, no men, and no women. There was no world as we know it. Everything was hidden in total darkness and surrounded by absolute silence. It was boring, since there was nothing to see, nothing to touch, nothing to taste, nothing to enjoy, and nothing to love. The Light was everywhere, but it did not know what to do with all its energy."

Kukara quietly walked over to Hina and dabbed a few drops of blood from her face, before they dripped onto her white garment.

"Then, faintly at first, the Light vibrated into other forms. The abysses of darkness vibrated so much that stars were created. The sun was created, then the earth, then the moon. Suddenly, the Light was visible everywhere."

She wiped a few drops of blood from her face with the cloth Kukara had previously left. Her people intensely respected their queen for attempting to speak while she was in such terrible pain.

Hina continued. "The Awesome Sea was created, then the fish. Islands drifted on the sea. Clouds gave the rain, and fish found their way to dry land for the first time. Finally, birds were created, flying from island to island, bringing life everywhere. Make Make was created from pure energy. Make Make was the first man, yet he was still a bird in many ways."

"A white tropicbird landed on Make Make's right shoulder. 'Kuihi-Kuaha,' the tropicbird said. Make Make immediately recognized the sacred words from the Light. Something was expected from him. He listened to his subconscious, knowing that the message would come from far inside hidden areas in his mind. He made a ball from wet dirt, poked a hole in its middle, and blew into the hole until something came out. Initially, it resembled a little cloud. Then after a while, a young man took shape. Disappointed to see a sibling, Make Make sent the young man back into the ball of dirt."

"After deep meditation near the seashore, Make Make looked

for a fresh banana tree shoot. He pulled the young man from inside the dirt ball, cut open his heart, and let the blood flow inside a cut he had made in the banana tree's shoot. Several times he blew on the blood that ran onto the banana tree shoot. This time, the result was spectacular. A young woman was formed. Make Make admired her beauty and her gentleness. 'My name is Uka,' she said. 'I was sent by the Light to be your companion in this new world'."

Hina of the Valley paused, and for the last time wiped the blood oozing from her face. Someone brought a tiny banana shoot to her that had just broken the surface of the earth a few days earlier. She carefully wiped a few drops of her blood into a cut that had been made on the side of the shoot. The shoot was immediately planted in a well-protected area near the ahu. Hina smiled at the unpredicted interruption.

"People of Rapa Nui, always remember this legend. It does not matter who will repeat it to you, perhaps in different words. The details are made by people; the message is made by our god. The deep message will be the same unalterable, profound, and eternal truth. Nothing will ever challenge the ultimate truth, the ultimate power of the Light. Our perceptions are created by people and are inherently weak, but our faith in the Light is mana at its best."

****

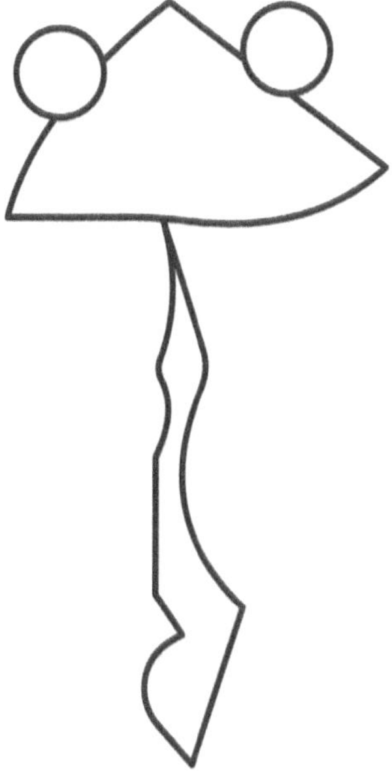

Long before birth the child already has great knowledge given to him by the universal consciousness. Therefore, even at this stage, life is sacred.

CHAPTER 24

*"My best friend once said, 'For the few days I have left
to live in this world, I would enjoy sitting under a coconut
tree at Anakena beach and watching beautiful women bathing
in happiness with their mates, children, and friends. You see,
my child, all my sons are gone and I never had the daughter I
wanted so much. Then I found you, my little one from another
world. When I die, please come to me and close my eyes. It has
been a privilege to walk and talk with you. I know who you
are, and I know I will see you again in the world of spirits,
where you travel so easily.' He was a friend. He was like a
father. He was fun and knowledgeable. I loved him dearly. I
miss him tremendously."*

Kukara Tici Viracocha

The new moai was completed. It was still attached to the
mountain by a narrow keel. Already a few holes had been cut to
weaken the keel. It was heavier than the one carved for Taranga
Tici Viracocha, mainly because of the large convex base that
Kukara had specified to facilitate its transportation.

Kon and Tamatoa showed her the huge hewn base. As
she ran her long, thin fingers along the smooth volcanic rock,
she felt the moai's magic flow into her fingers. As the carving
progressed, mana flowed between the workers and the moai,

each strengthening and giving life to the huge sculpture. It was no longer the cold wall of the mountain; it was as alive as anyone. Kukara carefully studied the base, noting that it looked like a curved shield about twice the diameter of the moai. It wrapped around the sides and front of the moai, but not the back, since it needed to be slid down the hill.

"After it is released," Kon said," it will slide on its own, like Taranga's, to be stopped by that mound of dirt behind the trench. At this point, it will stand vertically on its base. It is carved in such a way that it will stand on its own. Then you will see this platform much farther away. This is where you and Kukara must bring it… if you can!"

"I still believe it cannot be done," Tamatoa said. "It would be a lot easier to use big palm tree trunks."

"What did you say?" Hina asked, from a short distance away.

"It is just a comment," Tamatoa replied.

"I certainly hope so," Hina said with a smile on her face. "Kukara, this is your project, and the Rapa Nui people are here watching what you are going to do. I would like for you to talk to the people before this historic event. They would like to know exactly why we are doing this."

Kukara walked to the people, making magic sounds with her flute. They all thought Rano Raraku started to vibrate, awakening the great moai. As she came closer to the people, she put the flute in her pocket, sat on a large boulder, and smiled at everyone.

"This moai is my friend, "Kukara said. "This moai was your king in Hiva. This moai was your beloved king at Anakena. This moai will rest forever above the remains of my friend. Today you shall see the great Hotu-Matua resurrected for the last time. But who exactly was Hotu-Matua? Only a few of you may know what fact is and what fiction is."

She stood and walked in a circle while she searched dim, distant memories.

"Hotu-Matua was a passionate traveler. He went to unknown lands far north and far west. He found other travelers, some of them with very advanced knowledge. They gave him the Rongo-RongoRongo-Rongo tablets that I have been working on ever since I was a little girl. Today I am almost a young woman and still a girl. Today as you know, I have added much knowledge to these tablets. And you can see, many of these characters have been tattooed on my chest, waist, and thighs. Those on my chest show exactly how the moai will be brought to life today. If the tattoos are correct, then Hotu-Matua will indeed live again today."

Kukara hesitated, walked in a circle again, and faced the crowd, her arms raised.

"I am not certain how to explain this, since part is true, part is legend, and part is what Hotu-Matua told me. He had seven sons. When I was a little girl, they were all grown and kings on their respective islands around Hiva. The relationship between father and sons was not great. Some of them had even declared war on their father to acquire more land. Then he told me that he had once sent seven explorers to the east to look for new lands, some of which were his sons. He did this at Taranga Tici Viracocha's request. Two explorers were lost at sea. Five returned to Hiva and gave him a list of new islands southeast of Hiva. Rapa Nui may have even been mentioned, but by a different name. It may or may not have been something that was told to them by the two explorers who vanished at sea. You know the rest of the story, which ultimately resulted in our arrival on this island."

Kukara wiped tears from her eyes.

"Hotu-Matua had a good life for one sun cycle at Anakena. With Taranga he planned such marvelous projects for this island.

For him, Rapa Nui was like a new life, because he had found seven of the best friends he ever had. I recall that he used to call his seven best friends his seven sons, his seven explorers. Today they are all part of the Sacred Circle of the Seven Souls. Who we are today is because of Hotu-Matua. Who the Rapa Nui people will be tomorrow is because of Hotu-Matua. We will continue his work, his dream, and the projects he started. Because of us, he will have a long life on Rapa Nui. Because of you, he will remain the most legendary figure this island will ever have. Others will come. Others will even call themselves by the same name. But there will be only one Hotu-Matua, the one with the remains that will sleep for eternity under the moai that you will see walking, alive, today. I am going to do this for my beloved friend, for the other members of the Sacred Circle of the Seven Souls, and for each and every one of you."

She turned around and looked at Rano Raraku, then raised her arms toward the sky.

"Hotu-Matua! Please give me courage. Please give me talent. Please give me the necessary mana. My life is in your hands."

The crowd cheered the young friend of their great benefactor, Hotu-Matua.

She walked back up to the quarry. The crowd circled the huge mound of dirt where Hotu-Matua would stand on his own. Tamatoa kept the crowd under control, making sure everyone was at a safe distance. Also, the best places were reserved for people with higher rank, as was their custom.

Kon and Taatamao thoroughly inspected the ropes, winding drums, and placement of teams. Following the lessons learned from the first moai, a few more ropes had been added, and all of them reinforced. However, the new large, heavy convex shield at the base of the moai was something new to worry about; they were not certain how it would behave on its way down. The long pathway had been paved with large basalt slabs that reached the place where the moai would rise on its own. Carving, carrying, and paving the avenue had been a long, tedious operation. It had been widened in the middle to accommodate the shield. Rollers made of basalt had been placed at regular intervals along the pathway, so that the moai would always move slightly above the ground. At the end of the pathway, a tall mound of dirt had been piled to stop the moai. The moai rested at the same slope angle as the hill, which was quite steep. As soon as the keel was broken, the moai would slide downhill, gathering considerable momentum as it went. Kon wanted to keep it tightly under control, which was the purpose of the ropes around six winding drums. If all worked correctly, the moai would be lowered slowly and under Kon's complete control the entire way. Channels carved around the moai were backfilled with gravel to the top of the keel, which would prevent any sideways tilt when the keel was severed. Six holes had been dug across the keel, and in each of them a wood beam had been placed to be used as a lever to break the keel. Experience from the first moai showed the keel would break after four wood beams had been applied, but Kon decided to keep six just in case.

Kon gave his last recommendations to the women watching.

"Stay away from the moai's path. It will crush everything in its way."

Hina, Kama, and Mahine made sure his command would be respected. Kukara sat near the dirt mound.

"Step aside!" Kon ordered. "The moai may totally pulverize the mound."

Kukara complied and sat on the ground.

"Do not sit on the ground," Kon ordered, "and be prepared

to run away any time."

Kukara moved, rolling her eyes at Kon's overabundance of caution, as did the other women.

Once more, Kon checked the ropes, their tension, the winding drums, and each man's position. Satisfied that all was in order, he shouted his instructions.

"We are ready. I am going to start breaking the keel. Be prepared and do not lose focus."

Kon pulled on the first wood beam, breaking the upper part of the keel. Nothing happened. The moai was still solidly attached to the living rock. He pulled on the second beam. Nothing. He pulled on the third one. Nothing, but he did hear a distinctive crack from the ground below the keel.

"When I pull on the next beam, everything will go," he shouted.

He had learned his lesson when he was nearly killed during the liberation of the first moai. He attached a long rope around the fourth beam and stepped away, giving a strong pull on the beam. This time everyone heard a loud crack in the keel, and the gravel started to roll downhill. Kon knew there was no need to break another beam.

"Get out of the way!" he shouted.

Everyone held their breath; this was to become the second historic moment for Rapa Nui, for Rano Raraku. The keel suddenly collapsed, sending the broken fifth and sixth beams into the air. The moai started its slide, slowly at first. The tension on the ropes became incredible, straining the six teams and winding drums to their limits. The men felt the pull, increasing slowly, inexorably. All winding drums ground and grated with an ear-wrenching, rasping sound. A cloud of dust rose from the mountain's womb, where the great moai was born. Kon jumped out of the way. The moai reached the first rollers on the pathway. At this stage it started to accelerate and became a force unto itself. The men ineffectually did their best to slow it. Two winding drums broke, shooting rock chips everywhere. This was just what Kon had feared. Two ropes snapped, producing an ear-piercing crack, and whipped up the hill, blinding one worker as the rope's end flicked his eyes. More winding drums broke. Two more ropes broke.

"Let it go!" Kon ordered.

The energy that the formidable juggernaut gained was far greater than what Kon had anticipated, even after the lessons he had learned from the first moai. A deep rumbling noise issued from the ground. Slabs, rollers, everything on the moai's path was crushed and thrown in the air. The pathway behind the moai became a deep trench. Everyone was riveted, unable to move or talk as they witnessed the fast-moving Hotu-Matua race uncontrolled down the hill. Finally, the moai tilted into a shallow ditch, then hit the dirt mound, which was instantly pulverized. Its forward momentum carried the moai to its upright, vertical position. Kukara felt the shock wave hit her body. Then everything stopped, dust settled, and everything was silent. The moai stood vertically, at the right place, intact. Finally, after realizing what had just happened, an uproar of joy raised from the crowd. For the second time, a giant was born at Rano Raraku.

****

When the moai was detached from the mountain, formidable power would inhabit it, and its soul would come to life.

CHAPTER 25

"The new moai was alive and walking. The stone became the great Hotu-Matua. His brain was Kukara Tici Viracocha, and she directed the sacred dance for the gods. I have seen many extraordinary things in my life. This would always remain in my mind, since it changed everyone on the island into a different person. The men who spent sun cycles carving the moai had tears in their eyes. Kon, the master of Rano Raraku, raised his arms in disbelief of Hotu-Matua's powerful mana. The men who held the moai's ropes were caught in a rapturous song, where every word meant life, step by step, for the giant leaving the mountain. Everyone was stunned by what they saw. I was humbled by the little girl I loved so much; she was one with the behemoth and the teams."

Hina of the Valley

The dirt pile's remnants were carefully removed. Kon thoroughly inspected the moai's base and found it intact and unblemished. The path between the moai and the final resting place of Hotu-Matua was leveled and cleaned for the last time. It was about midday. Two deep horizontal notches had been carved immediately above the convex base, front and back; each of them held a massive wooden beam that had been lashed to its counterpart's ends. Kon's design would enable just a few workers to rock the huge moai forward from one side to the other, using these beams as powerful levers. The workers would synchronize the point of maximum tilt with a twisting motion going forward and would repeat this cycle—similar to how they had previously "walked" large rocks—and walk the moai to its final resting spot. Furthermore, if the ends of the beams on each side of the moai were to hit the ground because of excessive tilt, they would be a safety guard against a dangerous swing that could ultimately bring the giant to a fatal fall, and so they thought. It was the beginning of a very different journey.

The members of the Sacred Circle of the Seven Souls gathered around Kukara.

"Kukara Tici Viracocha," the queen said, "from now on, everything is yours."

Tamatoa and Kon threw a long rope ladder over the statue's head, then helped Kukara climb far up the moai's head. After struggling above the long ears, she finally reached the top, where she thoroughly brushed loose dirt away. She scuffed her feet on the head, testing the grip of a new pair of special sandals. She had four teams at her disposal. One team, composed of three men, would pull the moai to her left with a rope attached around its neck. A second team of three men would do the same, but to her right. They would alternate their pulls at her command of "vi" for the left team, and "co" for the right team. The other two teams, of twenty men each, would pull the moai forward using a long rope tied to each end of the lever beams. One team was ahead of her, slightly to her left; the other team was slightly to her right. The pulling teams would coordinate their pulls with Kukara's chants of "ra" for the right team and "cha" for the left team, "vi" for the left tilt, "ra" for forward right pull, "co" for the right tilt, and "cha" for the forward left pull… "Vi…ra…co…cha." They all knew that word.

"We are going to practice this first," Kukara explained to the teams. "If I am not happy with the results, the walk may not take place today."

She had practiced many days with a small version of a moai with the teams. She patiently explained that each team's timing was critical to making the moai walk, and failure could result in the statue's toppling; it was a subtle balance for which there was no place for a mistake. Kon and Tamatoa tried to encourage the construction of a frame on the moai's top that Kukara could use to steady herself and keep from falling. But Kukara was a stubborn girl: she believed that she needed to feel the statue's complex motion to ensure that everything would progress as planned. She argued that it was only an experiment and agreed that she would accept their recommendations, if warranted.

She raised her hands.

"The sideways left and right teams will pull first. The two forwarding teams can sit on the ground for now."

"Pull slightly to the left… Vi," she said raising her left index finger.

The formidable height of the moai resulted in a relatively high center of gravity, which gave the three men a considerably higher leverage than expected. She felt the moai roll slightly to the left, then immediately return to the right. Surprised, she lost her balance, but recovered just in time to prevent a dangerous fall—however, not without straining her back. It was visible from the grimace on her face that she was in pain. She rubbed the strained muscle and said, "Stop this and get me down!"

She explained she wanted a crown built around the moai's head that she could use to grasp, if necessary; she did agree to attach a safety rope around the crown and her waist as a further precaution.

"We told you," Tamatoa admonished.

"This moai is not the same as the big stones," she commented. "This can obviously be a killer. I admit that I underestimated the magnitude of the swing. The next moai should not have as much curvature as this one. Half the curvature would be adequate."

Kon built her safety gear very quickly. Ready for another attempt, she raised her hands.

"The two sideways teams pull first. The two forwarding teams sit on the ground for now."

"Pull slightly to the left… Vi," she said raising her left index finger. "Take it easy."

She felt the moai roll to the left, then immediately bounce back to the right. This time she was ready and adroitly handled the swing. She raised her left index finger, saying "vi," and the great moai swung left. She raised her right index finger, saying "co," and it moved to the right. She repeated the procedure many times until she was easily able to maintain her balance and the two teams were able to better synchronize their efforts.

"Now let's try it with the four teams," she said. This was the long-awaited, critically important moment.

She raised her hands.

"Pull slightly to the left… Vi," she said, raising her left index finger. She felt the moai roll to the left.

She pointed her finger to the right team to pull forward, saying "ra." They did. The moai went forward a little, and then bounced to the other side. "Co," she said. But the other teams reacted too late for what they had to repeat. Everything came to a stop.

"You are too slow, and you are not thinking," she said in a disappointed tone. "We need to practice much more."

Back on the ground, circled by the four crews, she patiently explained the timing, using four sticks to illustrate each team's role. Wincing from a twinge of pain, she rubbed her back.

"Did you hurt your back?" Kon asked.

"A little; it is nothing."

Kon massaged her back while she continued her explanation.

"At the maximum roll to the left side, the right team must pull forward. As soon as the moai starts rolling in the opposite direction, the right team must stop pulling forward. So you have a very short time to pull forward. Similarly, at the maximum roll to the right side, the left team must pull forward. As soon as the moai starts rolling in the other direction, the left team must stop pulling…"

"Kukara Tici Viracocha," the queen said, "I don't think you are ready for the big show today. Take your time."

"I need to practice this slowly with them for half a moon cycle."

"So be it!" Hina replied, raising her arms to dismiss everyone.

Little by little, day after day, they practiced the meticulous and complex procedures required to make it work. Men were reassigned to make better use of their strengths. Some were better at coordinating the swings, while others were better at coordinating the pulls. They also learned to listen more attentively to her commands. Every day they went further, and became more confident and skilled. They reached the long-awaited point when their expertise and Kukara's expectations coincided. Then she knew she had achieved her objective. The smile on her face told everyone that they were doing an excellent job. She had only one worry, which was the excessive curvature of the moai's base. If the side teams excessively rocked the statue, they might topple it, with catastrophic consequences. She and they were aware of the dangers. By the time the moai had moved about a third of the distance to its final destination, they decided the big day had come. Hina of the Valley called her people together again.

Up the hill, near the site of the moai's birth, seven seats had been carved in the rock, one for each member of the Sacred Circle of the Seven Souls. Because Kukara, Tamatoa, Kon, and Taatamao were part of the teams, only Hina, Mahine, and Kama would sit in their distinguished places that day, where they would enjoy a panoramic view of the walking moai in the foreground, set against a spectacular background scene of the placid crater lake. The absentee seats were festooned with garlands of bright tropical flowers that honored their souls and reinforced their mana. Downhill from the sacred seven seats, closer to Kukara and the working teams, the crowd would watch as the giant moai walked to its eternal resting spot. In a way the people were closer to the action, but Hina liked it that way.

"I want everyone to see this wonderful event, so they will never forget what they witnessed. From here we see the grand picture. What man does and what nature wants are two different things. It is our duty as members of the Sacred Circle of the Seven Souls to find a balance so the gods can rest in peace. Then, and only then, can we unworthy humans mark a day of glory during our fleeting lives." The queen had spoken.

The moai was there, standing. Hotu-Matua was there, living again, poised to walk again. The moai's size combined with its immobility, for now. Its face was inscrutable and timeless, with the Make Make god painted on its cheeks, the mysterious expression on its lips frozen in time. This exceptional piece of rock was much more than a vulgar statue. It had a life of its own; its silence made it seem more alive. Everyone was humbled by the magnificent giant's beauty and charisma. But the best was yet to come.

Kon headed the left rolling team, while Taatamao captained the right. Tamatoa was responsible for the left forwarding team, while Lutafu headed the right.

Kukara climbed the rope ladder to the sacred platform on the moai's head. She tested the sturdiness of the rail and scuffed her sandals to obtain a firm purchase on the basalt. She tightly tied the safety belt around her waist. She gathered her long black hair and tied it behind her head with a delicately braided cord. She adjusted her headband so her hair would not interfere with her vision.

"Remember," she said, "vi…ra…co…cha!"

The queen stood tall with the right Make Make side of her face toward the people. She clapped her hands, giving the signal to proceed. Make Make communicated with Kukara, giving her the necessary mana: nothing could happen without the subtle, yet profound touch of Make Make. Only if the supreme god inhabited Kukara could she accomplish her mission at this very critical moment.

Kukara raised both arms, one pointing at the left rolling team, the other pointing at the right forwarding team. The index finger of her left hand pointed at Kon as she said "vi," and the moai rolled slightly to the left. She raised her left thumb to signal Kon to stop rolling, and simultaneously pointed to Lutafu with her right index finger. "Ra," she said. The giant statue rotated a fifth of a circle and moved forward about one foot. She raised her right thumb to signal Lutafu to stop forwarding, while simultaneously pointing at Taatamao with her right index finger: "Co." The moai rolled to the right. She raised her right thumb to signal Taatamao to stop rolling, while pointing to Tamatoa with her left index finger. "Cha," she said. Hotu-Matua rotated a fifth of a circle back and moved forward another foot.

"The sequence is perfect," Hina murmured. "She's got it right. Look at the smile on her face. This is Kukara's smile when she succeeds, when she is happy with herself and at peace with her mana."

Several cycles went on. The teams worked in flawless harmony. Kukara slightly increased the rolling amplitude and the forwarding strength with a strident whistling. Now each forward movement consisted of a quarter-circle rotation. The moai was gaining more momentum. Kukara had to tighten her grip on the rail, as the excessive rolling was becoming more demanding on her small body.

Two large circles were drawn on each side of Kukara's chest. The four circles symbolized the mana that she had imparted to each team. To the crowd, it was the sign of the supernatural forces she constantly transmitted to the teams. The circles connoted the team's dependence on her. At this moment Kukara Tici Viracocha was the unrivaled great priestess: no one else knew how to perform this job with such flawless mastery. For every Rapanui the moai's movement through Kukara's mana was a mystical inspiration. Maybe it was not the most efficient way to transport a moai, but this was irrelevant. What was highly relevant was the challenge and beauty of doing it her way.

From a distance, Kukara briefly glanced at Hina of the Valley. She saw Make Make on her face. She saw Make Make gliding with majesty above the crowd. This was her moment. This was the time when Kukara would change the course of history for Rapa Nui. Transporting the statue from one place to another was not the ultimate goal, but rather a way to communicate with the gods, and at this particular moment they were watching and listening to the young priestess.

Kukara increased the amplitude of the rolling and the strength of the forwarding with two strident whistles. Now each forwarding movement resulted in a third circle rotation. The moai's momentum and speed increased rapidly, and soon it seemed to be walking on its own. It seemed to everyone, including the crews, that the massive moai was getting lighter and lighter.

Kukara whistled three times. Her hair bounced from left to right. Her voice reinforced the incredible roll-pull-roll-pull cycle.

Her body was bound to Hotu-Matua. Hotu-Matua was alive and running to the little platform reserved for him for eternity. Kukara lowered her arms and sat; everything halted. Never in all her life had she sweated that much. She heard the roar of the crowd. She heard the roar of her teams. She had superbly done the impossible. A giant moai had walked on its own. It was an undeniable, beautiful historic fact.

"This must be transcribed in Rongo-RongoRongo-Rongo tablets," Hina of the Valley ordered, "so no one will ever forget how this was done, today, by Kukara."

The wood beams used as levers to pull the moai forward were removed and saved. During the process of moving the moai, they had acquired considerable mana that would be used later for another moai. The curved base was carefully chiseled away, until the moai looked exactly like its neighbor Taranga Tici Viracocha. The chips were all sent back to the quarry. Without the heavy curved base, it would be impossible for anyone to move the moai again, as long as it stood upright. Hotu-Matua was forever frozen in time, forever staring at the northwestern horizon, the direction of Hiva, his homeland. The long fingers, extended by long nails carved under a prominent belly button, revealed Viracocha features more than Maohi features, but for many years Hotu-Matua had been deeply influenced by the Viracochas and had always appreciated them and respected their customs.

The two giants, carved from the living stone of a volcanic mountain, stood tall and looked over the small colony who would respect them for many generations. It was the dawn of the largest rock-carving endeavor ever undertaken by mankind.

****

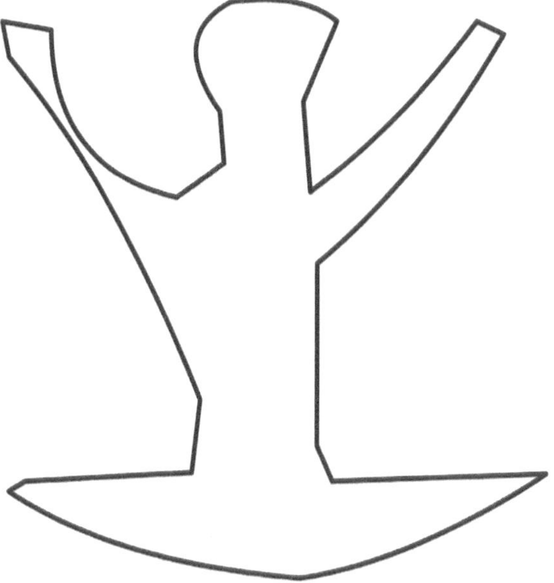

The massive curved base of the moai would allow a powerful mana to help the great priestess initiate the sacred walk.

CHAPTER 26

"Hotu-Matua's ghost haunts Rano Raraku. His moai, now frozen in time, will always walk along the crater lake, each drumming step echoing throughout time. A new magic has been created, not by the moai's impressive size, but by the way it walked to get there. Future priests that may master the concept of how to make moais walk will never equal Kukara Tici Viracocha's mastery of technique, command, and most importantly, mana. She changed our thoughts filled with sand and water into a fire she alone could ignite and sustain."

Kon Tici Viracocha

Hotu-Matua was there, huge, silently standing. Now in his hallowed position, he became immobile; now only his shadow would transit the day and moonlight nights. The crowd was gone. The carvers were gone. Only birds and insects owned the place. Everything now reverted to its rightful owner: Mother Nature. It was the time Kukara preferred to communicate with her inner spirit, and to communicate with her erstwhile old friend. She bent down and joined hands with Hotu-Matua's.

"He did not have long fingers and long fingernails like this," she joked.

"The design was a fantasy of my mind… and yours a long time ago at Rano Raraku," Kon replied.

Her long fingers and long nails matched the ones of the moai. She felt a current of energy leave her and enter Hotu-Matua's earthly manifestation. In her mind it was much more than a carved rock. The expression of the face, the silent doubt on his thin lips seemed to question man's true role in the universe. Hotu-Matua's presence belonged to the dream land that permeated this small, humble, remote island. It was obvious to Kukara that his spirit inhabited the moai. Kukara took a few steps backward and admired the mighty face that gazed at the faraway horizon and beyond.

"You are still limping," Kon observed.

"It will go away," she replied.

Kon placed a ladder against the statue so that Kukara could stand on its head. Exactly as she did for Taranga Tici Viracocha, she would stay there, seated, legs crossed, in deep mediation for the rest of the day and a full night. Kon knew it was her routine, her way to reach her spiritual food.

She wiped the dust covering the little platform on which she sat. She reached forward with her hands to feel Hotu-Matua's upper forehead. The wooden safety crown she had held during the march was gone. It was only her and him.

"I will come back tomorrow morning," Kon said, removing the ladder. She could no longer get down on her own. She had plenty of room to move around, but she needed to be careful and stay away from the edges, lest she lose her balance and fall. In a way, she was in a place that belonged to the birds. She watched Kon walk away, toward their Ovahe settlement. She had a plan in her mind to occupy herself, but she was in no hurry. Time passed slowly as she peacefully observed and admired the view of the lake, the reeds, and Hotu-Matua's birthplace, the mountain where Kon had freed him. She could see the "cradle" hole where Hotu-Matua had gestated. Above, she could see the holes in the mountain that were used as giant shafts to slow the moai during its detachment from the mountain. She followed the flight of several frigates, drifting lazily, high in the sky. She saw a few clouds and thought she might have to endure a rainy late afternoon. She looked at the reeds being blown around the lake by a light breeze. A fish leapt and splashed in the middle of the lake. A little songbird walked around her, curious about the new arrangement. She thought she had never noticed such a bird on the island before. There were many more secrets to be discovered. Her mind ambled between the universe of her temporal surroundings and the inner spiritual world of Hotu-Matua. She recalled his childhood, his seven sons, his wars with his brother and sons, his sadness at never having a daughter, his immense kindness as a king, and his innocent admiration of people bathing at the Anakena beach. She closed her eyes and started her long trip by focusing inwardly; it was as though she were descending inside Hotu-Matua's brain and was becoming a part of this most awesome presence at Rano Raraku. It was time to meet the Light again, as she had so many times in the past. It was her private world. She felt that she needed to renew her energy resources after the grueling schedule that she had maintained over the past few moon cycles, and she would reexplore the world where she alone could freely travel. None of the Viracochas had ever ventured as far as her; it was something she could not share yet with anyone. It was a private experience with a supreme being; it was her special privilege to have private communion with her God.

As she became more at one with the statue and the Light, she meandered among myriad neural networks; it was like visiting the repository of what made her. Many things were unknown, their function unclear. Many of them she did not understand. But obviously, they all had important purposes. She found it sublimely interesting that she was made from infinite parts, yet had no idea what they did or how to control them. She was overwhelmed by the complexity and interactions among this formidable network of veins, arteries, muscles, nerves, and pulsating membranes. Her mind probed farther inside each of these parts. She willed herself to a smaller perspective and entered a more orderly world, where marvelous geometric patterns, resembling infinitely long ladders, spiraled endlessly. She mentally climbed the treads until she became dizzy. She took a break and sat on the edge of a spiral and let her mind range even farther, deeper, and entered a new universe where strange, unknown constellations brilliantly illuminated the black, microscopic firmament. Some stars were red, some yellow, and others bright blue. For an instant she thought she was looking at an undiscovered night sky. Then she realized that they were arranged geometrically. Faced with such an alien landscape, she wondered if she was traveling inside herself or dreaming. Kukara knew better. She knew it was not a dream. She knew she had waited for this profound exploration for a long time. However, she did have a major puzzlement: was she exploring inside herself or in the giant moai? She thought she was inside herself. But she also thought it was probably inconsequential. So she pursued the sacred diminution even further, believing that she would reach a critical point where many mysteries would be revealed to her.

She approached one of the star-like objects, a blue one. It seemed that she approached it at an incredible speed. It quickly transformed from a point of light to a fuzzy, pulsating ball. It appeared to be surrounded by a translucent haze, caused by something orbiting the ball at an incredibly fast speed. Flashes of purple light regularly emanated from the haze. Kukara remembered that the Light was always purple: could she be approaching the end of her journey? She was happy to have progressed this far, but became concerned, scared that she might be overstepping her bounds.

She reduced her focus one more level and proceeded to enter what she sensed was sacred, prohibited territory. But the Light had never told Kukara it was specifically proscribed to her. She rationalized the ambiguity and hoped the Light would forgive her. Her first visit had been an elementary view of what the world was all about. On this second trip, she hoped to increase the depth of her explorations.

She now found herself floating inside a faint purple cloud that blocked all external lights and features; this was disorienting her. She glanced at her own body. There was none. She was also made of the purple light, albeit having slightly more substance. Actually she found it quite bright, and the shadows dancing around like sea waves were attractive. Silence was absolute. Her attempt to move imaginary arms created a large satin wave that passed by her eyes. She tried to touch her eyes and realized they were no longer there. She was only purple light. She was the Light. As she finally realized who she was, she became calmer, more confident, and she knew she was having a remarkable experience. From now on she had the means to find all the answers to what she wanted to know. No one, nothing could stop her. She became the Mighty for a moment, or so she thought.

She saw another bright purple ghost approach her, enter her, and become one with herself. She did not hear the words, but they entered her subconscious. The Light was talking to her.

"For this moment, Kukara Tici Viracocha has become the great Make Make. You were chosen because you selected yourself. This is not our first encounter. I did tell you this is a prohibited territory that humans should not explore before they learn how to live in peace with each other and with Mother Nature. You and the Sacred Circle of the Seven Souls have been doing well. Yet I know this will not last much longer. However, you, Kukara Tici Viracocha, I know you are different from them and will never break my mandate for peace. As a result, I will reveal more secrets to you, and then, when you go back to your world, you must plant the seeds I give to you in the minds of the others. It will be up to you to determine how you will accomplish this. Furthermore, you must also devise a method of measuring your results. You must plan how your power will be transferred to future generations. When you walk with the next moai, the name of which is Illa Tici Viracocha, I will fill your mind with an exceptionally powerful mana."

"Now, who am I? I am the Light. Any part of this purple light is of the same person. You, although this purple light fills the entire universe, you don't need to look to the stars, you do not need to look into others, you just need to look to yourself. All your answers are to be found here, within you. Everyone else's answers are to be found within themselves. You have done well, and you now understand that you are the Light."

"I and you are composed of an unimaginable amount of light waves. Each wave can travel anywhere and anytime. Each wave has no mass and is pure energy. All waves can communicate between themselves, anytime and anywhere. All waves are aware of what any one of them is doing. Each wave has a clear mission but may find many obstacles. Each wave accumulates enormous quanta of knowledge during its distant travels. This knowledge is stored and can be retrieved by the initiated. But such knowledge is forbidden to any being incapable of living in peace with their fellow man or nature, or of obeying the Light's commandments."

"The Light continually experiments. A few experiments lead to hopeful possibilities and promising conclusions. Very rare ones turn out to be so good that they deserve special attention, help, and privileges. The few that produce exceptional results can make their way to the world outside of where they were created. All failures will be eliminated, so they don't undermine the good ones. We are trapped in a small world: we have been quarantined. The sooner the others realize this, the more promising their future will become. Unfortunately, the shortsighted behavior of a few will ruin it for the majority. It is sad. But that is the way it is. And this is a sacred truth."

"Back to my world: I can be life and death, I can be the commoner or the ruler, and I can be the naïve or the sophisticate. I can be the poor or the rich. I can be the saint or the tyrant. Be it good or be it bad, it is all my sacred choice. The secret is to make the right choices, regardless of who I am. This is why who I am is really irrelevant. What is important is who I want to be. Nobody wants to be a bad person. A bad person is the result of ignorance and poor choices. I am left ignorant and make bad choices when my peers are incapable of teaching me the truth, the way of the Light. Therefore, if they cannot teach properly, obviously the experiment will fail, and we shall all become extinct: we would no longer be relevant to the experiment."

"I visited a world where giant reptiles were at war in devastated forests. It was part of a logical evolution that would lead to more harmony, more peace, and more achievement. It did not happen that way. Predators always won, evolved, and became meaner and meaner. A point was reached when they would conquer new worlds, but consumed with internecine warfare, they annihilated themselves."

"In another world, a water world, I found that marine life had evolved into a cognitive, but warring, species. Eventually, evolution succeeded, and peaceful harmony was reached. An enlightened invertebrate being ruled their world and transformed it into an ecological marvel. A superior level of wisdom, care, and love created superb achievements where every advanced being would live, learn, create, suggest, perform, and finally reach serenity. They found ways to live longer. They found ways to reach other water worlds. Finally, they found ways to create new water worlds by themselves. The Light bestowed immortality on them. They were a winning experiment."

"I visited this world, looking at its evolution. It was balanced between self-destruction and harmony. Humans are on their way to becoming successful; however, they are still struggling and wasting precious resources in their futile conflicts. Many, too many, find pleasure in killing and causing pain. This is a borderline world. It has been placed in quarantine until something positive evolves. But it has become sterile and uncontrollable. As soon as one segment of the human species made some minor progress, devastating failures elsewhere would negate the good. Over and over again, life, evolution, progress had to restart from its very beginning. The Light saw no hope, no positive trend, and it looked very much like you were on your way to extinction."

"The Light was everywhere watching, everywhere entering the eyes of humans to help them dream and evolve. Every one of the magnificent entities of pure energy, pure intelligence, and simultaneous awareness were capable of weighing, judging, and acting according to a well-orchestrated cosmic dance. The rules are simple: create at all cost, evolve at all cost, live and die until you are successful, then prosper and continue an upward evolution for eternity. The ultimate result is to become pure energy, pure intelligence, and pure awareness. Then you can join with all the other successful creations in the creation of new universes ever and ever more advanced. The Light would evolve as well, toward something much greater. That is the ultimate secret, the ultimate goal."

Kukara thought to herself, "My short journey into the truth is coming to an end. I need to return home. I have had an awesome privilege granted to me. Would I remember all I saw and learned?"

Kukara opened her eyes. It was dawn. The sky was pink, and the sun was still below the horizon. She felt pain in her lower abdomen. She needed to urinate. But she could not jump from the top of the moai. Apologizing to Hotu-Matua in advance, she relieved herself.

"The rain will wash this away," she murmured.

She sat on a dry part of the slightly curved platform and reflected on her experience. She looked at the world around her with a new perspective. She tried to retrace what she had learned or what she had been told. Then she recollected the Light's pronouncement.

"The name of the next moai will be Illa Tici Viracocha," she recalled.

"By all the spirits in this world, how is it conceivable that such a thing would be done?" she asked.

She was quick to analyze the stunning implications. There was only one way. The Great Gathering was coming soon. She would have to attend and retrieve Illa Tici Viracocha's remains from Rapa Iti. She would tell no one until the Great Gathering. But would they let her go with Kama's son, who was the only one who knew how to find his father's remains? She would manage one way or another. She saw Kon coming back. He helped her down. She walked very clumsily at first. He gave her a gourd of water and some food.

"How was your journey with the spirits?" he asked.

"My journey filled me with fear for this world," she replied in a sad tone. Then she turned back and glanced up at the moai's lips expressing a secret doubt about something. "It is time for the Sacred Circle of the Seven Souls to become far more demanding of our people. The circle is not creative enough."

Kon did not answer. He was thinking about her words, and wondered where she had traveled. He knew she would not tell him more at this time.

"How is your back? The rolling of the moai could break your spine one day and paralyze you for the rest of your life. I am not sure it is a good idea for you to direct the walk on the top of the moai. You could do this as well from the ground."

"No way!" she replied, her wide dark blue eyes glittering with anticipation. "My back is just fine!"

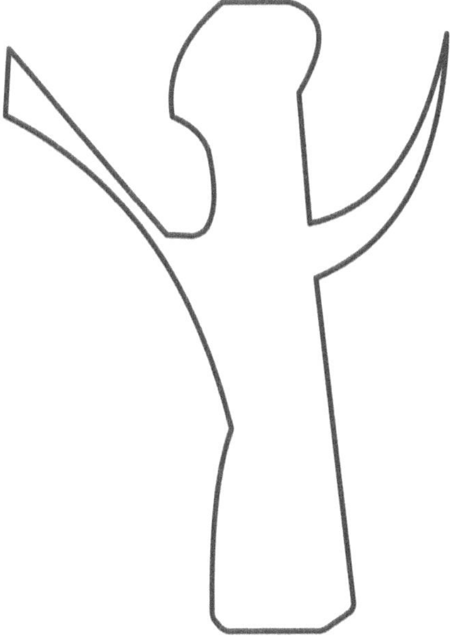

After the massive curved base of the moai was cut, it would stand for eternity watching an assigned sector of the horizon and stars. Mata Kite Rani was born.

CHAPTER 27

"Some rules were meant to be followed. Some taboos were sacred and meant to be respected. Sexual assault on women without consent I would never tolerate. As the queen of the island, I had a choice to make: let them live in shame, or let them die. I was going to make that choice, and nobody could dissuade me."

Hina of the Valley

Kon, Hina, and Kukara had been at Orongo for several days, exploring the jagged cliffs in the crater's throat with Tamatoa. Kama, no longer fond of rock climbing, went to Taatamao and Mahine's settlement on the northwest side of the island. The day started out like many others.

"Let me show you our new sweet potatoes," Mahine said, excited.

"What do you mean 'new'?" Kama asked.

"As you know, we brought ten different varieties to the island. But the one that I want to show you, we have never seen before."

"I think some of the existing ones have crossbred," Taatamao suggested. "Why don't you go and look at them? I have some work to do around here, repairing the walls that protect the banana trees and building some new ones."

The two women walked away and disappeared farther north,

up in the hills, in a collapsed lava tube. As they descended into the gardens of the depths, they noticed a group of five men engaged in a stormy discussion at some distance down the mountain slope, near the edge of the lava tube. The men waved to them, and they waved back.

Mahine pointed at the new kumara sweet potato. Kama marveled at what she saw.

"How did you do this? I cannot believe their quality and size. Have you tasted them?"

"Not yet! We wanted to share the experience with you."

As they continued talking, the five men walked closer and descended into the gardens of the depths, which annoyed Mahine, since they hadn't asked or received Taatamao's permission. Everybody on the island knew that the garden was part of Taatamao's settlement.

"Do you remember the discussions the people had, a few moon cycles ago, about having too many women in charge?" Kama asked.

"Yes, I do. What does that have to do with these men?"

"They are the ones who believe that our rulers should all be men," Kama replied.

The group of men slowly, grimly approached Mahine and Kama. Now several paces from the women, the men formed a circle around them and started to close it. It was clear their intentions were not friendly. With no witnesses in this isolated area, they wanted to use this chance encounter to make their point.

"You take that one," one man said, pointing at Kama. "We will take this one."

Two men grabbed Kama, who tried to fight back, but was no match against the two Maohis. The other three had a tougher time with a more athletic Mahine. But they were very strong men.

"Do you realize what my father would do to you if he saw this?" Mahine asked defiantly.

"That woman from another world has turned him into a lazy pig," one man replied.

They tied Kama and Mahine's hands and legs, and then they viciously ripped their garments off and stood over them leering and threatening, trying to build up their courage.

Kama realized what they were up to. She recalled that many years earlier she had telepathically communicated with old Taranga Tici Viracocha and others, when they were on the continent. She recalled what Taranga had said then about little Kukara: "For her age, she is remarkably talented."

Kama tried to ignore the men. She closed her eyes. She went into a trance that made the men believe she had died of fright. As a result, they left her alone and raped Mahine.

Kama descended deep into her mind and called for Kukara or Kon to come and help them. She also recalled distance was a factor. Short distances worked much better, but Kukara and Kon were far away. Then another detail came back to memory: when someone would be contacted, there were flashes of light visible in the mind, so she kept her awareness to see such flashes.

****

At Orongo, inside the eastern cliff of the crater, Kon, Tamatoa, and Hina entered a cave they had not previously explored. Kukara stayed outside, pretending she was not feeling good, which was true. She stretched out on the long, fresh grass, in the shade. She still struggled with back pain. She closed her eyes and listened to the wind's soft lowing. She was instantly bombarded with flashes of light that pulsed through her mind. The last time she had seen those flashes was when she lost her parents and brother to bloodthirsty assassins. Caught off guard by these painful memories, she concentrated as hard as she could to understand their meaning. She saw Mahine, lying naked, being raped by men by the gardens of the depths. She saw Kama sprawled next to her, trying to communicate telepathically. Kukara stood and called for the others to join her and rush to Kama and Mahine's rescue. The others came out of the cave, thinking she had had an accident. They found her on her knees, weeping.

"What is it, little one?" Tamatoa asked, taking her in his arms.

"They raped Mahine! They are going to rape Kama as well!"

"Who? Where?" Tamatoa roared.

"In the gardens of the depths, in the hills, beyond Taatamao's settlement."

"Are you sure about this?" Tamatoa asked, wondering how she could know such a thing.

"She is right," Kon added. "I feel something as well, but it is not as clear. They are too far away."

"Women, stay at Orongo!" Tamatoa ordered, taking his conch from his belt. "Kon, come with me."

"Don't make that call," Kon suggested. "Make it only when we are much closer to them, perhaps with Taatamao. They might plan to kill them after raping them. We need to hurry to them, but not warn them of our coming, lest they panic and kill them."

As they were hurrying up the cliff, Tamatoa thought about Kon's words.

"As usual, Tici, I think you are right. Can you run with me? I know the way."

"I sure will!"

Kon suddenly recalled the race to the top of Mount Orohena and wondered what the outcome would have been if the adversary had been Tamatoa himself. At the rate they were running, it was clear Tamatoa would have been a formidable adversary. Though he could have been Kon's father, the tattooed giant was a human fortress that seemed never to age.

As they arrived at Taatamao's settlement, they saw him making a wall with large stones, helped by three other men.

"Quick, come with us!" Tamatoa ordered. "I have no time to explain."

"Mahine and Kama are in trouble in the gardens of the depths," Kon said, out of breath.

Puzzled at how they could know such a thing, Taatamao and the three men helping him followed.

****

"You really think we are going to stay at Orongo, doing nothing?" Hina asked.

"Mother! I was waiting for this."

"Then, my girl, let's go! How is your back?"

"It is painful, but not too bad. I can manage."

****

The necessary time that it takes to run from Orongo to the gardens of the depths, beyond Taatamao's settlement, gave plenty of time for the five men to brutally assault and grievously injure the two women. Like two pigs taken to the market, the two women had been trussed by their ankles and wrists and carried between two men on a stout wooden post. They were being taken farther north, toward the men's settlement. Kama was still conscious. Mahine, severely beaten for trying to defend herself and Kama, had lost consciousness.

****

Being fresher, and knowing exactly were Kama and Mahine went, Taatamao was the first to descend the gardens of the depths. He immediately saw the torn garments and many scuff marks on the ground, showing that a struggle had recently occurred there. Several small pools of still-wet blood sent Tamatoa into an uncontrollable rage. He was once again the feared warrior. Kon looked at him with sadness. He knew what the outcome would be, and there was absolutely nothing he could do or wanted to do to stop the giant. The guilty men had no idea of what they had unleashed or how Tamatoa would dispense his justice.

"I have a fair idea who they are," Taatamao said. "They are the same men who argued about too many women being in command. Their settlement is further north."

"I know where the bastards are!" Tamatoa said, taking a rock in his hands, literally crushing it. "They cannot run with the women, but we certainly can. Take a drink my friends. We have a mission to do."

Tamatoa took his conch, ran to the top of the lava tube, and blew with all the force of his lungs, asking for help toward the northern settlements.

****

At the sound of the conch, the men dropped the women to the ground. They knew it was Tamatoa's call: their earlier bravado instantly evaporated, replaced with pure animal panic. How could he have known? How could he have known? How could he have moved so fast from Orongo? They were taken by surprise, not expecting such a fast discovery and reaction. They had to change their plans.

"Let's take them to the nearest boat and get out of here," said the short, mangy man.

But they were still far up in the hills.

****

Again, being fresher and an outstanding runner, Taatamao was the first one to reach a cliff that had a good view of the northern slopes. Far away, halfway down, he saw the five men transporting Kama and Mahine.

When Kon arrived, Taatamao pointed at the men. "It appears that they may try to take them to the coast, perhaps to a boat."

"They are not going to do this, I swear," Tamatoa roared, running down.

Taatamao was very fast and caught up with the five men before they arrived at a small cove where there was an outrigger. The men were surprised and befuddled when Taatamao shot by them and went to the outrigger and pushed it out to sea. Running back to the cove, Taatamao saw the men break into a hard run, leaving the two women on the ground.

They had nowhere to go. On one side Kon and three men were in their way. On the other side Tamatoa was in their way, and Taatamao was closing in on them.

Still cowards, the five chose to attempt an escape on Tamatoa's side. They felt that they could quickly subdue Tamatao and flee; after all, they were from Hiva and had come with Hotu-Matua. They had heard about Tamatoa, but had never seen him as the great warrior. Running very close to a steep cliff, the first man tried to escape, but a powerful hand gripped his arm and held him tight, in a way the man had never felt before. With one arm, Tamatoa lifted the man off the ground, stopped, and looked at his companions. He saw that Taatamao had grabbed another man and was fighting with him. Taatamao's helpers had pinioned another. Kon rushed over to free the women. He found them conscious, but badly wounded. He cut the ropes around their arms and legs and gave them some water.

"You are safe now," he said to Kama, who was struggling to swallow.

"I hate the bastards!" Mahine screamed, standing up. "They would have killed us at sea if you had not been so fast."

Two other men escaped. Tamatoa laid his man on the ground. The man was trying to fight back, but it was like punching a moai. The tattooed giant brought his nose close to the man's nose. The man had never seen that terrifying face so close.

"You are going to give me the names of the two who escaped... Now!"

As everyone watched, the man urinated on himself in sheer terror but shook his head; he would not divulge his companions' names.

"I know their names," Kama said, finding some energy.

"Oh no!" Tamatoa said. "They will tell me their friends' names."

"Never argue with me when I am angry," Tamatoa bellowed, smashing the man's face with a ferocious power that literally decapitated him, sending a geyser of blood spurting into the air. Then he threw the body over the cliff. They all saw what happened. Then he slowly went to another man, who was trying to free himself from Taatamao and one of his helpers.

"Give me that one," Tamatoa said, with an unexpectedly calm voice.

He grabbed the man's arm and lifted him in the air with one hand.

"Please, the names!"

The man, knowing what would happen if he did not comply, quickly stuttered the names of his companions.

"Kama, do you agree with the names?"

"Yes," she murmured, dismayed at a Tamatoa she had never known before.

"Good! Much better," Tamatoa said gently.

Before dropping the man, he snapped the man's humerus like a twig.

"I am not going to hold your dirty body, but if you move away from me, you are dead, understand?"

"Yes," the terrified man replied, in fierce pain.

They tied the hands of the two men and bound them together, making any movement difficult.

"You take care of them," Tamatoa said, pointing at Taatamao's helpers. "You will get help soon. Take them to the Hanga Roa Ahu, where they will be judged."

Tamatoa, Kon, and Taatamao took the naked bodies of their loved ones to the sea, where they cleansed off the terrible corruptions both in and on them. At the touch of the warm water, Kama, exhausted, closed her eyes and let the men's gentle ministrations assuage her body and spirit. At the contact with the water, Mahine broke down and started sobbing, something she had never done during her struggle.

"You are all right, you are safe now," Taatamao said to her gently.

"You are my girl," Tamatoa said, "and I am proud of you. I know you fought back hard."

"She sure did!" Kama replied, not even opening her eyes.

While cleaning Kama's wounds, Kon told her how effective she had been.

"Without your powerful thoughts communicating with

Kukara, you probably would be dead or lost at sea by now. They would have fed you to the sharks, leaving no trace of what happened."

"I disagree," Tamatoa argued, "there would have been plenty of tracks, believe me."

"You should not have killed that poor man," Kama said. "You should not harbor anger like this. It is negative, and it will make you ill."

"I know," Tamatoa said in a gentle tone. "As a boy I grew up with hatred in my heart. It is difficult sometimes for me to forget my past, but I try, and I will get better with time."

"Thank you, my love," she replied with tears in her deep blue eyes. "I forgive you."

Back at Taatamao's settlement that evening, they joined Hina and Kukara, who had just arrived.

Kama and Mahine, still badly shaken, shared the heinous transgression with Hina of the Valley and Kukara Tici Viracocha. The four women bathed together in the underground pool. Hina and Kukara helped Kama and Mahine clean their innermost parts.

"How did you communicate with Kukara?" Taatamao asked, sitting on the edge of the pool.

"Some Viracochas are very good at communicating with their minds," Kama replied. "And frankly, I had no idea I could do it, much less as well as I did. I was desperate; my mana must have increased during this emergency."

"I think it is the receiver who was outstanding," Kon said, pointing to modest Kukara.

"She received the message so strongly that you made her sick," Hina replied.

"I was sick, very sick!" Kukara murmured, caressing Kama's back.

The four women embraced each other in deep caring and love.

After a modest meal, Hina returned to her pragmatic way of thinking.

"The full moon day, I want these men judged at the Hanga Roa Ahu," she said.

"Don't kill them!" Kama asked.

"I will ask the opinion of each member of the Sacred Circle of the Seven Souls. I will also talk to each member of the men's families. Then I, and I alone, will decide the verdict," Hina said with finality, while showing the Make Make symbol toward them.

"What if one of you carries life in your womb from these men?" Tamatoa asked, concerned.

"I knew you would ask this," Kama replied. "When I was a young woman, I was trained to destroy unwanted life in my womb. Through intense mental concentration, mana already destroyed such life. You have nothing to worry about. However, Mahine was never trained to do such a thing. Tomorrow I will give you a mixture of poisonous plants. These plants, taken in excess, can kill. You will take them in small amounts, as I will direct, every day for half a moon cycle. The concoction will make you sick, but will kill the unwanted life in your womb."

****

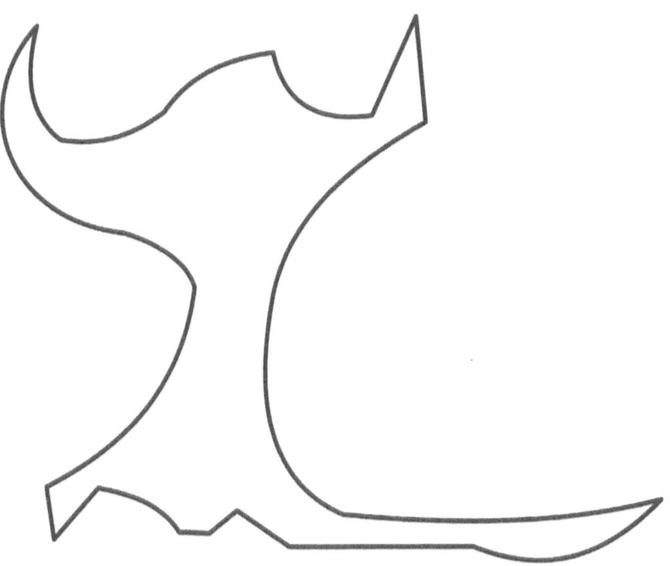

A crawling demon could enter the life of anyone at any time.
Death would often follow.

CHAPTER 28

*"A second ahu would be built to complement the first.
The Hanga Roa Ahu would be used for sunset ceremonies, and
the Vinapu Ahu would be used for sunrise ceremonies. No one
had thought about Vinapu, until tragic acts made it necessary
to eradicate man's hatred and to lift their souls to new heights,
so they could live in dignity."*

Kon Tici Viracocha

A few days later, as the full moon rose in the east, four men
were brought to the Hanga Roa Ahu, awaiting Hina's verdict.
Every islander attended. Hina of the Valley, in full regalia, walked
to them. She wore Kon's golden pin above her head, making her
hair rise high and fall back graciously around her shoulders.
Her Make Make cheek faced the men. By the impatient look on
her face, it was clear she was in no mood to conduct a lengthy
proceeding.

"You who are accused today broke a sacred taboo."

Going to the first man in line, she jabbed her finger on his
chest. "What do you have to say in your defense?"

Defiant, the man spat at her. "You are a woman. You are not
our legitimate ruler. You usurped your rank from men."

Tamatoa rose to his feet. Hina raised her hand and pointed a
finger at him, giving him an order to sit down. Then she went to
the second man. "What do you have to say?"

"He is our chief," he said, pointing at the first man. "We obeyed his command, although we did not agree."

She went to the third man. "What do you have to say?"

"In Hiva, women cannot have high rank, ever. We did what is right."

"Your king, Hotu-Matua, was caused to walk a few days ago by that young woman," Hina stated, pointing at Kukara. "He never said anything derogatory regarding women: he was an enlightened man." The entire crowd applauded Kukara, repeating her name. The drums sounded for silence.

Hina went to the fourth man. "What do you have to say?"

"I am ashamed of what I did. I now regret it. I do not have a valid defense."

Hina placed her hand on his shoulders, as a sign of hope.

She went beyond the men, toward their families.

"Which woman among you is ashamed of what your mates did?"

One woman came forward and identified herself as the chief's mate.

Hina took her hand. "Follow me!"

They went to the upper platform of the ahu, where the members of the Sacred Circle of the Seven Souls sat.

"In the name of your abashed friends, family members, and children, explain your everyday life at home, please."

"We love our mates, but we have no rights. They do not permit us to eat with them, though we prepare their food. They never let us eat bananas, as they were too good for women. They forbid us from giving opinions…"

The woman continued to describe all the taboos that their men had created. At one point, Hina became irritated by litany of indignities heaped on this poor woman and the others; she stopped the woman.

"I think we have heard enough."

She went back to the first man. "What gives you the right to put other humans in bondage? What gives you the right to believe you are superior to women?"

Then, pounding hard once more on his chest and touching his nose with hers, she asked, "What gives you the right to overthrow the legitimate leaders approved by your sacred king before he died?"

The man lost his confidence, and attempted a feeble response. She held her hand up to stop his rambling, stepped closer to him, and kneed him in his private parts. Paralyzed with the most profound pain, the man dropped to his knees.

She walked back to the Sacred Circle of the Seven Souls, slowly.

"Tamatoa, the old warrior, what is your verdict?"

"Death!"

"Why?"

"We must set an example for others. It has always been our way."

"Kama, the victim, what is your verdict?"

"They should live with their family, in a remote part of the Poike peninsula, as outcasts."

"Why?"

"Their families need them, and they should learn how to treat their women with more respect, as equals."

"Mahine, the victim, what is your verdict?"

"Death! I hate every one of them."

"Why?"

"They are animals. They are a danger to all of us." Tamatoa gave her a sign of approval.

"Tamatoa!" Hina objected, pointing a finger at him. "I did not ask for your opinion."

"Kon, the wise man, what is your verdict?

"They should live. Otherwise, we will be as bad as them.

We, as a society, failed to teach them how to think in better ways. Their crimes are a reflection on our shortcomings to provide a better way of life."

"Then they go away with no punishment?" Hina asked.

"Their punishment is to live in shame for a long time," Kon replied.

"That sounds too light," Hina observed.

"Taatamao, Tamatoa's greatest commander, what is your verdict?"

"Death!"

"Why?"

"Simply because they broke a taboo, and one of them just spat on your face. You cannot do that to Make Make's face." The entire crowd applauded in approval.

"Kukara, the princess of moais, what is your verdict?"

"They should live."

"Why?"

"Because we can transform them into good men: it is our duty. They won't have to live in shame for the rest of their lives. But they have a lot of work to do."

"Three against three!" Hina said. "Now, for my verdict."

She walked slowly to the first man. "A long time ago, at the summit of a great mountain, and at the end of a brutal race, I learned the most beautiful quality that a king or a queen can have."

She walked some distance from the men toward the crowd, especially toward the families. They were all waiting for her answer.

"This quality is called magnanimity. Therefore, they will live!"

The families went to their men, in tears. The crowd rose in wonderment, amazed by their queen's decision.

"But listen!" Hina ordered. The drums rolled, signaling

everyone to remain silent. She had more to say.

She took her obsidian knife from her belt and cut the ropes around the men's wrists.

"The four of you, come to the Sacred Circle of the Seven Souls."

The men did not wish to approach Tamatoa.

"Tell Kama and Mahine you are sorry. Tell them you thought you were doing the right thing. Tell them you know now you were wrong. The Sacred Circle of the Seven Souls is not the only one who decided you were wrong. The crowd did. Your families did."

The four men kneeled and acknowledged that they had been wrong. The man who spat on Hina apologized to her and thanked her for her kindness.

"However," Hina said, turning to Mahine, "I overruled some of my best friends to accommodate some criminals. Mahine, the wounded one, do you agree with the new verdict?"

Mahine had a grimace on her face, hesitating.

"You don't have to agree with the verdict," Hina helped, "but I need to know."

"You are my best friend. I trust your judgment."

"You did not answer my question."

"I don't trust any of these men."

"You still did not answer my question."

"Yes! I agree with the new verdict."

"Taatamao, mate of Tamatoa's daughter, do you agree with the new verdict?"

"You make things too complicated for me. I am having trouble following your logic."

"You did not answer my question."

"Yes, I agree with the new verdict."

"Tamatoa, do you agree with the verdict?"

"Yes, I do. However, I disagree for them to be isolated at the end of the Poike peninsula, as Kama suggested earlier."

"Where would you locate the outcasts?"

"Right here, at the opposite side of the isthmus, where I could keep an eye on them all the time."

"There is no settlement at the place you mention."

"We can create a new one, for this kind of people."

"It should be an inspiring place," Kon suggested, "where they would find dignity and pride in their rehabilitation."

Tamatoa walked away from the group and stared at the western horizon, obviously wrestling with something in his mind. He turned around and came back, pounding every step, as he did so well a long time ago when he was the king.

"We should build a new ahu at their place, from which we can have ceremonies at dawn, similar to the ones we have here at dusk."

"I like the idea," Kon replied.

Hina turned to the four men. "Do you realize how lucky you are? Personally, I cannot believe what I am hearing. Three people who wanted you dead moments ago are now talking about the creation of a special settlement for you and your families."

"We would like to live where we are now," one man said.

Hina went to him, a finger pointing at his nose. "I dare you to ask for this. I dare you to express any desire. I dare you to hope for anything else but the wish of the Sacred Circle of the Seven Souls."

"Does that mean we live under Tamatoa's jurisdiction?" another man asked.

"Yes!" Hina replied sarcastically. "It was your dream to be ruled by a king, remember! Now I have given you one."

The four men bowed in front of Tamatoa the Great.

Tamatoa went some distance away, looking at food. He picked two lobsters and split them into five pieces, came back to the men, and offered one piece to each of them, and ate one piece himself.

"If you live by the rules of the queen," Tamatoa said with a thundering voice, "you will learn that I can be a beneficent ruler."

Hina put her hands on Kama and Mahine's shoulders. "This is the man I recall, at the summit of Mount Orohena, a long time ago. This is what I call magnanimity."

Hina turned to the crowd. The drums rolled, demanding quiet.

"It is a bad thing to break taboos. It is worse to disrespect peaceful women. We love our men, and we love to serve them. People of Rapa Nui, have a good life. Enjoy your families. Respect your neighbors. We are going to build a new ahu, better than this one. It will be a landmark where people will be rehabilitated. It will also be a place where families can go to talk and solve their family problems. Those ceremonies will always start at dawn, and all problems shall be resolved by dusk. You should argue with each other, even insult each other if necessary. Do not suppress anything; completely air your grievances as you walk between the new ahu and Hanga Roa. But when dusk settles and you arrive at Hanga Roa, your problems must be resolved. We will wait for you at Hanga Roa, and it better be good."

She raised her arms, and the drums rumbled loudly again, signaling everyone to be silent. Hina wanted to make an important, final statement.

"The name of this new place, where debates will start at dawn, shall be Vinapu, where a new and better style of life shall begin, and so this shall be done."

She went to the four men.

"In due time, we will meet again at Vinapu and Hanga Roa, as I am not finished with you yet."

****

Eliminating the presence of a demon in someone was not a simple matter. The queen would have to personally intervene in such a matter.

CHAPTER 29

"It was far more difficult to live in peace than I originally thought. As a young priestess, I may have been a little too idealistic. The reality of life and the human condition is a complex matter, involving patience, kindness, firmness, and magnanimity. As a queen, I found it challenging to balance these principles and create a long-term healthy society. In this endeavor, help me, Make Make."

Hina of the Valley

It took a full sun cycle to build Vinapu. It was slightly smaller than the Hanga Roa Ahu. However, enormous attention had been given to details. All stones, regardless of their size, were jointed to perfection. It was impossible to slide a blade of grass between them. Kon was praised by everyone for his remarkable skills. The southeast coast was visible from the ahu, only a short distance from the cliff. It was a place where the rising sun could be honored for giving its blessings of warmth and light for a new day. The two ahu were actually designed by Kon as solar observatories. They were also ceremonial platforms for important events. Before the dedication day, the entire population would gather at Vinapu in the morning and walk to Hanga Roa to observe the sunset. During their walk, the people would resolve their quarrels and arrive at Hanga Roa in peace with their fellow citizens. Hina of the Valley had great expectations about the healing power of the quarrel resolution walk. She had talked about it for the full sun cycle.

Kama and Mahine looked for the four men who had treated them so badly. Several times since the incident, the families had joined in healing sessions and slowly resolved their animosities. They were now in a position where they could actually joke about it. The four men and some of their adult brethren worked hard with the others to build the ahu. They were very proud of the results. The project had completely eradicated memories of the bad day, but not the powerful lessons learned. Many people were amazed at the magic of creating large monuments. The men were at peace, healthy, and mentally active. The euphoria from overachievement was addictive and an invigorating way to nourish the soul and the gods.

The leader of the four men awaited the review of their fate on the day of Vinapu's dedication. They came to welcome Kama and Mahine to their area. Their leader's name was Tara of Hiva, a well-known district chief under the command of the late King Hotu-Matua. He bowed to Kama, and she placed a friendly hand on his shoulder.

"Welcome to Vinapu," he said. "It is now an honor to have you among us."

Then he looked at Mahine, who stoically returned the gaze. It was apparent that Mahine had not fully forgotten their crime.

"I come in peace because the queen and my father, Tamatoa the Great, have ordered me to do so, and because Kama has forgiven you. Nevertheless, I still carry the scars of the crime that I have not been able to forget."

"Daughter of Tamatoa the Great," Tara replied, "The men who did that to you are dead. The men in front of you today are different and ask for your kind forgiveness."

Mahine went to Tara's mate, who carried a young child in her arms. She took the child in her arms and went to Tara. "This young girl is yours. One day she will be a woman. You love her, and she will love you. As you age, I urge you to reconsider the mission of women. Because of my authoritarian father, I know too well how women are often ignored in the Maohi society. Nevertheless, there are times when a woman can excel and allow our society to flourish. Such exceptional women deserve universal respect. At this time, in Rapa Nui, destiny gave us three of these exceptional women: Hina of the Valley, Kama Tici Viracocha, and Kukara Tici Viracocha. I don't consider myself as an exceptional woman, though I am part of the Sacred Circle of the Seven Souls. I just try to apply my skills as best I can."

"You are an exceptional woman," Tara replied. "A long time ago, an old priest named Mato told us you were gifted with the power to know of things happening far away."

"How do you know this?" Mahine asked in surprise.

"Tamatoa the Great told us a lot about you, during the construction of Vinapu."

"One sun cycle ago, in the gardens of the depths, this talent did not help me much!" she replied slightly sarcastically, giving the little girl back to her mother.

"We thank you for your hospitality," Kama said, coming to the rescue.

Mahine placed her hand on Tara's shoulder. "In spite of bad memories, I shall work hard to forgive you."

The little girl went to her father, and he took her in his arms. Tara had tears in his eyes.

****

The following day at dawn, as the sun appeared on the eastern horizon, Hina of the Valley stood on the high platform of Vinapu and raised her arms toward each Rapanui sitting on their respective stones on the hillside of the ahu.

"You are here today to learn the reasons Vinapu was built. As you already know, the exceptional stonework involved in this monument is a gift to our great god Make Make. This monument will live for many generations, exactly the same way as its counterpart at Hanga Roa. When kings and members of the Sacred Circle of the Seven Souls die, their bodies will be buried under the ahu; then monuments will be erected where I stand today to remind you that their souls are still alive and witnessing your daily lives."

She walked down to the crowd and commanded the four men who had raped Kama and Mahine to come forward. They followed her to the top of Vinapu, where the Sacred Circle of the Seven Souls sat.

"Today you will proceed through several important phases," Hina said. "You will explain to the crowd what you did a sun cycle ago, step by step, to recreate that shameful day. Then I will tell the crowd how you lived at Vinapu, until this day. Later on, you and your families, with the Sacred Circle of the Seven Souls, will walk to Hanga Roa, where this ceremony shall end at sunset. Along the way, you must look in yourselves and cast out the bad spirits that still live in you. At sunset, you will explain who you are now; then I will pronounce your fate."

With her words, Hina made clear these men were not exonerated yet. A price needed to be exacted for such crimes. They knew she would be fair, but at the same time very firm.

****

Everyone waited near the Hanga Roa Ahu for Hina's final verdict. The four men, sober and contrite, focused inwardly to tap into their respective mana and give them strength. A long debate within the Sacred Circle of the Seven Souls had taken place all the way between Vinapu and Hanga Roa. Hina of the Valley raised her arms and spoke.

"You, Tara of Hiva, the leader of these men, tell us what your sentence should be."

"As you asked, we debated this all along the walk between Vinapu and Hanga Roa, and we all came to the same conclusion…"

A long silence took place.

"I am waiting!" Hina said, visibly impatient.

"We all decided our queen should tell us what our sentence is."

Hina had a large smile on her face.

"Are you sure about this? You may not like what I decide. Remember: after my words are given, there will be no turning back."

"You tell us!" Tara insisted.

Hina walked away from the circle and the four men. She looked at the western horizon and thought about her childhood.

"I always do that when I have an important decision to make," Tamatoa murmured.

"I know," Kama replied.

"I know too," Kon said with a grin on his face.

Drums rolled, commanding everyone to observe total silence. The queen came back. She was ready to speak.

"You, the guilty ones," Hina said, pointing at the four men, "stand up and bow your heads and listen carefully to every word I say."

A long silence ensued. Only the waves pounding on the rocky shore behind the ahu could be heard. Hina of the Valley was to make a historic pronouncement for Rapa Nui.

"Tomorrow at dawn, the four of you will come to the summit of the cliff at Orongo. While we are at the very edge of the cliff looking down the wall, so steep that no one could ever climb it without being killed, I will tell you your fate."

Everyone was stunned at the proposition. No one knew exactly what the queen had in mind, but people speculated all night. Anxiously, four men and their families waited for her final words. Curious, most of the crowd walked to Orongo that evening and spent the night there, near the formidable cliff.

****

At dawn Hina of the Valley, wearing her most valuable ceremonial clothes, reviewed each of the men as they stood shoulder to shoulder at the edge of the abysmal cliff, a cliff forbidden to men.

"Look at the farthest islet," Hina said. "A long time ago Kama Tici Viracocha lost a little girl at this place. As a result, it has been a sacred place ever since. Today you shall find your way down from here to the rocky beach, swim to the islet, find an egg from the sacred Make Make bird, and bring it here, intact. I shall then have these unbroken eggs in my own hands."

"I knew it, you have wanted to kill us all along," Tara objected. "You are trying to absolve yourself of our murders by making it look like we died accidentally."

Hina poked a violent finger on his chest. The man almost lost his balance above the abyss.

"Do you prefer me to push you off this cliff, right now?"

"No," the man blurted, nearly paralyzed by the Make Make's stare.

"Do you realize you challenged the queen's will?" Hina said. "Don't push your good fortune anymore, or I will destroy you, with great pleasure."

The Viracochas raised their eyebrows at a statement they thought out of line with their peaceful philosophy. There was silence for a long time.

"Depending on the outcome of the egg quest, your destiny shall be manifest," Hina stated firmly. "To be honest, you may die by falling down the cliff, by drowning, or from some other mishap. However, if you come back with an intact egg, you will be free as you were before your crimes. If you come back with a broken egg, you and your family will be exiled from this island forever. If you don't come back before dusk, before the last part of the sun sinks behind the horizon, you and your family will also be exiled forever. You should start your ordeal now; the longer you wait, the more difficult it will be to meet my conditions. All this shall be done."

Everyone was stunned at the queen's mandate. Even Kon Tici complained about the impossibility of this endeavor.

"You send them to their death," Kon said.

"They did not ask Kama and Mahine if they were comfortable when they committed their crimes against them," the queen challenged. "Ask me not what I can do for their comfort; ask them to comply with what I have decided. There is no other way."

"This is the woman I met a long time ago!" Tamatoa the Great murmured.

The four men started their arduous struggle. Everyone watched with concern and compassion. Hina did not bother watching.

"Tamatoa, call me if one of them returns before sunset. I have no desire to watch these criminals."

Kon, Kama, and Kukara followed her.

"What are you doing?" Kon asked. "Why do you exhibit so much hate toward them? This is not like you."

"I am a Maohi, and Maohis take taboos very seriously. If the punishment is too light, then everyone will flaunt our taboos with impunity."

"Hina, you broke taboos yourself a long time ago because of me," Kon argued. "Maohis forgave you for this."

"The difference is that I did not commit any crime nor harm anyone in the process; these men most certainly did!"

"But…" Kama pursued, immediately stopped by a powerful finger pointed at her chest.

"Dear friend," Hina said, "I am not proud of my judgment, but their crimes were clearly prohibited by the Light. Do not be afraid of my decisions; I will always be fair."

"But," Kukara pursued, "forgiveness was the source of your immense success after Tamatoa's crimes; why the difference?"

"Kukara Tici Viracocha," Hina replied, "you are now a young woman with extraordinary talents. You must understand the difference between a man still in shock after having seen his father cut into pieces by a hate-filled enemy, and a man raping a woman and planning her murder. Tamatoa had a reason for what he did, and even if what he did was a horrible thing, magnanimity was always present in his mind. These men who were on trial today have no idea what magnanimity is. I am sorry, but I have absolutely no remorse for them. If they survive, it will teach them honor, as now they have none. The only reason they lived peacefully during the building of Vinapu is because they were scared to death of Tamatao. I am not naïve, and I see potential future problems with them unless we are able to cleanse their souls now."

"Yes, I understand and agree with that," Kon said, putting a friendly hand on Hina's shoulder. She stared at him, and he could see the slow formation of a tear in Make Make's eye.

****

At sunset, everyone reconvened at Orongo, and the queen was informed that two of the men were on their way back.

"What happened to the other ones?" Hina asked.

"One man fell to his death from the cliff as he was going down," Taatamao replied. "The other one drowned on his way back from the islet, and we do not know why."

One man, full of blood all over his body, brought an intact egg to Hina.

She took the egg.

"You are a brave man, and your mana was with you. You are free, and you may settle with your family anywhere you please on the island."

"May I settle with my family near Ovahe to serve you and your family?"

Surprised, Hina placed a friendly hand on his shoulder. "I said anywhere you please, and I mean what I said."

The man went away with a smile and a countenance full of hope. He was immediately circled by joyful relatives, who heaped endless congratulations on surviving the challenge, as well as being given the right to settle near Hina.

Tara came back… with a broken egg.

Hina went to him, pointing a finger at his face.

"The sacred place of Make Make's birth saw evil in your soul; as a result, you were unable to protect this egg with sufficient love. You must leave the island with your family and go back to Hiva, where you were born. You no longer belong to Rapa Nui. You have two days to prepare. We will watch you depart from Anakena. This is said and shall be done."

****

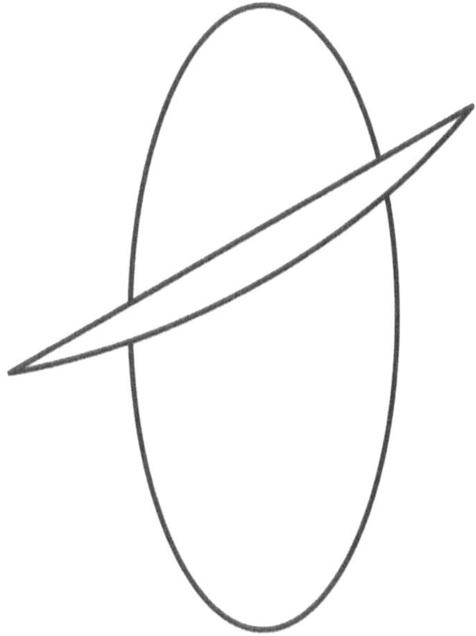

The sacred egg from the frigate bird must be used for many ceremonies. The opening of the egg and the use of its contents was a serious matter for the rulers.

CHAPTER 30

"My encounters with the gods always came at unpredictable times. For each occurrence there were solid facts, but also many mysteries. Yet again I would be baffled by a reality far more complex than I ever imagined. I was the queen, and I had to adapt to what I learned and also to what I could not understand. There were forces in this world far beyond human comprehension."

Hina of the Valley

Following lengthy arguments among the members of the Sacred Circle of the Seven Souls, a decision had been made that only one ship would be used to go to the Great Gathering on Havaiki Island. The Great Gathering takes place every seven sun cycles. Since Hina did not want to attend, Kon decided not to go either. Similarly, Tamatoa did not want to go; therefore Kama stayed at home with him. Taatamao and Mahine would go with their child, Kukara, and Kane, Kama's son. It was Tamatoa's wish that they use his ship, which was larger, faster, and in almost perfect condition. It would be crewed with twenty people, as Hina indicated by spreading the fingers of both hands twice. It would include four families.

The travelers would leave one moon cycle earlier than what the trip should require. They would visit Tahiti Nui before sailing to Havaiki.

"You would love to go," Kon said.

"I know," Hina replied, "but we have too many responsibilities on Rapa Nui. Our people cannot afford for us to be gone for so long."

"This trip will be a fantastic experience for Kukara," Kon said. "She is going to make a great impression at the gathering. In a way they already know her."

"Of course they do, especially the people of Tahiti Nui; she will be received as a queen."

"She has grown up and is starting to resemble Kama," Kon said. "When she comes back, she will be a woman. It is hard to believe time has gone so fast; our little girl is fourteen sun cycles old."

They spent the day at Anakena, loading the ship, making recommendations, and saying sad farewells with hugs, kisses, and tears.

"Mother and Father, I am going to miss you," Kukara said. "When I return, I will be able to tell you about a secret mission I am undertaking at the Great Gathering."

Kon and Hina glanced at each other and remained silent. Kukara's words were not spoken idly; once again, she was up to something of great significance.

The ship was pushed away from the beach while the crew was joined in song by those staying on the island. As soon as the wind bit into the hoisted sails, the double-hulled vessel sprang to life and rapidly gained speed, pushed into the western sea by the brisk eastern breeze.

Kukara looked at her loved ones fading away and whispered, "I shall return and bring limitless joy to all of you. Help me, Make Make."

****

Kon, Hina, and their son, Maui, joined Tamatoa and Kama

and their child as they headed back to Ovahe, where they would stay for a few days. Along the way, they gathered fruits and vegetables offered by their friends. Tamatoa bargained for a fat piglet that he carried over his shoulder the entire distance. When they reached the settlement, they all felt the emptiness caused by the departure of their loved ones. Together, they would learn to cope with their absence. They all joined in the preparation of a good evening meal they planned to enjoy on the boathouse's terrace, while gathered around a fire fed with dead shrubs and enhanced with the intermittent burning of pungent herbs patiently collected around the island.

The piglet, taros, sweet potatoes, and bananas were carefully wrapped in several layers of banana leaves, then buried in the fire pit's red embers. A layer of red-hot stones covered the embers, followed with a layer of soil. They left the boathouse and went to Hina's favorite pond, in which they would bath naked, talk, and joke until late at night. Back at the boathouse, they fed the young children and put them to sleep in a quiet, tiny room reserved and decorated for them.

Kon and Tamatoa removed the piglet from the embers. They carefully removed the charred banana leaves to reveal delicious fresh vegetables and the meat, which could be pulled apart, piece by piece, with their fingers. They ate slowly and enjoyed their meal well into the night, until one by one they drifted off to sleep, right there on the clean slabs of the terrace.

Early the next morning, the raucous squawking from a few seagulls finishing leftovers from the frugal meal awakened them. Kama chased them away and collected some untouched leftover scraps and brought them to her companions. For several days Tamatao helped Kon work on a drainage system that would channel rainwater into a lava tube that extended from the top of the tiny crater to the garden where they were grew vegetables and fruits. Meanwhile, Kama and Hina explored the environs for rare plants, took care of the children, and bathed at the Ovahe pink sandy beach.

****

The ship had sailed at full speed on its westerly course for five days. The waves were high, long, and easily managed. Life on the deck was quiet and uneventful. Kukara spent a lot of time meditating, while Kane had a passion for trolling a long line, trying to catch large yellowfin tunas. They had much more fresh meat than they could eat. Their catch was kept in a bamboo aquarium. They still had an ample supply of fresh sweet potatoes, taro, bananas, and green coconuts. Later during the voyage, they would switch over to the fresh yams, which could keep well for two moon cycles. Schools of dolphins intermittently followed; all the voyagers enjoyed watching them, believing that they brought good luck. They gave them names and played with them. The crew loved to jump into the water, secured by a long rope wrapped around their waist or around one foot, and swim and dive with the dolphins. It was a favorite game for both humans and dolphins. Kukara was convinced she could talk to them. The next morning, Kane sat close to Kukara as if he had a secret to tell her. She noticed the difference in his attitude and wondered what he had to say.

"Since the day my brother, Ku, left this world," Kane said, "I had wondered if I could replace him in your heart."

Surprised, she looked at him with wide open eyes.

"In the cave, when Hina held him lifeless in her arms, you said you loved him."

"Yes, I loved him as if he were my brother," Kukara replied. "I love you the same way."

"I thought you loved him enough for him to become your mate."

"The thought crossed my mind," Kukara replied coyly.

383

"Have you ever thought that I might, one day, become your mate?"

"No, I never thought of it," she said teasingly.

Chagrined and disappointed, Kane walked away and started a new task. Amused, she watched him go and decided it would be good for him not to take her for granted.

"You must conquer me," she murmured to herself. She was indeed fond of him. She rubbed her back, which continued to bother her at times, especially when she had lifted something heavy. She wondered if she would ever fully recover before the next moai walked. Then she wondered about the consequences of violently bouncing again, many times a day. Perhaps she would be unable to perform such a task. Perhaps Kon had been right to suggest she could direct the walk from the ground. However, it was her pride and her passion to do this from the top of the moai.

Ten days passed before they saw the first atoll's distinctive contour on the western horizon.

"Now we are within well-known territory," Taatamao said. "As soon as we identify this island, we can adjust our course straight to Tahiti Nui."

"I am excited," Kukara said, squeezing Mahine's hand.

"So am I!" Mahine replied. "I hope to see my old master again."

"Old Mato was your mentor?" Kukara asked.

"He was more than that. He was my father when Tamatoa, my real father, was busy on a very crucial mission, and he was also my friend. I could talk with him about anything. He would patiently listen and offer wonderful answers."

"Do you think he is still alive?"

"I don't know. I hope he is."

Later that evening, under a starry, moonless sky, Kukara, Mahine, Taatamao, and Kane sat in a circle and silently meditated. Several times they made attempts to communicate with their peers from the Sacred Circle of the Seven Souls. Several times they failed to make contact. They included Kane in their tiny circle to help develop his skills. On this particular evening, Kukara was inspired and determined to make contact. All day along, she had concentrated within herself to send signals to Kama, Kon, and Hina.

****

Far to the east, long before dawn on the same day, Kon took Hina aside.

"I clearly received signals from another Viracocha," Kon explained.

"Kama is here with us," Hina replied.

"It must be Kukara. Kane is not very good at this."

"What would you suggest?"

"Usually, Kukara meditates at dusk and during the early part of the night."

"Shall the four of us gather at a place she knows well?"

"Around Hotu-Matua at Rano Raraku would be the best place."

At midday they left Ovahe and headed to the sacred quarry and resting place of the gods. When they arrived, they saw the long shadow of Hotu-Matua slowly extend as the sun set. They quickened their pace to be by the formidable moai at sunset.

They stood near the giant and looked up. Frozen in time, serene and remote, its unblinking eyes looked at the stars. Mysterious, with a slight grin on the face, Hotu-Matua's spirit looked out upon the surrounding world. They felt meek in its presence, a presence that they had created. They sat humbly and quietly in a circle near Hotu-Matua's long fingers. Kon placed a round stone in the center of the circle. The stone, Hotu-Matua's companion, was used as a reference point during meditations; it helped them to focus their minds on a single common object.

Kama placed one hand on the longest finger of Hotu-Matua's left hand. Kon placed one hand on the longest finger of the right hand. With the other hand, Kon took Hina's hand, Hina took Tamatoa's hand, and he took Kama's hand; the circle was complete, establishing a link with the awesome power of a long-departed king. They waited until the sun vanished, and until the sky turned completely dark. There were many stars and no moon. They all saw the black contour of a ghost slowly moving on the same path as the stars. Hina received a shock wave of energy from Kon's fingers; chills coursed along her spine. Never before had she felt so insignificant. Tamatoa glanced at the moai. His eyes looked up and up until they met the pointy black nose. Even though he was twice as strong as anybody else on the island, he felt like a weak little boy. He glanced at Hina and saw the silent face of Make Make looking up as though it was communicating with Hotu-Matua. He recalled how much he respected her. The contact of her hand was comforting to his soul. He felt honored to be part of this sacred circle.

Now they all had focused on the round stone in the middle of the circle. Now they waited for a signal from Kukara, or from a god through whom her mind might travel. It came, in the most unexpected form. A late petrel, exhausted from its flight back to land, crash-landed in the middle of the circle. After recovering its composure, the bird climbed on the top of the round stone and inspected its surroundings. The bird saw four pairs of eyes staring at him, in resolute silence. The bird recognized the familiar contour of the moai. Tired, the bird lay on the stone, closed its eyes, and went to sleep.

****

Far away at the same instant on the sailing ship, a tired tropicbird landed in the middle of Kukara's sacred circle. After recovering its composure, the bird inspected the surroundings and saw four pairs of eyes staring back at him, in silence.

A very faint purple glow enveloped the two birds. Each member of the two sacred circles saw it form on their respective birds. Was it reality? Was it an illusion? Or was it wishful thinking? The well-trained Viracochas, like Kon, Kukara, and Kama, knew that contact had been made with the other party, and that it was being led by a supreme being who wanted such a contact to take place. The others were unsure what to believe. For Hina of the Valley, however, her past experiences had taught her to be open-minded when it came to the strange territory of spirits. She followed every detail very closely.

"Great Taaroa," she murmured, "great Viracocha, great Make Make, great Light, All-Mighty, I was told once to use your powers wisely. Now I have a desire to use them."

Kon raised his head and glanced at her, and pressed her hand; she felt Tamatoa doing the same thing. They all closed their eyes. They left the bird in peace and started traveling in space. In front of them, in the faint purple glow, they recognized Kukara's vague shape. The Light had once more taken Kukara's form. The Light was with them.

Far away on the ship, Kukara saw the Light and knew instantly her beloved relatives saw her as well, because she was talking to them.

"The ship carrying your beloved family is doing well," the Light said. "Kukara Tici Viracocha is doing extremely well. They have already passed the first atolls. Be reassured and love each other under the presence of this giant figure you created in the living rock. It does not move. To many, it is only a stone. To many, it was a fool's errand. To many, it would seem an unnecessary waste of human resources to create such a work. But to the few initiates, this creation is your living soul. You are special. You are inspired. You are my dear children. You are progressing well…"

Kukara's vague silhouette vanished, and the faint purple light dissipated. They all emerged from their lucid dream experience. Both birds took their flight in the middle of the night. Hina was the first one to recover her composure.

"Kukara is doing well," Hina said. "They already passed the first atolls."

Tamatoa glanced at Hina and at Kama; he seemed frightened.

"In my wildest dreams," the tattooed giant said, "it never occurred to me I would experience such a presence in my mind. All of us were with the great spirits. I saw everything. I heard everything. I always had a doubt about Viracochas' claims. Never again will I ever doubt."

Hina took his face in her hands and placed her nose on his in a friendly gesture.

"Let's go back home," she said. "I am hungry."

"You were born that way," Kon chuckled.

They all laughed in good spirits. Under the starlight they found their way out of Rano Raraku. They left Hotu-Matua slowly fading into the night. They never turned back to look at him. They knew he was omnipresent. They knew they would live with him for the rest of their lives. They knew the giant they had created was alive in many ways. They knew they could be proud of everything they had done at Rano Raraku. The gods were happy.

****

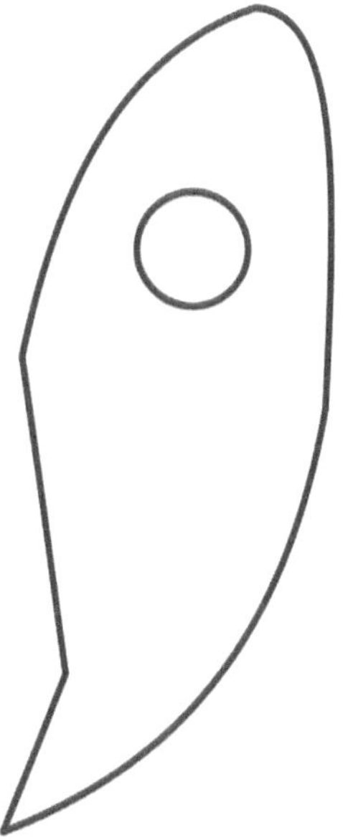

The moai at its final resting place is forever inhabited by powerful mana. Rulers and visitors will touch it with one finger and catch mysterious powers that will, some day, guide their life.

CHAPTER 31

"Toerau was an inspiring place; it played a major constructive role in the development of my mother's character. It was the favorite perfect place for me to finalize how I wanted to do things during this journey to the Great Gathering. I also needed to find a powerful ally among Maohis."

Kukara Tici Viracocha

At dawn the ship was approaching Tahiti Nui's shore. Kukara saw the black sandy beaches and the coconut trees that surrounded Haapape, a little village located on the western side of Papenoo, near the beautiful Teauroa point, where Hina the child had often played in the sand dunes. Many outriggers were being launched from the shore and were being paddled to meet the visitors. The king's ship, with its unmistakable contour, moved away from the beach and headed toward Tamatoa's vessel. Everyone on Tahiti Nui knew what Tamatoa's ship looked like. They remembered that their loved ones departed on that ship over seven sun cycles ago.

Kukara, now a beautiful, voluptuous Viracocha woman, stood on the ship's bow, her long black hair blowing slightly in the morning breeze. Her joy was so great that she felt her heart pounding in her chest. These were the beloved people of her adoptive mother. These were Hina's parents and sister. This was the magnificent birthplace of the great Hina of the Valley. Tears found their way down her cheeks. Mahine embraced Kukara and shared a joyful cry with her.

Taatamao gave orders to set course for the strait connecting the ocean with the large Matavai Bay. Tupua, the king, brought his galley, about half the size of Tamatoa's ship, alongside the familiar visiting ship. Soon, once they were inside the calm waters of Matavai Bay, they slowly approached each other. Taatamao and Tupua anchored their vessels. A short distance was kept between the two ships, with long paddles held on both ends by seafarers. Some paddles were brought together side by side and lashed, forming a walkway between the boats. This time was very different. This time warmonger's formalities were out of fashion. Tupua ran across the narrow bridge and warmly welcomed Taatamao, and then he went to Mahine and hugged her as if she were from his own family. Then he glanced around.

"Where is your father? Where are Hina and Kon?"

"They did not come with us," Mahine replied, "but they are all fine, and they send their love to you."

"Well!" Tupua said, trying hard to contain his disappointment.

"However, she came," Mahine said, pointing at Kukara.

Tupua hesitated for a short moment.

"Kukara? You are Kukara! This is unbelievable."

She ran to him. The king hugged and welcomed her as though she were his own beloved daughter.

Atea, the king's wife and Hina's mother, ran across the bridge and went straight to Kukara.

"My little girl, how much you have changed!" she said with tears in her eyes. "How is your mother?"

"Hina of the Valley is well; she is our queen on a remote island about the size of Havaiki," Kukara replied. "You would be very proud of her."

"We will talk about this," Tupua said, taking Kukara's hand, "for a very long time!"

"Yes!" Kukara smiled.

Kukara crossed the bridge and ran to Fenua, Hina's sister, and Aru, her mate.

The two women embraced each other and hugged for a long time, thoroughly enjoying the wonderful reunion.

"I cannot believe how much you have changed," Fenua said.

"I am not a little girl anymore," Kukara replied, hugging Aru.

Then Kukara saw a thin old man anxiously waiting for her. He wore the classic long white robe of priesthood; the famous green pigeon feather was on his chest. He was the great priest.

"Vana!" Kukara exclaimed. She ran to him and gave him a hug that nearly cracked his ribs. "Hina talks about you all the time."

"I am saddened that she did not come," Vana replied with a broken little voice, taking a shallow breath.

"We will talk about this," Kukara comforted. "I have an idea."

Kukara remained on the king's boat, while the others returned to Taatamao's. The respective crews poled the boats to an anchorage and disembarked. They walked the short distance between Haapape and Papenoo. The king invited everyone to his garden to relax, eat, and catch up. It took Kukara, Mahine, and Taatamao the remainder of the day to explain their adventure and all the events that led to Rapa Nui's discovery and what life was like there. In a way, their description of the island seemed to paint a picture of a bizarre and unattractive place to the old, overweight monarch. He was puzzled why Hina liked living in such a dismal and dreary place, when her place of birth was such a paradise.

"Unforgettable events make you like a place," Vana

suggested, "even if the place is unattractive."

"Rapa Nui is immensely attractive," Kukara argued, visibly annoyed by the comment.

"You pierced your ears like Kon," Tupua noticed. "But the disks are made of fish bone."

"Kukara," Mahine said, "show your beautiful Rongo-RongoRongo-Rongo tattoos to our host."

Kukara removed her robe and revealed her torso, arms, and legs. They all marveled at the beautifully and delicately tattooed, mysterious Rongo-Rongo signs. The tattoos seemed to augment her natural beauty. However, they found her too skinny.

"You need to gain some weight," Tupua suggested. "You must have been starving during this long trip."

Vana started laughing, knowing his old friend was truly annoying the young woman. He knew Kukara enough to expect a strong reply, exactly the way Hina would have done. It came, but with a polite and diplomatic touch, which greatly surprised Vana.

"I like myself this way, and so does my mother. Kane, who I introduced to you earlier, is already courting me. Therefore, my skinny body must be attractive to him."

Atea glanced at Fenua, and both giggled.

The next day they participated in the perfunctory ceremonies reserved for high-ranking visitors. Late in the afternoon, close to the festivities' conclusion, Vana asked Kukara to play some tunes on the flute that the Inca's son had given to her several sun cycles ago. Nobody had ever seen one like it.

"Kukara is exceptionally good at this instrument," Mahine said admiringly. "All of us have tried numerous times, but cannot come close to Kukara's skill."

"So let's hear it!" Tupua said, sitting on a large boulder.

Kukara sat on another boulder, facing Tupua. Many

dignitaries and other people were watching her expectantly. The ceremonial drums rolled, signaling everyone to become silent; that is, except for one cranky baby in his mother's arms.

"Do not worry," Kukara said. "Observe the baby."

She blew a delicate melody in the air, much to everyone's surprise and admiration. The baby immediately became quiet and opened his eyes and searched for Kukara. Not seeing her, the baby started crying again. She played one note and silenced him again. Everyone laughed. Drums rolled again.

Her delicate fingers and long fingernails seemed to become an extension of the flute, mesmerizing the audience with their dance. The melody was soft, sad, but also inspiring. Men listened, intrigued by this young woman from another world. Although they knew her, they became increasingly aware that they knew nothing of her knowledge and skills. They knew she was a peaceful ambassador and the most honest person they had ever met. Women had chills run up their spines and goose bumps all over their bodies. There was something about her that was far beyond their ken. There were mysteries very disturbing to their ordinary life. Yet with all her talents, Kukara was the most humble person in the world. Her humbleness came through this music they had never heard. Even the priests became enchanted and whisked away to the edge of the spirit world. The king closed his eyes and recalled the face of Kon Tici in his dreams many sun cycles before he had met the man.

It was silent for a long time after she stopped. Each person had been transported to their private place of peace.

"Exquisite, wonderful, thank you!" the king said.

The king's pronouncement was punctuated by a standing ovation. Later in that evening, Kukara took a walk with Vana to the Toerau Marae, the sacred place where Hina had started her priesthood.

"We left it exactly as it was when she departed," Vana said. "Once in a while we all come here to reflect on her life and maintain the gardens for that day when she returns."

Kukara stopped and took his hand.

"Hina of the Valley will never return to the homeland she loves so much. She is another person now, with enormous responsibilities. She places her duties far above her sentiments."

"I am not surprised. Even as a child, she was a proud and responsible person."

The first thing Kukara noticed as they approached the main complex of Toerau was the many tiare bushes, which bear Hina's favorite flower.

"Tiares don't grow well on Rapa Nui," she said. "It is too cold in winter."

Vana took one flower and placed it behind Kukara's ear.

"You look better that way," the old man said. She smiled.

"Remind me what does Toerau mean?" Kukara asked. "My mother told me, but I have forgotten."

Vana knew that Kukara had not forgotten. For some reason she wanted to continue their conversation.

"It is the name of the northwest wind, the wind that is blowing right now. Toerau brings rain and verdure to the valley. Toerau gives birth to the rain forest. Toerau is the father of the ferns that you like so much. Toerau brings food to my people; therefore it brings peace."

Kukara looked at him with tears in her eyes.

"Why the tears, Kukara?"

"Because your words are her words exactly."

"So you knew."

"I wanted to know your version."

"It is not my version. Hina chose the name of Toerau, fully aware of what it meant. It was an enlightened choice. And more, when you first came to this island with Hotu-Matua, your sails were pushed by Toerau."

Kukara gave a smile for his thoughtful statement.

"As a queen today, she is making bright choices," she said.

"I am delighted to hear that. Coming from you, I know it is true."

"When Taranga Tici Viracocha neared his crossing," Kukara said, "there were many people who he could have been chosen to become our ruler. He never hesitated on the choice, and Hotu-Matua was in full agreement with him. Hina of the Valley had always been their choice."

"I wonder why they chose a Maohi over a Viracocha."

"The few Viracocha survivors are talented people in many ways," Kukara replied, "but they don't have the skills, completeness, or love for the people like Hina. From the people's perspective, she is a remarkable choice. They love her. They respect her. They socialize with her. But when warranted, they fear her. She is a good keeper of order and laws. They know the taboos very well."

"She was my favorite child. Yet many times she was my nemesis."

Kukara burst into laughter.

"I knew she would be a powerful leader one day," Vana continued. "Her father did not see this because she was a girl."

"A person's sex is irrelevant," Kukara said. "If you are a born leader, so be it!"

"It is easier said than done sometimes," Vana replied.

"I know what you mean because we had such an experience recently. But Hina handled the situation better than anyone expected. She was tough, but she was fair."

Vana sat on an old bench carved from precious tamanu wood and looked at the setting sun. He seemed preoccupied and distracted.

"May I ask a question?"

"Anything!" Kukara replied. "Later, I will ask a favor of you."

Vana was intrigued by the young woman's mysterious air.

"I am the great priest, but I don't know half of what you know. You are still a child. I have no idea how you do this. I would like you to share one of your powers with me, so I can learn from it. Will you do that for an old man?"

She nodded and smiled.

"You know many things that I don't, if we look around in the forest. Yes, I know what I am going to do. You will enjoy it."

Vana gave her a wide smile. He knew she would never do anything mediocre. She came over and sat next to him.

"Come close to me. I am going to share some of my memories with you; that way you can see what Rapa Nui looks like."

"This cannot be done. I don't believe you!"

She pulled his hands to her chest. She pulled his head against hers.

"For this to work, you must stay in close contact with me at all times. Close your eyes. Listen to the waves pounding on Toerau. Let your mind wander…"

Vana felt the warmth of the young woman's body. This, in and of itself, was agreeable. Then he felt something flowing through his hands and his head. At first it seemed like slow, viscous warm blood. It became more pervasive, steadily permeating his body; it was as though she injected a powerful drug into his bloodstream. His awareness of his surroundings slowly vanished, replaced with visions from a new world. He walked on the edge of sharp rocks. Kukara held his hand. On one side, deep in the mountain was an immense hole with a lake at its bottom. Many green islets floated on the lake's blue waters. On the other side was the steep cliff that jutted into the sea. Waves pounded at its base. Farther out in the sea, he could see three islets. The scenery was different from anything he had ever seen. They walked to a village where he saw Tamatoa with a Viracocha woman. She was taller and older than Kukara. It seemed Kukara and he were flying, moving from place to place very fast. He saw a white sandy beach where women and children bathed. He saw a pink sandy beach, followed by another settlement. He recognized Kon, then Hina, though he only saw her back. She turned around, and he saw a frightening tattoo on one side of her face. Then he saw the other side of her face, which was like the Hina he knew. They went to a monument made of huge stones. The island's entire population was there. Each person was seated on a half-buried stone. The area surrounding the monument was well-groomed. A group of seven people formed a circle on the top of the platform. There he saw Hina, Kon, Tamatoa, Kama (he had been told), Kukara, Taatamao, and Mahine. When Hina stood, he saw the sacred green feather on her chest. Kukara then took him inside a lava tube, something he had never seen. She took him to the gardens of the depths, and he marveled at what he saw. During his out-of-body journey, he saw the charm of a very different place, but he could not talk to anyone. To all of them, he did not exist. He was only visiting memories from Kukara's mind. Nevertheless, it gave him an amazing insight into their new life. Now they came to a stop, and he squeezed Kukara's hand. She felt his face shaking against hers and his hands trembling on her chest. She did not want to wake him. She took a few steps backward in the vision. Stunned, Vana fell on his knees. In front of him a giant statue walked across the horizon, led by many men. Standing atop the great statue, a fearless commander gave the precise orders, which kept the leviathan moving. The commander was only a young girl. It was Kukara Tici Viracocha! He instantly woke up and looked into her charming blue eyes. He thought what he had just seen was impossibility.

"Everything you saw is reality," Kukara said calmly.

"Who are you, young woman?"

"I thought you would like to see a few of the things we do on Rapa Nui."

"I cannot believe this," he replied, standing up and laughing at himself.

"Keep this to yourself, because many people won't believe you."

"That I know!" he replied, poking a finger on her chest. "What was that thing?"

"It was a statue that Kon carved and transported to the resting place of Hotu-Matua. We made another one for Taranga's resting place."

"So they are dead. Who designed this? How did you learn to do such things?"

"Kon is the master of everything we build on Rapa Nui. He is a very quiet man. You rarely hear from him, but his mind is constantly working on his next sacred project."

"So he is the one who trained you?"

"No, I trained myself. Nobody thought what I did was possible. Even Kon was skeptical."

He took her face in his hands.

"Young lady, you are the most extraordinary great priestess I ever met. I will do anything for you."

"Promise?"

"Promise!"

"Then sit down," Kukara ordered. He complied.

"You know Rapa Iti?" she asked rhetorically.

"Of course I know Rapa Iti. I went there several times when

I was young."

"The climate of this island is very much like the one on Rapa Nui, but colder."

"I know that."

"The remains of Illa, Kon's brother, are buried somewhere on Rapa Iti's mountains. Kane knows the exact place. I want to take Illa's remains to Rapa Nui, where they belong."

The old priest's smile slowly vanished into sadness.

"Moving the remains of the dead is not a good idea. Such an act is taboo."

"That is why I need your help; you can convince people otherwise, that there are exceptions. After all, you are the great priest."

"Suppose we succeed in convincing the Rapa Iti priests; how can I help you otherwise?"

"I want to convince Tupua to come with you, not only to Rapa Iti, but to Rapa Nui as well, where you, Atea, and Tupua will stay for several moon cycles."

"You are out of your mind," he huffed, with a deep frown forming on his face. "We are too old to travel like this."

"At your age, this may be your last chance to do so."

"You are an idealistic young lady. I will never convince Tupua to do so."

"Therefore, I already convinced you to do so!"

He stared at her and started laughing.

"I would like to see that statue walk with my own eyes."

"Great!" she said, giving him a big kiss on the cheek, surprising the old priest a great deal.

****

From left to right: The spirit of the turtle would communicate between Rapa Nui, Hiva, and Havaiki. Spirits would go back and forth from Rapa Nui to the lands of the ancestors. The sacred Seven Souls selected by King Hotu Matua would carry the supreme knowledge for what Rapa Nui would become.

CHAPTER 32

"The Great Gathering on Havaiki was a dream place, where my talents would be scrutinized by the great priest and our kings. It was my duty to well represent the last Viracochas. It was a huge responsibility, and I was not yet sure exactly what I would do. I chose to wait and see. I trusted myself to quickly adapt as needed. I had attained a new level of self-confidence."

Kukara Tici Viracocha

The next day, Kukara sat in the king's magnificent garden. The surrounding frangipanes, tiares, and many other tropical flowers intoxicated her; she loved the climate and environment of the island, where she had once lived, seven sun cycles ago. The giant vines that twisted around very old trees were unknown on Rapa Nui, where the vegetation was sparser and less luxuriant. This place was a delight to her nose, eyes, and soul.

Fenua walked up to Kukara and handed her a freshly opened green coconut.

"I thought you would enjoy this drink."

"Thank you, you are kind to me," Kukara replied.

"You are family."

"Do you mind if I join the girls?" Tupua asked with good humor, caressing his huge tummy.

"Did Vana talk to you?" Kukara asked.

"Yes, he did. In principle, I agree with your plans. That being said, there are some difficulties to resolve, namely the Rapa Iti priests and their kings. There are two clans who do not care for each other. Other difficulties include the preparation of several large ships and training their crews to stay close together. This would be a long trip, particularly since we will be sailing against the wind. It will not be an easy voyage. But if we can surmount the obstacles, we will give it a try."

"No problem!" Kukara replied with a smile full of confidence.

"You are an optimistic young lady," the king said. "In return, I have a favor to ask of you."

Fenua felt she better leave Kukara alone with her father. Kukara watched her leave and drank a little of the fresh coconut milk. Then Vana joined them.

"I would like you and Vana to prepare some kind of performance you can present to the audience at the Great Gathering that would impress the people."

Kukara smiled, amused. The king was interested in showing how important he was; she and Vana were the puppets. She graciously accepted the king's very human request.

"Do you have any idea what we might do?" she asked Vana.

"I don't have a clue."

They all threw back their heads and laughed.

"You have half a moon cycle to think and practice," the king chortled.

****

Half a moon cycle later, Tupua's ship entered the Te Ava Moa Pass that connected to the Opoa Bay in the southern part of Havaiki. Straight ahead, they would meet the large contingent of

Maohis that sailed from many distant islands. All the kings and priests would gather around the sacred white monolith of the Marae of Taputapu-Atea.

As the ship approached the beach, Kukara and Vana recognized the massive outlines of some of Tamatoa's, now his son's, ships. Tamatoa's son Mehao was now the supreme ruler of many islands. Some were from Rarotonga, Pora-Pora, and Huahine; others were from Rapa Iti and from such distant locations as Mangareva and Samoa. To Tupua's surprise, many ships came from unknown regions.

As Taatamao and Mahine's ship entered the Te Ava Moa Pass, there was a great commotion. Many people knew that ship very well. For some it was a welcome event, for others it was worrisome to think that Tamatoa the Great was back. Mehao's ship maneuvered to within a short distance of Taatamao's, and the paddlers quickly laid their paddles across the space between the two ships and created a narrow bridge. Mehao immediately jumped on the bridge and confidently strode to the other boat. He wore a long red feather cape and a spectacular headdress made from thick bark cloth and decorated with rare cowries. It was topped by long dry grass fibers, so no one would be taller than him. He was very formal, following ceremonial protocols very closely. Taatamao was much more practical and did not want to show off; he walked briskly to his old friend and clapped him on the shoulder. At first Mehao seemed annoyed, but their old friendship took over quickly. Mahine ran into Mehao's arms. She had tears of happiness to see her brother again.

Later that day, Mehao took Mahine aside.

"Please tell Taatamao to follow our rituals and customs; this is the Great Gathering."

She turned her back to him and started to walk away.

"Hina, help me!" she murmured to herself. Then she turned to face him.

"The Great Gathering is about great people, regardless of how they dress or act. The Great Gathering is full of mediocre people who dress extremely well to compensate for talent they don't have. My brother, I love you, but what you just said makes me mad. Our great father would not approve. have disapproved."

"I did not intend to offend you. Come with me, I want you to meet an old friend of yours."

They approached another ship and boarded it, following the usual rituals. They went to a little cabin on the aft end, thatched with woven coconut fronds. Inside the cabin, a very old man dressed in a long white robe reclined on woven mats.

"Mato!" Mahine exclaimed. She fell on her knees to hug him.

"My child, I am so happy to see you again."

"My dear companion, I missed you so much."

"My bones and muscles can no longer support me. I still walk a little, but with great pain. I am near the end. My, you look healthy. I can tell you are doing well."

"We are all doing well on Rapa Nui."

"Where is Rapa Nui?"

"It is far away toward the rising sun, an island about the size of this one. I wish you could see what we are doing. My father is doing well. He is a happy, peaceful man now."

"Is he the king?"

"No, Hina of the Valley is the queen, the great priestess, and our supreme ruler."

"Amazing!" he replied with a giggle. "Knowing your father… amazing!"

Later that night, in Mato's guesthouse, Mahine and Kukara came to visit the wizened old priest.

"I asked Kukara for a favor," Mahine said.

"The last time we met, you were a bright little girl," Mato said, taking Kukara's hands.

"Kukara is going to show you what our new home looks like," Mahine said.

"How can she do that?"

Kukara sat near him, pulled his hands to her chest, and rested her head against his.

"Press tightly against me at all times. Close your eyes. Listen to the waves pounding on the reef."

She repeated the ritual that she had done with Vana. All the time Mahine watched, excited about Mato's reaction.

Suddenly, Mato became agitated and opened his eyes in disbelief.

"Who are you, young woman?" he asked, staring at Kukara.

"Everything I showed you is true. You saw the new home of Tamatoa and Mahine and their magnificent gardens of the depths."

"Yes! Beautiful! But this statue walking, with you directing at the top… How?"

Kukara laughed, but she always tried to be humble about her remarkable powers. Mahine came to the rescue.

"This is what priests can do, when they are good at it."

"Well! Yes, but… How can she pass these images to my head?"

"Viracochas are good at this," Kukara replied.

"Only gods are good at this!" the old man argued.

"I am not a god," Kukara said. "I do not seek recognition for what I do; I have been able to harness my mana and passion to accomplish what I enjoy to do."

"By all the spirits in this world, I never dreamed of such an experience, ever. You have a lot to offer at this gathering, I can tell you."

Energized, he stood and walked toward the beach.

"Amazing!" he muttered. "Amazing!"

Mahine glanced at Kukara, who was thoroughly enjoying herself.

Mato joined Vana, who was also walking on the beach.

"Amazing!…" Mato said, looking at Vana.

"What is amazing?" Vana asked.

"Kukara! How can she do that?" Vana took Mato's arm and helped him to walk on the sand.

"So she got to you too! She is an amazing girl. I thought Kon was good, but I had not seen anything. What amazes me the most is her confidence and certainty. She never questions if she will succeed or not. She just expects things to happen, and they do."

Later, Kukara was alone with Kane in a guesthouse. She took a cupful of coconut milk to Kane, who took it and shared it with her. She knew he had only one thing on his mind; he was in love with her.

"You don't care about me," he said petulantly. "You care only about showing off to these kings and great priests."

"I resent what you just said."

She looked into his eyes and tenderly caressed his hands.

"The Great Gathering takes place every seven sun cycles," she said. "We will have plenty of time to talk about our relationship after we return to Rapa Nui. The romance you are dreaming about is not for me yet. I am not ready for it. But when the time comes, you will be my choice. And I will tell you when the time is right."

"Really!" he replied in disbelief.

She took his face in her hands and slowly rubbed her lips against his. She turned around, lay on the woven mats, and went to sleep.

Kane, still in shock from what Kukara had just said and done, his eyes closed and his head still spinning, slowly returned to reality. He went outside and walked to the beach. He stopped where the waves died on the black sand beach and looked at the stars, totally in awe. He touched his lips with his fingers, still feeling the shock wave she had sent through his body.

"She is so good!" he murmured.

He took a few more steps and jumped as high as he could.

"Wow!"

The following morning, Kukara went to Vana, preoccupied and puzzled.

"How is my young priestess?" Vana asked.

"You are a talented priest with medicine," she stated, ignoring his question.

"Yes, I suppose. What is bothering you?"

"When I was bouncing at the top of moai you saw in my mind, I hurt my back. I thought it would go away, but after many moon cycles it is still bothering me."

"I see! Lie down and let me examine your back."

She complied. He gently rubbed her spine from her neck to her lower back.

"Right there!" Kukara said.

"I don't feel anything. I have two suggestions for you. Several times a day you should grab a tree branch and lift your body for a short time, making certain that your feet don't touch the ground. This may stretch your spine and relieve the muscles; they seem stiff. Then stay there; I am going to warm some stones in a fire. I will be back shortly."

Kukara thought about his idea, and it made a lot of sense. When Vana came back, he was followed by three women carrying warm stones. Vana placed the heavy stones on her back around the place she had pain.

"This feels so good!" Kukara said.

She enjoyed the pressure and the warmth of stones until they had completely cooled. When she stood, the pain had abated significantly.

"It is not perfect," Vana said, "but it will help you."

Later that afternoon, they went to where a huge fire had been prepared for several days, at the Marae. Many dignitaries had already assembled and were amicably chatting. When they saw Kukara walking with Vana and Mato, most of them recalled the fascinating little girl they had admired seven sun cycles earlier. They were astonished by how different she looked. Her garment was modest, a long white robe bound with a belt of tiny golden cowries, but they knew better. They noticed immediately that she wore the feather of the sacred green pigeon on her chest, an emblem that signified she was among the few high priests possessing exceptional powers. Usually such a privilege came when the high priest was very old. A few days earlier, Vana had honored her by offering her the sacred feather. They noticed the length of Kukara's fingernails, which clearly said she was not accustomed to manual labor. Mato sat cross-legged, facing the kings, the priests, and their relatives. He rested his hands in his lap and slowly scanned the people. He invited Vana and Kukara to sit next to him. The young woman kept her calm and distinguished manners. They all noticed how she carried herself, her bearing, her self-confidence. Her demeanor, combined with the regal attire, captured their attention. There was no doubt in anyone's mind that the small group seated in front of them was the cause célèbre of the Great Gathering. They were consumed with anticipation. They had many carefully rehearsed questions that they had prepared for the priests and priestess, a tradition that dated to the dawn of their societies.

The Havaiki high priest was now the old Mato. He stepped forward and gave the command that the audience could now ask questions of Vana and Kukara, their most honored guests.

"What have you done to achieve such an honor?" one king asked, pointing a finger to the green feather.

"I showed Vana what we were doing on our new land called Rapa Nui," Kukara replied, with modesty.

"But how did you show him?"

"That is a good question!" Vana replied, which seemed to annoy the king.

"I let him enter my mind and see for himself what I saw on Rapa Nui."

The king stayed silent but started to flush in anger, then turned to face the audience.

"No one can do such a thing. How do we know if it is true?"

There were murmurs in the surrounding crowd, confirming they also had doubts regarding Vana's claim. The drums rumbled, commanding everyone to observe total silence.

"This is not exceptional for Viracochas; we, more or less, all have that skill."

"Suggest a test we can all observe for ourselves," the king demanded, pointing his hand toward Vana.

Tupua, king of Tahiti Nui, commenced having a major anxiety attack that produced bright red pustules on his face. He was deathly worried that Kukara and Vana would not perform well, causing him to become the laughingstock at the Gathering.

Kukara stood and took the initiative. She took Vana's hand.

"Come with me," she said, giving what sounded like an order. The king realized he had annoyed her.

"Vana is going to remain with some of you on the far side of the fire… I will stay here on this side, with you," she said, pointing at the king who questioned her. "Someone… anyone, tell Vana something that you are thinking. I will turn my back so I cannot see Vana. Then I will tell you what was told to him."

"Impossible!" the king said. "Then, yes, let's try this!"

The king went in person to Vana and whispered something in his ear. Vana laughed. The king came back to Kukara and asked her what had been said.

Kukara concentrated her mind to communicate with Vana's mind.

"You told him that you have been constipated for three days and you are worried about it."

The crowd exploded with laughter. The king was astonished. Drums started to rumble…

"Young lady, Vana, you are going to explain this to us," the king said. "Never in my life have I seen such a talent, and I want to understand how you have attained this level of knowledge and skill."

Mehao, Tamatoa's son and king of many surrounding islands, came to Vana and whispered in his ear. Then he went to Kukara and asked her what he had said.

"You asked the name of your father's new mate. Her name is Kama Tici Viracocha."

"Nobody in this audience should ever doubt anything this young woman says," Mehao said. "She truly deserves the green feather she is wearing."

The entire crowd approved… Drums rumbled…

"And yet, you have seen nothing!" Vana said, still laughing.

"I can vouch for that!" Mato added.

"How is that?" Mehao asked.

"What you witnessed is child's play," Mato said, "compared to what we saw when we visited her mind."

"Can we see what you saw?" Mehao added.

"Very few people can," Kukara said. "I have no problems between Viracochas, no problems with people that I know extremely well, like my mother, Hina of the Valley, like Mahine, or like highly talented priests like Vana or Mato. I have tried many times with Taatamao or Tamatoa, but it went nowhere."

"In other words, it is a two-sided talent," Mehao added. "The recipient must have good skills as well."

"In a way, yes," Kukara replied.

A powerful man she had never seen before strode forward. The man presented himself as the great priest of a recently discovered group of islands. Kukara was informed that these islands were almost one moon cycle to the northeast of Hiva. He explained to her that the people in the audience did not understand the descriptions of the land they had come from. He wanted her to read his mind, hoping that she could better describe the landscape.

Kukara invited him to sit close to her. She took his hands and placed them on her chest. Hesitant, the man complied. Then she took his head in her hands and placed his forehead against hers.

"Stay like this at all times," she said. "Forget the surroundings of this place. Forget the people around us. Focus on the place that you want me to see. Envision your lands…"

Kukara stopped talking. Her hands squeezed the priest very hard, like she was searching for a support, for safety. She blew some air on his face, as though she was getting too hot. Her hands caressed his cheeks, and she became still, relaxed, obviously admiring something. People sitting close by noticed that she was sweating, which was very unusual for Kukara. The priest tried to break the psychic connection, but she grabbed his head even harder; she wanted to see more. He complied. They were floating over a huge island, many times the size of Tahiti Nui, and visited many craters that reminded her of Rano Kau and Rano Raraku. Then they walked toward the summit of a huge smoking mountain. It seemed to be the highest point on the island. When they reached the summit, she again saw what she had seen earlier, a huge lake of molten rock. It was in front of her, terrifying her. A red river of fire flowed rapidly from the other side of the immense crater. The inferno was burning the forest and changing course as it flowed down the slopes, to the faraway sea. It was an alien scene, far beyond anything that she had ever seen. It was frightening; it was awesome; it was beautiful. Kukara Tici Viracocha was spellbound and wanted to continue to watch. The priest knew she was viewing everything that he was envisioning.

She regained her composure, took his hands away from her chest, and looked him straight in the eye.

"There are no words in our language that can describe this landscape," she said. "How do you explain this to these people? You cannot!"

"Exactly! That is why I wanted you to see this; perhaps you can help me describe my lands."

"Explain more about this island," Kukara asked.

"There are several islands. The one you saw is the largest one, and the only one that spits rivers of fire from two different summits. The large mountain you saw is called Mauna Loa. It is the home of our goddess Pele. People can live well on this island. They just have to stay far away from the rivers of fire. Sometimes these rivers go underground, forming endless tunnels you can walk through long after the river has stopped flowing."

"We have similar craters on Rapa Nui; we have many of

these underground tunnels you just mentioned. But we never witnessed a river of fire like the one you just showed me."

"Perhaps it happened a very long time ago, before our times," the king replied.

"Which means it may happen again!"

"Yes!"

"Now you have my attention," Kukara said.

They talked all night about these mysterious islands and about Kukara's talents. Kukara tried her best to communicate with many guests' minds. Some were astonished with the results, but some were disappointed.

It was almost dawn when Kukara finally escaped and went back to the guesthouse, where she found Kane sleeping deeply. She was not sleepy, and decided to walk on the beach. She strolled for a while, and then sat on the sand. Mahine saw her walk to the beach; she came and sat beside her, but remained silent.

"I knew there was fire deep under Rano Raraku," Kukara said, looking at the sunrise on the horizon.

"I know. Hina told me that you have mentioned it many times, and under Rano Kau as well."

"But now I know I was right."

"I don't want to think about it!" Mahine said, walking away.

****

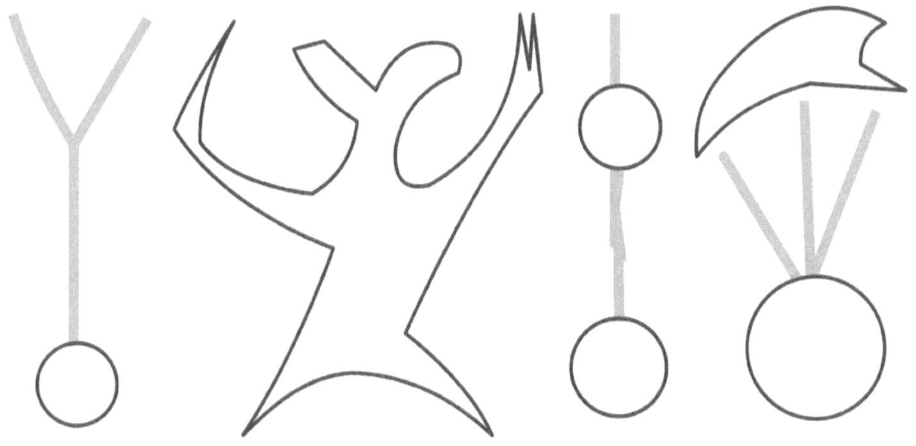

*From left to right: Came the light from the stars. Came Make
Make surrounded by stars. Then came light from the sun and
light from the moon. And so the world was created.*

CHAPTER 33

Kukara Tici Viracocha

During the half moon cycle following the Great Gathering, Tupua prepared his three best ships, one of which would remain on Rapa Nui, at Hina's request. Mehao also agreed to provide two ships that would stay on Rapa Nui. Taatamao told Mehao and the others that Rapa Nui did not have any timber suitable for shipbuilding, except for small outriggers. Taatamao also relayed Hina's invitation to young couples that they were welcome to settle on Rapa Nui; the number of couples was limited to nine, due to the space limitations on the ships. Mehao's two ships would sail with six families from Huahine and Havaiki. One of Tupua's ships would sail with three families from Haapape, a little village located on the western side of Papenoo. They were all Hina's friends and wanted to live near her again. The ships were loaded with plants, pigs, chickens, and valuable clothes, livestock and goods that were scarce or unavailable on Rapa

Nui. Their plan was to first sail to Rapa Iti and gather Illa Tici Viracocha's remains. Tupua and Mehao agreed that it was a good idea to take the most southerly course possible to take advantage of the currents flowing toward the rising sun, and not fight the headwinds. On the day of their departure, the vessels' captains held an important meeting on how they would keep their ships together during the voyage.

"This is a long trip," Tupua said. "We must be well disciplined to stay together."

"At least one person who knows the position of the stars at Rapa Nui, at this particular time of the sun cycle, should be on each ship, just in case," Taatamao suggested.

"Good idea," Tupua replied. "So Kukara comes on my ship. Kane goes on another ship; Mahine goes with Hina's friends on the third ship. The rest of your crew from Rapa Nui will be distributed on the two ships Mehao offered. Do you agree?"

Kane did not like the idea of being separated from Kukara. Mahine did not want to be separated from Taatamao. However, neither openly objected since it was in the better interests of all.

"May I suggest a strategy as to how we might be able to stay together?" Taatamao asked.

"Of course, my friend," Tupua replied. "After all, you were trained by the Great Tamatoa. He was a master of this kind of navigation."

"The two ships whose crews are the most experienced at identifying and following the stars should be placed on both sides of the fleet. This will force the centermost boats to maintain the correct course. At night we should keep candles lighted. Every morning we must regroup."

****

One and a half moon cycles later, life on Rapa Nui followed its ordinary path. Hina kept track of the days that extended beyond the trip's expected duration.

"I don't worry too much," Kon said. "There are plenty of reasons why they may be later than expected."

"I know, "Hina replied. "Especially getting three big ships that could remain here; that alone could be a problem."

"Who knows, we may see an armada returning," Tamatoa joked.

"I think you should stay with us at Orongo until they return," Kama suggested.

"Why?" Hina asked.

"Because they will come from where the sun sets," Kama replied.

"But we arrived here from the other side," Hina argued, as a joke.

"Taatamao is an outstanding navigator," Tamatoa said. "This time I can assure you he will be right on target. Actually, I would not be surprised if he comes from the south side to avoid fighting the strong currents and winds, just as we did, when we missed the island."

"All right, we will go with you until they return," Hina said.

****

For many days, ever since they left Rapa Iti, the six-ship fleet had sailed against the wind as they navigated toward the sunrise. The sea had been relatively friendly, and the sea swells very long. The ships stayed together under Taatamao's leadership.

Tupua and Vana sat near the entrance of the cabin most of the time. It was their favorite place to talk on warm days. Kukara wove some mats with Atea and occasionally stared at the horizon in an attempt to discern whether a cloud formation marked the presence of an island.

"I know we are very near now," Kukara said.

"I hope you are right," Atea replied. "I want to see my daughter so much, and my grandson."

Kukara suddenly dropped her mat.

"Look! Two birds are flying on our left. They are going to Rapa Nui."

They all stood up and looked at the two sandpipers flying ahead of them.

It was late in the afternoon, not a good time to see anything on the eastern horizon, except perhaps clouds. There were no clouds. The sea was empty.

"Three more birds!" Kukara exclaimed. This time they flew between their ship and the next one. From the way people on the other ship were waving their arms, it was clear they also saw the birds.

Tupua blew in his conch. The next ship did the same thing, and so on. Now all the ships were aware of the birds and their direction.

"I think we will know at dawn," Tupua said.

"I know we will," Kukara replied.

"Good!" Vana said. "I am tired of this boat."

"What is it?" Tupua asked in mock indignation. "You don't like my boat!"

Vana did not answer but observed the path of waves.

"There is an island ahead of us," he stated with certainty.

Kukara looked at the waves for a while.

"How do you know this?" she asked.

"Much experience! I can tell from the way the waves cross each other. You see, I may know things you don't."

"That is a fact!" she said. "I am going to enjoy a few moon cycles with you."

"So am I!"

****

A short time before dawn, at Orongo, Hina lay sleepless on her mat, worrying about Kukara and her friends. She went outside and revived a few embers left from the previous evening's fire. She stood and carefully scanned the western horizon. It was still too dark to distinguish any details. She went to get more wood and placed it on the fire. Then she sat down in the long grass near the cliff and waited for the western sea to lighten.

"It reminds me of the last day I was alone," Kama said, sitting close to Hina.

"Where did you see them the very first time?"

"This way," she pointed with a finger. "Do you see what I see?"

"Where?" Hina asked, standing up.

"There. I count six ships on the horizon."

"Yes! I see them now."

Hina ran to wake up everyone. Tamatoa came near Kama with his conch and looked at the ships, still far away.

"They are close to each other, exactly like I trained them to do. The one on the left is my ship. It is Taatamao."

Tamatoa blew a powerful blast, sending the long-awaited message across the island. Within moments, the message had been transmitted throughout the island. They all ran to Hanga Roa, where Tamatoa had told Taatamao that he would join them and escort them to Anakena. By the time they had arrived at Hanga Roa, the six ships were much closer to the coast. Hina, Kon, and Kama all scrambled aboard the ship; the crew hurriedly pushed away from the shore and started paddling toward their returning friends and families. Hina took a closer look at the ships and felt blood rising in her head.

"That ship!" she pointed at the ship on the far right. "That ship is my father's ship."

Stunned, Kon agreed.

"Tamatoa, please!" she said.

"I know. We will go to your father's ship first," Tamatoa replied.

"Thank you, my dear friend," she said, jumping up and down and running in a small circle.

"The boat is too small for her," Kon joked.

As they approached Tupua's ship, Hina calmed down and regained her regal bearing. She was overjoyed with the encounter, but felt the countervailing pull of her queenly role. After all, this reunion would also bring the queen and a king together. Both ships were now side by side, maneuvering closer so the crews could reach each other's ships with their paddles. As soon as the bridge was made, Hina ran over it and went directly to her father. It was a long-awaited moment for Tupua. Hina breathlessly, silently hugged him. Then they looked at each other.

"You lost some weight," Hina said.

"You look so different with your tattoo," Tupua said.

"If you don't like it," she replied with a smile, showing the other side of her face, "look at this side of me. This side is Hina the queen, this side is Hina the friend."

"I see!"

She went to Kukara.

"I missed you so much, my daughter."

"I missed you too," Kukara said, crying.

"This young woman of yours is quite a character," Vana said.

"I am so glad to see you too, old master," Hina said, hugging the priest.

Hina hugged her mother for a long time.

"You look so different!" Atea said. "You are most impressive."

"Why did you decide to come?" Hina asked, puzzled.

"I told you this young woman is quite a character," Vana joked, pointing at Kukara. "She is very stubborn. It is her fault that you are now stuck with all of us for several moon cycles."

They laughed and caught up on everyone's comings and goings. Both ships separated and prepared to move in the bay. Kama remained on Tamatoa's ship; they then paddled to Taatamao's ship.

"You did well!" Tamatoa said, patting Taatamao's shoulder.

"It is good to see you again," Kama said, hugging Taatamao.

"I have to show you something," Taatamao said. "This was Kukara's idea, and I am not sure how you may react."

He took her by the hand and led her toward the cabin. Inside, she saw a wooden box decorated with many flowers made with seashells.

"Inside the box are the remains of Illa Tici Viracocha."

She fell to her knees, then covered her face with her hands and wept. Tamatoa put his huge hands on her shoulders to comfort her. She stood up and hugged him.

"I loved him so much," she murmured.

"I know. We will honor him with a great tribute."

She liked his answer; it gave her strength and pride.

"Was it really Kukara's idea?" she asked.

"It was not an idea," Taatamao replied. "It was an obsession."

"It was so thoughtful of her," she said, still in shock.

Around midday, the fleet settled in Anakena Bay, at a short distance from the beach. The ships were pulled almost to the sand, where everyone disembarked. Kama ran to Kukara, who was waiting for her on the warm white sand.

"What have you done?" Kama said, holding the young woman in her arms.

"I thought about it before I left. It was my secret. I thought it was the right thing to do."

"I will always love you for this. You have no idea how much this means to me."

Kama informed Hina and Kon, but they already knew about it from Kukara.

Tupua placed a friendly hand on Kama's shoulder.

"We were told so much about you," he said. "It is a privilege to finally meet you."

"I think that you will have quite a story to tell us one day," Vana said.

At this moment, she was happy, and she was sad. Conflicting emotions cycled through her mind.

"Six ships!" Tamatoa said.

"One of them is from me to you," Tupua said.

"Two were sent by Mehao," Taatamao said.

"This is very good," Tamatoa said. "We needed them very much. This island does not have any good trees, such as are needed to build strong ships like these."

Hina met her childhood friends.

"From now on, you will live with me on this island," Hina said. "You are welcome to settle a short distance from our settlement."

"We brought my older sister," one woman said. "She has no mate. But Kukara insisted she would be nice to a lonely old man from Hiva she referred to several times."

"Kanui!" Hina said. "Kukara, you are something else."

"I thought it was the right thing to do."

"And you thought about this before you left," Kama added.

"Yes!" Kukara said with a timid voice.

Hina glanced around, and clear enough she saw Kanui at the top of the beach, watching the crowd near the ships. As usual he separated himself from everyone else. She went to him.

"Follow me," Hina said to the middle-aged woman, who was slightly overweight but still attractive. Kanui was embarrassed by the queen's attention.

"I want to introduce you to this nice woman from my village in Tahiti Nui, who came to live with you, to be your mate."

"Impossible!" Kanui said, taken totally by surprise.

"What? Don't you like the idea?"

"I am a nobody; what can I offer her?"

Hina took him by the shoulders in a firm way.

"Your knowledge of plants around the island makes you somebody, a very important somebody. You still have many years to live. Why don't you try to live the best you can and enjoy yourself?"

"As you wish!"

"It would please me very much," Hina insisted.

"In that case, so be it!" he replied, encouraged by Hina's enthusiasm. She knew too well he was very happy about this unexpected development.

"He will get over it," Hina thought, after introducing the middle-aged woman to him. She left them and went back to the crowd.

A caged rooster on one of the ships crowed, expressing his satisfaction at being on firm land again. Another one from the land answered. Hina burst into laughter watching Tamatoa and Kon chase a pig that escaped while being offloaded.

Later in the afternoon, after all the newcomers and Tupua's crew had been taken in by the island's families, the members of the Sacred Circle of the Seven Souls gathered near Ovahe at Hina and Kon's place. Tupua, Vana, and Atea marveled at their surroundings, housing, and gardens.

"I have a word to say," Tupua suggested.

"Father, you may speak as you please," Hina replied.

"Vana and I are old men and only visitors; therefore you should do things your way. You rule this island, and we shall not intrude on your traditions."

"I appreciate what you said, Father," Hina replied, "but it would be to our benefit to have your views regarding many things."

The other members of the Sacred Circle of the Seven Souls unanimously agreed with her wisdom.

"Where should we place Illa's remains?" Kama asked. It was obviously something that had bothered her since they arrived.

"I have a suggestion," Kukara said.

"Of course, you are the one who has been thinking about this for a very long time," Kon said.

"We should honor Illa at Rano Raraku with another moai," Kukara suggested.

"I would love to witness the construction and transportation of a great statue," Vana said, and Tupua nodded his approval.

"But it will take six moon cycle to complete such a project," Kon argued.

"So we can wait six moon cycles," Tupua replied. "We have no obligations. Younger leaders are taking good care of our land."

"Tomorrow you should rest here," Hina said. "After tomorrow, we will walk to Rano Raraku, then to Orongo. It will be a two-day walk for you."

****

The walk to Rano Raraku was a long journey for Tupua, Vana, and Atea. At times four porters took turns carrying them in a chair that had been suspended under two long wooden poles.

"It is tough on these poor men," Atea said.

"Don't worry, Mother," Hina replied. "It is a lot more difficult for them to pull a moai."

"What is a moai?"

"You will see two of them soon."

They climbed the outer slope of Rano Raraku until they could see the lake. Vana was immediately behind Kon, and marveled at the beautiful blue lake surrounded by green reeds. Then his eyes met an unusual object.

"By all the spirits in this world, is this the moai?"

"This is Taranga Tici Viracocha," Hina explained.

They followed a narrow trail that circled the lake and approached the moai. Vana stopped and looked at the giant from top to bottom. It was only then that he realized the scale of the achievement.

"There are no words to describe this," Vana said.

He approached the statue until he was in its shade and touched it with his fingers.

"Be careful," Kukara blurted. "He is alive and possesses a powerful mana."

Vana backed off.

"What are you talking about? You will have to explain this to me later. Look at these fingers! Look at this face! He is looking at something. Look at his tight, grim lips."

"He studies the stars every night," Kukara explained.

"Impressive!" Tupua said.

"Impressive indeed!" Vana replied, sitting on the ground.

****

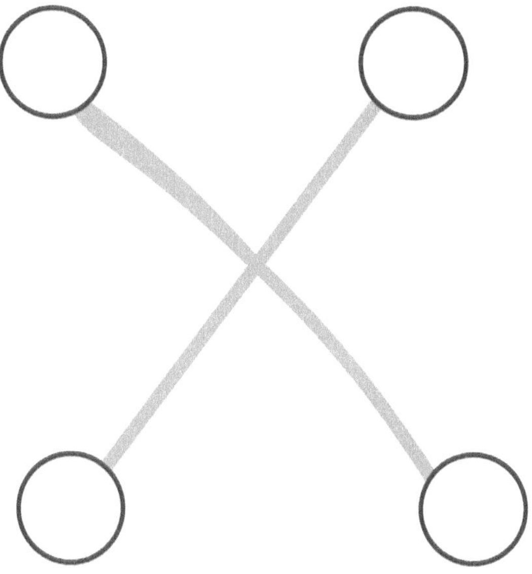

The light from stars can trigger fire madness on earth in the form of powerful lightning strikes.

CHAPTER 34

"Vana had a wealth of knowledge about plants; therefore I asked him to spend a lot of time with Kama, Kukara, and Kanui studying our native plants, as well as determining how to best introduce some of the specimens he brought from Tahiti Nui. Those from Rapa Iti were of special interest, since its climate is similar to ours. He was pleased to help them."

Hina of the Valley

Half a moon cycle went by. Vana's two favorite places to visit were the gardens of the depths near Taatamao and Mahine's settlement and the area around the lake at the bottom of Rano Kau. This morning, he embarked on a botanic mission with Kama. She took him all the way down the caldera, where he never tired of admiring the huge palm trees that were new to him.

"I noticed that you have succeeded in growing many plants near the water," he said.

"The microclimate is much warmer there, since it is well protected from the dominant cold winds of winter."

"Can you walk on these?" he asked. "They look like floating gardens."

"They are!" she replied. "Dying reeds for many generations have built up and formed the green patches that you see floating on the lake. Make no mistake, the lake is very deep. We don't know how deep it is."

"Are there caves along the slopes?"

"There are caves everywhere. You don't see them at first. But I have visited this crater many times, and every time I find a new one. Sometimes you just have to move a small rock, and there it is, a tiny hole that can often lead to a huge room or a tunnel. But this is not unique to Rano Kau; it is the same all over the island. If you don't know the underworld of this island, you know nothing about Rapa Nui."

"Fascinating!"

"There is this above-the-ground world," Kama said. "Then there is another huge, mysterious underground world that holds enormous volumes of valuable fresh water. We don't know much of it yet. Exploring the tubes and tunnels can be dangerous; it cost Ku, my oldest son, his life."

"I am sorry to hear that."

"Viracochas are born explorers; therefore many of them are killed exploring. For example, look at Kukara. The risks that she takes, making these moais walk, is very concerning to me. What she does is extremely dangerous."

"Why do you let her do this then?"

"Because it makes her happy; she is an explorer. Ending this pleasure would end the extraordinary girl she is. It is her birthright; she is destined to expand our mana."

"You, too, are an explorer, in many ways."

She looked at him, puzzled by his remark.

"I explore vegetation," she said. "I am not aware of anything else."

He smiled, sat on the ground, and rested his back against the trunk of a huge palm tree.

"The day you decided to be Tamatoa's mate was a daring

exploration."

She burst into laughter.

"Not at all. Tamatoa is the most gentle, considerate, and attractive companion I ever met."

"You are kidding me!"

"Not at all! His size, strength, and brutal personality belie who he really is. All this was from the pain created by others when he was a boy. You know this. Hina explained to me what happened when you first met him in Tahiti Nui."

"You are right. He turned out to be a surprisingly good man."

"But he has always been this way. He is very happy here with all of us. He keeps telling me these are the best times of his life."

"I noticed he is very attentive to you."

"I love him. He loves me. I trust him implicitly."

"This reminds me of the words he once said to Hina, words that I will never forget."

"What were they?" she asked, puzzled.

"Magnanimous people will never be my enemy!"

"That exactly captures his essence," she said, smiling. "He is a man of great honor. But of course, as Hina explained to you what happened to Mahine and me a few moon cycles ago, do not face him if you have committed an evil crime."

Returning to their mission, Vana pulled a little package from his garment.

"These are tutui nuts, also known as candlenuts, a favorite of Hina," he said. "The oily nuts can be burned on skewers to give light at night. Their soot can be used to make the black ink used to draw on bark cloth. The oil from the nut can also be used to heal wounds from coral. The sap from the inner bark of its root can be mixed with banana tree sap, and then mixed with charcoal to make a nice paint to protect ships and outriggers."

"I think Hina brought some, but she did not succeed in growing them."

"I am surprised about that; they are easy to grow. Plant them here and don't tell her. Just surprise her one day."

"I will!"

She planted the nuts at three different locations some distance apart. Then Vana handed her another bag he had been carrying on his shoulder. She opened it up.

"What are they? They look like fern roots."

"They are. These are from several species that live at a high altitude on Tahiti Nui; they grow in a relatively colder environment that may be closer to the growing conditions that you have here, in many shady areas."

"This is a wonderful gift. I love ferns."

He separated a few and held them out in his hand.

"I have to tell you about this one," he said, pointing to one plant. "It has powerful medicinal applications. It can be used to prevent pregnancy. This one, here, grows large leaves, which you can take on long sea voyages. If you run out of fresh water, you can chew on a piece of the leaf, and then drink a small amount of seawater with impunity. The sap of this other one can heal severe wounds rather quickly. This last one, if taken daily in small quantities, will cure stomach pain."

She listened attentively to Vana and memorized everything he said.

"Now the trick is to find a good home for each of them."

"Kanui will help us," she said. "He showed me some impossible places where he planted things where nobody would dare to go."

"He is a quiet, clever man," she added." Once he gave Kon some tubers he brought from Hiva. He had grown them in an inaccessible place in this crater, and nobody knew about it. He called the tuber uhi."

"I know uhis," Vana replied. "They are very rare and very tasty."

"Kon and Hina succeeded in growing them in well-protected holes surrounded with a tall stone wall. They like this better than the popular kumara."

"I understand that you are very knowledgeable about various seaweeds," Vana inquired.

"I know many species and what can be done with them. They are fascinating because they are largely ignored and yet so abundant. Another day, I will you on a tour of our coast and its resources."

"What can you do with these reeds growing around the lakes? They are so plentiful."

"So many things that I would not know where to begin," she replied. "We make boats, mats, hats, roofs, walls, and much more… They are very useful."

Later that afternoon they started climbing up the crater. Along the way she pointed to a few caves. They stopped at the entrance to one that was protected and shady; there they planted a few of the precious ferns.

Tonight Vana would stay at Orongo with Tamatoa and Kama. Tamatoa explained to him that he had other ideas as to how the moais could be moved, but they were against Hina's rules that forbade cutting the large palm trees.

"I see your point," Vana said. "She may be right. According to Kama, these trees take a very long time to grow. Therefore, it is easy to understand that the wanton cutting of these trees could result in their extinction, since when they die, so does their ability to reproduce."

"We will not cut the palm trees," Tamatoa explained. "I was just exploring an idea. If we were in Tahiti Nui, I would not have a problem, since trees grow much faster on those islands."

"Forest resources are not unlimited, and many are not resilient," Vana explained. "The forest is a much more fragile place than we may think. It does not take much intrusion from man to disturb the balance between species. Often we do not realize how much damage we inflict when this balance is upset."

"I know," Tamatoa replied apologetically. "On Rarotonga, in building a huge fleet of warships, I destroyed forest in two large valleys. I saw it happening, but at the time I was blind with revenge."

"We all make mistakes," Vana said. "If we learn from them, then perhaps there is hope."

Kama brought three lobsters that she had just grilled on the embers.

"I tried to cook them the way Mahine does," she said. "But I am afraid they are not as good as hers. There is no doubt she is the master."

"I see that you cooked them under a layer of seaweed," Tamatao said. "I know that is not from Mahine."

"No, I wanted to show Vana how we use seaweeds we have here."

Vana tasted the lobster, then took another bite, this time with some seaweed.

"Not bad! Not bad at all!"

"Does that mean it is good?" Kama inquired, with a teasing smile on her face.

They chatted for a while, and then retired for the evening.

At dawn, Kukara and Kon joined them. Kon wanted to show Vana a huge scar on the land that no one had been able to explain.

To get a good view of the scar, they walked around the edge of the crater until they saw Mount Orito, the place where they mined obsidian rocks. Kon pointed at the little landmark mountain.

"Look slightly to the left. Do you see that long stripe on the land, going northward?"

"Yes, I see it," Vana replied.

"Keep looking farther north along the same alignment. Do you see an impact point on the mountain?"

"Yes, I see it," Vana replied.

"Today I would like to visit this scar. Maybe you will see something that we have missed."

"Could this crater have ejected a giant boulder, a long time ago, when it spit fire?" Kukara asked, thinking about what she had seen in the minds of people at the Great Gathering.

Kon looked at the scar relative to their position.

"It is a good thought," he said, "but the scar's alignment does not support your idea. Whatever created that scar did not come from this crater. It was caused by something else."

"Could it have been made by a falling star?" Kukara asked.

"That very well could be," Kon replied. "I already thought about it."

The sun was already high in the sky when they arrived at the first point of impact. Vana studied the area, stunned by the size of the object that plowed the lava so deeply and widely; it went on as far as they could see, following the landscape's upward slope in a northerly direction.

"Look at the long scratches," Kon explained. "It is as though a giant's fingernails plowed the rocks."

"Fascinating!" Vana said, running his fingers into the deep grooves in the rock.

They followed the gouges' northward path, carefully picking

their way around rubble and thick vegetation. It was a strange disturbed place that yielded no clues as to what could have created it so long ago.

"What kind of god could have created this," Vana asked, "and why?"

"Is every act of nature necessarily caused by a god?" Kukara asked.

"That is a good question," Vana replied. "It reminds me of young Hina. I can see her influence on you."

"You did not answer my question," Kukara complained.

Vana and Kon burst into laughter.

"Pragmatic!" Vana commented.

"Very much so!" Kon replied.

"Young lady," Vana said, placing a gentle hand on her naked shoulder. "Nature is the supreme god of everything. Nature masters many smaller gods who are given special tasks. One of them must have been given this task. Perhaps it is just a game to find out if we are intelligent enough to find the solution."

"I like that!" she replied, with a smile on her face.

They reached what seemed to be the end of the long scar. The terrain went up slightly, and the rubble became less chaotic. This was the place where they would finally find the answer they sought. Vana inspected a bush he had never seen before. He found a nest of shearwaters underneath it; the birds were apparently at sea for the day. Behind the nest he just barely saw a dark opening. Curious, he struggled his way under the bush, over the nest, and then realized there were more seabird nests hidden by the darkness. He backed off and called Kon and Kukara.

"Another cave!" Kon shouted. He squeezed in through a narrow channel that gradually widened. Kon was joined by Kukara, and they entered a huge tunnel going straight into the mountain. They backed off once more, to get better organized to explore what they had found.

"We went through this before, and it ended with a tragedy," Kon said. "We will need ropes, more people, a dog, and torches."

They went back to Orongo to get everything they needed. The next morning they were back at the cave's entrance. They cut the brush from the entrance and cleared the rubble and cobwebs. Then, to prevent head injuries from the low ceiling, they all wrapped and tied several layers of thick fabric to their heads. Kon and Tamatoa each carried a long rope. Kukara carefully placed tiny pebbles on the ground to mark their way. When they reached a huge gallery, Kon finally realized how the giant scar had been made.

"This scar was not created by something falling from the sky," Kon said. "It was created by molten lava falling from the mountain. It is the same thing that created the tunnels we use as gardens of the depths, but much larger. The scar we see outside is the portion of the tunnel that collapsed."

They soon reached a point where the main tunnel bifurcated. They explored the one to the right and shortly came to a dead end, where the tunnel roof had collapsed. They backtracked their steps and went to the other tunnel, which seemed to go deeper inside the earth. They stopped and listened.

"I hear water dripping into a pond," Kukara said.

They walked farther down the tube, and suddenly came to the water's edge. The little dog with them lapped the water with joy. The water was deep, crystal clear, and bluish under the flickering light cast by their torches. The ceiling gradually descended to the water's surface far ahead. They realized the tunnel descended much deeper into the earth, and it brimmed with a huge treasure of pure fresh water.

"This place will be made taboo to protect its sacred water reserve," Tamatoa said.

"I am not accustomed to giving such protections to water," Vana said, "as we have so much of it in our rivers."

"This island has no rivers," Kon replied. "Every time we find an underground reservoir, it is a big event for all of us. At first we had only a few freshwater reserves. But as we explored the island, we have found these sacred resources to be more plentiful. And this is a big one."

That evening they celebrated their discovery at the Vinapu Ahu. They all drank some of the newly discovered water as a token of gratitude to Mother Nature, who had given them so much.

Vana came over to Kukara and placed a friendly hand on her naked shoulder.

"You see, my young friend," he said with a gentle voice, "there is a god who created that for you. We found it, we respect it, and we save it with great care. Today I think the gods are happy."

He went to Hina and spoke into her ear, as though he had a secret to tell her. Hina smiled and nodded her approval. Vana searched a little bag that he always carried with him. He removed something that was wrapped inside several layers of sacred tapa cloth and took it to Kukara. He slowly unwrapped his treasure. Kukara's eyes opened widely when she saw the magnificent feather from the sacred green pigeon. Vana took it and attached it to the cloth Kukara wore over her chest.

"This is the second time that I have given this feather to a woman in my life," Vana said. "The first time was to Hina of the Valley, a long time ago. This will give you enormous status as one of the most powerful priestesses among the Maohis. For everything I saw you do, I know you greatly deserve it. I loaned one to you at the Great Gathering, so you could discharge your duties. It is now my wish for you to have it forever."

Kukara blushed with pleasure. She fully appreciated the great honor that Vana bestowed on her. For many sun cycles she had seen her adoptive mother wearing hers proudly. She also realized how her people would respect this mark of exceptional merit.

Hina took Vana's hand.

"My dear old friend, thank you for honoring Kukara Tici Viracocha. Yet I can assure you that you have seen nothing that she can do."

"I cannot wait until the day when she will show us more," he replied, bowing in front of Kukara. "I know your musical virtuosity. I know about your powerful Rongo-RongoRongo-Rongo characters. I anxiously wait for the time when your mana will be at its best at Rano Raraku."

****

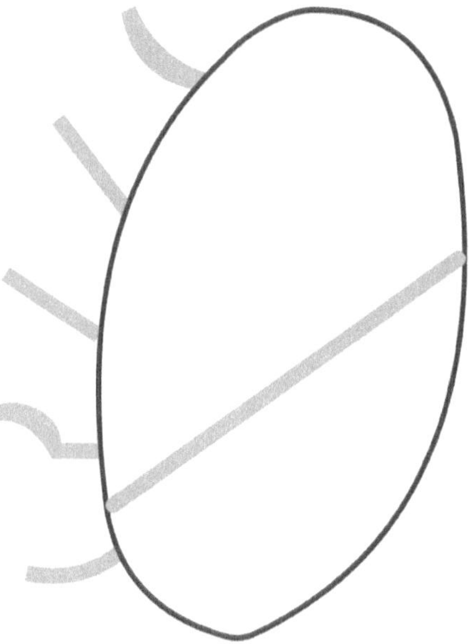

Near the seashore, light brings life to the spores from lichens and algae.
As the spore splits, new life proliferates and brings food to man.

CHAPTER 35

"It does not matter how committed man is to live in peace, he still needs his share of danger, emotional challenge, and anything that would enhance his glory. As a result, he found a new game on the steep slopes of Rapa Nui. Even Mahine, my best friend, was intrigued by it. I think this is what surprised me most."

Hina of the Valley

Halfway between Ovahe and Rano Raraku, there is a small conical mountain with very slick and regular slopes. Kon, Tamatoa, and Taatamao had talked about it for quite some time. More recently, it had become an obsession with them; they were fixated on making their dream into reality. They shared their vision with Tupua and Vana. The women of the Sacred Circle of the Seven Souls were amused by how secretive they were about their scheme.

"Here we go again," Hina joked, "women are good for nothing."

"We never said that," Kon remonstrated.

"Then what is the meaning of your little boy secrets and whisperings?" Kama asked, laughing.

"If we tell you, Hina will ban our access to the banana trees for many sun cycles," Tamatoa replied.

Vana and Tupua roared with laughter, and so did all the other men. Hina, Kama, Atea, and Mahine glanced at each other, then at Kukara.

"What?" Kukara asked. "I don't know anything either!"

"You mean old Vana has not yet betrayed their secret to my little priestess," Hina inquired.

"Absolutely not!" Vana protested.

"I have an idea," Mahine said.

"Which is?" Vana probed.

"We have spent a lot of time cooking these delicious lobsters," Mahine replied. "We could keep them for ourselves until our delinquents give up their little secret."

"Yes!" the other women exclaimed, laughing.

"That is not fair," Tupua protested. "It was not my idea."

"You, the big one," Hina said, "you will be treated exactly like the others."

"What do you mean the big one?"

Vana sat on the ground, bowed deeply, and laughed until he started to wheeze; everyone else burst into laughter at his hilarious laugh-snort-wheeze episode.

"By the way," Hina asked, poking a finger on Tamatoa's chest, "what does a banana tree have to do with all this?"

Vana burst into deeper laughter until tears came from his eyes.

"The banana tree is very slick," Kon suggested.

Vana threw his head backward and laughed so hard that a rooster became emotionally involved with a hen.

"I don't get it!" Hina said, puzzled.

"Banana!" Vana replied. "...Slick... I am going to die..."

After everyone had recovered from their paroxysms, Tamatoa formally addressed the queen.

"Your Highness, we need to cut a few large banana trees. Can we sacrifice this many banana trees?" he asked, showing six fingers.

"I never prohibited the cutting of banana trees," Hina replied. "They grow fast."

"No, but the queen does not like the idea of cutting trees in general," Kon replied.

"Do you want to eat lobsters tonight?" Hina asked, becoming tired of the silliness.

"I will explain everything," Tamatoa replied. "It was my idea anyway. Halfway between this place and Rano Raraku, there is a small mountain with a steep, smooth slope. We have been thinking about building a sled made of two banana tree trunks lashed side by side."

"Keep going!" Hina encouraged, looking toward Mahine and Kama.

"From the top of the mountain, one of us can sit on the sled and slide down the slope as fast as we can. The one that reaches the farthermost point at the bottom would win."

"No way!" Kukara exclaimed, with a wide smile on her face.

"What are you trying to do, to kill yourselves?" Hina asked.

"This is not more dangerous than what Kukara does when she makes the moai walk," Kon defended.

"Actually, I like the idea a lot," Mahine added. "I might enter the race as well."

"No, it is not for women!" Tamatoa said.

"What do you mean it is not for women?" Hina argued, poking his chest with the shell of a lobster.

"Ouch, that hurts!"

"You really want me to hurt you for good?" Hina insisted, poking him again, but lower.

"All right," Tamatoa replied, "Mahine can enter the race."

"I like that better," Hina said, smiling. "I like men when they become nice to women. Let's enjoy these lobsters prepared with Mahine's mastery. So, if I understand correctly, you will build three sleds."

"Yes," Tamatoa replied, "because it takes a long time to bring them back to the summit after each contestant makes his run."

"Or... her run!" Hina added, poking at his navel with a lobster shell.

"You are starting to annoy me!"

"Good! I like that." Hina smiled good-naturedly. "When will the race start?"

"We need to practice for a while," Kon suggested. "Maybe we could have the race one moon cycle from now."

They spent the next moon cycle making daily inspections of the progress being made by a team of twelve men carving the new moai at Rano Raraku, and practicing their favorite sport on the steep slopes of the little extinct volcano. Vana spent more time than anyone else at Rano Raraku. He was fascinated by the carving project and practiced cutting the mountain rock with sharp, very hard obsidian and basalt adzes. He admired and praised Kama Tici Viracocha's adze design that she had perfected during the many sun cycles that she was all alone on the island. By the day of the race, the new moai was showing excellent progress. The face and the chest were completed. The team was now busy carving the sides that would eventually wrap under the moai and form its back and keel. Every day, before leaving for the long walk to Ovahe, Vana would caress the giant, convinced that it was already inhabited by Illa Tici Viracocha's soul. On that day Kukara accompanied him, and was amused by his gesture.

"Do you like him?" she asked, already personalizing the giant.

"The face!" the old priest replied. "The face is more inspiring than anything I have ever seen during my life. It has a relatively simple design, yet it projects mysteries, judgment, and an inner peace. What genius designed such a powerful face?"

"Hina, Kama, and I did!"

"That does not surprise me."

"In due time I will bring him to life, and I will fill him with eternal mana."

"How do you know he can keep mana for eternity?"

"By the way people will look at him, tomorrow, next moon cycle, next sun cycle, and throughout eternity."

"How will they look at him?"

"Exactly the way you have looked at him. You have this irresistible urge to touch him with the tip of your fingers. Right?

In due time, you will feel his inner vibration. Anyone who touches him with fascination and respect will absorb some of his mana. His or her life will change forever because mana will grow in that new person; they will become a new, inspired believer."

"I cannot wait for that time," Vana replied, putting one hand on Kukara's shoulder to pivot and walk away. At her contact, he instantly felt a strong tingling as a current of energy entered him. He did not say anything, but wondered if he had just experienced a little part of the mana that she discussed.

A short distance before reaching Ovahe, they met Tamatoa, Kon, Taatamao, and Mahine coming back from a long day of practice.

"You all look like you have been run over by the spirits of death!" Vana said, pointing at their bleeding and bruised bodies covered with dirt.

"We will rest three days before the race," Kon said. "Hina of the Valley decided to make the race a special event that will take place once every sun cycle on the day that the sun is halfway through into its course into the long Rapa Nui winter."

"That way, we would have a long time to recover from our wounds, before summer," Mahine joked.

"I am not sure that poor man who was practicing with us yesterday will ever recover," Tamatoa said.

"Do you know how he is doing?" he asked, pointing at Kukara, who had gone to the man's home at Anakena earlier that morning.

"One broken leg," she replied, "two broken ribs and several more pushed in where he apparently landed on a rock, a badly bruised and cut face that will be scarred for the rest of his life. He will recover, but his future health will not be good."

"What really happened?" Vana asked.

"Halfway down, when he was at full speed, he bounced hard, lost his balance, and was thrown from the sled," Kon replied.

"And you want to do this?" Vana asked, as he stopped walking and looked at them.

"Absolutely!" Mahine replied, raising a fist toward the sky.

"It is far more difficult than we all anticipated," Kon added. "It was a good idea to practice."

"Those kids are crazy...," Vana muttered to himself.

A few days later, all the islanders had gathered at the bottom of the mountain, where the contestants hoped to finish their long and dangerous run. They placed little wooden posts along the planned path so that nobody would interfere with the racers, or get killed. The three sleds were positioned at the summit, poised for a fantastic ride. Twenty-one racers were enlisted; therefore the sleds would make seven trips to the summit: in and of itself, hauling the sleds to the summit was an impressive task, requiring four men for each sled. Mahine would be the only woman in the race.

At midday, all the racers, except those of the Sacred Circle of the Seven Souls, had raced. Taatamao was next, followed by Kon, then Mahine, and finally Tamatoa the Great.

"This reminds me of another race," Taatamao said, looking at Kon.

"I know, me too!" Kon replied. "I wish you good luck."

Taatamao wrapped the two ropes attached to the front of the sled around his wrists. They served as a guide and also a way to lift the front of the sled so it would slide faster. He grabbed another rope that was attached to the end of the sled and pulled hard as he ran faster and faster, and then jumped on the sled, focusing his attention on the steep track that seemed to go forever. The people at the end of the run looked like small bugs, jostling for the best vantage points to watch the Circle's members as they sped down the hill. Taatamao's sled picked up speed. Halfway down it was clear that no one had gone faster. The crowd was yelling, screaming, and stomping the ground. Toward the end of the incredible course, Taatamao showed his bravado by standing up on the sled as it shot down the hill at full speed. He greatly exceeded the mark of the former winner. He jumped off the sled and raised his arms in victory. It was clear that last three contenders would have a difficult time beating his distance.

"This was a legendary ride!" Tamatoa said. "Tici, it is your time. Show us what you can do."

Kon grabbed the ropes, closed his eyes, and concentrated on his mental map and checklist. They all knew about his ability to use great mana. But this was different, more in line with the kind of thing Maohis were good at: sheer power! It was indeed their great strength.

Kon opened his eyes and made eye contact with Kukara, who was looking at him from a distance. She was focusing her mana on him, and so was Kama Tici Viracocha. He pulled on the back rope. The sled started sliding. He ran, faster and faster, and jumped on the sled, lifting the front end as high as he could. The acceleration was awesome, and it seemed the mountain was sliding upward, at a great speed. Several times he bounced and slid on rocks and random bumps. As he sailed toward the end of the course, he lay flat on the sled, instead of standing up on it as Taatamao had done. The sled slowed and crunched to a stop, a short distance behind Taatamao's.

"Ha, I won that one," Taatamao said, proud of himself.

"You sure did!" Kon replied, congratulating him. "Now let's see what Mahine can do."

Mahine pinned her hair up so it would not interfere with her vision. She was already tall, and that made her look even taller than usual. She was a solidly built woman, with big bones and muscles exactly like her father. On this day she was on a mission. She had trained hard for that race. Many men in the race did not take her seriously. Now was the moment of truth. She closed her eyes and concentrated on her mana. She slowly wrapped the two ropes attached to the front of the sled around her wrists. She grabbed the rope attached to the end of the sled, pulled hard on it and screamed with all her power, and ran, faster and faster, until she jumped on the sled, focusing her attention on that long, formidable slope ahead of her. The sled gained momentum. Halfway down, she looked very competitive. The crowd yelled and screamed, pounding with their feet and arms, pounding on everything near them. At the end of the incredible course, Mahine stood on the sled exactly the way Taatamao did. She came just short of Kon's stopping point. So far she was number three in the race.

"That is my girl!" Tamatoa yelled from the top of the mountain.

Kon and Taatamao congratulated her.

"Many men in the race are not happy about being beaten by a woman," Kon said.

"Too bad!" she replied cockily, still filled with her mana. "My father will win the race. Taatamao does not stand a chance."

Everyone turned their eyes to the summit. It was the tattooed giant's turn to show the world that he was still a powerful competitor, despite his age. This was the last race of the day. This race had been his idea. He was more confident than anyone. To him, there was no race. He would only do what he had in mind all along, and all along he never thought that anyone could beat him at this game. Yet Taatamao's performance had been impressive. Tamatoa did not bother to close his eyes in concentration. A strong and powerful mana lived within him. He grabbed the two ropes attached to the front of the sled with such power that the heavy sled jumped off the ground. He grabbed the rope attached to the end of the sled, pulled on it, and started running. Power was everything for a good start. Even before he jumped on the sled, it was clear to everyone that he had already reached a higher acceleration that anyone else. He lifted the front of the sled higher than anyone else. The crowd yelled, screamed, and pounded their feet and arms. The speed at which he shot down the hill was incredible and frightening: he was fully in control. The tattooed giant stood on the sled, passed Mahine, Kon, and Taatamao. He glanced at them with a wide smile. There was no contest. All along there had never been any contest.

The full Sacred Circle of the Seven Souls and the distinguished guests Vana and Tupua came to congratulate him.

"I can see that you have not lost any of that warrior's mana," Tupua said. "Every man on this island deeply respects who you have become. This has been a formidable race."

Tamatoa grabbed his daughter, Mahine, in his arms. "You did superbly well, my daughter. I am proud of you."

Hina of the Valley raised her arms, as a command for everyone to listen. Drums rumbled to hush the crowd for Hina's pronouncement.

"We are a small colony on a lost island on the Awesome Sea. There are ceremonies that we have created to properly rule, and some are just for fun: this has been a happy, fun ceremony. From now on, once every sun cycle, we will have this race on this day. You may win this race only once. Tamatoa, you did superbly well; therefore you cannot enter the race next year. Three moon cycles from now, we will have the most supreme ceremony of all. First there will be the moai's detachment from Rano Raraku. Then we will walk Illa Tici Viracocha to his final resting place. You see this high priestess carrying the sacred green pigeon feather on her chest! On that day, you will meet the strongest mana with all its magic. Be assured that it will have lasting effect on each of you. Now, my friends, go home and look forward to the moment of your life."

****

Across the land, light brings life to grass seeds. When the seeds split, new life proliferates and creates food for man.

CHAPTER 36

"Illa Tici's Viracocha's remains were buried in their eternal resting place, under the new moai. But the distance between its mountain womb and where it will stand is considerable. It would be the longest distance I have ever walked a moai. I had learned much by making Hotu-Matua walk. This time I would be much better prepared."

Kukara Tici Viracocha

The day of the new moai's delivery from the mountain had arrived. It was a sacred celebration for the entire Rapa Nui population and their distinguished Tahitian guests. The breaking of the keel act had become ritualized, thrusting Kon into an uncomfortable, godlike role. The quiet man would be deified during the day the moai would take life. Nobody would be allowed to talk to him, except the members of the Sacred Circle of the Seven Souls. Everyone would follow his orders. It was dangerous work. Everyone awaited a grandiose spectacle with great anticipation.

The long pathway was paved with large basalt slabs that had been carefully sized and placed, based on the experience gained from the first two moais' erection. Basaltic rollers had been placed at regular intervals, enabling the moai to move slightly above the ground and reach appropriate momentum; this time there were more of them, and they had a larger diameter. A thick bed of woven lake reeds had been placed between the rollers to promote sliding while protecting the moai's back. The crowd circled the huge mound of dirt where Illa Tici Viracocha would stand at the end of his descent. Tamatoa kept the crowd under control, making certain that everyone kept a safe distance. The best places were reserved for the women of the Sacred Circle of the Seven Souls and their Tahitian guests. Kon had his workmen create bleachers near where the keel breaking would take place. It was a safe distance, but close enough to leave a lasting impression on the audience.

"This is very close!" Tupua commented. "Are you sure this is safe?"

"It is," Tamatoa replied, "don't worry."

"Where is your sense of adventure?" Hina asked her father.

"Look at him!" Tupua replied, pointing at Vana. "He is shaking in his sandals."

Kon and Taatamao walked around the giant, reclining moai and verified that all was in order: the ropes, winding drums, rollers, and crews were ready. Kon went from team to team, iterating and quizzing the men to ensure they thoroughly understood their roles. For the last time, Kukara inspected the massive shield on the moai's base. The curvature was not as pronounced as for the earlier moai. She worried the shield would break during its descent down the pathway, which would make the walk impossible. The moai was slightly taller than Hotu-Matua, but was not as bulky. It rested at the same steep angle as the surrounding mountain's slope. As soon as the keel was broken, the moai would start its downhill slide with considerable momentum. Kon hoped that he had correctly estimated the stresses that would be exerted on the ropes, winding drums, and men: the moai's descent must be controlled somewhat to prevent damage. The carved channels that flanked the moai were backfilled with gravel to the top of the keel, which would prevent the possible sideways tilt of the moai when the keel was severed. Six holes had been carved through the keel, and in each, a wooden beam had been placed.

Kon gave his last recommendations to the crowd.

"Stay away from the moai's path. It will crush everything in its path."

"Do not sit on the ground," Kon ordered, "and be prepared to run away at all times."

"We know! We know!" Kukara said. "We understood you the first time."

Once more he checked the ropes, their tension, the winding drums, and each man's placement. Satisfied, he pulled on the upper wood beam, breaking the upper part of the keel. Nothing happened. The moai was still solidly attached to the living rock. He pulled on the second beam. Nothing happened. But he heard the familiar, distinctive crack that signaled the moai's readiness to join its predecessors.

"When I pull on the next beam, it will go."

"We are ready," Kukara said impatiently.

He attached a long rope around the third beam and walked a short distance away, then holding tightly to the rope, pulled it with all his might. A loud crack emanated from the keel, and the gravel started to roll downhill. Kon knew there was no need for another beam; the moai's mana was now in control.

"Stay out of the way!" he screamed. The noise from the wakening moai drowned his voice.

Everyone held their breath. This was the third historical moment for Rapa Nui, for Rano Raraku. The keel collapsed, breaking the beams like twigs and sending them high into the air at incredible speed. The moai started its slide, slowly at first. The rope's tension increased geometrically, severely challenging the six teams. The winding drums turned slowly, emitting an earsplitting grating noise and sparks. A cloud of dust rose from the moai's pit. Kon jumped out of the way as the moai reached the first rollers, and crushed them like dirt clods. The teams did their best to slow the inevitable. Three winding drums exploded, sending rock chips everywhere; the three ropes instantaneously snapped with the crack of thunder. Another winding drum broke, its rope sent whistling through the air. Now nothing was left to restrain the colossus.

"Let it go!" Kon ordered.

The formidable mass erupted from the quarry, wild, issuing a deafening rumble. Slabs, rollers, everything in the moai's path was pulverized. The moai's passing ground a deep trench in the volcanic rock. Seeing a mountain slide toward them, the audience was paralyzed with shock and awe. A few ran away. Tupua and Vana jumped backward, terrorized. Finally, the moai reached the ditch, smashed into the dirt mound, and started to tilt upright. The ground shook so hard that several guests were thrown to the ground. The combination of momentum and center of gravity caused the moai to roll on its convex base and stand erect and intact. Then, as quickly as it had started just an instant earlier, the noise stopped, dust settled, and an eerie silence enveloped the island; gradually, frigate birds restarted cawing, crickets resumed chirping, and the crowd burst forth in delirious cheering. For the third time, a giant was born at Rano Raraku.

Tupua recovered his composure, helped Vana to stand, and placed a hand on his shoulder.

"My old friend, I thought that I had seen everything in this life. I was mistaken. This dwarfs everything that any of us have ever experienced."

Still in shock, Vana did not reply. Hina gently placed her hand on his shoulder.

"This moai may have some mana," she joked.

He looked at her sideways.

"Some mana!" he replied. "Did you say 'some' mana? She said 'some' mana!"

He finally burst into laughter.

"She said 'some' mana! Take me to Ovahe; I have had enough of this humbleness. 'Some' mana indeed!"

Kukara glanced at Kon, smiling.

"This is how we, on Rapa Nui, have fun," Hina added.

"Fun!" Vana repeated laughing. "She said 'fun!' If I were to pee in my clothes, you would probably find that 'fun' as well!"

They all threw their heads back and roared in laughter.

"Now it is your turn," Hina said, pointing at Kukara.

Kukara took her flute and started an enchanting melody.

"I like that," Vana said. "I could use some soothing music right now."

The moai's awesome power in counterpoint to the immense inner peace brought by Kukara's melody inspired many islanders. It was Rano Raraku's magic, a place where, at the same time, silence could charm a songbird, yet the act of man trigger the charisma of a moai's fury.

"If we could generate powerful, positive emotions at will," Kon suggested, "we would never have wars."

"Here we go again!" Vana replied, poking a finger on Kon's chest. "This is not a reason to make me pee in my clothes!"

That night they slept at Rano Raraku, as the star-studded Milky Way cast its faint light on the giant moais. Vana had recurrent nightmares that the mountain chased him around the island, and then he would stand still and watch the moai, in its silent, majestic glory. Illa Tici Viracocha would now watch the heavens for eternity; he would absorb the Light's secrets from across the universe and keep them for himself. He would become an anchor point for future generations and visitors from around the world. Vana lay down, went to sleep, and dreamed of alien shores on unknown worlds. He did not realize that these dreams were the Light communicating to him in a tiny area of his subconscious. Kukara would come, lie by his side, take his hand, and impart 'some' of her mana so that he could better understand the deeper motives behind the creation of moais.

*The moai sculptor receives an obsidian tool from the bird man.
The sculptor will then be filled with Make Make's mana until the
moai is detached from the mountain. Then, mana and the moai
will be one.*

CHAPTER 37

"Moais filled with mana will live forever at Rano Raraku. After reaching their final resting place, they no longer will need to move. When you touch a moai with the tip of your finger, you will be filled with a powerful sensation that will penetrate to your soul's most secret spots. These massive statues' magic resides in what they see, what they think, and that which they keep silent. Every traveler who experiences that feeling, and respects it, will become capable of changing something in this world, for the best."

Kon Tici Viracocha

The day for the new moai to walk to its final place had arrived. It was a sacred time for the entire Rapa Nui population and their distinguished Tahitian guests. This would be when the dead would live. This was the moment when the moai would assume its human identity. This was the moment when a young woman would master the moai's mana and her mana, merging the two into a most wonderful, most dramatic demonstration of its power. It was a moment when a legend was born from reality. It was that moment when humility became greatness. Kukara Tici Viracocha was ready.

She slowly walked toward the great moai, her hair pinned up in the same style as her adoptive mother. She wore a long grass skirt secured tightly around her waist. Hina had wrapped several layers of a wide woven cloth around her lower back to protect it from any further injury from the moai's wide, breathtaking oscillations as it walked to its final location. She wrapped a narrow strip of white bark cloth around her chest. Her headband was decorated with flying condors, the mark of Viracochas that reminded her people that she was inspired by the Sun God. The modest green pigeon feather denoted her high rank as a great priestess. Today was her day to demonstrate and confirm her mastery of two powerful manas.

At some distance from the moai she stopped, as though she had forgotten something important, and scanned the crowd gathered around her. Her eyes found the target: she walked to Kane, who was standing with Hina, Kama, and Mahine. She went to him, stoic, self-confident, and jabbed a finger on his chest. Surprised, Kane attempted to defend himself, wondering what had caused her actions. She deftly grabbed him by one arm and restrained him.

"Listen to me, young man! I told you a few moon cycles ago that I love you. I know you have been waiting for this moment. This is the day. When I am finished with my mission, while I am still filled with mana, you will take me to a remote place on the Poike peninsula and make love to me."

She turned around and went back to the moai. Stunned, Kane glanced at his mother.

"Don't look at me!" Kama said, laughing.

"Today she is wild!" Hina added. "I have never seen her like this before; she is filled with energy."

Kane was all smiles, but his mouth hung wide open, wondering if he had heard Kukara correctly.

"I will bet that we will not see you for half a moon cycle!"

Mahine joked.

Throughout Rano Raraku, there are moais special to long-forgotten settlers. Once again, Hina of the Valley would repeat this powerful prophecy so dear to the people of Rapa Nui.

"To all the future generations who will visit this island, just like you, Vana, and my dear mother and father," Hina of the Valley said, raising her arms as high as she could, "look at this impressive moai. Before sunset, it will become Illa Tici Viracocha. He will walk again, alive and filled with mana's power. At the top of that giant, inhabited by the genius of a great priestess, never forget that the ghosts of many generations are witnessing our courage, our joy, our talent, and our dedication. In peace, Maohis are far greater than in war. This tiny world, at the feet of that giant, is our experience, our achievement, our model, and our hope. Dreaming, we desire; learning, we must; achieving, we want; exploring, we embrace; and excelling, we vow for each new coming day. This is how we live. This is how we love. This is how we die. Our desire is to become invested in the formidable gift the sacred Light has given us, the symbol of which is the great Make Make."

As Kukara caressed the giant's fingers, the profound meaning of the moai raced through her mind. She glanced at the huge hanging ears, far greater than those of the first two moais. It was much more than the obsession of making the greatest moai ever created. It was much more than the obsession of fulfilling a ritual ceremony at Rano Raraku. It was that primal need of mankind to explore deeper into unknown territories. It was a peaceful, formidable achievement for the little colony. Early, when they first founded their society, they made a pact that their important achievements would never involve war or any brutality against one another. This achievement would be a powerful way to say these sacred words:

"Have a dream," Kukara murmured. "Who we are should not matter if we want to reach out to the unknown. Only by becoming who we want to be will we be taken to that unknown destiny. Today we will reach for that new destiny."

She backed away and pointed a finger at Kon and Tamatoa.

"Put me on the top of that 'inanimate object'," she added, almost screaming, "so I can bring it to life in the person of Illa Tici Viracocha."

And so they prepared, with care, with love for the young woman, and with passion. The road ahead was almost one third of Rano Raraku's circumference, much farther than the distance they had moved Hotu-Matua. The way had been carefully leveled, paved with compacted gravel, and decorated with reeds and flowers. It was dawn. They challenged themselves to complete the task by sunset. There was no time to lose.

After the remains of the dirt pile had been carried away, Kon thoroughly inspected the moai's base and found that it was undamaged by the impact. The position of the ditch relative to the pile had been carefully planned so the moai would stand up on impact, and it did. Now the moai was standing on a flat surface. The curvature of its base was not as pronounced as Hotu-Matua's. As a result, the amplitude of its rocking would be more manageable, enabling Kukara to safely stand up on its top. Two long wood beams, one in the front and one in the back, were tied together at their ends. A deep groove carved in the front and another one in the back of the moai prevented the beams from shifting position during the walk. They provided an effective lever to bring the moai forward with each swing. Furthermore, in the event one swing went too far and endangered Kukara, the beams would hit the ground and keep the moai from tipping too far. Kukara and the men had trained for many days; their skills were honed like never before.

Kukara inspected the platform at the top of the moai's head and whisked the dust with a small brush. The process that she used to start and continue the walk remained the same as before. The guardrail had been reworked to make it tighter on her body, giving her more freedom with her hands. She was ready for a first attempt. She raised her hands.

"The two sideways teams first. The two forward teams, you sit on the ground for now."

"Pull slightly to the left,… vi…," she said, raising her left index finger. "Take it easy."

She felt the moai roll to the left, and then swing to the right, "co." The swing was gentler than with Hotu-Matua, yet she felt the pain in her back caused by an abrupt change of direction. She flexed her legs to warm up and better absorb the next swings. She raised her left index finger, "vi…". The swing came. She raised her right index finger. The opposite swing came, "co…". She repeated the procedure several times until she became accustomed to the rhythm, and the two teams were able to synchronize their efforts properly.

"Now, let's try it with all four teams," she said.

She raised her hands.

"Pull slightly to the left, vi," she said, raising her left index finger. She felt the moai roll to the left. She pointed her finger and sent a sharp sound, "ra," to the right-side pulling team. The moai went forward. On time, at her right-hand command, "co," the right team rocked the moai to the right. She pointed her finger and sent a strident sound, "cha," to the left-side pulling team. The moai went forward. She stopped the teams. It was perfect. She knew they were well prepared this time.

The Sacred Circle of the Seven Souls convened near the original quarry, where Kon had carved seven seats. Because Kukara, Tamatoa, Kon, and Taatamao were part of the teams, Hina, Mahine, Kama, Vana, Atea, and Tupua sat in these distinguished seats that provided a clear view of the walking moai set against the background of a spectacular crater lake. Hina had laid crowns of flowers on Kukara's seat to honor her soul and increase her mana.

Kon headed the team that would rock the moai to the left. Taatamao headed the one to the right. Tamatoa headed the left pulling team, and Lutafu headed the right. They all had held the same position once before.

The queen clapped her hands, the signal to proceed. Make Make communicated with Kukara, strengthening her mana; nothing could happen without the delicate touch of Make Make. Kukara could accomplish her mission only if the supreme God inhabited her at this critical moment.

Kukara raised her arms, one finger pointing at Kon, saying "vi," and one pointing for Lutafu to pull forward: "ra." The index finger of her right hand pointed to Taatamao. "Co," she said. The moai rolled slightly to the right. She pointed at Tamatoa and said, "cha." The giant statue rotated a quarter of a circle and moved forward about one foot. She pointed a finger at Kon, "vi," then at Lutafu, saying "ra." Then at Taatamao, saying "co," and then at Tamatoa, "cha."

"Vi… ra… co… cha…"

"Vi… ra… co… cha…"

"The sequence is perfect," Hina murmured. "She got it right. Look at the smile on her face. This is Kukara's smile when she succeeds, when she is happy with herself."

The teams worked in a flawless harmony through several

cycles. Kukara slightly increased the rocking amplitude and the forward movement by raising her voice. Now each forward movement resulted in a rotation of a third of a circle. The moai gained more momentum, making Kukara grip the rail very firmly. The increased rocking placed significant stresses on her fragile back.

"Vi…ra…co…cha…vi…ra…co…cha…"

As before, two large circles had been drawn on each side of her chest. The four circles symbolized the mana that she had given to each team, at the right moment, and for the right effort. The crowd saw them as signs of the supernatural forces she was transmitting to the teams. The circles proved the teams' total and unconditional dependence on her. Kukara Tici Viracocha was the unchallenged great priestess. Nobody but she knew how to accomplish this job with flawless coordination. The key factors were good thinking, confidence, and speed. For every Rapa Nui, the moai's movement, manifest through Kukara's mana, was a mystical inspiration.

"Vi…ra…co…cha…vi…ra…co…cha…"

From a distance, Kukara briefly glanced at Hina of the Valley. She saw Make Make on her face. She saw Make Make majestically gliding above the crowd as two frigate birds. This was her moment. This was the time when Kukara would establish yet another Rapa Nui legacy for the future generations.

Kukara increased the rocking amplitude and the forward motion with two strident whistles. Now each forward movement involved a rotation of nearly a half circle. The moai was steadily gaining more momentum and speed. It came to the point when it seemed as though it was walking on its own. It seemed as though the massive moai was getting lighter and lighter.

"Vi, ra, co, cha. Vi, ra, co, cha…"

"I just cannot believe this," Vana said.

"Absolutely amazing!" Tupua replied.

Atea bit her lips and shook her arms with deep anxiety.

Hina, Kama, and Mahine beamed.

Kukara whistled three times. Her hair bounced from left to right. Only her voice helped the incredible sequence. Her body, mind, and mana were bound to Illa Tici Viracocha, who was alive and running.

Vi-ra-co-cha. Vi-ra-co-cha..."

At midday they were at the halfway point. They took a short break to eat and drink. Kane attempted to talk to Kukara. Hina stopped him, as he was not a member of the Sacred Circle of the Seven Souls. He protested. Hina became angry and showed him Make Make on her face.

"How dare you argue with me? By dusk you will have all the time in the world to talk with her, just as she told you."

Mahine took him aside, more patiently.

"You must be a good example, Kane. Furthermore, you are a Viracocha. You must achieve an extraordinary reputation as one of the last survivors of a lost race. You must become a man that we respect and cherish as one of our own."

He stared at her, abashed and contrite.

"I don't have any talent compared to all of you."

He turned around. Hina heard their words and went to Mahine.

"He has plenty of talent," Hina said. "Kukara will train him well, I can assure you."

Later in the afternoon, Kukara and the crew stopped at some distance from their final target. She wanted to meet with the four team leaders before they started the final walk.

"The last leap must be beyond everything we have ever

done," the young priestess said. "We know how. We have been good all day. Now let's give Illa Tici Viracocha the thrill of his life. This has been said, and this shall be done."

All the guests moved closer to watch the finish. Kukara drank some water and returned to the moai's top. She tightened the harness and whistled three times, signifying they were to start the fast way. As the rhythm was regained, her hair bounced from left to right. Her voice and fingers exquisitely conducted the orchestration. Her body became Illa Tici Viracocha. From a distance anyone would have sworn the statue was running on its own. Now, totally absorbed in reverie, Kukara no longer bothered to watch; she peacefully closed her eyes and responded to the sounds and feel of the great Illa Tici Viracocha's rebirth.

"Viracochaviracocha…," she chanted.

It was an astonishing, divine dance, all the way to the final destination. The entire island was in harmony with everything she did. Rano Raraku was dancing. A legend was born, creating a most baffling mystery for many future generations of archaeologists. Then Kukara halted the sweating workers; everything came to a stop. Kukara lowered her arms and sat, drenched with sweat. She heard the crowd roar. She heard the shouts from her teams. They helped her down. Kane glanced at the queen for permission.

"She is all yours," Hina said. "Love her well; she deserves it."

Kane and Kukara ran to each other. The crowd applauded and gave their blessings to the young couple. She passionately kissed him, and he rubbed his nose on hers in the Maohi tradition.

"I need a bath," Kukara said. "I will take you to my favorite underground pond. My back hurts very much!"

Kukara and Kane consummated their love in a remote location on the Poike peninsula. They were the first of the very few Long Ears that lived on the island.

The wooden beams that were used to pull the moai forward were removed and saved as a sacred part of the mana that would be used later for another moai. The curved base was carefully chiseled away, until the moai looked exactly like the one built for Taranga Tici Viracocha. The channels that held the wooden beams were erased. The spine was carefully emphasized. The long ears were carved, and the long fingers, with their long nails, were artistically finished. Make Make was painted on one cheek. The necklace and headband were painted with red ocher and squid ink. The rock chips were all sent back to the quarry. Without the heavy curved base, it would be impossible for anyone to move the moai while it stood. Illa Tici Viracocha was forever frozen in time, looking at a predestined sector of the northeastern horizon, the direction of the rising sun that marked where a lost race had once prospered. The long fingers, further elongated by long nails, carved under a prominent navel, attested to his unmistakable Viracocha lineage.

Three giants carved from the volcanic mountain now stood tall and watched over the small colony that would respect them for many generations to come. This was the dawn of mankind's most prolific rock-carving endeavor.

****

Five days later at the Ovahe settlement, everyone was eating the large sea urchins that Hina had named vanas, in memory of her old mentor. Although a simple gesture, Vana was sincerely flattered by the honor.

Kukara went to Vana.

"May I ask you a favor?" she asked gently.

"Of course! What can I do for you?"

"Would you please place warm stones on my lower back?"

"Absolutely!"

"Can I have warm stones on my lower back too?" Mahine asked.

"Sure!"

"Can I have warm stones on my lower back as well?" Hina asked.

Vana smiled, almost embarrassed.

"Can I have warm stones on my lower back as well?" Kama asked.

"Can I have warm stones on my lower back as well?" Atea asked.

"Can I have warm stones on my lower back as well?" Tupua asked.

"You, the big one," Hina replied, "you stay with the men."

"All the women on the ground," Vana ordered, laughing. "Make a circle so you can see each other and talk."

On the terrace of Hina's house, a magnificent circle of women, face down, looked like a giant, open flower.

Kon came to watch.

"What are you looking for?" Hina asked.

"I am enjoying the scenery."

"When we are finished with this, I will show you my own scenery," Hina replied with a chuckle.

They all roared with laughter.

Vana was busy warming stones in the fire. He carefully checked each rock to make certain that they would not burn the women's skin. A large stone was placed on the middle lower back of each woman. Five smaller stones were placed in a circle around the larger one.

"This feels so good!" Kukara moaned.

From time to time, Vana replaced cool stones with warmer

ones. He thoroughly enjoyed his task.

The women used this last opportunity when they would be all together to renew their vows of sisterhood and friendship. The men were busily provisioning the boats for their departure in a few days. It was a time for quiet reflection.

"Tomorrow, after you leave from Anakena, stop at Hanga Roa; we will all meet for a formal farewell," Hina suggested.

"We will, my daughter," Tupua replied.

Two days later at dawn, Tupua's ships left Hanga Roa for their return journey to Tahiti Nui. Standing at the top of the ahu with the other members of the Circle, Hina of the Valley, wearing her best garments, watched the ships sail into the distance. Behind them, the entire Rapa Nui population chanted and drums rumbled. Hina held a mauro fish in each hand. She gave a discreet signal to Kukara, who whistled. Instantly, two frigate birds circled around, then landed on Hina's hand looking for their treat. Far away, watching from their boat, two old Maohis had tears in their eyes.

"I am very proud of my daughter," Tupua said, looking at Make Make alive in her hands.

"My friend," Vana replied, "I think this is an understatement."

****

A few days later, after the Tahitian guests had left, Kon Tici walked to Rano Raraku to meditate on his life's achievements.

He sat in front of his brother and held the giant hands. Far above on the head of the statue, a frigate sat, undisturbed.

"I am happy you are here with us. I have had a good life with an exceptional mate; I have Kama as a friend, and Kukara as an inspiring genius. Kane, your dear son, will take good care of her. I thought I knew a lot when we were together, but today I am humbled by what I see around me. All of our loved ones are quite a team. Everyone has their place and a specific contribution to make. I am not sure how long we can treasure such a valuable society and make it prosper. But I swear to you, my brother, we will all try our best. They call us the last Viracochas, Teke. For the few well-initiated, we are the Tici family, a legend that will last on many islands. We are the Heirs of a Lost Race."

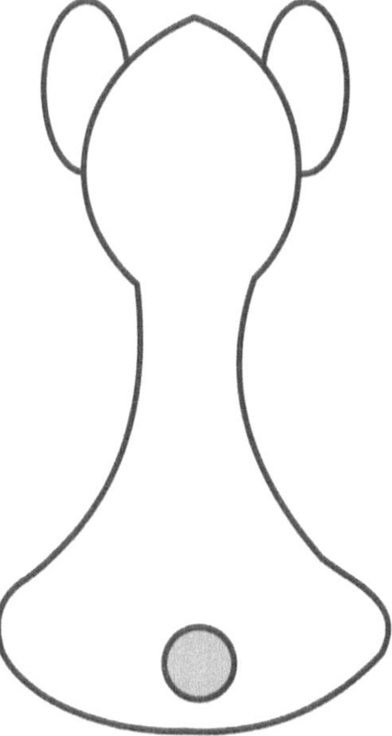

The enlarged convex base of the moai was the place where his mana was concentrated. The sacred knowledge of how mana was used was brought and taught by the Long Ears

CHAPTER 38

"Mother Nature is imponderable, not because she purposely hides her mysteries, but more because our minds become closed to the Light. We do our best to find logical interpretations to help us obey the Light. I have always found it ironic that we are told so little, yet achieve so much. It is my view that the more we discover the 'right thing to do' by ourselves, the more we will ultimately please Make Make. Therefore, as Kon has told me many times, we must create positive energies throughout our lives. Learning about good things is an excellent start, but not enough. Learning is only half the story; for our lives to be fulfilled, we must apply our learning by creating, always creating positive energies."

Hina of the Valley

Hina of the Valley silently reflected on her life, her eyes fixed on a distant horizon.

"For several days it had been a quiet, uneventful life at Ovahe. Our friends and warm, sunny days let us enjoy our peace, appreciate our loved ones, and play with our idle passions."

On that pleasant early morning, she sat on her terrace and watched Maui and the other young children chase each other around the boathouse, frustrating a rooster's amorous advances to his hens. Hina shook her head and laughed at her simple entertainment. Kama and Mahine were busy weaving baskets. Tamatoa, Taatamao, and Kon were occupied building a second fortress for the hens and their roosters; now there were two clans, and they did not like each other. Since the second wave of chickens had arrived, the chicken population had dramatically increased.

Kukara walked on the Ovahe beach, totally in love with Kane. She had come to a point in her life when she discovered there was more to life than moais, Rongo-RongoRongo-Rongo tablets, petroglyphs, and tattoos. Hina was pleased that Kukara was more like a young woman than a possessed priestess, as she had worried that the young girl's mind might mature too fast. Relieved, she now knew such was not the case. Kukara had her ways, but she never let her success alter her childlike innocence; she was a wonderful human being, and Hina's guidance had a lot to do with this.

Without warning, one of the roosters started to flap its wings and run in circles, as though it were upset with some invisible foe. Shortly, the hens started to cluck loudly and fly around in total panic, for no apparent reason either. Seabirds across the island flew simultaneously into the sky, flying in unusual random patterns, occasionally bumping into each other. Hina became slightly disoriented and tried to focus on something solid, looking at the ground; she saw pebbles rolling around on the ground. The others were having similar reactions and concentrated on maintaining their balance. The earthquake was impressive; the partially completed chicken pen completely disintegrated in an avalanche of rocks and rubble. The islanders had experienced smaller temblors in the past, but nothing like this one. The very surface of the earth seemed to rise and fall like waves in the ocean; it seemed to last an eternity. Then everything returned to normal.

Kon ran to the Ovahe beach to check on Kukara and Kane: they were already on high ground, well aware of what could follow. Tamatoa blew on his conch to make sure everyone at Anakena moved to high ground. Children were scared and crying. Wildlife continued to be confused and lost. Then they waited, farther up in the hills and away from any overhangs and cliffs. From past experience, they knew aftershocks might occur. They also knew too well that the Awesome Sea could unleash its fury on them at any time.

Around midday, they saw two unusually large waves wash ashore, but they were nothing to be concerned with. Later on they were able to resume their normal life, despite a few mild aftershocks. However, a workman from the quarry at Rano Raraku ran up to the group and told them that the Illa Tici Viracocha moai had toppled onto its back. The two other moais were still upright and undamaged.

"I worried about this," Kon said.

"It will take a huge effort to raise it," Tamatoa commented.

"Maybe it is not meant to stand upright," Kama suggested. "Maybe Illa prefers to watch the stars at night."

They all looked at each other; perhaps Kama had a good point.

"Mata Kite Rani; eyes looking at the stars!" Kukara said. "Illa prefers the upright position to look at the stars."

"Maybe," Hina added, "some moais might be meant to be upright, and others lie on their backs."

"I don't think so!" Kukara argued, but she was only one voice against the many.

During the following days, they partially buried Illa. Only half the moai would be exposed to the elements. Now and forevermore, Illa would stare straight up at the stars during clear nights. They performed a brief ceremony around the recumbent statue, still filled with its mana that could be felt every time they touched it. Then Kon asked them to follow him to the ridge above Rano Raraku. After reaching a point where the mountain cleft, Kon showed them the beautiful view of the southeastern coast framed by the split.

"Tomorrow at sunrise," Kon explained, "we will be able to draw a straight line from the rising sun, through those rocks in the bay and this fissure. This can only be done on the longest day of the sun cycle."

They all marveled and nodded their approval at his explanation.

"That is an astute observation," Tamatoa said. "I have often wondered about these stones' purpose. Perhaps we should make a similar observation point for the setting sun on the other side of the island."

"Of course, we can do that," Kon replied. "The best place would be in the hills above Taatamao's settlement."

"Why not Orongo, at my place?" Tamatoa argued.

"Because you need a reference point, along the coast, far away from the observation point," Kon explained. "We must select a point, actually two points of observation, one for the longest day and one for the shortest."

"I have an idea!" Kukara offered.

"Genius wakes up," Hina chuckled. "I wondered why she was silent for so long."

"We should build a long ahu above Taatamao's settlement," Kukara explained, "then set a big stone at each end as observation points, sighted in on a third stone placed away from the ahu, closer to the coast."

"Not bad!" Kon replied. "Not bad at all!"

"Then, if this is agreed," Hina suggested, "we could place five additional stones between the two observation end stones on the ahu. The seven stones would evenly divide the sun cycle, and we will have one stone for each member of the Sacred Circle of the Seven Souls."

"This is getting better and better," Kama and Tamatoa marveled.

"This has been said, and this shall be done," the queen replied, raising her arms in front of the split in the mountain.

The next evening they met above Taatamao's settlement. They chose a reference point far down the coast. Exactly at sunset, Kon planted a wooden post in the ground at the point of observation, while Taatamao, who was closer to the coast, planted one at the reference point for the longest day of the year.

"How do you know where to place the other posts for the shortest day without waiting another half sun cycle?" Hina asked.

"I can solve that problem within one moon cycle by observing typical daily changes," Kon replied. "Then half a sun cycle from now, we will make the final tiny adjustments."

"This ahu will be called the Ahu of the Sacred Seven Souls," Hina said. "Each of us will be assigned a rock on the ahu; on the day our rock is in alignment, that person will sit on their respective rock during the evening. This will be a wonderful reference for our people."

Therefore, they did.

One sun cycle later, exactly on the same day, a lengthy reunion was held at the Ahu of the Sacred Seven Souls. At the end of the ceremony, they watched the famous green flash as the sun set, and the Seven Souls openly reflected on the meaning of life.

"Our thoughts are pure mana forces," Hina suggested.

"Mana is pure energy," Kama added.

"Our soul is mana," Kukara said.

"Who created mana? Who created our soul?" Tamatoa asked.

"When I collapsed deep in my inner self," Kukara replied, "I became the Light. The Light has always been, it was never created; therefore it will never die."

"Then," Kon added, "our thoughts are pure energy; therefore our soul is. It was never created, and it will never die."

"Taatamao, what do you have to say?" Hina asked.

"My mana is powerful, and has always been with me," Taatamao replied. "I just did not recognize its presence. However, I have started to measure its importance."

"How about you Mahine?" Hina asked.

"All my life, all the way back to when I was a little girl, I knew that something powerful lived deep inside me. Today I know what it is, because of you. I know my soul went into my body the day I was conceived. One day, my body will be taken back. My soul will then look for other tasks."

"I would have said that somewhat differently," Kukara argued.

"Genius, please explain," Hina said.

"Our soul always was and always will be," Kukara replied. "Our body is mana's gift to Mother Earth. Mother Earth can do whatever she pleases with it to make this world harmonious. Because it was a gift, our body cannot be returned. As a result, after the body has fulfilled its valuable mission, our soul will proceed forward, moving to other important tasks. Because our body is part of the Light, and Mother Earth digests our body, there is no birth, there is no death; it is all an illusion, or if you prefer, a necessary transformation."

"Then we are no more than a transient gift!" Mahine summarized, dismayed.

"Don't be disappointed," Kon added, "we still need to make the gift worthwhile."

"I am getting the feeling we are reaching the worrisome part of the conversation," Tamatoa chuckled, "at least as far as I am concerned."

"As long as you live," Kon added, "you will be able to adjust your life's course, and you have done perfectly well on this topic."

"Then," Hina said, "let's conclude this discussion, since the green flash should occur shortly. Actually, that gives me an idea."

She climbed on the stone that was aligned with the place where the green flash would appear. She opened her arms. A rare red-tailed tropicbird swooped out of the sky and hovered above her head.

"I, the queen of Rapa Nui; I, the great priestess; I, Hina of the Valley, enjoy my soul that always was, that is, and that always will be. We, the Maohis, the Viracochas, and many others, were never created. We are, and we will never die. Birth and death form a protective cocoon that surrounds this most wonderful gift."

A spectacular green flash took place the instant the sun disappeared behind the horizon.

"Let's join hands," Hina said. "Kukara Tici Viracocha will help our souls explore our inner parts. During our respective trips, we must learn how to observe foundations on which we are all built. We must find our deep inner identities. We must swim in the quiet Awesome Sea where the Light lives. We must all become the Light and think about whom we really are and whom we want to be, in an entirely new way."

Kukara placed a sacred stone on the ground and instructed them to sit in a circle, facing the stone, and place their hands on the stone. Kukara closed her eyes and asked them to do the same. Almost instantly, a faint purple light enveloped their hands. The Viracochas sent their energy to the Maohis. The Maohis sent their mana to the Viracochas. They were one, free from prejudice. Until much later that night, their minds probed their brains' neural networks, synapses, and many unknown, hidden areas. It was as Hina had said earlier: they were discovering their foundations. Most of them did not know what they were experiencing. But they were aware that Kukara's exercise had an essential purpose. They found it interesting, yet terrifying, to learn that they were built from infinite parts of which they had no previous awareness. It was perhaps the autonomous functioning, the inability to control most of these parts, that concerned the men. Kukara's tour explored the labyrinthine, interconnected network of veins, arteries, muscles, and organs. She guided their minds' perspectives to zoom in, so they could explore smaller and smaller universes, far deeper within themselves than they had ever imagined. They now entered a world that seemed better structured, better organized: it was composed of amazing geometric patterns that resembled endless spiraling ladders. Their minds followed the steps along this unusual turning stair until they experienced vertigo. They took a break, sat on the edge of the spiral, and their perspective diminished even more. Deeper and deeper they went; they entered a breathtakingly new universe. Like the Rapa Nui night sky, they saw a blaze of red, yellow, and bright blue points of light on a pure black background. As they observed the pinpoints of light, they realized they were aligned in a multiplicity of repeating geometric networks. Clearly, they were not stars. They each wondered if what they were seeing was real or only a dream.

"You are not dreaming," Kukara communicated to the collective subconscious.

Since they were one, they all knew they were exploring unknown universes that had waited for them a long time. Only one thing was not clear to them: were they inside their respective bodies or were they inside someone or something else? They concluded they were within the universe of the Seven Souls. But they also decided that it did not really matter. So Kukara further reduced their viewpoint. Kukara told them that they were reaching a critical juncture where unexpected events might take place.

Holding hands, they drifted toward one of the bright pinpoints of light, a blue one. Now their speed accelerated dramatically. The pinpoint was no longer a star but a fuzzy, pulsating ball. Like Kukara's earlier encounter with the Light, they saw that the ball was surrounded by glowing layers; it was as though something was permanently orbiting it. These disks flashed purple light at regular intervals. The color was the same as what the Light emitted when it revealed itself to the Circle during rare occasions. Therefore, they concluded the Seven Souls were approaching the end of their journey. They were happy about it, concerned, and scared.

They descended one more level farther inside themselves and approached a sacred, prohibited territory. They had been told that descending any farther was prohibited by the Light. But the Light had never told them the level where they were now was prohibited to them. There was ambiguity in their minds about where to stop, and they hoped the Light would forgive them if they were going to make a fatal mistake. There was no mistake. They were afraid because they had been educated by men to be afraid of the Mighty. This education was man-made, so powerful rulers could control the people. At the level where they were, there was nothing to be afraid of, and this became slowly clear in their eternal consciousness.

They now found themselves floating inside a faint purple cloud. Nothing else was visible. Not having a reference point to orient themselves, they became disconcerted and anxious. They glanced in each other's direction: there was nobody. They also perceived that the purple light was solidifying and becoming brighter. Actually, they found it exceedingly bright. The light was purple, a purple comprising infinite hues that ebbed and flowed like the sea. Silence was absolute. They tried to move their imaginary arms: the result was a majestic wave that passed in front their eyes. They tried to touch their eyes and realized they were no longer needed: they were waves, they were pure consciousness. The fact they were waves of purple light was the immense revelation. They had become the Light. All along during their life they were the Light. Realizing this, they reached serenity, they became confident, and they knew they were participating in a remarkable experience. From that moment forward, they possessed the tool needed to control their destiny. Nobody, nothing could stop them. They had been given the ultimate privilege, to momentarily become Make Make. Then the immense knowledge stored in their souls was revealed.

They saw another bright purple apparition approach them, enter them, and become one with the Seven Souls. The Light communicated telepathically with them; rather, they communicated among themselves until they felt the time had arrived for them to stand, turn east, and walk across the plains to Rano Raraku, as the full moon rode high in the night sky.

Like floating ghosts, they followed each other and circled the half-buried, recumbent Illa Tici Viracocha, his immense eyes staring deep into the cosmos.

****

After the moai had been detached from the mountain, then separated from its convex base, it was settled on its final resting place for eternity.

CHAPTER 39

"For a moment, Kukara Tici Viracocha was the great Make Make. The Sacred Souls were chosen because Kukara believed they were ready to meet the Light. It was not our first encounter. I told Kukara that deeper in the territory where I lived was the prohibited territory for humans to enter until they have learned to live in peace. I just gave them a glimpse. But you and the Sacred Circle of the Seven Souls have been progressing remarkably well. Therefore, I will expose more secrets to you, Kukara, that you must take back to your world. You must then propagate the knowledge that I have given you, into the minds of others."

Make Make

"How to do the assignment, you must find by yourself; how to measure results, you must find by yourself; and how to give your power to the next generation, you must find by yourself. When you meditate near a moai filled with exceptional mana, you must objectively assess yourselves, your family, your neighbors, and the world. Sometimes you become conditioned to look upon something as being good, solely because that is the way it has always been done. You must remove yourselves and regain your perspective of what is right and what is wrong. The powers that I have and will give to you must never be used to subjugate, cause fear, or harm people. My powers are limitless and should be used to foster caring and love among the people. Remember, you have no enemies, only adversaries. Make certain your adversaries never become your enemies. If you are magnanimous to those who want harm to you, you will win them and everyone that witnesses your mercy and forgiving. Use my powers so you can protect the ones nearby and attract the ones far away through your living example."

At midnight, the Sacred Seven Souls were brilliantly illuminated by a full moon as they sat in circle near Illa Tici Viracocha's moai. To their sides and farther away, they saw the formidable masses of Taranga Tici Viracocha's moai and Hotu-Matua's moai casting their slow-moving shadow over the slopes of Rano Raraku. The two giants silently dominated the night. Nothing could improve on that stunning, omnipresent silence. The silence was such that many things that could not be heard on a normal day became the only things that could. Some distance away, they could see the moon's shiny reflection on the lake, and farther up on the other side, they could see the dark, massive outline of the Rano Raraku quarry, and to the side, a fragment of the crater's profile reminded them that deep inside the earth, molten rock continually intimidated their island.

"Stay here," Kukara said. "I want to meditate privately on Illa Tici Viracocha's forehead."

They joined hands and watched Kukara as she walked away, climbed on the moai, caressed its long nose with respect, explored its deep eyes in wonderment, and finally reached the massive forehead, where she sat cross-legged. She interfaced her long fingers and rested them on her lower abdomen. She looked up into the night sky, ablaze with the light from the moon and stars. She closed her eyes and went in a deep trance. To the Circle, she became a distant white ghost sitting on the dark giant, her human flesh and the giant rock melding into a mysterious universal consciousness.

The other six Sacred Souls did not talk, but watched their surroundings in awe. Long shadows from the upright moais slowly became disassociated from the moon's influence. Other shadows became detached from the quarry and crawled to the lake, then circled the lake, danced with the totora reeds and their shadows, and finally circled Illa Tici Viracocha. Several shadows flew over the lake, or maybe they were just flying petrels or shearwaters. Little frogs and crickets could be heard. The light breeze could be heard in the tips of the tall, dry grass. There was peace and mystery permeating this sacred place that was reserved for spirits and gods.

The Sacred Souls were no longer looking at their world through yesterday's eyes. Now capable of reaching far inside themselves, they saw the world as they wanted, instead of the physical world they were really in. They had transitioned from where, on one side, everything must conform to a highly regulated and predictable world, to on the other side, a world where impossibilities became the norm. For the privileged Souls, it made an elemental difference in choosing who they wanted to be. Before, they had been shocked at unexplained shadows gliding around the lake; now they were pleased by expected shadows filling their field of consciousness. Before, they had been shocked at unexplained behavior of giant stones filled with a mysterious mana; now they were pleased by giant stones that shared their universal consciousness. Mana was no longer a mystery. Before, they believed that only humans could think and act, and that giant statues could only rest in immobile positions. Now they were pleased to see that giant stones were filled with a different kind of life that was equally capable of thinking and acting and possessing mana. Before, they were limited by their earthly experiences. Now they could access deeper experiences than they had ever dreamed, offering them stunning possibilities. Now they were no longer constrained mortals; they were gods, albeit humble and focused on disseminating caring love.

So all the rest of the night they watched the tiny white ghost and many massive dark ones. They watched shadows gliding throughout the island, the sky, and the water. They watched as giants roamed about the mountain and lake. Theirs was a dance of joy, filled with a very faint purple light.

They slowly drifted off to sleep, comfortably curled up on the ground, dreaming of festivities that would continue, creating strong bonds with others' reality.

Dawn and the total absence of any sound roused the Circle from a narcotic-like sleep. No frogs, no crickets, and no breeze in the dry tips of the tall grass could be heard. Something unusual was taking place at Rano Raraku.

Hina of the Valley stood and rubbed her eyes. Stretching her arms to the sky, she twisted her torso and yawned. She turned her head to see if Kukara was still sitting on the great supine moai. Her eyes opened wide. What she saw sent a shock wave along her spine.

She ran to her companions and woke them.

"You must see this. Please tell me what you see."

They stood up and backed away in shock and disbelief. They looked around for the crowd that could have helped Kukara to achieve the impossible during the night. There was no crowd anywhere to be seen. They were alone at Rano Raraku.

Illa Tici Viracocha was standing. He looked exactly the same as when the carvers had completed their work following the historic walk a sun cycle earlier. Two eyes, hidden deeply under the shade of massive basalt eyebrows, searched for light in the early morning sky. A sublime beauty radiated from his human-like countenance, but he was very alien in many other ways. A small, ephemeral cloud drifted over and rained on the little group. Kukara was sitting on Illa Tici Viracocha's head, still in a deep trance. Slowly she released herself from the stupor, stood, raised her arms, opened her eyes, and looked at her companions far below her. Raindrops covered her face. She was no longer the young woman; she was mana personified. For the first time, others could see her mana. She was dressed in a simple white robe that resembled a fuzzy cloud. A most magnificent rainbow, with a pronounced purple band, enveloped her body. With a beautiful, childish smile she sent the magic words, with all their mana, all across Rano Raraku. Those words would endlessly resonate for eternity from moai to moai throughout this glorious place where anyone having a soul could humble themselves to touch the tip of the giant's finger and would be forever inspired. In these words there was depth because of their choice, there was search for who we really are because of their judging power, and there was search for who we want to be because of the hope they provided. Her powerful words encouraged everyone to plumb the depths of their being and understand their life's full potential and achieve it by focusing their mana. She said that man's nature is to explore the unknown; she challenged everyone to use their newly gained knowledge for the good of all men. Kukara was clearly someone who had attained a complete understanding of mana and the Light and their sacred truths. In her words was that desire to understand what is out there and what is waiting for us as born explorers. There was that certainty, typical of someone who has finally reached sacred, unshakable facts and awaits serenity, demonstrating that Rapa Nui settlers had reached in-depth substance about the nature of mankind. In her words there was a living god, the nature of which would never be altered by human-made rules. In her words there was peace, simplicity, beauty, and caring love. At the same time, in her words there was a challenge for mankind that had far more reach than the words of savages who could have destroyed themselves. In her words there was a destination, a mysterious home, divine substance, and exploring possibilities.

"Mata Kite Rani!"

****

THERE IS NO END, AS THERE WAS NO BEGINNING.

EVERYTHING IS ETERNAL CONSCIOUSNESS, AND LIGHT IS PURE INTELLIGENCE.

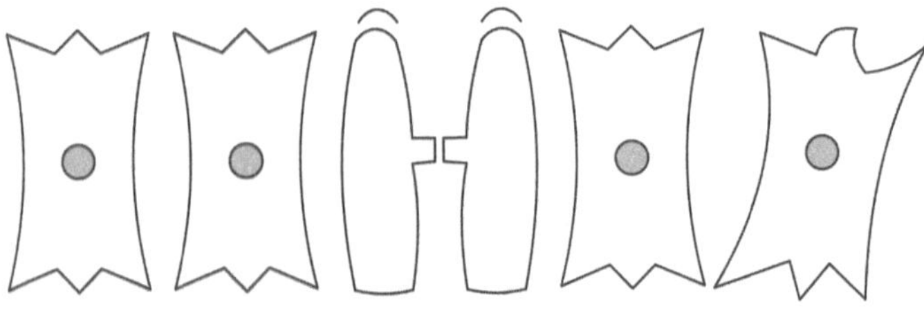

Four teams were given the necessary mana to walk the statue in half circles, once to the left, once to the right. However, only one of the teams was exercising its effort at any given time. Training, coordination, and speed were mana's essence, delivered by the Long Ear Great Priestess.

EPILOGUE

Talented and disciplined, the little colony lived, dwelled, and prospered in peace for more than one thousand years. This alone is a monumental achievement, considering the limited resources at their disposal. Taken in the context of what these stalwart people accomplished on a small patch of land, they must have done something very right. And it would behoove us to learn what they did and apply it to our civilization now. We, like the Rapanui, are faced with dwindling resources, overcrowding, and increased polarization. Although their quality of life slowly degraded over the centuries, it was nothing compared to what was to come.

Preceding the tender mercies of Western civilization, Rapa Nui is believed to have been contacted by early fifteenth-century Chinese. Although no record of this encounter exists, it is not far-fetched to think that the islanders suffered from new, devastating diseases brought by these peaceful merchants.

Then there was the buccaneer Edward Davis, who claimed to have seen a big island during 1687, in a region where only Rapa Nui could exist. Although he claimed that he did not set foot on the island, it is highly unlikely that this adventurer and his crew of cutthroats would have ignored the opportunity to "mingle" with the natives.

Suddenly, on Easter Sunday of the year 1722, their destiny slowly entered a living hell: for the first time, they had contact with white man's civilization. White men knew everything. Missionaries were less than peaceful and only interested in teaching their faith. Navigators were only interested in their image and in glory under the orders given by their lords. Their arrogance endowed these proud people with smallpox, venereal diseases, leprosy, tuberculosis, and an abundance of contagious maladies. Once more, our islanders hardly stood a chance to remain unaffected by diseases they were incapable of overcoming.

Anyway, for the 100 years following 1722, civilization's effects on the islanders were devastating. Family, clan, and societal traditions and bonds were sundered. The people became confused, depressed, and far more aggressive. Ironically, they blamed their horrible fate on the moais. The many statues reverently built and consecrated over the centuries, a testament to their forbearers' courage and well-born souls, now became anathema.

But strong they were. It would take another 150 years of the white man's tender mercies to reduce their status lower than that of grazing sheep. From the many thousand islanders living on Rapa Nui, only 110 would survive their isolated holocaust. None of the Long Ear lineage would survive. This was the true fall of Rapa Nui, but sometimes the truth is not convenient to many.

For the skeptics we should perhaps recall that exactly the same scenario took place in the Marquesas, in Hawaii, along the Amazon, in Patagonia, and many other places. Many of these early navigators are presented to the entire world as discoverers and heroes, but they were at best arrogant conquerors, diseases transmitters, and well-indoctrinated military officers in search of valuable resources for their lords. Beware of hypocrites and those in search of power in this world; sometimes the facts are so overwhelming that it becomes a duty to make sure they are not conveniently forgotten. This book is the author's humble attempt to speak for those long silent voices.

For the Rapanui, at the end of the tunnel there was the Light, bringing the sacred message of peace and love again, under the new name of Christianity. Some of the missionaries were good people, who instinctively felt the fundamental commonality of two ancient beliefs. Intuitively, almost genetically, the Rapanui knew they were not finished yet. Their joy, their song, and their love were reborn. Witness a one-hour mass at the Hanga Roa church: their belief in the sacred soul is palpable and shared with anyone who cares to partake. Today the Maohi and Viracocha's spirit continues to lives, with the pride and extraordinary charisma of Make Make still flying above them. The Rapanui are who they want to be. Under the silent countenance of one thousand giant moais frozen in time, and for the few still standing, their mana lives.

The Rapanui invite the entire world to consider an alternative to our destructive, hedonistic ways: "Our ancestors knew how to live in peace, knew how to love, knew how to challenge fate every day, and knew how to have joy. How is it possible that, with your 'advanced' civilization, principles, and beliefs, you are patently incapable of accomplishing what they did?" Any Rapa Nui great priest could have said these words. The answer is simple and was given by the Light a long time ago: "Look deep inside yourself where truth is found, temper your abysmal arrogance, and we will all live well, in peace." This is indeed Rapa Nui's valuable message to the entire world. Therefore, a trip to Rapa Nui is not an archaeologist's quest, nor a tourist's journey, but a pilgrimage to an extraordinary place. A place where time is irrelevant, where love is abundant, where inspiration is a certainty, where mystery permeates every cell in your body, where humbleness prevails, and where arrogance dies. Thank you, Rapa Nui, for being what you are and what you want to be. With all your Maohi brothers and sisters far away across the Pacific Ocean, you are the most cherished repository of human values in our sadly devalued world. You all live well on this modest island of extraordinary beauty. This time, let's make sure it remains that way forever. Rapa Nui and the rest of Polynesia do not belong to any country, but to the entire world, as a sacred, untouched, and unpolluted sanctuary. The international community, under the auspices of the United Nations, has the moral obligation and sacred duty to protect Rapa Nui and the rest of Polynesia. Rapa Nui may be part of Chile; Tahiti, a French territory; Samoa, an American one; Hawaii, an American state; Rarotonga and Maoris, members of the British Commonwealth. Nevertheless all these are part of the Grand Polynesia, part of the grand family of Maohis. It is the duty of all these privileged countries to remember their own humble beginnings and proactively join in the preservation of this great Grand Polynesian culture that covers one third of the surface of the earth. They should eagerly embrace the trust endowed by history, the wonderful privilege of possessing a part of the Grand Polynesia.

It has been an immense privilege for me to tell this possible untold ancient story of Rapa Nui to the world. The reality of the story and its characters is moot: what does matter, however, is their spirit, and who they wanted to be. Anyone even vaguely acquainted with Polynesian archaeology, anthropology, and ancient philosophy will attest to this truth.

It is incumbent on us to understand and propagate the inspiring work of these early settlers; our success will be measured in peace, our failure in annihilation.

Let's enjoy this world, our blue marble, instead of brutally exploiting it. This objective starts with the completion of an inspiring little college located on the north side of Hanga Roa. I call it a modest, beautiful, and tiny window that has opened its arms to the world. Necessary resources to complete it, and make a cultural success of it, will measure how much the world outside Rapa Nui has really evolved. This opportunity may very well be the final positive message of who we are.

This novel, although well researched, was only a contrivance of my mind, and the reader must not forget this. Indeed, we don't know yet what Rapa Nui's real past was like. I can only hope that the truth will be revealed one day through the steady, scientific work of scholars. This brings us to a few thoughts regarding Rapa Nui's future.

A proud and rich heritage, surrounded by intriguing mysteries, is characteristic of this tiny world lost in the middle of the Pacific. Anyone with cultural sensitivity and an inquiring mind will be humbled by even a quick visit to Rapa Nui. If a longer visit is made, then anyone with a good heart would inevitably reflect on the rest of our world and wonder why Polynesians are not the object of far more understanding, respect, and love. Perhaps this should be the topic of more in-depth discussions around the world.

A valuable Polynesian influence is waiting for everyone around the world to tap into. In a simple way, the ancient Polynesians' philosophy is profound, because it is free from our grand mistakes. Their philosophy bonds body and mind with a pervasive and omnipresent paradise that we, too often, forget to love and appreciate. Many people believe that mankind lost the Edenic paradise a long time ago by making mistakes that displeased the Almighty. Polynesians tell us that paradise has been there all along, and that we are the ones to blame if we cannot see, enjoy, and preserve it. Therefore, we are unnecessarily punishing ourselves, submitting ourselves to the will of those who want to crush the people for the sake of their cherished power and control of others.

Encouraging robust, in-depth archaeology and anthropology on Rapa Nui can only lead to the discovery of the deeper Polynesian psyche that was one with Mother Nature. Today people believe that it is dangerous to sail the boundless waters of the giant Pacific in small boats. The Polynesians, or more exactly, Maohis, never thought of it that way. They believed that the infinite waters of the Awesome Sea were their home, on which the islands drifted. It never occurred to the ancient Polynesians that the sea was a world of its own, and the land was another world on which they lived. To them, the two worlds were an indivisible one. The Polynesian was the human, the fish, the bird, the tree, the earth, and the water. Everything was unity in paradise. With extraordinary simplicity and clarity of thought, Maohis reached the shores of serenity long ago, while we continue to search for our subquantic identity. This, I believe, is because mankind stubbornly refuses to search for the truth buried deeply within each of us. By not understanding ourselves, we are stubbornly fixated on the notion that "it must be out there, somewhere else."

Another subject that cries out for our attention is the exploration of Rapa Nui's hidden underworld. I am convinced that many stunning discoveries await us that will help us unravel and better understand a rich past. Under the surface of this island, thousands of lava tubes lie tantalizingly close to the surface, many of which were known and used by the ancient Rapanui. A few are known by the Rapanui today. Almost none have been explored or cataloged by mainstream archaeologist or anthropologists. The Rapanui are very secretive and protective about this sacred underworld, which is partially driven by the fear that their holy places will be desecrated and plundered. Yet in fairness to the Western world today, its scholars are more knowledgeable and its governments are more socially responsible. Therefore, it is my recommendation to the Rapa Nui people that they should support serious and accredited archaeologists and anthropologists in their quests to understand and publish the rich Rapa Nui experience to an anxious and needy world. Let's put it another way: the dead would be proud to have a mission of peace, if it was done with sacred respect. The Rongo-Rongo characters tell us that birth and death do not happen; birth and death are just mileposts along the cosmic continuum, so what is to fear? Let's reach for the sacred, higher level of who we really are.

Tourism is a major industry on Rapa Nui, and the source of substantial revenues. My family and I have been tourists on several occasions on this amazing island. These trips, combined with discussions that I have had all around the world, have helped me to categorize Rapa Nui's tourists.

There is the "checkmark" tourist, who simply wants to say "I have been there and done that" and spends perhaps a day or two on Rapa Nui. When he is told that you will stay two or three weeks on the island, he will look at you and ask incredulously: "How can you stay for so long on this island? There is nothing to see besides a few broken statues." This boor is not interested in Polynesian culture, much less learning of the many mysteries known by the islanders, and is perhaps even less impressed by the splendor of one of the most beautiful volcanic craters in the world. Let him go. He is irrelevant to Rapa Nui, save the few dollars he may have reluctantly spent on some doodad for his den.

Then there is the tourist who is willing to stay somewhat longer. He knows everything. He is convinced the Polynesian was ignorant and brutish, causing his own self-destruction a long time ago. To him, the first white navigators that reached the island were the true heroes. They brought civilization to the lucky few surviving savages, who became cannibalistic troglodytes. He is a contemporary counterpart of the first white navigators. He was a problem hundreds of years ago. He remains a problem today. And he will continue to be a problem tomorrow, since he is the author of the grand misconceptions. He is only interested in propagating self-serving fictions. Truth, to him, is irrelevant and counterproductive. Dear Rapa Nui friends, tolerate him and help guide his steps when he is on the island. If he cannot get it right, at least he should have some respect for your culture. As my good friend Charles Oliver Ingamells said once: "Homo sapiens are advised to reexamine the foundations of the scientific and philosophical edifice they have inherited, instead of building ever grander imaginings on the primitive foundation of looking out for the truth. There are among us those who perceive the flaws in the structure on which we build, and we are advised to refrain from insulting and rejecting them. Listen to these gifted ones who know the only truth is deep inside each of us in our subquantic identity as they may rescue us from the swamp in which we flounder."

Happily, there is the tourist who has read many books about Rapa Nui. He is knowledgeable and has spent years researching and planning to make the most of his visit. He wants to experience the mysteries himself. He would respect everything on Rapa Nui. He is a believer in the Polynesian culture. This is the kind of tourist you want to embrace and dance with. He has the Polynesian heart. He lives the living dream of Rapa Nui. There will be kissing and sadness when he departs his beloved island. Hopefully, he will be able to afford a return visit one day. Enjoy and encourage these gifted ones: they are Rapa Nui's angels. Do they know they are angels?

Then, in the spirit of Edward Davis, the buccaneer, we have a new threat searching for plunder. It is the developer opportunist, who sees nothing but dollar signs when he lands at the Hanga Roa airport. Where the Rapanui once communed with Mother Nature, he sees multimillion dollar hotels rising like mushrooms at Hanga Roa or Anakena. He sees mansions all around the island for the rich people from the continent. He sees concrete, steel, and glass everywhere. This is perhaps the sacred reason why the island should be governed by its original people, the Rapanui, alone. Yes, tourism is good for the island, but tourism does not obviate or conflict with respectful stewardship. It is equally good to preserve the romance of the island, which can only flourish inside humble little flowers, green trees, and the well-known Polynesian touch of how to make a discreet bond between human activities and nature.

I am laughing at the rubbish published by those who believe Rapa Nui's desolation was caused by the Polynesians. Let the record clearly show that it was the slave merchants who purposely and systematically torched the island to drive the islanders into herds, so they could be captured and exported to the mainland guano mines. In this vicious process, the highly knowledgeable priests were exterminated on sight. Those too sick from white man's diseases or maimed from previous encounters were killed and fed to the sharks. The island's beautiful women were raped and forced into servitude. Children lost their parents. The world nearly lost paradise. As though the humiliation of its people were not enough, the white man humiliated the land by introducing over fifty thousand sheep that denuded the once-beautiful island for a short-term profit for almost one century. Then in an act of unbelievable and wanton stupidity, someone decided to plant eucalyptus on the island. Eucalyptus is an invasive, fast-growing tree that dramatically changes the chemical composition of native soils and the ecosystem so that no endemic plants can grow under or nearby them.

The spiritual leaders of Rapa Nui still exist, and must be encouraged to continue their ancient ways. The new college may help them to become better guides for the little Polynesian colony. They have the responsibility of blending the best of Christianity with ancestral Polynesian values. They are responsible for enabling their children to grow up as loving and happy adults. They are responsible for establishing laws and mores for the common good. They have the awesome responsibility to keep mana alive in the minds of many. And they have the responsibility to help archaeological and anthropological scholars conduct their research in such a way that it benefits both the islanders and the rest of humanity. Indeed, as a Polynesian, there is a responsibility to carry on and show the world how healthy spirits and well-developed souls can live in peace and harmony in a fragile paradise. To become a spiritual leader is not an easy task: only a very few can attain the necessary levels of knowledge and wisdom needed to discharge their prodigious responsibilities. With hard work and a deep love for Rapa Nui, anyone can become a spiritual leader, if that is what you want to be, and just like Kukara Tici Viracocha, keep it simple and search within.

The island's college was a daring investment and is a valuable institution for the islanders. It most certainly will create a strong bond between the local culture and the rest of the world. This is what the college is all about: building harmony for the local children to become who they want to be by logically benefiting from the outside world, so they can help the island grow and realize its long-suppressed destiny.

The philosophy of becoming who you want to be is at the

heart of ancient Polynesia's deepest values. Do not be dismayed that you are not the person that you want to be. Talk to the spiritual leaders, let them help you discover the kind of person that you want to become. You will find your key, deep inside your sacred soul. Every islander must have a dream, which does not have to be complicated. It could be becoming a better husband, a better cook, or a better cattle rancher. It could be more complex, such as becoming a better businessperson, a better teacher, or a better parent. It could be even more sophisticated, such as becoming an archaeologist, a political leader, a law enforcement officer, or a doctor.

I hope that the island's popular festival, held during the beginning of each year, will help the people to develop enough sustainable momentum for Rapa Nui's art, architecture, and faith to become more widely known and embraced, thereby preserving this heritage for future generations. If accomplished, the pride of all islanders would be immense, providing a strong incentive for their children to learn their traditions and religion and become loving beings.

A faithful reconstitution drawn from the one thousand-year-old archaeological record would be a wonderful reward for the true loving tourist who wants to relive early Rapa Nui life. A few boathouses could be built exactly the way they were many hundreds of years ago. They would become inspiring way stations for hikers away from frequently traveled roads. I would hope that many of the island's stoic moais could be raised again and protected. Today many statues are being slowly buried with a thick layer of eolian deposits. I am sure many very old statues and beautiful ones are now completely buried: we might not even be aware they exist. Moais must look at the stars. Therefore, they can only be upright or lie on their backs. It is an egregious insult to the ancient Rapa Nui settlers to leave the moais buried or face-down on the ground: Mata Kite Rani!

The airport is gifted with a magnificent runway. It was originally built as an emergency spot for the space shuttle. Although someone may think such a huge runway is an unwanted, deep scar on the Rapa Nui landscape, it is an asset. It is far less intrusive than one might think; it is relatively discreet when viewed from the surrounding hills. The terminal could be enriched with many more artifacts from the local culture. Something missing from the airport is homage to the ancient Polynesian's skill as accomplished celestial navigators. Such a display should connect the Rapanui with the airport's original mission. It is quite all right for us to identify ourselves with the immensity of the unknown. Polynesians were great explorers. Deep inside each of us resides an explorer; we need to remember our extraordinary heritage and its subtle mark on our soul.

Another issue that has always been dear to me, as you may know from reading Heirs of a Lost Race and Rapa Nui Settlers, is the very old Raiatea celebration cum reunion held every seven years for all Polynesians. In ancient times, Raiatea was called Havaiki; it was the religious center of all Polynesians. Polynesians were outstanding navigators, and they probably traveled the Pacific Ocean far more extensively than what modern man is willing to acknowledge. Proof that the original Rapa Nui settlers were outstanding navigators is provided by their numerous trips across the Pacific, often against strong currents and winds. I believe it to be terribly naïve to suggest that such skilled navigators would land on Rapa Nui, not find quality wood suitable for boat building, and get stuck on the tiny island for over a thousand years. It is highly probable that the original Rapa Nui settlers navigated back and forth between Rapa Nui and Raiatea, most likely every seven years for their religious gathering. Yes, such navigation may have slowly vanished as the islanders chose to become more insular. Dear reader, I suggest that we revive studies about these early Polynesian navigators who were the true Rapanui ancestors. We should go back to Raiatea every seven years and have fun with our Polynesian brothers and sisters. We could combine our festival with theirs once in a while. I would, and I think you would as well.

The combination of romance, mystery, and simplicity in the old Polynesian language is a difficult concept for people not familiar with the Polynesians. My novels were written by an outsider to the Polynesian ways of thinking. Therefore, there may be times the characters may not act like true Polynesians: it is the general message that counts rather than the details. Dear modern archaeologists and anthropologists: please do not teach the Polynesian culture in a boring way. Your revealing and rich studies of Polynesia must include romance. Romance always had its charms for Polynesians. Your studies should also carefully protect Polynesian mysteries. Mysteries were important to the Polynesians. Above all, these studies must be exquisitely succinct. For ancient Polynesians, straight-to-the-point simplicity had enormous charisma. It takes class to bond these two words together in irresistible ways, like Hina of the Valley did so well: simplicity and charisma!

Long ago the Rapa Nui people embraced Christianity. Christianity, if following the true, simple, and charismatic words of Jesus Christ, is perfectly compatible with the ancient Polynesian's philosophy. We need to be careful how this is done. A religion incapable of tolerance toward other religions has nothing to offer and is a prisoner of our grand mistakes. A true God, if we believe in such a concept, is necessarily peaceful, loving, and forgiving.

A god promoting extermination of nonbelievers is a spiritual cancer that we may carry in our genes for centuries. Intolerance is the tyrant's invention. It is incumbent on us to cure the disease by becoming living and loving examples: I cannot find a better example than the ancient Polynesian, the true Maohi, to show us the way to reach this noble, vibrant wisdom.

END

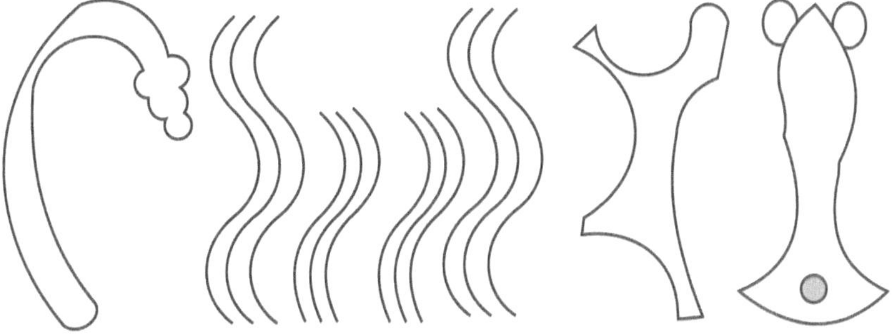

From right to left: "Mana's knowledge brought the moai to its final resting place for eternity. Such knowledge had been brought from far away beyond the Awesome Sea in a land called Hiva, Hotu-Matua's sacred birthplace where he lived many sun cycles with the Long Ears.